Fly Away Home

Also by Jennifer Weiner

Good in Bed

In Her Shoes

Little Earthquakes

Goodnight Nobody

The Guy Not Taken

Certain Girls

Best Friends Forever

Jennifer Weiner

Fly Away Home

SIMON & SCHUSTER

London · New York · Sydney · Toronto

A CBS COMPANY

First published in the USA by Atria Books, 2010
A division of Simon & Schuster Inc.
First published in Great Britain by Simon & Schuster UK Ltd, 2010
This paperback edition first published by Simon & Schuster UK Ltd, 2011
A CBS COMPANY

1 3 5 7 9 10 8 6 4 2

Simon & Schuster UK Ltd
1st Floor
222 Gray's Inn Road
London WC1X 8HB

www.simonandschuster.co.uk
www.jenniferweiner.com
Simon & Schuster Australia
Sydney

A CIP catalogue record for this book is available from the British Library

ISBN (UK) 978-1-84739-025-7

Printed in the UK by CPI Cox & Wyman, Reading, Berkshire RG1 8EX

For Joanna Pulcini and Greer Hendricks

Fly Away Home

PART ONE

Something About Love

SYLVIE

Breakfast in five-star hotels was always the same. This was what Sylvie Serfer Woodruff thought as the elevator descended from the sixth floor and opened onto the gleaming expanse of the lobby of the Four Seasons in Philadelphia. After thirty-two years of marriage, fourteen of them as the wife of the senior senator from New York, after visits to six continents and some of the major cities of the world, perhaps she should have been able to come up with something more profound about human nature and common ground and the ties that bind us all, but there it was—her very own insight. Maybe it wasn't much, but it wasn't nothing. If pressed, Sylvie also had some very profound and trenchant observations to make about executive airport lounges.

She took a deep breath, uncomfortably aware of the way the waistband of her skirt dug into her midriff. Then she slipped her hand into her husband's and walked beside him, past the reception desk toward the restaurant, thinking that it was a good thing, a reassuring thing, that no matter where you were, London or Los Angeles or Dubai, if you were in a good hotel, a Four Seasons or a Ritz-Carlton—and, these days, when she and Richard traveled they were almost always in a Four Seasons or a Ritz-Carlton—your breakfast would never surprise you.

There would be menus, offered today by a girl in a trim black suit who stood behind a podium in the plushly carpeted entryway, beaming at the patrons as if their arrival represented the very pinnacle of her day and possibly of her lifetime. Richard would wave the menus away. "We'll do the buffet," he'd announce, without asking whether there was one. There always was. "Of course, sir," their waiter or the maitre d' or today's black-suited girl would murmur in approval. They'd be led through a richly appointed room, past the heavy silk drapes, elaborately tassled and tied, past mahogany sideboards and expensively dressed diners murmuring over their coffee. Richard would deposit his briefcase and his newspapers at their table, and then they'd proceed to the buffet.

There'd be an assortment of fresh fruit, slices of melon, peeled segments of grapefruit and orange and sliced kiwis, arranged like jewels on white china platters. There were always croissants, chocolate and plain, always muffins, bran and blueberry and corn, always bagels (yes, even in Dubai), always shot glasses layered with yogurt and muesli, always slices of bread and English muffins, arrayed next to a toaster, and chafing dishes of scrambled eggs and bacon and sausage and breakfast potatoes, and there was always a chef in a toque and a white jacket, making omelets. Richard would ask for an omelet (spinach, as a nod to health, and mushrooms and Cheddar cheese—he liked onions, but couldn't risk a day of bad breath). Once the order was placed, he'd hand off his plate to Sylvie and return to their table, to his *New York Times* and his *Wall Street Journal* and the eternal consolation of his BlackBerry, and Sylvie would wait for his food.

The first time her mother, the Honorable Selma Serfer, had seen Sylvie perform this maneuver, she'd stared at her daughter with her mouth open and a dot of Crimson Kiss lipstick staining her incisor. "Seriously?" she'd asked, in her grating Brooklyn accent. Sylvie had tried to shush her. Selma, as always, had refused to be shushed. "Seriously, Sylvie? This is what you do? You fetch his eggs?"

"He's busy," Sylvie murmured, shifting the plate to her right hand and tucking a lock of hair behind her ear with her left. "I don't mind." She knew what her mother was thinking without the Honorable Selma, first in her class (and one of seven women) at Yale Law, former chief judge of the state of New York, having to say a word. Sylvie should mind, and Sylvie should be busy, too. Like her mother, Sylvie had gone to Barnard and Yale. Sylvie was meant to have followed in Selma's footsteps straight up to the Supreme Court, or at the very least practiced law for more than two years. Selma and David Serfer's only child had been intended for better things than marriage, motherhood, committee work for various charities, and collecting her husband's breakfast.

Ah, well, she thought, as the chef swirled melted butter in a pan. She was happy with her life, even if it didn't please her mother. She loved her husband, she respected what he'd accomplished, she felt good about the part that she'd played in his career. Besides, she knew it could be worse. In cities all over the world, women went hungry, were beaten or abused; women watched their children suffer. Sylvie had seen them, had touched their hands and bounced their babies on her lap. It seemed churlish to complain about the occasional small indignity, about the hours she'd spent campaigning, face smoothed into a pleasant expression, mouth set in a smile, hair straightened into an inoffensive shoulder-length bob, wearing hose that squeezed her middle and pumps that pinched her toes, standing behind her husband, saying nothing.

Normally, it didn't bother her, but every so often, discontent rose up inside her, spurred by some unpleasant reminder of her unrealized potential. A few months ago, the forms for her thirty-fifth reunion at Barnard had arrived in her in-box. There'd been a survey, a series of questions about life after college. One of them was *Tell us how you spend your time. If you're working, please describe your job.* Before she could stop herself, Sylvie had typed *My job is to stay on a diet so that I can fit into size-six St. John knit suits and none of the bloggers can say that my behind's getting big.* She'd erased the words immediately, replacing them with a paragraph about her volunteer work, the funds she raised for the homeless and the ballet, breast cancer research and the library and the Museum of Modern Art. She'd added a sentence about her daughters: Diana, who was an emergency-room doctor right here in Philadelphia, and Lizzie, vexing Lizzie who'd given them such heartache, now several months sober (she didn't mention that), with her hair restored to its original blond and all those horrible piercings practically closed. She'd added a final beat about how for the last fourteen years she had been lucky enough to travel the world in the company of her husband, Senator Richard Woodruff, D-NY. But sometimes, late at night, she thought that the truth was the first thing she'd written. Whatever ambition she'd possessed, whatever the dreams she'd once had, Sylvie Serfer Woodruff had grown up to be a fifty-seven-year-old professional dieter, a woman whose only real job now that her daughters were gone was staying twenty pounds thinner than she'd been in law school.

So she'd lost herself a little bit, she thought, as the chef sprinkled cheese into the pan. So life hadn't been perfect; bad things had happened, mistakes had been made. But hadn't they built something together, she and Richard, and Lizzie and Diana, and wasn't that more important, more meaningful, than anything Sylvie could have done on her own? What kind of career would she have had, anyhow? She wasn't as good a lawyer as her mother. She might have been quick, and smart and well-read, but her mind wasn't built to spring and snap shut like a trap the way her mother's was. She could admit, if only to herself, that she was bright but not terribly ambitious; that she lacked a certain something, aggression or tenacity or even just desire, that magical quality that would have lifted her from good to great. But she'd found a place for herself in the world. She'd raised her girls and been a help to her husband, a sounding board and a concierge, a scheduler and a speechwriter, a traveling companion and a co-campaigner. So what if every once in a while late at night she felt like all she had to show for her years on the planet were miles logged on a treadmill that took her nowhere and a number on the scale that was becoming increasingly difficult to maintain? So what if . . .

"Ma'am?" The chef was staring at her, spatula raised. The omelet sat in a perfectly browned half-circle in the center of the pan.

"Sorry," she said, and held out the empty plate toward him like an orphan in a Dickens novel, an orphan asking for more.

He slid the omelet onto the plate. Sylvie collected the slices of whole-wheat bread she'd popped into the toaster. She added a pat of butter, a pot of marmalade, the wedges of cantaloupe that Richard would ignore, and a single slice of bacon, well-done, the way he preferred it (he'd want more than one slice, but there was his heart to consider). Richard was reading the Op-Ed page and talking on his phone, with a cup of coffee steaming at his elbow, so busy multitasking that he barely looked up. She set his food in front of him and tapped his shoulder. "Eat," she said, and Richard smiled, put his arm around her waist, and gave her a quick squeeze.

"Thank you, dear," he said, and she said, "You're welcome," then went back to gather her own joyless meal: fat-free yogurt, a single stewed prune, a mini-box of Special K, a glass of skim milk, and, as her reward, a scoop of the oatmeal she could never resist, deliciously creamy, the way it never got at home. She'd add a little butter, a swirl of brown sugar, a splash of cream, turning it into something that was more like pudding than breakfast.

She'd eaten only a few bites when Richard dropped his

crumpled napkin over the remains of his eggs. He'd ignored the fruit, as she predicted, and the bacon was gone, the way she knew it would be. "All set?" he asked. She wasn't. But she nodded, rising as he stood, gripping the starchy elbows of his suit jacket as he kissed her, lightly, on the lips. Her schedule was in a manila folder, tucked into her purse, and had been beamed to her iPhone as a backup, along with her speech. Richard would be attending a fund-raising coffee for a state senator, a rising star in the party who was being groomed for bigger things. This would be followed by a lunch at the convention center with CEOs of some of the nation's largest hospitals, bigwigs looking for breaks on the import taxes they'd pay to have their MRI machines assembled in Japan. Meanwhile, Sylvie, who hated public speaking, would be locking her shaking knees, hiding her sweating palms, and delivering an address to the Colonial Dames, a Philadelphia variation of the Junior League, about how, if each of them gave just what she spent each month on highlights and lattes to the Free Library, they could buy hundreds of books and expose thousands of children to the joys of stories. It was a speech she'd given dozens of times and would doubtless give dozens of times more before her husband's third term ended in four years. And after that? "Sky's the limit," Richard used to say, when they were young and dreaming, lying on the flimsy mattress in their apartment on Court Street in Brooklyn, where the floors tilted so severely that if you put anything round down against one wall it would roll to the other side of the room.

They'd lived in Brooklyn back when telling people your address made them treat you with the solicitous courtesy they'd extend to pioneers who'd just set off west in a covered wagon. Back then, Richard owned two suits, one navy blue and one brown, both purchased at an end-of-season clearance sale at Bloomingdale's and paid for, in part, with a gift certificate that Sylvie's parents had given her for Chanukah to buy her own working-girl wardrobe. He would rotate his suits Monday through Friday—blue, brown, blue, brown, blue—and on Saturdays, he'd drop them off at the cleaner's. Every morning they'd walk to the subway together, and Sylvie would follow him down the stairs, thinking how lucky she was to have found this man, her Richard—slim-hipped, broad-shouldered, his light-brown hair thick and unruly, no matter how carefully he combed it, the hair of a little boy who'd just rolled out of bed, with his briefcase swinging jauntily in one hand. *That's my husband,* she would think. She'd want to shout it to the sky, or at least to the other women she'd catch looking him over, their eyes making the drop from his face to his ring finger. *My husband. Mine.*

"Husband," she whispered, standing on her tiptoes (Richard was nine inches taller than she was, a solid six foot three, a presidential height, she sometimes thought) and letting her lips graze his ear. Almost imperceptibly, he shuddered. "Wife," he whispered back. Richard had always been ticklish. In bed, she'd drag the tip of her tongue along the edge of his ear, nipping at the lobe with her teeth, and he'd tremble, muttering her name. At least, he used to. Sylvie frowned, or attempted a frown—the Botox she'd gotten the week before was making it hard to furrow her brow—and tried to remember how long it had been. Over the past months—maybe even the past years—things had slowed down, not in an alarming fashion, but in a manner that Sylvie had come to believe was normal for long-married couples. They made love once or twice a week, sometimes with dry spells of a week or two (or three, or four) when Congress was in session and Richard spent the weeknights in the rented townhouse in Georgetown. She missed it sometimes, but she thought that the kind of sex they'd had at the beginning—every night, sometimes twice a night, once in the thankfully empty sauna at a resort where they'd gone for a law school classmate's wedding—that was the sex you had in the early days, and then things settled down, they had to, or else how would anyone get any work done, or raise children?

Richard gave her a squeeze and planted another kiss in the center of her paralyzed, poisonous brow (perfectly safe, the dermatologist had assured her when he'd come to the apartment with his doctor's bag full of needles and his mouth full of reassurance). "I'll see you tonight," he said. Sylvie watched him walk out of the restaurant, BlackBerry in one hand, briefcase in the other, through the lobby and then out to the curb, where a car would be waiting, the way, these days, a car always was. *My husband,* she thought, and her heart swelled, the way it had when she was a young bride watching Richard descend into the depths of the subway station, ready to rule the world.

She was in the backseat of her own Town Car by four o'clock, an issue of *The Economist* open in her lap, reading the latest news from the Middle East as the car crawled through a five-mile backup on the New Jersey Turnpike. The region was clenched in a typical August heat wave, the air a humid steambath that left everyone sticky and ill-tempered after even the briefest venture outside. She was planning her movements, how she'd exit the car and enter her apartment building with the least time possible spent in the humidity—she had a cocktail party to attend, and she didn't want to have to redo her hair—when her cell phone rang. Or, rather, her cell phone belched. Lizzie, her youngest, had set it up so it would burp instead of ring, and Sylvie hadn't been able to figure out how to make it stop. The phone burped again, and her best friend Ceil's face flashed on the screen. In the picture, which Sylvie had taken outside the Buttercup Bakery, Ceil was devouring a red velvet cupcake, and had a dab of frosting on her nose. Sylvie had snapped it and had threatened to post it on Facebook. Not that she completely understood how Facebook worked, or had any idea of how to post things there. The threat alone had been enough to make Ceil laugh. As she hit the button to answer the call, Sylvie noticed two missed calls, both from Richard. She'd call him back after she was through with Ceil, she decided, and lifted the phone to her ear. "Hi!"

"Oh my God," Ceil whispered. "Are you watching?"

"Watching what?" Sylvie felt the first genuine smile of the afternoon on her face. There was probably some gossip about a star whose sex tape had leaked to the Internet or who'd been photographed exiting a limo, sans panties, or maybe more news about the Academy Award–winning actress whose husband was fooling around with a tattooed white-supremacist stripper, and her best friend couldn't wait to discuss it.

When they'd met at Barnard all those years ago, Ceil Faraday had had a Mia Farrow pixie cut and a face as round and sweet as a bowl of rice pudding. She'd arrived at the dorm with a trunk full of Fair Isle sweaters and pleated plaid skirts that she'd taken to the nearest consignment shop as soon as her parents' station wagon had pulled onto the West Side Highway. She'd spent the hundred dollars she'd gotten to buy black leggings, black turtlenecks, a pair of fringed suede boots, a woven Mexican poncho, and an eighth of an ounce of excellent pot.

At Barnard, Ceil had been a drama major who'd spent large portions of her college career pretending to be a tree, or the wind, or the embodiment of feminine anima. ("Or maybe I'm supposed to be Eve," she'd told Sylvie, perched on the window seat, blowing Virginia Slims smoke out into the night. "The director says he'll let me know Monday.")

The two of them had bonded instantly. "You're so exotic," Ceil had said, taking in Sylvie's tousled dark curls, her olive-tinged-with-honey skin, her hazel eyes and prominent nose. "Does exotic mean Jewish?" Sylvie had asked, bemused, and Ceil had beamed, clapping her hands in delight. "Are you Jewish? Well, that's excellent! Come on," she said, dragging Sylvie toward the bottom bunk, which her mother had made up with a flowered comforter and down pillows that smelled of sachet. "Sit down and tell me all about it!"

Sylvie had given her an abbreviated version of her life story, with Ceil's wide eyes getting wider with every revelation. "Your mom's a judge?" she said. "Wow. My mom ran for the PTA once, and she didn't even win." Sylvie told her roommate that her parents had both grown up working-class, in Brooklyn, both of them the children of immigrants—her father's family from Russia, her mother's from the Ukraine. They'd met at Bronx Science High School, two smart, fast-talking strivers who'd spent their childhoods translating for their Yiddish-speaking parents wherever English was needed—at the bank or the post office or the department store. Both Dave and Selma had been told, since they were old enough to hear and understand, that they were destined for great things in the New World—with the implication being, of course, that their children would do even better.

Selma had gone to Barnard, then Yale, and Dave had gone to Columbia on a full scholarship, then Wharton for business school. He'd made his first million in commercial real estate by the time he turned thirty, and he and Selma had made Sylvie the year after that. Sylvie was their only child, the repository of all their hopes and dreams, which were detailed and extensive. If Selma and Dave had been expected to succeed, to go to college and then graduate school, to become professionals, then Sylvie, her parents intimated, should at least be president by her forty-fifth birthday, if she hadn't already been named empress for life. In the apartment on West Eighty-second Street where she'd grown up, expectation was like oxygen. It filled every breath she took, every particle of the atmosphere. Sylvie could have no more announced that she didn't want to be a lawyer than she could have told her parents that she planned on growing a second head.

"So you're rich?" Ceil had asked, in her guileless way.

Sylvie winced. Ceil's mother, elegant and blond in a Lilly Pulitzer shift and pearls, and her hearty blue-eyed dad, who'd worn a cotton sweater tied around his shoulders, had just left the dorm, looking as if they were on their way to lunch at the country club. The Farradays were probably still on the staircase, with Sylvie's mother, dressed, as usual, in a black skirt, white blouse, and flats—her philosophy was that money spent on clothing was a waste, because her robes covered everything—and her father, who stood just a shade over five foot three and always had a cigar clamped between his stained teeth. Sylvie wondered what they were talking about. She suspected that Ceil's parents didn't socialize with many Jews, and as for Selma and Dave, Shaker Heights, Ohio, might as well have been on the moon, populated by a race of bizarre aliens who'd encourage their kids to go to football games and drive-ins instead of the library.

"We do okay," Sylvie had said, turning toward the closet and starting to hang up her clothes.

Ceil had persisted. "Do you live in a mansion?"

"An apartment," said Sylvie, feeling relieved, because "apartment" didn't sound ostentatious and Ceil wouldn't think to ask a New Yorker's follow-up questions—what neighborhood and how many rooms and did they have views of the park?

Ceil and Sylvie roomed together for all four years of college, much to Sylvie's parents' unspoken but palpable dismay (they called Ceil the shiksa princess behind her back and, eventually, to her face). After graduation, Sylvie went to Yale. She found a sunny apartment on Edgewood Avenue—she and a medical student named Danielle each had a tiny bedroom, and they shared the living room with its working fireplace, the bare-bones kitchen, and the seventy-five-dollar-a-month rent, but they never bonded the way Sylvie and Ceil had, probably because both of them spent so much time in the library (and maybe because her new roommate had no sense of humor at all). Sylvie ate Sunday brunch at the Elm Street diner and took yoga classes at the Y down the street. Ceil, meanwhile, realized her New York dreams. She moved to the Village and took classes in dance and movement and voice. She never landed more than bit parts off-Broadway and had a speaking part (in reality, it was more of a grunting part) in a single laxative commercial before making the transition to marriage, motherhood, wealth, and the complacent life of a lady who lunched, shopped, and wrote large checks to laudable organizations. Still, Ceil had never lost her ability to wrest drama from the most commonplace situations. Once, she'd sent Sylvie an urgent e-mail, the memo line—MUST SPEAK TO YOU NOW—written in all capital letters. It turned out that a married actor had left his movie-star wife for the nineteen-year-old nanny—had, in fact, announced his defection on that day's installment of *The Howard Stern Show,* to which Ceil was addicted—and Ceil felt the need to discuss this development immediately, if not sooner.

"Is it juicy?" Sylvie asked, and adjusted her phone against her cheek. She had one of those space-age headpieces that fit inside her ear, but she'd never been able to figure out how to make it work reliably, and was too embarrassed to ask her daughters or her assistant to explain it again.

There was a pause. "You don't know?" asked Ceil.

"I'm on the New Jersey Turnpike. What's going on?" Sylvie settled more comfortably into the seat, readying herself for the soliloquy Ceil would doubtlessly deliver about New Jersey. Ceil hated suburbs and conformity and any place where people lived that wasn't the right neighborhoods of Paris or Manhattan, even though she, herself, was leading as white-bread a life as possible, with her ex-Cornhusker husband named Larry, her twins Dashiell and Clementine, and the granddaughter named Lincoln whom she carted to Little Mozart music class every Tuesday (the normalcy of that, she insisted, was leavened by the fact that her daughter was a lesbian, and that Suri Cruise had attended one of Lincoln's makeup classes).

"Oh, God," Ceil said, and from the urgency in her voice Sylvie could tell she hadn't called to gossip. "You need to find a television set right this minute. They're saying . . ."

"What?" Possibilities raced through Sylvie's mind—another terrorist attack? A bombing, a plane crash? An assassination? Something to do with her daughters? With Lizzie? (Even in her panic, she knew that Diana would never do anything that would end up on TV, unless she was being credited with some scientific discovery or medical advance that Sylvie would have to spend the rest of her life pretending to understand.) "You're scaring me."

"It's Richard," Ceil said, her voice shaking.

Icy bands tightened around Sylvie's heart. "Is he all right?" But even as she asked the question, she assured herself that Richard was fine. If he wasn't, she'd have been told. Her driver, Derek, or her assistant, Clarissa, sitting ramrod-straight, with her spine hovering inches from the seat, beside him—if something was wrong, really wrong, they would have been informed by now. There were procedures in place, calls she would have gotten. Ceil started talking again, speaking rapidly in her ear.

"You know what? Don't. Just never mind. Just come home. To my house, okay? Come straight here, and don't watch the TV, Syl, promise me you won't, just get here as fast as you can."

"Ceil. Tell me." Sylvie gulped, pushing the panic down. "You're scaring me to death. Tell me what's going on."

From a hundred miles away, she heard her friend sigh. "I'm watching CNN right now, and they're saying that Richard had an affair with one of his legislative aides. They're saying that he went on vacation with her, to the Bahamas, and got her some cushy job in the D.C. branch of the law firm where he used to work."

Ceil paused. Sylvie pressed her lips together, clutching the telephone in her right hand, pressing her left hand flat against her thigh. She felt as if she was in a roller coaster that had crested the steepest hill, and all the track was gone. She was in free fall. Not Richard. Not her Richard.

"Sylvie? Are you still there?" Ceil, cheerful, straightforward Ceil, who could get a whole room laughing with her reenactment of her stint as Anonymous Constipation Sufferer #3, sounded like she might have been crying. "Listen, honey, it kills me that I'm the one who has to tell you this, and I . . ."

"Let me call you back." She punched the button that would end the call, and leaned forward, feeling her three waistbands—the skirt, the control-top pantyhose, and the girdle she wore beneath them—biting at her flesh vengefully, as if her outfit was trying to strangle her. "Can we find a rest stop?" she asked as the telephone burped and displayed her husband's face. She ignored the call. There was a quaver in her voice, but, she hoped, not one obvious enough for the pair in the front seat to notice. And she'd asked politely. Sylvie was always polite. It was a reaction, she thought, to her frequently profane mother, who'd once made the papers for telling a plaintiff's attorney that he needed to buy her dinner if he was going to treat her like he'd been doing, because she insisted on dinner before getting fucked. Sylvie had made a point of raising her own daughters, headstrong Diana and dreamy Lizzie, to be polite, to be considerate, to think of others, and to remember, always, that manners mattered. Even when Lizzie was in the throes of her drug use, Sylvie liked to think that her younger daughter had said please and thank you to her dealer.

In the front seat, a look passed between Derek and Clarissa, and in that look Sylvie saw that what her friend had told her was true . . . or was, at least, being reported as true. Sylvie felt a scream swelling in her throat, demanding release. Her husband. Another woman. And it was on TV. Her hands wanted to sweat, her knees demanded to quiver. She wanted to eat something: a warm chocolate-chip cookie, a strawberry malted, a square of baklava, dripping with honey, a bowl of oatmeal big enough to swim in, with melted butter pooling on top . . . *Calm down,* she told herself, and settled her purse in her lap. *You're being Syllie.* That's what Ceil said, during the rare instances when Sylvie gave in to emotion, and Ceil, drama queen Ceil, who would turn the opening of a can of soup into a ten-minute performance, complete with intermission, would tell her to calm down, to stop being Syllie.

She tapped at her assistant's shoulder. "I really need to stop."

Clarissa turned. Her eyes were so wide that there was white all the way around the blue-green irises. Her cheeks were flushed, and her honey-colored hair, normally smoothed into the sleekest chignon this side of the ballet barre, was sticking out in a tuft over her left ear.

"Please," she said, speaking to Derek, telling him, in a tone that brooked no discussion, what to do and where to go.

DIANA

"Hello there," Diana said briskly, opening the door of the exam room. The patient, a good-looking guy in his twenties, waited on the table. She looked over his chart and gave him a friendly smile. At her last evaluation, her students had given her excellent marks for her skills and her teaching, but they'd said her bedside manner needed improvement. "She scares me," one of the little scut-monkeys had written, "and I'm not even sick!"

"Mr. Vance?" she said, making a point of using his name. "What brings you here today?"

He smiled back, his eyes intent on hers. In jeans and running shoes and a long-sleeved cotton T-shirt, he was the picture of ruddy good health, so unlike the majority of the people she saw, who usually looked wretched and exhausted from sitting for hours in the dingy, poorly lit waiting room. Usually they smelled bad, too, the hospital's odor of antiseptic and body fluids clinging to their skin like an invisible film. But this guy, as she approached him, smelled like soap and spice and warm, male skin. "I've just been feeling weird lately," he said.

"Weird?" Diana asked, setting his chart back into the plastic holder on the back of the door.

"Feverish," he amplified. He was still smiling, his white teeth gleaming, radiating vitality. He had a head full of thick black hair, strong shoulders and long legs, an ease in his body as he sat eyeing her appreciatively, as if he could see right through the lab coat and the clothes underneath it, as if she was standing in front of him naked, or maybe just wearing her lacy black panties and bra.

"Well, let's take a look." She turned away, feeling like she was stepping out of a spotlight, and took a moment to collect herself as she pulled a thermometer strip out of the drawer and smoothed it over his forehead. "Unbutton your shirt, please."

His fingers—long, capable-looking, a little bit of crisp black hair on the knuckles—moved lazily over the buttons. His eyes never left hers as he slipped the shirt over his shoulders. He was bare-chested underneath it. A mat of soft black curls, the same color as the hair on his head, covered his chest, and the smooth, tanned skin of his shoulders gleamed under the lights. Diana swallowed hard and checked the strip.

"No fever."

He shrugged. "That's strange. I've been feeling so hot lately."

"Let's take a listen." She bent over his healthy, handsome body, sliding the bell of the stethoscope down his chest, listening to his heartbeat, steady and strong. She was so close that his breath rustled her hair. "Breathe in, please." His chest rose as he did it. She slid the stethoscope over to his back. "Any other symptoms?"

"Well . . ." He paused, then took her wrist in his warm hand, pulling it down to the bulge at his crotch. "I've had this swelling."

Her fingertips brushed the denim. She gasped, jerking her hand back, feeling her face flush. "Mr. Vance. Please! I'm a professional."

But he was on his feet by then, his hot chest pressing against her crisp white lab coat, his arms circling her, the swelling between his legs pressed irresistibly against her belly. "Please, Doctor. You've got to help me." He took her hand again, gently this time, and slipped it into the waistband of his jeans. She felt the heat of his skin, the coarse curls of his pubic hair before her fingers wrapped around the throbbing length of his erection.

"Oh, my," she breathed.

"You see?" he whispered in her ear. "That's not normal, is it? Do you think it's a tumor?"

"I'm not sure," she whispered back as he nuzzled the side of her neck, his big white teeth nipping gently at the skin. "Maybe I'd better have a look."

"Oh, Doctor," he sighed as she unbuttoned his fly and took his hot length in her hand. "Does my insurance cover this?"

"I'm sure we can work something out."

She pulled his boxers down over his hips. His cock brushed the side of her face, hot and smooth and gorgeous. She rubbed her cheek against the silky skin, hearing him inhale.

"Suck it," he groaned, his hands in her hair. Diana put her left hand on the delectable curve of his ass, cupped his balls in her right. That was when her BlackBerry started buzzing.

"Shit!"

"Don't answer," said Doug. "You're on break, right?"

"I've got to take it." She got to her feet, engorged and throbbing between her legs, and pulled her BlackBerry out of her pocket. But it wasn't the front desk paging her to tell her that the food-poisoning lady needed fluids or that the guy with chest pains was crashing. Instead, a number with a 202 area code was flashing on the screen. Her heart, already pounding, seemed to pick up the pace even more. Her father knew how busy she was. He wouldn't call her during her shift, on her cell phone, unless something major was happening.

My dad, she mouthed. Doug nodded and rebuttoned his pants.

"I'll see you later," he whispered, and she waved at him, distracted. He breezed out the door—back to class, she figured. Doug was twenty-five, an intern she'd met three months ago in the very exam room they'd just been using. And she, Diana Katherine Woodruff, was a married mother of a six-year-old. *Never mind that,* she thought, *never mind that for now,* and lifted the phone to her ear.

"Dad?"

"Diana?" Her father's voice sounded shaky. *Lizzie,* she thought, her hands clenching. A familiar, impotent fury filled her. Something had happened to her sister Lizzie again, or Lizzie had done something stupid and gotten in trouble . . . and Lizzie was minding her son.

"What is it?" she asked, smoothing her hair and stepping out into the hallway. "Is it Lizzie? Is Milo okay?"

"No. No, honey, Lizzie's fine. It's . . ." He paused, which was strange. Her father was a practiced public speaker who could deliver an address on everything from the don't ask/don't tell policy to the cash for clunkers program with hardly a pause or an "um." "I'm going to be on the news tonight."

This wasn't unheard of, and it certainly didn't merit a phone call. Usually his chief of staff would send an e-mail blast to friends, family, and key supporters (translation: big donors), telling them to set their DVRs when her dad was on the news. "Why? What's up?"

He cleared his throat. "Need to tell you something, sweetheart."

Diana felt nausea twist in her belly. Her father never sounded unsure of himself. Whether it was the time she'd fallen off her bike and needed stitches in her chin, or the televised address he'd given after the planes had hit the Twin Towers on 9-11, his voice was rich and resonant. He sounded reassuring, no matter what he was saying . . . but now he sounded almost frightened. Was he sick? Was that why he was calling her? She ran down a list of potential problems—heart disease, hypertension, enlarged prostate. Ugh. Her father cleared his throat, then kept talking.

"Last year a woman came to work in my D.C. office as a legislative aide, and we . . . she and I . . ."

Diana pushed the door to the break room open with her shoulder. It smelled, as usual, like the ghost of someone's departed burrito, like sweat and adrenaline and, faintly, of what she'd come to think of as eau de ER—blood and urine and feces and vomit, the smell of illness and of fear.

"What?" she asked, her voice loud in the empty room. "What are you saying?"

"We had an affair. It didn't last long, and it's over, but I helped her get a job, and someone found out about it—about us—and it's probably going to be in the news tonight."

Diana slumped against a row of pale-blue-painted metal lockers with the BlackBerry pressed to her ear.

"It's over," her father repeated. "That's the important thing. It didn't last very long, and it . . . it was never . . . I wasn't going to . . ."

Her thumb hovered over the button that would have ended the call. She wanted desperately to press it, to silence her father's voice, to unlearn what he'd told her. She wanted it to be five minutes ago. She wanted to be back in the exam room, on her knees, investigating Doug Vance's mysterious swelling.

"I wanted to tell you," her father was saying, "before you heard it somewhere else. I'm sorry, Di. I'm sorry." His voice cracked.

She wondered where he was calling from. His office in Washington, with its big leather chair, family photos on the desk, and a framed copy of the Bill of Rights over the bookshelves? The back of a Town Car, with a briefing binder in his lap, the day's papers folded by his side?

Diana reached for the television remote and pointed it at the set bolted to the ceiling. It was tuned to CNN, and, as the picture came into focus, she saw her father walking somewhere—in D.C., she presumed—with his arm around the waist of a curly-haired, chubby young woman. The young woman smiled as her father bent his head, saying something in her ear that made her laugh. *Sources are reporting,* a voice coming from the set said, *that Senator Woodruff may have paid lobbyists to get his former assistant and rumored mistress, Joelle Stabinow, a job at the D.C. branch of the New York City law firm where he was once a partner.*

"You got her a job? This woman?"

"It wasn't anything illegal." Her father's voice sounded calmer, more assertive. "She was qualified. She finished at the top of her class at Georgetown."

"Excellent." She sounded brittle, like her mother after too long on a receiving line. "Tell her congratulations from me."

"Diana. There's no need for that tone."

"Oh? Do you want me to sound happy?"

"Of course not. I'm not happy about it. I really screwed up here."

"Ya think?" But really, she wasn't in a position to say anything. How could she condemn him, given what she'd been doing when he called? Down on her knees in front of a med student, her student, a man who was not her husband, a man she had no business touching. At least she had the sense to be discreet, to lock the door.

"It'll pass," her father was saying. "It'll be a one-day story. There wasn't any fiscal impropriety, no taxpayer dollars, no—"

She cut him off. "Did you tell Mom?"

"I've been trying to reach her," he said. "She's not picking up. Neither is Lizzie."

Lizzie. Diana's heart sank. Her father paused. "Do you think you can tell your sister, if I don't reach her first? It'll kill her to see this on the news."

"Fine," Diana snapped. *Here we go again,* she thought, with her in her familiar role as responsible big sister keeping little Lizzie safe from the big, bad world.

The break room door swung open and Doug Vance poked his head in. He looked at Diana, then up at the TV set, which was now showing a commercial for a weight-loss program. "Everything okay?" he whispered.

"I'll speak to you later," Diana said to her father. She hung up the phone, slipped it back into her pocket, and turned to her . . . what was Doug, exactly? Her boyfriend? Her lover? Her man on the side?

"Everything's fine," she said, and did her best to sound as if she believed it.

Doug gave her a puzzled look. "Catch up later?"

"I'll text you." That was how they communicated, by texts, like love-struck teenagers, all abbreviations and emoticons: Need 2 C U. U R MY HRT. Silly little things, and yet she cherished every letter, every emoticon. Doug moved her, in a way that no one, including her husband, ever had.

As if to confirm that unhappy truth, her telephone spasmed in her pocket. She lifted the phone to her ear. "Hi, honey."

"Diana?" asked Gary, whose voice was low and rattly, due to his extensive allergies and the hay fever he seemed to have for ten months out of the year. He sniffled, cleared his throat, and said, "Um, did you hear about . . ."

"I saw."

Gary paused, fumbling for the words. "Are you okay?"

"I'm fine." She crossed the room and opened her locker. There were her running shoes, a pair of shorts, a sports bra, and a ripe T-shirt that she'd shucked off after a lunchtime five-miler two days before. It would do. She tucked the phone under her chin and started unbuttoning her lab coat. "I'm fine," she repeated. "Why wouldn't I be? I didn't do anything wrong."

"Well, right," Gary stammered. A great stammerer was her Gary. "I mean, of course not. But it's just . . ."

"It's a shock." She shoved her feet into the sneakers, then bent and gave the laces a hard yank. "It's appalling."

"It's a surprise," said Gary. "I thought your dad was one of the good guys." Gary sounded as if he was on the verge of tears. No surprise there. Of the two of them, Gary had always been the crier. He'd cried at their wedding and when Milo was born, both occasions during which Diana had remained dry-eyed (although, to be fair, during the birth she'd also been heavily drugged). Gary, she'd thought more and more frequently as the years went by, was more of a girl than she was.

"Listen," he was saying, as Diana pulled the running bra over her head. "I know we were supposed to go out tonight . . ."

"And we should," she said, grimacing as the fragrant T-shirt settled over her shoulders.

"Are you sure? We can reschedule."

She shook her head. This was typical Gary, looking for any excuse to stay home on the couch. "We can't reschedule. We've already rescheduled twice, and the gift certificate expires next week." They'd won the dinner at Milo's school auction last year. She'd bid for it, paying too much money and not caring—it was for charity, and Gary would never take her anywhere fancy without some prepaid prompting.

His voice was very small. "You don't think people will stare?"

"Let them stare." She banged her locker shut. "I have to go."

"I'll see you at the restaurant," he said before she ended the call. Instantly, her telephone started buzzing again. She reopened the locker, threw the phone into her purse, retrieved her iPod, slammed the locker shut again, and walked swiftly past the receptionist on duty, a pale, pie-faced thing named Ashley.

"I'm taking my break," she announced; Ashley cringed and nodded and started to say something before Diana cut her off.

"I need you to call my sister," she said. "Lizzie Woodruff. Her number's on my contact sheet. I'll be back in forty-five minutes. Please ask her to meet me here."

"Yes, Doctor," Ashley whispered, and then Diana pushed through the door to the stairs, taking them two at a time, until she came out on the steaming, humid pavement. Then she went running down Spruce Street, east toward the Delaware River as fast as she could, with music pounding in her ears and her blood pounding through her body, until a stitch burned in her side and her breath tore at her throat and the pain pushed everything out of her mind except putting one foot in front of the other.

LIZZIE

It was a scramble getting Milo out of the brilliantly blue swimming pool, into the changing room, and then into his clothes: his khakis and boat shoes, the button-down shirt and the ski cap he insisted on wearing even in the summer heat. Lizzie ended up with no time to do anything but pull on her ribbed tank top and her long, lacy white skirt, slide her feet into her flip-flops, loop her old Leica around her neck and her purse over her shoulder, grab Milo's backpack, and race through the swimming club's door out to Lombard Street to hail a cab.

By the time they arrived at the hospital they were fifteen minutes late, and Lizzie was a wreck—pink-faced, frizzy-haired, with something unpleasant that she hoped was gum and feared was worse clinging to the sole of her shoe. Also, she'd forgotten her bra. She'd barely noticed, but it was the kind of detail that would not escape her sister. She was sweating, and the unpleasant taste of copper filled her mouth. Ashley hadn't said what her sister wanted, but Lizzie had never been summoned to Diana's workplace in the middle of the day and could only assume that the news was bad—that she'd screwed up something, that she was in trouble again.

Diana was waiting for her by the ER desk, perfect as ever, buttoned up in her lab coat, wearing a slim pearly-gray pencil skirt and matching high heels, as put together as she'd been that morning, except her face was beet red and her hair, slicked back in a twist, was wet.

"Are you okay, Mom?" Milo asked in his gravelly voice, and Diana softened, the way she only did for her son, and bent to brush her lips against his forehead and smooth his dark bangs out of his eyes.

"I'm fine. Did you bring your Leapster? Can you go sit in the waiting room by yourself like a big boy for ten minutes? Aunt Lizzie and I need to have an adult conversation."

Once Milo was parked on the couch, playing some improving game, Diana pulled Lizzie into the empty break room and closed the door behind her.

Lizzie, who thought she'd figured out the reason for this impromptu visit, was prepared. As soon as the door was shut, she started talking. "Look, I know what you said about McDonald's, and I read all the information you gave me." This was a slight exaggeration—she'd glanced at one of the articles in the stack that Diana had left on her bed, but had gotten so grossed out by the descriptions of cattle mistreatment and beef preservatives that she'd shoved it in the drawer of the dresser and never looked at it again.

Diana lifted an eyebrow—Diana could do that, could lift her eyebrows one at a time. Lizzie plowed ahead. "He said he was the only kid in his class who'd never been there. And we only went once, and I paid with my own money, and he had the Chicken McNuggets with milk, not soda, and I got him a cut-up apple on the side . . ."

Diana cut her off with a wave of her hand. Her nails were perfectly filed, gleaming ovals. Lizzie snuck her own raggedy fingertips, with their bitten tips and peeling red polish, into her pockets.

"Dad called."

Lizzie blinked. "What's going on?" Her sister's tone triggered a familiar sensation, the feeling of a trapdoor opening in her belly. For years, Lizzie had thought of her parents, and even her sister, as sort of like Greek gods—distant and capricious and unknowable, larger than life, or at least smarter than average, given to hurling their thunderbolts and their decrees down from Mount Olympus, not really caring what kind of damage they'd do to the normal people like Lizzie. Like savvy mortals throughout time, Lizzie had done her best to escape their notice. She was polite and cheerful when spoken to, and tried to keep a low profile the rest of the time.

Diana found the remote on the break room table and pointed it at the set. CNN came on the screen, and there was their father, Senator Richard Woodruff, D-NY, with his arm around the waist of a woman who was not their mom.

"Oh." Lizzie stared at the screen. A sick feeling rose in her throat as she caught the words *extramarital affair.* She knew this feeling, that nausea, the clamminess in her armpits and the small of her back. At twenty-four, Lizzie Woodruff was well acquainted with shame. She'd just never had the occasion to feel it on behalf of another family member—not impeccable, brilliant, successful Diana; not her gracious, elegant, eternally appropriate mother; and certainly not her father, a man everyone looked up to, a man everyone respected. She swallowed hard, wiping sweat from her upper lip.

"Oh," she said. "Oh, jeez."

"Yeah," said Diana, lips curled. "Oh, jeez." Lizzie was still staring up at the screen, which showed a picture—a photograph pulled from a computer, Lizzie thought—of the same woman, now dressed in a bikini, sitting cross-legged and laughing on the bow of a sailboat.

"Christ," Diana muttered. "You'd think one of these bimbos would own a one-piece."

"Did you talk to Mom? Is she okay?" Lizzie whispered. She twisted her hair in a knot and secured it with her elastic band, then started pacing.

Diana pulled her phone out of her pocket, hit a button, listened, then said, "Mom? Hang on. I'm going to conference in Lizzie."

Lizzie's telephone trilled its ringtone, the bouncy melody of Lady Gaga's "Just Dance," from the depths of the embroidered, sequined purse that she'd bought for ten dollars on Canal Street. Diana made a face—at the purse, or the ring tone, or Lizzie's inability to locate her phone, Lizzie wasn't sure. She rooted around, fingers brushing against lipstick and crumpled bills and Kleenexes and the cartridges for Milo's Leapster, feeling dizzy and desperate to find someplace dim and fragrant with the smell of old beer and cigarettes and drink white wine, chilled so cold that the first glass would give her a headache, which the second glass would instantly cure, or maybe rum and Cokes, her old favorite, syrupy-sweet, so easy going down, making the world pleasantly blurry.

Finally, she found her phone at the bottom of her purse. "Hello? Mom?"

"Girls?" Sylvie's voice was pinched and small.

"What's going on?" Diana demanded.

"I don't know," said Sylvie. "I'm in a car, on my way back up to New York. I've spoken to Ceil, but other than that, I don't know what's happening."

"I talked to Dad." Diana's words were clipped. "He says he was having an affair, and he got her a job. And he's sorry. Which of course he'd say."

"Oh, God." Sylvie's voice was a croak. "As soon as I speak to your father I'll call you back. Until then, just wait. And be careful. I'm sure reporters will call you, and you shouldn't say anything."

Diana barked laughter. "Oh, really? You don't think I should go down and make a statement?"

"Diana," said Sylvie. Diana rolled her eyes. Her mother could be terrifying, and never more so than when she was angry.

"Maybe it was innocent. Maybe that woman just needed, you know, a father figure. Maybe it was nothing. Maybe they're just friends."

"Oh, for God's sake," said Diana. The scorn in her voice could have been bottled and sold as a chemical weapon. "Fifty-seven-year-old senators are not friends with their twentysomething aides." She exhaled noisily. "I bet there's e-mails. Or more pictures. Or something. There's always something. Not to mention," Diana continued, looking pointedly at her sister, "the press is probably going to write about all of us."

Lizzie wondered when the details would come out and marveled at her sister's ability to always see the worst in any situation . . . including, of course, Lizzie's own. She remembered once, for her birthday, her parents had taken them to a state fair. Lizzie had been eight, almost out of her mind with excitement about the Tilt-A-Whirl she'd be allowed to ride and the cotton candy she'd be given to eat. Diana, at fourteen, hadn't wanted to come at all, and had spent the ride upstate gazing out the window and heaving noisy sighs.

The day had been wonderful. A cheerful round man in a suit and bow tie, the mayor of Plattsburgh, had met them in the parking lot. "So you're the birthday girl?" he'd asked, bending down with a soft grunt until he was eye level with Lizzie. The mayor had whisked them to the front of every line. He'd made sure that Lizzie sampled every delicacy—the grilled sausage and sweet peppers, the fresh-squeezed lemonade, the Steak on a Stake, the soft-serve custard and fried dough—and had squeezed her close, beaming, for a newspaper photograph.

Back in the car, sticky and sleepy and full, Lizzie had said to her sister, "This was the best day ever," and Diana, with her face turned once more toward the window, had said, "You know the whole thing was a photo op." Then she'd explained to her sister exactly what a photo op was, and how her father needed people in Plattsburgh to vote for him, which was why she, Diana, had been stuck wasting her Saturday in this stupid cow town when she could have been in the city with her friends. Lizzie had managed to hold back her tears until it was too dark for anyone in the car to see that she was crying. She'd thought the man had given her treats and taken her picture because it was her birthday; that she'd been the one they'd been fussing over.

Sylvie, meanwhile, was urging Diana to be patient, not to judge until they knew for sure what had happened. She gathered herself, asking, "Are you two all right? Lizzie, are you handling this okay?"

"*I'm* fine," said Diana. She sat down in a metal chair and crossed her toned, tanned legs, swinging the right one hard over the left. "Thank you for your concern."

"I'm okay," said Lizzie, who knew why her mother had asked about her first. Of course Diana was all right. Diana was always all right. The world could be crumbling to rubble at their feet and Diana would be going for a run through the ruins. Lizzie took an experimental breath as, once more, the television set showed footage of her father with his arm around that other woman. *Sources report that the senator gave Stabinow significant raises during her employment, then helped her find a six-figure job at a prominent D.C. law firm,* said the voice on the screen, as the video dissolved into a still shot of the woman graduating from somewhere, beaming in her cap and gown. "I'm all right," Lizzie said more strongly.

"You'll be sure to go to a meeting tonight?" asked her mother. Diana recrossed her legs and glared at the row of lockers as if they, too, had offended her. Diana was not a believer in meetings, or in what she called, with quote marks you could almost hear, "the culture of recovery." Diana thought that if you had a problem, you dealt with it on your own, with willpower and cold showers and fast five-mile runs.

"I'll go," Lizzie said, trying to sound like her sister, solid and smart and in control.

"I'll call you soon. I love you, girls," said Sylvie, and Diana and Lizzie answered that they loved her, too, before Diana broke the connection. She put her phone in her pocket and snapped the television off.

"I can't believe this."

Lizzie couldn't, either. Couldn't, and didn't want to. "Maybe it isn't true."

Diana rolled her eyes again. Her talent for dashing Lizzie's hopes, for puncturing Lizzie's balloons, hadn't diminished at all in the years since they were girls. "Of course it's true! Dad said so."

"Not to me," Lizzie said stubbornly.

"And there's video."

"Maybe it was Photoshopped." Such things could happen. Hadn't there been some kind of movie-star sex tape later proven to be a fake? And what about the time that talk-show hostess's head had appeared on a magazine cover on top of someone else's body?

"It wasn't. God!" Diana bounced back to her feet.

Lizzie edged toward the window, turning away from Diana's rage. She looked at her phone—her father had called her twice, probably while she'd been coaxing Milo out of the water, and it was almost five o'clock. "Milo needs dinner."

"Fine," Diana snapped. "Take him to McDonald's again. Take him to Wendy's. Get him pizza. Whatever he wants. I don't care."

"Are you going to tell him?" Lizzie asked.

Diana lifted one hand to her face and swiped at her forehead, and when she spoke, she sounded, for the first time, unsure. She walked to the window to stand next to Lizzie. The blue of the sky had deepened, and the angles of her face, the line of her lips were lit by the twilight glow. Lizzie reached for the camera that hung against her chest, then stopped her hands. Diana hated having her picture taken, and now was definitely not the time, even though she didn't think she'd ever seen her sister looking so beautiful, or so sad. "I don't know," Diana said, and then startled Lizzie by asking, "Do you think he needs to know?"

Lizzie thought it over. If Milo was in school or camp, surely the other kids would have overheard their parents' conversations and would possibly be talking about it. But school was out, and Milo had refused to go to computer camp or cooking camp or, heaven forbid, sports camp, which meant that he went for days without talking to anyone but his parents and Lizzie. He hardly watched TV—his mother carefully monitored his screen time, and what he did see was mostly nature documentaries, which Diana approved of, and cooking shows, which Milo loved.

"Maybe we shouldn't tell him yet," said Lizzie.

Diana gave a brisk nod, herself again. "Okay," she said. "Give him dinner. I'm going to stop at home to change. I'm going out with Gary tonight, remember?"

Lizzie slipped her phone back in her purse. The two of them walked into the waiting room and found Milo sitting with his Leapster abandoned on his lap and his gaze trained on the television set.

"I think we've all got scandal fatigue," said a redhead in a sweater that struck Lizzie as too low-cut and clingy for TV, or for someone who was old and emaciated. "Giuliani, Spitzer, Edwards, Sanford . . . what's surprising at this point is the politician who doesn't have something on the side." She gave a bright little laugh as the screen filled with a shot of Milo's Grandpa Richard, murmuring into the curly-haired woman's ear. "The only interesting thing at this point is how the wife's going to behave. If she's going to stand up at the press conference or make him go sleep in the barn."

"Those are the options?" The host sounded amused. "Stand by your man or go sleep in the barn?"

"Personally, I'd respect it if one of these women told her guy to go sleep with the fishes," said the redhead. Her collarbones bounced up and down as she giggled at her own wit.

"Let's give the senator credit," said the young man in a bow tie who sat at the table beside her. "At least he didn't use taxpayer money to pay for hookers. Or tell his constituents he was hiking the Appalachian Trail."

The redhead gave him a thumbs-up. Her face was tight as a tambourine, but Lizzie could see blue veins bulging across the backs of her hands, and her skinny fingers looked like claws. "Bonus points for that."

What if it was your dad? Lizzie wanted to call, assuming the brittle, bony old crone had ever had a father, that she hadn't been hatched in some conservative think tank's laboratory. *How would you like it, if it was your father, and I was the one on TV, laughing at him?*

Lizzie marched to the television set and stood on her tiptoes, trying to change the channel. "Miss," called the woman behind the reception desk. "You can't touch that!"

"Yes, she can," said Diana. She knelt down in front of Milo and started talking to him in a low, comforting murmur. *Nothing to worry about,* Diana was telling her son. *Everything's okay.* Lizzie strained and stretched until she hit the power button. When the set was off, she turned and beckoned for Milo, who was even paler and more somber than normal, looking even more like a miniature banker whose job it was to tell young couples that their mortgage applications had been denied.

"Mommy's going back to work," Diana told her son. "Aunt Lizzie's going to take you home." She bent, hugging him. "I love you miles and miles."

"Miles and miles," he repeated, then gave her a high five, a low five, and a fist bump before smoothing his bangs again and tugging his hat down securely over his ears. Lizzie reached for her camera again—she'd love to have a picture of that, of her sister being decent and gentle and sweet. Then again, she made her hands drop. Diana mustered a smile, gave her sister a tight nod, and slipped back into the ER. Lizzie took Milo's hand.

"Aunt Lizzie?" he asked in his gravelly voice as he followed her into the hallway. "Why was Grandpa on TV?"

"Well, you know, he's a senator."

"He makes laws in Washington," Milo recited. "But who was that lady? They said she was his girlfriend."

"You know what?" Lizzie said, and took his hand. "Let's talk about your delicious dinner. We don't have to worry about Grandpa right now."

SYLVIE

As the car swung into the rest area, Sylvie grabbed the door handle, and the instant the tires had stopped, she yanked the door open. Avoiding Clarissa's pained gaze and Derek's murmured "Ma'am?" she hurried through the heat of the parking lot, up the concrete stairs, and into the rest stop.

There, in the wide, tiled entryway that smelled of frying food and disinfectant, Sylvie stood as if frozen, head tilted back, staring up at the television set as it broadcast CNN. Travelers flowed around her: harried mothers with toddlers in their arms hustling into the ladies' room, senior citizens making their slow way toward the Burger King, or stopping to peer at the giant maps on the wall. Sylvie ignored all of them, letting them walk around her, barely hearing their "excuse me's" and "watch it, lady," and "hey, that's a real bad place to plant yourself." Over and over, the same snippet of film played on the screen: a woman, her head bent, curly brown hair blowing in the wind as she walked through an apartment building's door, followed by footage of Richard (blue suit, red-and-gold tie from Hermés she'd bought him last Christmas) on a standard-issue podium, delivering what was undoubtedly a standard-issue speech (together, they'd written one on education, and one on the environment, and one on Our Leaders of Tomorrow, which could be tailored for an elementary school or high school audience and padded for college graduations). Words bubbled out of the speakers, but Sylvie could no longer make sense of them. It was as if her mind was a Venus flytrap: it had ingested the pertinent facts, then snapped shut tight, refusing to let the words back out for further consideration. *Sources are reporting . . . Joelle Stabinow, a former legislative aide, a Georgetown Law School graduate who frequently traveled with the senator . . . donor-funded junkets at tropical resorts . . .*

The pictures cycled past again: the young woman, then Richard. Her brown hair. His red tie. And now, another picture of the girl, in a bikini that Sylvie never would have attempted, not even at her thinnest. The girl—the woman, Sylvie supposed, because that was the politically correct term—sat, cross-legged, on the wooden deck of a boat. Her belly pushed at the low waistband of the white bikini bottom, her breasts pressed at the cups of the top. No Special K and skim milk breakfasts for this one; no five A.M. sessions with a Pilates Nazi who'd bark, "USE your CORE," as if Sylvie were a dog failing obedience class.

So Ceil and Diana were right. This was real. She must have made some noise, some cry of dismay. Clarissa, who'd appeared at her elbow, looked at her sadly, but said nothing. Then again, really, what could Clarissa say? Sylvie was certain that the topic of how to handle it if your boss's spouse was caught in a sex scandal had not been covered at Vanderbilt, where Clarissa had gotten her degrees.

She tried to speak. "I think," she began. But whatever she'd thought was interrupted by a man who'd come to stand next to her. He was a beefy fellow in blue jeans and a plaid shirt. Red suspenders kept the jeans aloft. He had a grease-spotted Burger King bag in his hand.

"Boy oh boy," he said, as if Sylvie had started a conversation;

as if, in fact, she'd been waiting all day to talk with him. "Here we go again with this. Pigs. All of them. Pigs."

"Pigs," Sylvie repeated.

"Okay," said a young woman in jeans and dark-framed glasses, "okay, fine, but why are they wasting their time reporting on this? There's a war going on. People are dying." She gestured at the screen, where the words SEX SCANDAL crawled underneath the knot of Richard's tie. "And this is what the news shows are doing? Following politicians around to find out where they're getting their rocks off? Like, who even cares?"

"Who," said Sylvie, like an owl.

"She's not even that hot," offered a fellow in a Giants jersey. Sylvie was unsurprised to see that he had a weak chin and teeth that pointed in several directions. *Everyone's a critic,* Ceil always said. "Shit," said the Giants fan. "If I was a senator, I'd get, like, Miss Universe to sleep with me."

"Nice," said the girl in the glasses . . . but she said it quietly, so that the Giants-jersey guy could pretend he hadn't heard.

"I think it's a disgrace," said the man with the Burger King bag. "He's probably got daughters her age."

"Daughters," Sylvie repeated. She was aware, behind her, of the desperate glance Clarissa was undoubtedly shooting at Derek, a glance that telegraphed that this was developing into a Situation, that Steps Must Be Taken before Sylvie did something or said something to worsen this crisis before it could be massaged and managed and spun. Clarissa had gotten as far as placing a tentative hand on Sylvie's shoulder and uttering the word "Ma'am?" when Sylvie's bag (Prada, but discreet, with just one small label sewn underneath the handle) slipped out of her grasp and thumped to the floor. The fellow with the Burger King lunch knelt to retrieve it. "Ma'am? You all right?"

Sylvie looked down at herself: her sheer hose and plain

pumps, her expensive navy-blue knit skirt and jacket, a little too tight at the bust. ("Crunches!" she could hear her trainer exhorting. "Presses! Flies!" And his favorite, "Push-aways!" which meant pushing yourself away from the table.) *My husband is fucking a legislative aide.* There was a small reddish stain on the toe of the man's work boot. She could feel her throat clenching tight, and the pressure of tears building. She could smell onions, the onions Richard denied himself in his morning omelet. It was a poor place for a life to end. But that was what was happening. Her life, the one she'd built over decades, the one she'd made alongside Richard, her life as his wife, her life as she'd known it, was ending, unraveling, coming apart right here in a rest stop on the New Jersey Turnpike.

Sylvie pressed her fist against her lips. Clarissa's face, pale and worried, swam into her sight as she interposed her body between Sylvie and the man. "Mrs. Woodruff?" She shot a look over her shoulder and lowered her voice. "Sylvie? Are you all right?"

Sylvie's telephone burped. The man picked up her purse. Hoping that it was Ceil again, that sensible Ceil could somehow explain this all and make sense of it for her and tell her that things would be fine, Sylvie located her cell phone and lifted it to her ear.

"Hello?"

"That crotch!" Selma hollered, in her unmistakable hoarse, loud Brooklyn accent. "I knew he was no good for you! The first time you brought him home I knew it! I never liked the way he smelled!"

"Ma." The single word had exhausted her. Sylvie pressed the telephone against her face, hoping that no one in the crowd had realized who she was. It was unlikely—the average American, if pressed, probably wouldn't be able to pick a Supreme Court justice out of a lineup, so the chances of a senator's wife going undetected were high. *Bathroom,* she mouthed to Clarissa, and carried the telephone into a stall as her mother continued to talk.

"Insect repellent. Took me years to figure it out, but that's exactly what he smells like. Bug spray. You should have married Bruce Baumgardner. You remember the Baumgardners? They lived on seventeen. Carpet stores."

Sylvie didn't answer. "Are you gonna divorce him?" Selma asked. "If you are, you tell me first. I know all the best family law guys." Sylvie shook her head. This was surprising. As far as she knew, her mother had always liked Richard. He sent flowers on Selma's birthday, and on Mother's Day, and on the anniversary of Sylvie's father's death. He picked up takeout from the Carnegie Deli once a month when they went over for dinner, and always held doors and offered to carry Selma's bags and picked up her favorite See's candies when he traveled to California. Sylvie twisted on the toilet seat as her mother's voice spilled into her ear. "Bruce lives in New Jersey. His wife was running around with some fellow she met in her yoga class . . ."

"Yoga," Sylvie repeated. Her voice was hollow, and her skirt, as she sat on the toilet, was bunched in an unflattering way around her hips. The word had always sounded strange, but never more so than at this moment.

"They split up and he moved into the basement while they're waiting for the house to sell." Selma paused, perhaps realizing that a revelation of below-street-level tenancy did not put Bruce in the best light. "It's a finished basement. With a half-bath."

"Ma, this isn't a very good time . . ."

"Sylvia, listen to me, because this is important," Selma continued. "If you do a *60 Minutes* interview, don't wear teal."

Her head was spinning. The word *teal* sounded just as odd, as foreign, as *yoga*. "What?"

"Teal. Hillary wore teal. After the whole mess with Gennifer Flowers? Where Bill said he'd caused pain in his marriage? Teal wasn't a good look for her and I don't think it'd be good for you, either."

"Ma . . ."

"Washes you right out. Wear red. Red says you're strong and you're not going to take it. And you're not. Going to take it. Are you?" Selma paused to take a breath. "Oh, and make sure it's that Lesley Stahl who interviews you. Not the African-American fellow, the one with the earring. He's very abrupt."

"Ma." Sylvie sagged sideways against the wall. With her fingertips she touched the sagging skin beneath her eyes, the hound-dog droops that the Botox doctor hadn't been able to fix. "Ed Bradley's dead. I'm not going on *60 Minutes*. Please stop calling my husband a crotch." From underneath the stall door she saw Clarissa's black heels and slim ankles. There was a soft knock on the stall door. "Mrs. Woodruff?" her assistant whispered.

"Ma, I have to go."

"Can I give Bruce Baumgardner your number?"

"No!"

Her mother's grating voice softened, as if she'd remembered that she wasn't sparring with opposing counsel or interrogating a hostile witness. Sylvie's father used to be the one to calm her with a quiet word or a Yiddish endearment, but Dave had died of a stroke five years ago, leaving Selma alone and unmodulated. "Are you all right?"

Sylvie considered. She'd just learned that her husband was carrying on with a legislative aide, a woman who was probably half her age, a woman who, she thought with rising horror, could possibly be pregnant, was at least of an age where she could get pregnant, like John Edwards's mistress had, so she was a very long way from "all right."

"Poor Sylvie," said her mother. "You should call Jan for the keys."

"Keys?" said Sylvie.

"To the Connecticut house," Selma said, as if this was obvious. "I'll come up and visit once you get settled. Remember what I said about teal." Her mother paused, the way she had before closing arguments. "I love you, sweetie. Always. I'm here if you need me."

Sylvie ended the call, tucked her telephone into her purse, and stepped out of the stall. Clarissa stood back respectfully while Sylvie washed her hands and dried them in one of those high-tech blowers. Then, head bent as if buffeted by a heavy wind, she followed her assistant back out to the Town Car, where Derek hurried out to hold the door.

In the backseat, she slipped off her shoes and then, with some wriggling, her panty hose, which had dug bright-red ridges into her hips. She yanked them over her thighs, her knees and ankles and kicked them onto the car floor, considering her husband, whom she'd loved for so long and thought she'd known so well. She remembered the first time Richard had brought her home to Harrisburg, to the tidy two-bedroom ranch-style house where he'd grown up and where his parents still lived. Richard's father was bluff and hearty, proudly bald, with a barrel chest and a booming voice and an undying love for the Philadelphia Eagles. "How do you like my boy?" he asked, pounding Richard on his back (this back-thumping, Sylvie would come to learn, was what the male members of Richard's family did in lieu of expressing emotion or conversing with each other). Cindy, Richard's mother, was a small, timid woman who didn't walk so much as scurry, and who barely said a word after her whispered "hello." (Maybe, Sylvie thought, Richard Senior pounded her back, too, which was what had given her such a cringing, flinching manner.) She'd made a casserole for dinner, something with cream of mushroom soup and ground beef—Richard's favorite, she'd murmured, scooping it onto thin china plates. She'd put Sylvie's serving in front of her, then suddenly frozen, looking as stricken as if she'd served her son's girlfriend a stewed human hand. "Oh, no . . . is that okay for you? Can you eat it?" she asked, her voice so soft Sylvie could barely hear it. "I can make something else . . . it's no problem at all . . ." Sylvie, puzzled, had assured her that the casserole was fine, and told her, once she'd tasted it, that it was delicious, rich and filling, the perfect meal for a cold winter night.

Later, tucked up against Richard in his old twin bed, with her toes touching his calves, she'd asked why Cindy had been worried. Richard said he guessed that it was because there was cheese in the dish, along with the beef, and that, even in a land bereft of Jews, his mother had enough of a rudimentary grasp of the principles of keeping kosher that she was worried Sylvie wouldn't be able to eat meat with dairy.

"We should write a book," Sylvie said, fitting her body against his with her cheek against his chest and her hands cradling the back of his neck. "*My First Jew.*" He'd rubbed his fingertips gently against the top of her head.

"I'm checking for horns," he told her. She'd slipped one of her hands down the front of his pajama bottoms, whispering, "Me, too." They'd made love for a long, slow time, neither of them making a sound until the very end. Richard, as usual, had fallen asleep almost immediately, but Sylvie lay awake, listening to Richard breathing beside her in this strange little house, as the wind whistled through the trees, thinking that she had never felt so safe, so content, so loved.

In the back of the car, through the bottom of her purse, she could feel her telephone buzzing and burping. She pulled it out and looked at the screen, hoping, again, for Ceil. Instead, Richard's face flashed into view—Richard in their bedroom, smiling at her as he stood in front of the blue-and-white wallpaper. His hair was mostly gray now, but his optimistic grin hadn't changed at all since she'd first met him. Sylvie punched IGNORE. She wasn't ready for that conversation. Not now. Not yet.

Donor-funded junkets to beach resorts, the newscaster had said. She remembered a trip Richard had taken to Martha's Vineyard, a three-day weekend that spring, a Democratic National Convention retreat where current congressmen could look over the party's new faces and decide who had a future, who would get their endorsement and their time during the coming campaign season. Richard himself had been coronated at just such an event, that one at the South Carolina shore. Sylvie would have tagged along, but it was Ceil's birthday and they'd made plans to go to the Museum of Modern Art and a spa after, and a new sushi place after that. Richard had dug his golf clubs out of the storage unit in their building's basement, and Sylvie had tucked a bottle of sunscreen into his suitcase because Richard always forgot. He'd come home on Monday afternoon, the top of his head bright red the way she knew it would be (the next day, it would start to flake and peel, and she'd remind him to exfoliate in the shower and moisturize when he was done). When he'd kissed her, before dropping his suitcase off in the bedroom for her to unpack, she hadn't felt like anything was off, or wrong, even though it seemed that he'd been sharing his bed with his aide for those three nights.

Sylvie yanked at her waistband, wishing she could take off the too-tight skirt, feeling, again, like she couldn't breathe. Her phone was buzzing and beeping and belching. She glanced at the screen. Richard, again. She ignored it, thinking about e-mails and photographs, wondering how bad this could get. Numbness was creeping over her body, freezing her toes and her fingertips, turning her legs and arms into blocks of wood. Her brain, however, was no longer clamped shut. It was clicking and humming, whirling and turning, busily dredging up scenes and sound bites from political scandals both recent and long past. There was the senator who'd been busted in an airport men's room after soliciting sex with strangers (male strangers, and how Sylvie's heart had broken for his poor wife, standing beside him as he insisted that it was all a misunderstanding, that he wasn't really gay!). There was the governor whose aides had said he was hiking the Appalachian Trail when in reality he was visiting a ladyfriend in Argentina. That one had been a big topic around her house for weeks. "Do you realize," she'd told Richard, sitting cross-legged in the armchair of his office, "that I'll never get to be anyone's Argentinian mystery woman? Do you understand what a tragedy this is?" Richard had kissed her, saying, "Don't be so sure. You've still got time."

Was he cheating on her then? Had the joke been on her, the gullible, guileless wife who was just as much a dupe as poor Jenny Sanford down in South Carolina? Her hands tightened into fists as her telephone sounded. Richard again. She clicked IGNORE, and then, squinting at the tiny screen, she accessed the Internet and made her way to the most recent news story, which she read with one eye open and one at half-mast. *Sources say the senator took his mistress on a taxpayer-funded long weekend in the Bahamas, where they shared lunches of fresh crab salad and tropical fruit and played backgammon in a beachfront cabana.*

Sources. She wondered about that—a former aide, a disgruntled ex-staffer, someone who'd been fired or not promoted fast enough? She moaned out loud—but softly, so that Clarissa and Derek wouldn't hear her—and clicked through the story until she found a picture of the woman, Joelle. She stared for a long moment, looking at the tiny image, wondering what Richard saw in this other woman, an ordinary woman, pleasant-looking enough, a hopeful, happy expression as she gazed up at Richard. What struck her immediately was the resemblance.

When she and Richard had met, that was how she'd looked: big-busted, heavy-hipped. Back then, she'd favored necklaces of colorful beads that she bought on street corners in New York, and cheap, dangly earrings that usually ended up tangled in her hair. She'd drunk wine from bottles with screw-tops, and she'd been a social smoker of cigarettes and an occasional smoker of pot. She'd had a closet full of black tights and bright skirts, fringed scarves, tunics and peasant blouses to wear with them. She'd pull her curls off her face and twist them in a knot skewered with a pencil. *Wild child,* Richard had called her, cupping her head and pulling her into a kiss.

She and Richard had met in law school. There were twenty-three women in their class of one hundred and seventy, a group that included a future first lady (her husband, the future president, had been a year behind them). Among her classmates, Sylvie had been, if not royalty, then at least someone with a reputation, the daughter of Judge Selma Serfer, who'd once taught at Yale and who returned each year to lecture the 3-L's on gender and the law. Richard had a reputation, too. He'd played football back in Harrisburg and Penn State, and was tall and well muscled, with a shock of unruly brown hair. He was obviously smart—anyone at Yale would have to be. But Richard did not cultivate the air of bemused indifference that most of the other boys worked hard to achieve. In class, while they leaned back in their chairs, legs stretched presumptuously in the aisles, cuffs unbuttoned and frayed, he'd be bent over his notebook, scribbling frantically as if intent on getting every word down, his jacket hung neatly on the back of his chair and his plaid shirt buttoned to the throat. When the professors asked for volunteers, his hand shot up, his sleeves exposing an inch or two of knobby white wrist . . . but when he talked, his voice was low, and warm, and persuasive. He was never flustered, never unprepared, and seemed to relish the attention that Sylvie dreaded, and which she constantly received.

The professors would always find her, homing in on her face amidst the rows of students. They'd make a point of reading her name out loud, savoring the syllables. "Ms. Serfer," they would say, teeth buzzing over the "Mzz." "Any insight you can offer us on *Griswold v. Connecticut*?" She'd answer correctly. Sometimes she'd even get a little sassy. Asked if she'd read a certain opinion, she'd say, "Well, my mother wrote it," and pause before adding, "so, no."

In their first year of law school, Sylvie had dated a few of those cool, indifferent boys. Neil was a New Yorker whose parents knew hers, who'd been at Columbia while she was at Barnard and who seemed more interested, Sylvie ultimately decided, in a merger than a romance. (When Neil had shown up at their ten-year reunion with a male ballet dancer he'd introduced as his partner, she hadn't been entirely surprised.) Then there was Evan, who had pale skin and a beautifully molded throat, who'd dressed so handsomely and had such a nice way about him that it took her months to notice that he didn't seem as interested in the specifics of Sylvie's life as he did in whether her father might be in need of new in-house counsel.

Richard had arrived in New Haven with a girlfriend, a little blond thing who'd followed him from Penn State and was enrolled in Yale's School of Nursing. Sylvie would see the two of them around campus, Richard bouncing on the balls of his feet as he walked, gesturing as he spoke, and the little blonde gazing up at him from his side. Then, at some point, the little blonde disappeared.

She and Richard had been in classes together, in the library together, probably even at parties together, but they didn't speak for the first time until a funeral in December of their second year in law school. One of their classmates, a thin, intense dark-eyed boy named Leonard King, had fallen off a fourth-story roof late one night. ("Fallen off" was the official version, the one printed in the *Yale Daily News* and the *New Haven Register,* which referred to his death as a "tragic accident." Among his classmates, Leonard's death was widely assumed to have been suicide.)

All of the 2-L's attended a memorial service in the campus chapel. Leonard's parents had wept distressingly in the front row, his mother tottering on her heels before her husband and a son who was a younger, bespectacled version of Len wrapped their arms around her and followed Leonard's coffin out the door. Sylvie, in a black lace-trimmed skirt and a thin blouse several shades lighter, the most appropriate clothes she'd been able to find, had been shivering, picking her way across the slush and ice when suddenly Richard was beside her. "Let me give you a hand," he said. He reached for her backpack.

"No, I'm fine," she said. Richard's thin-soled dress shoes slid on a patch of ice and the next thing she knew, he was flat on his ass beside her.

"Ow," he said, startled. "Ow, shit!" His legs were splayed out in front of him, his socks drooping, his pants legs riding up, exposing his hairy calves. She grabbed his hand to pull him upright but couldn't get enough purchase with her silly high-heeled shoes, so she wound up on top of him, her chest pressed against his, both of them on the wintry, wet ground, laughing until tears ran from her eyes. She knew it was ridiculous, and that poor Richard's pants were soaked and probably ruined, but the day had been so terrible, and it felt good to laugh.

Richard finally got to his feet, then pulled Sylvie upright. "You okay?" he asked, and she nodded, her cheeks flushed from the cold and, maybe, from the feeling of his solid chest against hers.

He picked up her backpack, and they started walking together back toward the campus. "I have to say," he told her, "this wasn't how I thought our first conversation would go."

She looked at him sideways. He'd imagined a conversation they might have? That was pleasant to consider.

"You're Selma Serfer's daughter, right?"

She nodded, feeling less pleased. None of her other fellow students would ever bring up Selma, and all of them took pains to act surprised when Sylvie mentioned her mother, as if they were learning new information, when, of course, they all knew exactly who Sylvie was and to whom she was related.

"Watch your step," he said, pointing out an iced-over puddle. "Learn from my mistakes." Once they were past it, he said, "I'll bet it was something, growing up with a mother like that."

"Honestly, I just wish she was a better cook." As soon as the words were out of her mouth, she regretted them—it was a horrible thing to say, an antifeminist thing to say—but Richard had just nodded.

"It's a choice, right? Preeminent legal mind of her generation or makes a good potpie. And speaking of pot . . . pie . . ." He waited for her to laugh, then said, "My housemates and I are having a party Friday night."

Sylvie lifted an eyebrow—as an undergraduate, she'd practiced this maneuver in the mirror until she could raise her left eyebrow independently, which served her well in class. "Oh, yeah?"

He rattled off his address. "Nine o'clock or so. You wanna come?"

She wanted. Later, when she did sit-downs with the women's magazines, which would run an eight-hundred-word profile of the senator's wife alongside a head shot and her recipe for chewy molasses cookies, she would tell the story differently. She'd say that she and Richard had met in the library, instead of on their way back from a funeral, which sounded grim, like it foreshadowed tragedy. She never told anyone how Richard had fallen, and how she'd gotten her first good look at her husband-to-be with his bottom soaking in an iced-over puddle. She didn't mention that the first meeting had included a discussion of the Honorable Selma, or that their first real date had been at what turned out to be a typical beer-soaked, dope-smoky law school bash.

Richard lived in a rambling house with a half-rotted porch jutting off its front wall and a decaying couch beside the front door. Everything in the kitchen, every glass and plate and piece of cutlery, even the blender in which someone's girlfriend was frothing margaritas, was coated with a thin film of grime.

She arrived at the party just after ten o'clock. Richard was in the kitchen, waiting for her, which made her feel giddy, as if she'd been drinking champagne. Taking her hand, he led her down a narrow hallway into his little bedroom, which was, surprisingly, neat as a monk's cell. "Quieter in here," he called over the music. Sylvie looked around. There was an old Kennedy/Johnson campaign poster over the desk, an American flag on the opposite wall, and Janis Joplin on the stereo. The bed was neatly made, with a worn red-and-green plaid comforter tucked in tightly at its corners. Sylvie sat at the edge of the bed with her legs crossed. She bet herself that this was Richard's boyhood bedspread, that he'd brought it with him from home to college and then on to New Haven. She bet, too, that his parents hadn't replaced it; that somewhere in Harrisburg, Pennsylvania, there was a bed with just a sheet on it, maybe piled high with laundry, or clothes meant to be given away, but bare underneath, in a house that was very different from her parents' apartment on the Upper West Side, and her own pink-and-white bedroom, where the rolltop desk and canopied bed still stood, waiting for her to come home.

"Get you something?" Richard's face was flushed, from his jawline down the length of his throat, and she could smell him—

sweat and soap and shampoo and liquor. In his hand was a tumbler of something amber on ice—a seven-and-seven, she'd later learn, Seagram's whiskey and 7-Up. Most of the men she knew ordered whiskey, straight up, or what she'd come to think of as the beer of the proletariat—Pabst or Schlitz or Old Bohemian—but Richard liked his sweet drink and refused to change. It was one of the first things she admired about him.

"I'll have what you're having," she said.

When the bedroom door opened she got a blast of heat and noise from the party. Janis had been replaced by the Doors. When Richard came back, he handed her a drink, then sat on the bed beside her. "So," he said. "Sylvie Serfer." With one fingertip he traced the edge of her neckline, an embroidered peasant blouse that she'd pulled on over a denim skirt, tights, and a pair of fringed suede boots three sizes too big that she'd bought at a thrift shop and worn with three pairs of socks. "I like your shirt."

"Thanks." She pulled back a bit, alarmed at the unexpected intimacy; alarmed even more at how much she liked it. She wanted Richard Woodruff to press his palm against the skin the shirt left bare, to push her back on the bed and kiss her. She could smell the liquor coming off him. His eyes were bright and his gestures a little too expansive as he stood up and did an imitation—startlingly apt and a little cruel—of their Contracts professor, who had a body shaped like a bowling pin and wore shirts that exposed a simian froth of chest hair.

"So," she said, and set her drink down on a book-crammed nightstand (there were the familiar textbooks, and a dog-eared copy of *Catch-22*). "Tell me why you want to be a lawyer."

He smoothed his hair with the back of his hand and tipped his glass against his mouth. "Ah, the cross-examination begins. How about you go first?"

Sylvie shrugged. "With me it was dynastic. I didn't really

have a choice." This was true, although she'd never actually proposed an alternate career to her parents. She was smart, she could write, and in light of her mother's outsize successes, law seemed a given. But even though she was outspoken, and could be funny (and, like Richard, could occasionally even be mean), she had a far more conciliatory nature than Selma. She could sense injustice but lacked her mother's boundless passion to correct it, to wade into battle over and over again. As a girl, she'd been fascinated with nuns, with the idea that you could go to a place cut off from the world, where your job would be to pray, and make bread, or cheese, or something simple like that. (Of course Selma had turned this knowledge into one of her prize anecdotes. "My daughter," she'd say to her friends, and the audiences who turned out to honor her, "the first Jewish nun.") Sylvie finished her drink, feeling the whiskey burn her throat, wondering, a little fuzzily, whether a man could be a cloister, a monastery, a place where you could be enclosed and kept safe from the world.

"How about you?" she asked.

He looked at her thoughtfully from where he stood in the center of the room. He'd kicked his shoes off. Barefoot, he looked even more like an overgrown boy, a kid who'd been allowed to stay up late. "The truth is, I wanna be president."

She stared at him a moment before starting to laugh. President! That was another surprise. Most of her classmates would have given an answer involving justice. They would have talked about suffering, and the law as a tool to address it; they would have given examples from their years digging latrines in the Peace Corps or their summers interning at Head Start in Harlem, or offered up some anecdote from their own lives: an uncle bankrupted after he couldn't pay for his wife's hospitalization, a field or forest despoiled by developers.

"President?" she said, and Richard gave a charming shrug.

"One thing you gotta know about me, Sylvie . . ." And, in an instant, he was sitting beside her again, one warm fingertip back at her neckline, then dipping lower. "I am nothing if not ambitious."

This was the moment she could have pushed him away and gotten to her feet, exclaiming indignantly that she wasn't that kind of girl, that they hadn't so much as been to a movie together, that he hadn't even bought her a sandwich, let alone dinner. But she found herself both aroused and bemused by this half-drunk, earnest hick, with his bare feet and his plaid bedspread and his ambition. Was he serious about being president? Was he serious about her?

"Tell me how it's going to happen." He kissed her cheek, then used his fingertips, delicately, to free her copper earring from her hair. "You're going to get your law degree . . ."

"Got a job lined up already. Manhattan D.A.'s office this summer," he said, his voice low and confident, rumbling against her skin. "They'll hire me full-time soon as I graduate." He took her in his arms, eased her back onto the bed, and rolled on top of her. The one-quarter of her brain that was still processing information, instead of the feel of Richard's mouth against her neck, was thinking, *Drink talk.* Although maybe not. Someone had to be president, so why not Richard? Good backstory; nice-looking; state school to please the common folk, a Yale law degree to delight the snobs and the intelligentsia. The world could do worse.

"Then I'll go into private practice for a while. Make some money. Build my war chest." He bent down to tug at her boots, and if he noticed the three pairs of white athletic socks that came off with each one, he was nice enough not to comment. "Then I'll run for the New York State Assembly. Then the U.S. Senate."

"They're going to vote for you?" she murmured, as he climbed back onto the bed beside her. "They don't like outsiders."

"Oh, the good people of New York are absolutely gonna vote for me," he said, sliding his hand up her shirt and unhooking her bra one-handed. "We'll have lived in Manhattan for years by then."

She pushed him a few inches away, lifting her body up on her elbows so she could see his face in the dim light. "We?"

"I've had my eye on you for a long time, Sylvie," said Richard. "You're a sweetheart," he said. Before she had time to savor the compliment, to enjoy the taste of the word *sweetheart,* he added, "You're also the most organized person I've ever seen. Your notebooks are something."

"You're hot for my notebooks?" she asked, her amusement back and growing stronger. Her notebooks, she had to admit, were something—cross-tabulated, color-coordinated, with different colors for each class and a different color ink for each topic.

"You ever seen mine?" he asked, and leaned up on one elbow, reaching over to his desk and producing a battered black-and-white composition book. His handwriting was a mess, his notes were almost illegible, and, Sylvie noted a little smugly, he only ever used black ink. "I saw those notebooks, and I thought, *That's the girl for me.*"

Later, it would occur to her to ask the obvious question, which was *Why?* Of all the girls at Yale, many of whom took excellent notes, why had he chosen her? Later, she would wonder whether Richard had sought her out because she was Selma Serfer's daughter, because her status (relatively wealthy, from an educated and influential family, a native New Yorker, resident of perhaps the one city in America where being Jewish wasn't an automatic political drawback) had a luster that would make his own homespun, small-town scholarship-boy story even more impressive in contrast. But that night she didn't ask. She let him take off her top, let him press his bare chest against hers, crooning her name—*Sylvie, Sylvie, Sylvie*—and thought that he had what she didn't: an agenda, a plan. It was almost like a fairy tale: once upon a time, there was a boy from Harrisburg, Pennsylvania, who grew up to be president. Richard would write the story; he would draw the map. She would help him navigate, and together, triumphant, they would arrive at the destination he had chosen, where they would, of course, live happily ever after. *Do you trust me?* he'd ask her—this was on their second date, when he'd taken her to a matinee, and out for Chinese for dinner. They were in bed together, naked beneath the Kennedy poster, about to have sex for the first time (another detail she'd never shared with a reporter), and when he'd asked his question, she'd answered with the words of a bride: *I do.*

They'd gotten married right after law school graduation, in a ceremony in Yale's chapel conducted by a Supreme Court justice, one of Selma's friends. Sylvie remembered Richard's father talking too loudly, whacking her own father on the back repeatedly, and giving a drunken rehearsal-dinner toast in which he'd referred to Sylvie as "the little lady." Selma had smiled tightly, and Richard's mother had whispered apologies in the ladies' room, but privately, Sylvie hadn't been offended. Secretly, she'd liked the way it had sounded.

Her parents had offered to help with a down payment for a place near them, on the Upper West Side, but Richard had refused.

"I know they mean well," he said, twisting from side to side on the narrow bed in his New Haven apartment, "but I just wouldn't feel right, and I don't know how to tell them without sounding like an ungrateful bastard."

"Well, let's figure it out." She got off the bed and sat cross-legged in the folding metal chair that was the only other seating in the room. Richard, meanwhile, sprawled flat on his back, arms and legs and even fingers extended, as if that would help the words come more easily. Sylvie picked up a notebook and, after considering her pen selection, chose green ink. "We'll start off by saying how overwhelmed and grateful we are."

"Grateful," he repeated, nodding. "Overwhelmed."

"And then we'll tell them . . ." She paused, hearing Richard's voice in her head. "That you think it's important to make your own way in the world, like they did. To learn as you go."

"That's not gonna sound like I'm an asshole?"

"It won't," she assured him. That was the first speech, the first of many, that she'd helped him write . . . and never mind that she hadn't completely agreed with its substance, that she would have been more than happy to take the loan and move into a place that didn't have mice and a bathroom with barely enough room for a toilet and a tiny sink and a shower stall where the curtain stuck to your body unless you positioned yourself just right.

They'd moved into the apartment on Court Street in the Carroll Gardens neighborhood of Brooklyn. Richard had gone to work at the D.A.'s office, as planned, and she'd been a summer associate in the trust and estates department of Richter, Morgan, and Katz. Two years later, she'd had Diana. A year after that, Richard had left the D.A.'s office and become a partner at a big firm downtown. Buoyed by his six-figure salary and the promise of bonuses, they'd moved from Brooklyn to Manhattan, into a classic seven two blocks away from Central Park with a big living room and floor-to-ceiling windows, a place someone in Richard's firm had found for them, perfect for entertaining. With its cramped kitchen and small bedrooms and lack of closet space, the apartment was less perfect for raising a family, but Richard hadn't seemed to notice and Sylvie hadn't complained. Years later, when he'd come to her in the hospital after Lizzie was born and said he was going to announce his run for the state assembly the next week, and asked if she was ready, she'd set the baby, fed and freshly changed and swaddled, into her bassinet, sat up as straight as she could without her stitches pulling, and told him, "Absolutely."

Over the years Sylvie had decorated their apartment, choosing dishes and furniture that looked good enough for dinners for twelve and cocktails for forty but could withstand the assault of children; a pair of couches slipcovered in canvas, good Persian rugs. After Lizzie came home she hired a nanny named Marta, who lived two subway stops down from their old stop in Brooklyn. Richard's work, his campaigns, the researching and the scheduling and the speechwriting, kept her as busy as a full-time job would have, and the extra set of hands turned out to be invaluable. The girls, Lizzie especially, loved Marta, the soft-boiled eggs and toast fingers she'd cook for breakfast, the chicken and rice she'd prepare for dinner. On the weekends they begged to be taken to her apartment, where Marta lived with her husband and two teenage sons.

As soon as she was on her feet, Sylvie swapped her maternity clothes for power suits with towering shoulder pads, which she'd wear with sheer black panty hose and sneakers, the better to walk miles on the sidewalks, distributing window signs and pamphlets. Instead of colorful beads and inexpensive bangles, she had the pearls Richard had given her as an anniversary gift, and a drawer full of Hermès scarves. Once he was elected, she managed his district office, helping handle constituent service, ghostwriting his speeches, doing research, drafting bills. She did step aerobics in the 1980s, spinning in the 1990s, yoga and Pilates in the new millennium. She did Atkins, and South Beach, and Weight Watchers, and Weight Watchers online. She kept those twenty pounds off, and made other improvements. Any woman would have if she'd seen herself in the *Times,* in a picture snapped at a press conference, hair flying around her head, mouth hanging open and double chins on full display. Now Sylvie's hair was chemically straightened every three months and dyed every two. She'd had a breast reduction and a tummy tuck when she was thirty-five, and liposuction done on her chin and cheeks ten years after that. She wasn't thin—at least, not the bone-thinness of some of the other ladies-who-lunched and politicians' wives she'd met, women who looked, in real life, barely more substantial than the cardboard cutouts of the president that people posed with while waiting in line for the Washington Monument—but she was thin enough so that she didn't cringe every time she saw a picture of herself.

Of course, not everyone approved of her choices. "You look so ordinary," Ceil once cried, years ago, after they'd split a bottle of wine at lunch. Ceil had apologized, thinking that she'd insulted her friend, but secretly, Sylvie had been pleased. *Ordinary* was good. *Ordinary* meant that no one would notice you, or post your picture, or make fun. Ordinary meant that they'd leave her alone, her and her daughters, and that was all the blessing Sylvie could wish.

Sylvie's mother was even less impressed with her daughter's efforts. "What happened to you?" she'd ask, staring at her, perplexed, as if she could no longer recognize her own daughter. Sylvie remembered her mother's reaction the first time she'd brought Richard home, three months after Leonard King's funeral. Her mother had studied Sylvie's husband-to-be from across the table, watching as he struggled to eat her brisket, which had been roasted until each slice had the consistency of a scab. "He's going places," Selma had said, tapping one knobby finger against her red lips, while Sylvie washed the dishes and Richard and Dave watched football in the living room. "But I think he's the kind of man who just needs a woman along for the ride." Sylvie hadn't answered. She knew the truth was that

Richard didn't just need her along for the ride, he needed her help, her advice, her behind-the-scenes counsel . . . and, unlike her mother, she'd never craved the spotlight. She didn't mind invisibility or a permanent spot in the passenger's seat.

She also hated being a lawyer. She'd survived law school, where you could read about the great cases and argue about procedure and precedent and justice, but being a lawyer, especially in trusts and estates, wasn't about justice; it was about moving mountains of paper from one side of the desk to the other. When Diana was born Sylvie had left her firm and grabbed hold of new motherhood like a drowning woman clutching a piece of driftwood. Twelve weeks had stretched into six months, then a year, then three, then four, and when Diana was five she'd gotten pregnant again, not entirely accidentally, although Richard thought otherwise.

Diana had been a handful—headstrong and bossy, walking at nine months and uttering her first word—"more!"—at ten. Then, when Lizzie came along, after a difficult pregnancy and an emergency C-section, she was underweight and wrinkled, like a tiny and miserable old man in the pink dresses Selma brought to the hospital. Lizzie was also illness-prone, allergic to everything but the air and sometimes, Sylvie suspected, that, too. Between the two girls—Diana with her demands and her schedule and her Gifted and Talented enrichment classes, Lizzie with her acid reflux and her asthma—not even Selma expected Sylvie to go back to work. There were doctors' appointments to make and keep, games and practice to organize and witness, play groups to attend and homework to check and at least one frantic trip to the doctor or the pharmacy to pick up penicillin or replace a lost inhaler every month.

Eventually, it became easier to let Marta take the girls down to the subway or load them into cabs, to let her take Diana to her rehearsals and practices and deal with Lizzie's music lessons and bad moods. Marta, who was Sylvie's mother's age, short and no-nonsense, with lace-up orthopedic shoes, cardigan sweaters, and gray hair drawn back in a bun, was endlessly patient and, after her own boys, delighted to have two girls to dress up and coddle. Marta was patient in a way Sylvie wasn't. She could handle the elaborate arrangements for playdates and keep straight the names of the mothers of the girls' friends and the dosage of Lizzie's allergy medicine while Sylvie focused on her husband's work, her husband's world. Marta could deal with the girls, but only she could take care of Richard.

And look where that had gotten her, she thought, as the car glided out of the tunnel and up Eighth Avenue, past fast-food restaurants and dry cleaners and drugstores and the ubiquitous chain coffee stores that had sprouted on every corner. Look at her now. The numbness she'd felt since the rest stop restroom was starting to scare her. It wasn't right. Shouldn't she be crying, weeping, wailing, on the telephone with her husband, pleading with him to leave his young plaything behind? Yet she didn't feel like crying, or begging. She felt as if she'd been frozen, until she let herself think of her daughters, how they would be dragged down into the mud, how they would be shamed. Then she felt herself swelling with fury, and that scared her, too, because it was so atypical. She got annoyed—what wife, what woman, didn't?—but she could count the times over the years that she'd been truly furious at Richard on one hand, and have several fingers left over.

The car pulled up in front of their building. There were photographers clustered on the sidewalk, a dozen of them, sweating in the heat, some with television cameras and others with digital cameras, plus a few reporters holding notebooks and tape recorders, outnumbered by the photographers and video people. In this case, Sylvie reasoned, everyone knew the story. It was the images they were after, the money shot, the picture worth a thousand words of the disgraced wife lifting the cup to her lips and taking her first bitter sip. Derek put the car in park, then turned to face her. "How about we go around the back?"

"No," she said. She wouldn't be bullied, she wouldn't be shamed, she wouldn't slink through back doors as if she was the one who'd made a mistake. She had raised her head, reminding herself that she was Selma Serfer's daughter, when the first of the photographers spotted the car. In an instant, they were surrounded.

"Sylvie!"

"Mrs. Woodruff!"

"Sylvie, any comment on the senator's affair?"

Clarissa winced. Derek squared his shoulders and opened his door, then hers. "Just stay close." Sylvie grabbed her purse. She left her panty hose crumpled on the floor of the car, pushed her feet back into her shoes, bent her head, and stepped, barelegged, onto the sidewalk. She tried to make herself as small as possible, head tucked into her chest, arms tight against her sides, ignoring the shouts of "Mrs. Woodruff!" and "Is it true he paid the girl off to keep quiet?" and "Did you know about the affair?" and "How long's it been going on?" and "Are you planning to divorce him?"

Derek, big and substantial as an armored tank, led her through the heavy glass doors. Once they'd swung shut, the din subsided. The lobby was empty except for Juan the doorman at his desk. When she looked at him, he dropped his gaze. Sylvie wondered if Joelle had ever been here, whether Richard had snuck her up from D.C. for some afternoon delight while Sylvie was visiting that summer camp for kids with cancer or shopping at Bloomingdale's or Saks for one more unremarkable suit she'd wear to one more event where she would stand behind her husband, nodding like one of those dolls she couldn't remember the name of, the one cabdrivers sometimes kept in their back windows.

"You gonna be all right, ma'am?" Derek asked.

"Bobblehead," said Sylvie. That's what those dolls were called. Once, in the back of a taxicab, she'd seen one that looked like a Chihuahua. When Diana had been ten, she'd begged for a dog for her birthday, and Sylvie had said, "Someday." Diana, ever the stickler for specifics, had asked when, and first Sylvie had told her when Lizzie was out of nursery school, then kindergarten, and by then Diana had wanted a pony more than she'd wanted a dog and had let the matter drop without forcing her mother to tell her one of the unpleasant truths of her marriage: she took care of Richard, and it was a job that left little room for taking care of anything else—not a dog, not herself. Sometimes not even her daughters.

"Ma'am?" Derek was staring at her, the worry on his face plain to see. Sylvie felt suddenly, tearfully grateful. What had she done in her life to have a good man like Derek, a man with his own family and, she was sure, his own cares, worry about her?

She took his hand—it felt big and warm as a hot-water bottle—and squeezed it. "Thank you," she said.

He nodded. "I'll be praying for you and your girls." Derek had driven her for the past five years, and this was she longest sentence she thought she'd ever heard him say. Her throat closed, and all she could do was nod. He pushed the glass doors open again—there were more shouted questions, a fusillade of flashbulbs, and then the doors swung shut and he was gone. Sylvie walked across the lobby's black-and-white tiled floors, past the potted palms and gilt-framed mirrors, and punched the button that would summon the elevator.

The doors slid open on the tenth floor. Sylvie stepped into their apartment, her heels clicking on the floors, seeing it as if for the first time and realizing that she'd created, over the years, a version of those fancy hotel rooms in which she and Richard stayed. Everything was correct, everything was attractive, everything was in its place and as it should have been, from the green-and-ivory botanical prints over the fireplace to the carved teak elephant ("Quirky!" her decorator had said. "Whimsical!") in the center of the dining room table. She might have liked that elephant, with its sturdy legs and upraised trunk, if she and Richard had stumbled across it in some faraway flea market, or if one of her daughters had given it to them as a misbegotten anniversary gift, but now it was all she could do not to send it smashing to the floor. It had nothing to do with her, with them; and this apartment wasn't a home, it was another version of Richard's office, another place made for his use and his comfort.

Feeling outside her own body, like this was all happening in a movie she'd rented and watched by herself, she made her way down the hall. The door to Richard's office was shut, the television set was on, and she could hear a woman's voice, her own voice, coming from the speakers. She grimaced, almost groaning out loud. That silly Valentine's Day interview she'd given the *Today* show, when they'd talked to long-married couples about love. She hadn't wanted to do it—she hated being on camera almost as much as she hated public speaking—but Richard's chief of staff had convinced her that it would be good for Richard's brand. Once, they'd said "image," but these days it was all about the brand, and Richard's needed some rehabilitation, ever since he'd been one of a handful of Democrats to vote against the financial regulation the president had tried to ram through Congress the previous fall.

Tell us one of your favorite memories of your husband, the interviewer, a chic blonde with a discreetly lifted face, had asked. Sylvie, who'd known the question was coming, told the story that they were now rerunning on the news, the tale of a disastrous plane trip she'd taken from Miami to LaGuardia when she'd been a young mother, traveling with both girls. "Lizzie, my youngest, had gotten sick. She started screaming as soon as we left the runway, and the only time she stopped was to throw up. I felt like everyone on the plane was staring at me, thinking, *Isn't there something that woman can do?* I felt . . ." Sylvie heard her television-self inhale. "I felt like a failure. Like I was the worst mother in the world." The interviewer—childless herself, if Sylvie remembered right—had made a cooing, sympathetic sound and, Sylvie remembered, had leaned forward, patting Sylvie's knee. "We got off the plane, and I handed Richard the baby, and I remember he hugged her, and me, and all of us, and said, 'Don't worry, it's all going to be fine,' and just the way he said it, the way Lizzie smiled at him, I believed it."

"Lovely," the lady had murmured. Sylvie had smiled, thinking that she hadn't actually felt reassured at that moment in the airport, dripping with sweat, in the puke-stiffened blouse that Lizzie had thrown up on somewhere over Virginia. What she'd actually been thinking was that she had married a man incapable of shame. She, herself, had been desperately embarrassed—by the woman sitting behind her who'd asked for earplugs, raising her voice above Lizzie's shrieks, and the old biddy in the aisle across from them who'd commented, loudly enough for Sylvie to hear, that in her day children weren't allowed to behave like that. She knew she'd remember those women's faces, and everything they'd said, for days, possibly weeks, maybe even longer, and that Richard, if he'd been on the plane, probably wouldn't have noticed them at all. He'd have simply bounced the baby in his arms and sung "New York, New York" to her, loudly and off-key, impervious to the stares and rolled eyes and loudly heaved sighs of his fellow travelers. You couldn't embarrass Richard. He was immune to shame the same way some people never caught colds. It was why she thought he actually could be president someday—unlike the vast majority of people walking the earth, he could withstand a campaign, and all the things his opponents would say about him; he believed in himself, and no amount of criticism could convince him that he shouldn't.

"The senator's wife, in her own words," said the announcer. "A little ironic, given the events of the day."

Sylvie put her hand on the door to her husband's office, breathed deeply, then pushed it open.

DIANA

"Leaving," Diana snapped to the woman behind the desk—Ashley, or her replacement, she didn't wait long enough to see—and stomped out into the steaming night. Ideally, she'd run, but she'd done eight miles already that day: her usual five in the morning, and then another three that afternoon, after she'd gotten the news. More running would mean no sleep, and she needed her rest. She was back in the ER again tomorrow.

Her phone buzzed in her pocket. Gary again. "Yes?" she said. She hated the shrewish way she snapped at him, like he was the lowliest med student, but she knew that if she didn't force him to get to the point—assuming, as ever, that there was one—she'd be listening to him clear his throat and sniffle for minutes that she didn't have to waste.

"Just making sure you didn't change your mind."

She maneuvered around a clutch of stroller-pushing mothers. "I told you I'd call you if I did."

He paused. "If you're sure . . ."

"I'm sure," she said, and hung up before he could tell her that he wasn't.

She walked faster and faster, wishing she could move fast enough to outrun her own unhappiness, and the bad thing she was doing.

That June, she and Gary had celebrated their seventh anniversary. Maybe the thing with Doug was just the seven-year itch, a fling, a symptom of something so common and run-of-the-mill that there was actually a name for it. She considered this thought and dismissed it. What she had with Doug was better than anything she'd ever had with Gary, which led, inevitably, to the question she found herself wrestling with more and more frequently: Why had she picked Gary in the first place?

She blamed her parents. She recognized it as a cliché, that everyone these days blamed their parents for everything, but she knew that watching them had, inevitably, colored her own view of the world and influenced every decision she'd made, particularly the ones about love, about marriage, about the way she'd chosen to build her own life and her family.

Her earliest memories were of waking in the predawn hours, the city still a gray lunar landscape outside her window, and listening to her father sneaking down the hallway. *It's the boogeyman,* she would think, her body rigid in her bed, before her waking mind asserted itself and said, *No, that's just Dad leaving.* She would hear a creaking floorboard, the refrigerator opening and shutting, the hiss of the coffeepot, the hinges of the closet door as he removed his topcoat and picked up his briefcase. These sounds would be joined by her mother's lighter step, the sound of a cup clinking on the counter, a plate being set on the table. The two of them would talk, quietly, a murmur punctured by laughter, until finally she'd hear the front door open, then shut. A minute later, there would be more noises—water running, the refrigerator door again—and then her mother would go back to bed. Marta would come at seven, in a white shirt and cardigan and elastic-waisted polyester pants, with her big glasses and her gray bun. Marta was the one who would give the girls their breakfast, who would inspect their uniforms and make sure they'd brushed their teeth and escort them to the bus stop for school.

This was what had defined her childhood—her mother, who doted on her father and had little time for Lizzie and Diana; and her father, who was gone so often, who'd miss Girl Scout dinners and soccer games and academic awards ceremonies. Once she'd asked him about it. "Daddy," she'd said, standing in the doorway of his office, "why are you away so much?"

He'd invited her to sit in the big leather armchair on the other side of his desk, and he'd closed the door and answered her seriously, as if she was an adult. He told her that he was doing the work of the people, and that sometimes serving the people—the big-*P* People—meant he was less available for the little-*p* people that he loved. "It's hard for me," he'd told her. Diana suspected he was lying. She'd seen the looks on her friends' fathers' faces—how some of them would yawn, or joke about spiking the Gatorade at the soccer games, how they'd sneak out to check the scores during the winter choral concert, and how one of them had actually fallen asleep and slipped right out of his folding chair during sixth-grade graduation. She thought that whatever her father was doing in Washington was maybe more fun than watching eight-year-olds chase a ball up and down a field, or listening to them sing Christmas carols (and one obligatory song about Chanukah) every December; that maybe her father's work pleased him in a way his daughters didn't.

Back in her room that night, Diana had lain on her bed for so long that her mother came in to make sure she was all right. "Does your stomach hurt?" she'd asked, a worried look on her face. Diana had said no. "Is anything else bothering you?" Diana had shaken her head. Alone again. Breathing in the scent of Downy and cotton, she had arrived at two important decisions, goals that would shape her life. The first was that she'd be so outstanding, so remarkable, such a credit to her school and her team and her choir and her family that every parent would wish she was their kid. Her parents would be forced to pay attention.

They'd be peer-pressured into loving her, shamed into it by the endless stream of straight A's and coaches' praise and how every other parent would offer Diana as an example of what their children could do if they just worked hard enough.

The second was that when she was grown up, she would marry a man who didn't have to worry about big-*P* People, who only had to take care of the little-*p* people he loved.

By the time she met her husband, during the first year of medical school, Diana had lived up to the first promise. She'd been a standout student not because she was the smartest or the most talented, but because she worked harder than anyone else, putting in hours at the library, skipping parties and plays and shopping excursions to give her dioramas one more dusting of glitter, her papers one more round of edits, her clothes one more touch-up with the iron.

She'd never be petite or sexy, with her sister's flawless skin and honey-blond hair and the kind of adorable cuteness that naturally made guys want to protect her. She took after Grandma Selma's side of the family—strong jaw, big nose, features that were unobjectionable but would never be described as pretty (she'd overheard "handsome" once, as in "Diana Woodruff's a handsome woman," and had spent years trying to forget it). The running kept her BMI in the healthy range. She couldn't do much about her height—at five foot ten, she towered over some of the guys who would have been prospects otherwise. Nor could hard work shrink her big hands and big feet, but she could dress well, in dark-colored, well-cut clothes, and keep her thick hair long and dyed a pretty shade of auburn. She got facials and manicures, and put on her makeup before leaving the house—the black liner and shimmery cream eyeshadow and mascara that made her deep-set eyes look bigger and brighter, the lipstick that made the most of her thin lips.

She'd met Gary at a bar, the one around the corner from her apartment, the one she'd fled to after Hal had dumped her.

Hal had been her boyfriend at Columbia, a tall, pale-skinned, freckled, drily witty boy who sat in the back of the psychology class she'd taken as a respite from the hard sciences. Hal was rumored to be one of the editors of the wickedly funny underground humor magazine that appeared at irregular intervals in stacks on the steps of Low Library. *Out of my league,* she'd thought, and tried to keep from looking too long at his lanky body, and thinking about how soft the feathery hairs at the back of his neck would be if she touched them. One day after class, Hal had surprised her. "Excuse me, Diana," he'd said. His voice was surprisingly deep for someone so skinny, and her heart fluttered at the sound of it—she had no idea he even knew her name! "I've got a proposal for you."

"What's that?" She tried to sound cool, but her mouth was instantly dry and her palms just as instantly sweaty, as Hal explained himself: they needed a girl to pose in front of a urinal to illustrate a story in the magazine, and would she be interested?

Diana had laughed out loud. "You need me to stand in front a urinal? Why?"

"Ironic juxtaposition," he'd said, and she'd laughed again and agreed to do it. After the photo shoot, which had involved Hal squinting through the viewfinder of his Nikon and saying things like, "Could you try to look a little more desperate?" he'd taken her out for coffee, touched the tip of her nose with his finger, and said, in his deep voice that resonated right through her, "That was very convincing."

With one brush of a fingertip she'd felt her whole body heat up. *Oh,* she thought, looking at him mutely, feeling something that was almost desperation quickening her pulse. She liked him in a way she'd never liked a boy before. "Hey," he'd said, and she'd felt herself turning toward his face like a flower toward the sun. From the way he looked at her, half smiling, she could see that she wasn't imagining this; she knew that he liked her, too. "You want to see a movie Friday night?"

Just like that, in the manner of college students, they became a couple. They'd walk around the Columbia campus with their fingers interlaced. After classes, they'd go to his dorm room, a tiny single, and have sex, two or three times, and sleep curled in his narrow bed.

Hal could surprise her into bursts of laughter. He could make her weak in the knees just by kissing her cheek and could make her breathe hard just by nibbling the back of her neck. They'd dated from Halloween of senior year through the hell of finals and papers and the whirlwind of graduation, and into a blissful summer of trips to the Hamptons and the Jersey Shore, picnics in Central Park, and sex wherever they could find a little privacy. Then she'd gone off to Philadelphia for med school, and he'd stayed in New York City to be a paralegal by day, stand-up comic by night. They talked on the phone for six weeks until she had two free days in a row and took a train to Penn Station, armed with zinc and vitamin C for the cold he'd been complaining about.

Instead of taking her to his apartment, which she'd heard about but hadn't seen, Hal walked her to a pizza shop, sat with her at a booth in the back, blew his nose into a paper napkin, then took her hands and said that they were through.

"But . . . but what happened?"

"I'm not sure." Hal looked anguished, pale and exhausted. "I'm just not feeling the same anymore. It's like my brain changed. Maybe it's the drugs."

Her heart jumped. "You're on drugs?" Oh, God, she thought, her mind flashing to images of all the nights she'd found Lizzie puking or passed out, the trips to rehab and family therapy sessions with well-meaning, soft-voiced PhDs.

"You know I'm on drugs." Now Hal just sounded impatient. "The Sudafed, and the Claritin."

Diana stared at him as her fantasies of forcing herself to hold his hand while he confessed to trying marijuana for the first time at eleven swiftly receded. "The Claritin changed the way you feel about me?" He toyed with a pizza crust and didn't answer. "I know I haven't been studying medicine for that long, but that strikes me as improbable." She waited for him to smile, and when he didn't, she said, "I'd feel a little better if it was at least something illegal that made you not love me anymore. And you don't, do you?" She paused, waiting for him to say, *Of course I still love you!* Hal said nothing. "You don't love me," Diana repeated. She felt as if her body were collapsing, crumbling in on itself. She should have gone to med school in Manhattan. She should have come to see him sooner. She should have . . .

Hal dropped his eyes. "I'll always be here for you."

"I'll always be here for you," Diana jeered back at him. "The official motto of Dumpsville. Population: me." Hal winced—watching *The Simpsons* together had been one of their routines, and usually a reference like that would make him smile. Now he just looked sad.

Diana slid out of the booth and walked out the door with her head held high. She managed to keep it together through the subway ride and the walk to her parents' apartment building. Then, in her bedroom, the tears came, and with them her resolve. Hal had been her first real boyfriend, her first true love, and while she'd never been the kind of girl to daydream over a white dress and a wedding, still she'd imagined herself as a young bride and young mother, imagined living with Hal, raising a family with him, growing old in Hal's company.

Back in Philadelphia, Diana purged her apartment of every sign of her ex-boyfriend. The books he'd given her, the sweatshirts and boxers he'd left beneath her dorm-room bed, the Valentine's card she kept tucked into her mirror, all of these went into a contractor-size trash bag, which she tied in a double knot and left beside the door.

She couldn't go through it again. No more romance, no more breakups that left her gutted and heartsick. No more boys like Hal who would kiss her as if they were drowning and her mouth held the world's last breath of air. Certainly no men like her father, handsome and charismatic, who'd want their women to traipse after them like camp followers, fitting their lives to his wishes. No more.

Breathing hard, she went into the bedroom, did her hair and makeup, and wiggled into a tight black dress. *I am going to get drunk,* she thought, shoving her feet into high heels and stalking out the door.

There was a bar at the corner, and there was a guy at the bar, a tall guy, her father's height, who stopped talking to the bartender and turned to stare as Diana gulped down her first glass of white wine. "Hey," he said as she finished her second glass. "You okay there?"

"I'm fine."

"I'm Gary." When she'd first glimpsed him she'd thought, uncharitably, that he had a face like an elbow, all unpleasant angles, tiny, muddy eyes and a sharp, jutting nose. His body, underneath his shirt, looked just as bony and unwelcoming. But then she considered more generously. He had a nice smile. Straight white teeth, a kind face. He slid a twenty-dollar bill across the bar, and already that was better than Hal, who'd insisted on splitting the cost of everything right down the middle. She drank more wine, smiled at him, and thought, *Screw Hal,* who wasn't good enough or strong enough for her anyhow; Hal, whom she'd once heard remarking, *Diana's got a bigger set than I do . . .* and, the hell of it was, he'd said it knowing that she might have overheard, and in a tone suggesting that she wouldn't be offended if she had.

Gary, she learned through her thickening haze, worked in communications for a Philadelphia-based pharmaceutical manufacturer. He had funny stories about approving TV spots for the latest drug for erectile dysfunction without saying either *erection* or *dysfunction,* because it turned out that both words made men uncomfortable. He'd had the same job since finishing business school, and when she asked if he liked it, he shrugged and said, "They call it work for a reason." Not too ambitious, she'd thought, letting him buy her another drink. Then again, she was ambitious enough for two people. Maybe even more. Hal had made that clear.

Eventually, they were the only people left at the bar, and just before last call, Gary pulled her against him and started kissing her, his thin lips pursed and aiming for her mouth but making contact primarily with her nose. Stumbling out into the darkness, giggling in an almost Lizzie-like fashion, Diana thought that this was what regular girls felt like: her college roommates, who'd hooked up with guys as casually as trying on sweaters at the Gap. This was normal, this was fun, this was a harmless way to get over Hal, to feel like she was desirable and womanly instead of a bitch with a bigger set of balls than her boyfriend.

Gary lived in Society Hill, in an apartment on Pine Street, where he slept in a bare-walled room on a mattress on the floor. He held her hand tightly in his own sweaty one as he led her up the stairs, and gazed at her with an awed look on his face as she wriggled out of her black dress and tossed it at him. "Oh, God," he groaned. "You're so hot!" He sounded, she thought fuzzily, like a fourteen-year-old gawping at his first centerfold. Quickly she found herself on the mattress and there, less than two hours after meeting, they consummated their love, in a ten-minute episode that ended with Gary panting, red-faced, his sunken chest drenched in sweat, and Diana flat on her back, feeling as if she'd undergone a minor dental procedure—a little violated, slightly sore, stretched in places she wasn't used to stretching, but nothing that a few Advil wouldn't help.

So the sex wasn't great, she thought as they kissed, bumping noses and teeth as sweat dribbled from his forehead onto her breasts. ("Sorry!" he'd cried, wiping her off with a pillowcase.) True, Gary had jammed his fingers up inside her like he was trying to extract the last olive from the jar, and his kisses were the dry pecks of a maiden aunt. But the night had served its purpose. When it was over, and she lay in the crook of his arm, Gary looked down at her, light-brown eyes warm, with just the tiniest spit bubble in the corner of his mouth. "That was incredible," he said. Diana couldn't detect anything but sincerity in his voice or in his eyes. So maybe that was great sex for him. Maybe this was great sex for everybody, and there was something wrong with her. Either way she should stop thinking so much—another trait Hal had faulted her for.

Gary slid his hand over her belly, and tugged at her pubic hair in a not entirely pleasant fashion. "What can I do for you?" he asked.

Can you turn into someone else? Diana couldn't stop herself from thinking. *Can you turn into Hal?* She pushed the thought away and then, using her own fingers to guide Gary's, she showed him what to do, eventually succeeding in producing a ticklish spasm that she supposed was, at least technically, an orgasm.

So much for my one-night stand, she thought, pulling on her dress as Gary snored.

Walking the street at three in the morning, panties in her pocket, looking for a cab, she thought she would never see him again. Never seeing the guy again seemed to be how most of her friends' hookups ended, with neither party brokenhearted, or even much worse for the wear. He'd wanted her, and that was what mattered.

When Gary called her the next day, when he found her address and sent pink tulips to her apartment the day after that, she'd been surprised and charmed. He was pursuing her. In all of her previous relationships, the more loving one had always been her. Maybe she'd give Gary a try and see what it felt like to be on the other side, the one who was desired, who was pursued. True, Gary, with his rattling chest and runny nose, didn't make her heart flutter, but Diana figured she'd see plenty of fluttering hearts in her professional life. If she found his kisses less than enthralling—if, in fact, the first time she'd felt his tongue brush against her own she'd felt briefly revolted—well, there was more to life than kissing. Besides, she'd slept with him. Diana had slept with a grand total of only three other guys—Hal, her love, and Craig, in summer camp, and Paolo, the exchange student she'd dated for six months her sophomore year at Columbia who'd had a disconcerting tendency to fall asleep immediately after and, in a few humiliating instances, during the act. To Diana, sex meant something; it meant she couldn't put him aside or discard him like a book she'd started and decided she didn't want to finish.

She dated Gary through the fall and winter, then brought him home that spring, for Passover, to meet the family. She remembered how, over her mother's dining room table, she'd looked into his eyes and thought, *He will never leave me.* This thought was a comfort to her. It was also a helpful counterpoint to the thought she'd had just seconds before it, which was, *He's maybe a little bit dumb.*

Of course that wasn't true. Stupid people didn't go to Penn, then Rutgers, where Gary had earned a master's degree in business. If he occasionally looked doltish at certain angles—his mouth slightly open, his eyes wide and glassy, as if he'd just been given a really hard word at the spelling bee—well, that was simply an accident of bone structure and genetics. He was dependable, and he loved her, and he would never leave her . . . and she wasn't so desperately, blindly in love with him that she'd let go of her goals and dreams and give herself up, the way her own mother had.

Sylvie had the entire meal catered, and Gary, who'd never tasted gefilte fish before, ate an entire piece and even asked for seconds. When it was time to clear the table he'd practically leapt to his feet and started clearing and scraping and packing the leftovers in Tupperware. "He seems like a fine young man," Diana's father had said, before slipping into his office to take a phone call from the head of the Rules Committee. Diana's mother, typically, had watched Richard go and said nothing to her oldest daughter except "If you're happy, I'm happy."

The next afternoon, a gorgeous, soft April day, Gary had walked with her to the Columbia campus, where she'd been invited to a young alumni luncheon during the school's spring break. She was just about to kiss him goodbye and go through the gates on Broadway when she caught sight of a familiar figure across the street—Hal, holding hands with a leggy blonde. Diana felt her heart speed up. She knew Hal so well, his every gesture and expression, and she could tell, from his body language, that he was trying to decide whether to greet her or just keep walking. Her first impulse was to grab Gary's arm and hustle him onto campus, to pretend she hadn't seen her old boyfriend who'd dumped her so cruelly, but by the time she'd reached for Gary, Hal had crossed the street, calling, "Hey, Diana!"

Awkward introductions were exchanged while the two couples stood on the sidewalk between a hot dog cart and the ivied brick wall separating the campus from the street. "This is Maeve," Hal said. Diana took her in—the boot-cut jeans, the tight button-down shirt, the expensive eyeglasses and ironic sneakers. Undergrad, she guessed, a theory confirmed when Maeve told them she was waiting to hear from grad schools for next fall. Diana looked at Hal, in his khaki shorts and alt-rock-band T-shirt and running shoes, and thought, *He probably can't get a woman with an actual job to go out with him.* Then her bravado faded and her heart crumpled as she wondered whether he'd courted this Maeve with the same lines that had worked on her, whether he'd lain in wait on the library steps and said the words *Ironic juxtaposition.*

Maeve laced her fingers with Hal's. Diana took Gary's arm, knowing how good, how solid and grown-up he looked in his khakis and button-down; how, unlike Hal, he had put away childish things. He was a man, she thought; a man, not a boy . . . and on the heels of this happy realization came another one: *I can make this work.* True, maybe the chemistry between them wasn't great, but what was chemistry compared to compatibility and maturity and two grown-ups who wanted the same things? She could marry him, she thought, and stick to her timetable: a wedding by twenty-three, a baby the year after that.

"You look good," Hal said to Diana, his voice low.

"You, too." With her mind made up and the matter settled, she could afford to be generous. "How's stand-up?"

Stand-up, it emerged, wasn't good. Hal tried to sound optimistic, speaking vaguely of some opportunities on the horizon, a regular gig at an open mike night and a spec script he was writing, but Diana quickly forced him to admit that he was still earning a living as a paralegal, still living with five roommates in a two-bedroom apartment in a sketchy neighborhood in Harlem . . . and, of course, still dating college girls.

"Nice to see you," she said, offering Hal her hand, explaining that her attendance was expected at the young alumni luncheon. Then she slipped her fingers through Gary's and, beaming, kissed him. His lips were still too thin, his mouth entirely too wet . . . but none of that mattered. Her mind was made up. Diana would bring all of her will to bear on the subject of Gary and their marriage (that Gary might not want to marry her had never even crossed her mind) . . . and her will had never failed her, not in the classes she took or the races she'd run. It would not fail her now.

"So do you think you guys will get married?" Lizzie asked. This was in August, right before Diana was starting classes again, and Lizzie had come down to Philadelphia to spend the weekend. Diana and Gary had taken her to their favorite brunch spot, then to the Museum of Art, where Lizzie was visibly bored, and on to the Mütter Museum of medical oddities, where Lizzie had spent hours photographing the collection of syphilitic skulls and taking close-ups of some of the two thousand objects that had been removed from people's throats.

"Maybe," Diana had answered, turning her back to her sister, unhooking her bra, and slipping it through the sleeves of her shirt.

"And you like him?" Lizzie's disbelief was as palpable as the scent of sandalwood and pot that clung to her clothes.

"Yes," Diana said, twisting her hair into a knot on top of her head. "I do."

Lizzie peered into the screen of her digital camera, training the lens on the ceiling, with her blond hair fanning out over the bedspread. "Why?" she asked.

Diana sighed. "Because he's a good guy."

"He's boring," Lizzie said, punctuating her assessment with the shutter's click.

"Because he's not passing out at the table or stealing Grandma's silver?"

Lizzie fiddled with the lens, then snapped a picture of the

crown molding. "Boring," she repeated, swinging the camera toward Diana and punctuating her assessment with another click.

Diana turned her back again. She hated having her picture taken, hated the way she looked so massive and overpowering through Lizzie's eyes and Lizzie's lens. She thought of telling her sister that, unlike her, she couldn't afford to be picky, because she was never going to have a dozen guys to choose from. With hard work at the gym and at the mirror, where there was always something to pluck or wax or exfoliate, Diana rated herself acceptable: a six-and-a-half on the one-to-ten scale. Lizzie, with no work at all, looked like a woodland sprite, a busty little thing meant to wear a toga and a crown of laurel leaves and strum a lyre on a mountaintop. Diana looked, her exchange-student boyfriend had once told her, like the goddess Diana, Diana the huntress, born to sling a bow and a quiver full of arrows over her broad shoulders and go out and kill something for dinner.

Lizzie set down the camera, rolled onto her side, and swept her hair back over her shoulder. "You know that he spits when he talks."

Diana sighed. She knew. You couldn't spend five minutes with Gary and not know. "He can't help it," she said, stepping into her pajama bottoms. "And by the way, you could have been a little more subtle." At brunch, over banana-and-ricotta-stuffed French toast and a spinach-and-blue-cheese frittata, Gary had asked Lizzie where she'd be applying to college, and Lizzie had lifted her napkin and ostentatiously wiped off her cheeks before answering.

Her sister snorted. Lizzie was a great snorter. She could get away with it. On Lizzie, it was cute. "Subtle?" she said. "I thought I was going to drown. How can you like him? He's a . . ." She lifted the forefinger and thumb of each hand into the shape of an L and a 7, then touched them together, forming a square.

"He's nice," Diana said, feeling her face heat up, hoping that Lizzie's critique would not extend to Gary's looks. He did have those gentle brown eyes and good teeth and thick dark hair, and he was tall, but his face was all unpleasant, aggressive angles, and his body was bony and unwelcoming.

"Bor-ing," Lizzie repeated, lifting her camera again. "I liked Hal."

Diana turned away from the lens. "Hal," she said tightly, "has moved on." She got into bed beside her sister, rolled on her side, and shut her eyes.

Maybe love was a myth anyhow, a brew of hormones and fantasy, evolution's way of getting men and women together long enough for them to procreate, back in the day when girls got pregnant at twelve, were pregnant or nursing for the next twenty years, and were dead of the plague by forty. She was trying for something infinitely more obtainable than true love: a man with whom she could build the partnership she craved after all those years of listening to her father's stealthy early-morning departures and late-night returns, her mother's whispering and cosseting, and the way she had eyes only for her husband. She would find a man who would respect her as an equal and a partner; a man who would love her and never leave her, a man, unlike her father, who wouldn't give her a ring and then spend the next ten, twenty, thirty years taking things from her, chipping off little pieces, eroding her confidence and independence until there was nothing left but a shell in a St. John suit.

She'd have one child, a girl, she hoped. They'd take a week's vacation at the beach each summer, with the daughter holding her hand, stopping to consider driftwood and shells and sea glass. A cozy house with a fireplace and a little garden or a yard in the back. A husband, of course: someone to share popcorn at the movies, to carve the turkey on Thanksgiving, to hang Christmas ornaments, to kiss on New Year's Eve, to help her (it was morbid, but inevitable) handle her parents' old age and eventual death, because God knew that Lizzie would be useless. When Gary had proposed, pulling a box out of his pocket and saying, "Will you be my girl forever?," Diana let him slip the ring on her finger, let him kiss her lips, and whispered, "Yes," in his ear. She had told herself that she would have exactly the life she wanted, even if he wasn't exactly the man she'd dreamed of having it with.

By the time she arrived at their redbrick row house, still fuming from the afternoon's revelation about her dad, she'd sweated through her shirt, and her face was flushed. The living room was cool and quiet, the television off, Milo's Legos were stacked neatly in the corner, and the leather couch Gary had brought into the marriage was wiped clean. The room still looked unfinished, with its walls bare and its built-in bookcases mostly empty. Diana had big plans—there was a blue-and-white Chinese export vase she'd had her eye on in an antiques shop on Pine Street; an alpaca blanket, like a soft gray cloud, that would look perfect on top of the couch; the blown-up black-and-white photographs of Milo as a baby and a toddler that she'd meant to have framed and hung. So far, she was having a hard time putting together the time and the money to keep the room and, indeed, the whole house from looking as though the three of them had moved in the week before. *Can't we just buy a couple of chairs?* Gary would ask. *Do we really have to eat on a folding table?* Diana had patiently explained that if they were going to spend the money, the things they bought had to be right. It wouldn't do to just buy the first table that fit in the space, to hang just anything (or, worse yet, Gary's poster of the Phillies celebrating their World Series win) on the walls.

Milo and Lizzie were upstairs. Diana could hear water running in the bathroom, and her son's laughter as Lizzie shepherded him out of his clothes and into the tub. Gary, thank God, was nowhere to be found. She felt herself relax as she set down her bags and walked up the stairs, knowing that she'd have a precious twenty minutes to herself to get ready for dinner before facing Gary and the rest of the world.

LIZZIE

She'd been pronounced clean and sober and been sprung from the place in Minnesota at the end of June. A taxi had been waiting to take her to the airport at noon—Lizzie had been bemused to learn that rehabs had official checkout times, just like hotels. There she'd sat in the Northwest waiting area until her five o'clock flight was called. She felt more visible than she had in years, although, in her long skirt and flip-flops, her tank top and her denim jacket, she could see that she didn't look any different from the other young women in the terminal, the ones on their way to visit their grandparents or start their summer jobs. That was the thing about drugs—or, at least, it was the thing about painkillers, which had been her particular vice: taking them let her be present but absent, visible but gone. In the airport, sitting cross-legged on a black vinyl chair with her camera in her lap, she felt more *obvious* than she'd ever been before; as if she were gigantic, like everyone was staring at her, like she'd gotten a tattoo on her forehead, where no one could miss it, a scarlet A, not for *adultery* but for *addict*.

She thought she'd be going home, to her parents' place in New York City. Instead, her sister had grudgingly agreed to hire her for the summer. The plan, which had undoubtedly been cooked up by Lizzie's mother, was for Lizzie to babysit Milo, but Lizzie knew the real situation: her parents wanted big sister Diana to babysit her. Lizzie would be on Milo duty from eight in the morning until six o'clock every night, with Tuesdays and Thursdays off, because those were Diana's days home from the hospital. For her services, she was to be paid ten dollars an hour. "You know," Lizzie said, when she was on the phone with Diana, "the going rate's a lot higher."

"I'm aware of that," said Diana, in her clipped, impatient tone. There were hospital noises in the background, and her pager was beeping, too. "It includes room and board. And I think that you'd find on the open market you wouldn't get the going rate. Given your history."

Given your history. Trust Diana to find a way to remind her of it, to place her transgressions clearly in the forefront and keep the hierarchy clear. "Fine," Lizzie said, and hung up. She'd packed up her stuff, said goodbye to the staff and the one counselor she'd liked. She'd spent her last afternoon in the facility shooting with her beloved Leica, a present her parents had given her for her twenty-first birthday. ("You have to take care of it," her father had said, in a tone suggesting that she wouldn't.) "Why you wanna take pictures of this place?" one of the other patients had asked, as Lizzie peered through the viewfinder at the scarred metal of the doorless bathroom stalls. "It's so ugly." Lizzie had shrugged, not bothering to explain that what she was in search of was what all the photographers she most admired had been after: not beauty, which was easy, but truth.

She snapped shots of the meeting room with its cigarette-burn-scarred floor, the stained mattress of the narrow bed where she'd slept, a nurse's tired face in the slanting light that crept in through the blinds as she doled out pills into paper cups. Then she'd flown up and out of Minnesota, and Gary, her brother-in-law, had met her in Philadelphia. From the look on his face, Lizzie figured she was the last person he wanted living in his house, caring for his son. She greeted him cheerfully, even made herself lean in and kiss his cheek, but Gary barely said a word as he heaved her bags into the back of the minivan and drove her to the row house on Spruce Street, just a few blocks away from the hospital where Diana worked.

Lizzie had been determined to show her big sister that she wasn't a fuck-up; that she was a responsible, mature adult who'd put her bad times behind her. She'd come prepared with guidebooks and bookmarked websites, lists of museums and activities suitable for children Milo's age. She'd offered to shoot a family portrait, or a series of candids of Milo playing with his friends, something her sister could hang on her empty walls. But Diana nixed the idea. "We had a professional do a family portrait at Christmas," she'd said. As for Milo, who never left the house without a hat covering his ears and his *Field Guide to Insects* in his pocket, as far as Lizzie could tell he didn't have any friends. Nor was he impressed with Lizzie's offers to take him to the Japanese teahouse in Fairmount Park, to the Please Touch Museum or the Franklin Institute or even the indoor water park in Cherry Hill, and he resisted her ultimate bribe, a chance to use her fancy camera to take his own photographs. All Milo wanted to do was stay holed up in the air-conditioning, reading the collected adventures of *Captain Underpants,* and *Diary of a Wimpy Kid*, occasionally venturing down to the corner, where he'd squat in front of a tree planted in a small square of dirt and look for bugs.

After she'd been there for a week, watching Milo, dressed in shorts and a T-shirt and a ski cap with ear flaps, lying on the couch turning pages, waiting for him to dirty a dish so she could leave him alone long enough to wash it, he'd sat up and looked at her slyly. "Aunt Lizzie," he whispered. "Do you think we could . . ." He glanced to one side, then the other. ". . . watch TV?"

"Sure," she said, wondering what had taken him so long.

Milo whooped and bounded to the kitchen. He came back dragging a step stool, which he pulled over to the entertainment unit. Then he climbed to the top step, stood on his tiptoes, and pulled the remote off the uppermost shelf, where it had clearly been hidden away from him.

Lizzie noted this with growing concern and tried to remember, amid the pages and pages of instructions she'd been given, what Diana had told her about her son's entertainment options. She flipped through the five-page single-spaced alphabetized document and found nothing between SNACKS (organic only, fruits and vegetables preferred, absolutely nothing with high-fructose corn syrup, which was bullshit, because Marta had given her and Diana Little Debbie snack cakes every afternoon until they were in high school and the two of them had turned out fine, at least weight-wise) and TUCK-IN (two books, lights out at eight-thirty, and a bed check fifteen minutes later to make sure he was sleeping). Maybe there was something under ENTERTAINMENT, but best to go straight to the source. "Hey, Milo," she said. "Are you allowed to watch TV?"

His face fell. "Only thirty minutes of screen time every day, and it has to be educational."

"Ah." Lizzie found a listing under SCREEN TIME and saw that he was right. Which was total hypocrisy. From the minute loathsome Gary walked through the door until the minute he went up to bed, he had the box on and blaring at a volume suggesting that there was an eighty-year-old man in the living room. "Did you have any, uh, screen time today?"

He chewed on his lip. "I played Math Blaster on my Leapster."

Lizzie considered. "How about this? You get twenty minutes of TV, and tomorrow, first thing, we'll go to the park."

Milo narrowed his eyes. "Deal." He turned out to be impressively adroit with his parents' fancy setup, manipulating the remote to get a bunch of screens and speakers working. Within minutes, he and Lizzie settled back on the couch to watch something called *Yo Gabba Gabba!*, a program that Lizzie decided had to have been produced by a bunch of supremely stoned teenagers (and she was uniquely qualified to know).

"Who is that?" She peered at the TV set, where a skinny black man dressed in orange, with a towering fur hat on his head, capered into the screen's center and opened a silver boom box.

"DJ Lance Rock!" Milo crowed, showing more animation than he had during Lizzie's stay so far. On the screen, DJ Lance Rock pulled a series of dolls out of a suitcase—there was a pink one, with a bow on its head, and a robot, and what looked like a green ball of yarn, with rubbery arms and legs.

"That's Foofa," said Milo, pointing. "And Plex, and Brobee."

"Jesus," said Lizzie, as, onscreen, a red, ribbed rubber doll began to dance. "That one looks like a dildo!"

Milo giggled. "What's a dildo?"

"Um." This adventure was not, perhaps, getting off to the best start. "It's kind of a grown-up thing. Hey, do you ever watch *Sesame Street*?"

"That's for babies," Milo said, as the puppets, who'd somehow magically become life-sized, did a dance and sang a song about sharing. "Dildo, dildo, dildo," Milo chanted under his breath, and Lizzie giggled—she couldn't help herself.

"Um, Milo?" she said, when she'd managed to stop laughing. Her nephew looked up at her, all innocence and trust and fake-fur-lined hat, and Lizzie decided that the bigger deal she made about the forbidden word, the more he'd probably say it. "Nothing," she said. "Never mind." She left him in front of the TV and went to the kitchen to make his dinner—organic chicken nuggets Diana had shown her in the freezer, strips of red pepper, a bunch of green grapes, and half a sweet potato that she cooked in the microwave, then mashed with butter and cinnamon. She arranged everything on a plate, found a placemat and a napkin, and congratulated herself on how nice it looked. Milo was halfway through dinner when the door swung open and Diana marched through it.

Lizzie held her breath as her sister bent to kiss her son. "Did you have fun today?" Diana asked, and Milo swallowed a mouthful of sweet potato, nodded vigorously, and said, "Hey, Mom? What's a dildo?"

Diana glared at her, lips pinched and eyes narrowed. "Excuse me. I must use the facilities," Lizzie murmured, and slipped upstairs, deciding that it would be prudent to give Diana and Milo some alone time, and maybe take herself out to dinner. She pulled off her overalls and grabbed one of the relics she'd unearthed from the trunk in the back of her mother's closet: a long white cotton skirt, only slightly frayed and yellowed with age. She added a pale-pink tank top, the bangles and the beaded necklace she'd also liberated from her mother's closet, then pulled on her sandals, looped her camera around her neck, and swept her hair in a loose bun that left tendrils tickling her cheeks. She tiptoed past Milo's bedroom door, holding her breath as she listened to Diana explaining that some words were grown-up words, and scribbled a note—"back soon"—to leave on the kitchen table. Then she grabbed her purse, and stepped out onto the street lined with three-story red brick row houses that looked the same as they must have a hundred years ago, minus the streetlights and the skateboarders.

She wandered west for a few blocks, moving slowly, bangles chiming with each step. She bought a slice of pizza on Pine Street and ate it as she walked toward Independence Hall, drawn by the noise of chanting and singing. Some kind of demonstration was taking place. It was a warm, sultry night, and the wind carried the sweet scent of pot. Lizzie could make out the winking firefly light of a joint passing from hand to hand. She turned her head, struggling not to remember the slowed-down syrupy sensation a few bong hits could bring, and fired off a few quick shots of the crowd—a girl and a boy entwined on a blanket, a burst of fireworks flaring against the black sky. Then she strolled down Market Street until she came to a place called the Franklin Fountain. Its wooden sign was painted in an old-fashioned font, and its menu featured phosphates and malteds. She peeked through the window and was charmed by the pressed-tin ceiling, the marble counters with an antique cash register, the glass jars of pretzels, and the boxes of vintage gums and candies, and how one of the men scooping ice cream had an actual handlebar mustache. A malted sounded like just the thing. Lizzie could almost hear the clink of the long-handled spoon against the sides of the chilled metal cup, and she had money in her pocket, her pay for the week.

Bells jingled as she walked inside. Ceiling fans paddled lazily through the warm air, and the tiled floor felt cool beneath the soles of her sandals. After buying her drink and pocketing her change, she'd made her way to the back of the shop, where a table for two sat empty. Unfortunately, the table beside it was taken by a pack of four noisy guys in T-shirts and khaki shorts. College kids, or maybe even high school boys.

"Well, hey there," one of them had said, looking her up and down, taking in the long skirt, the beads, her mother's scarf, which she'd pulled out of her purse and twisted around her hair on the way. She'd given him a neutral smile and taken a seat, poured herself a glassful of her malted, and looked at the camera's square display screen, mentally editing the shots she'd taken on her way down.

"Nice camera," one of the T-shirt boys said.

"Thanks," she said, without lifting her eyes, flicking through images of fireworks and treetops and the couple on the blanket. My summer in Philadelphia, she thought, a little sadly. When she looked up, the boy was still staring at her.

"You wanna take my picture?" he asked.

"I don't really do portraits." In a flash of inspiration, she added, "And I'm almost out of film." Maybe he wouldn't notice that it was a digital camera. She could be wrong, but he didn't strike her as a connoisseur of the visual arts.

"Aw, c'mon! I'll pose for you." The guy lifted his shirt, displaying a hairy chest and disturbingly pink nipples, as his friends whooped and high-fived.

Lizzie set her camera on the table and got to her feet, thinking that she'd have the server pour her malted into a to-go cup and head back to Diana and Gary's house, but the boy grabbed her camera and aimed it at Lizzie. She heard the click of the shutter and felt her throat tighten. The camera was expensive, and it was pretty much the only nice thing she owned that she hadn't trashed or lost or traded for drugs.

She held out her hand. "Can I have that back, please?"

The boy sneered and raised the camera above his head, affording her an unobstructed view of his sweat-stained armpits. Ick. Behind the counter, one of the clerks said, "Sir, give her the camera back."

"Not until she takes my picture," said the boy. He turned and started snapping shots of his friends, who were also pulling up their shirts, egging him on.

A man at another table got to his feet. He walked over to the boy, stood right in front of him, and said, in a low, carrying voice, "Give her the camera back."

The camera thief looked the man up and down. Instead of shorts and a T-shirt, the man wore khaki pants and a button-down khaki shirt with a green tie. A patch depicting Independence Hall was sewn to the shirt's breast pocket. He had a round face, short brown hair, and wore wire-rimmed glasses.

"Or what?" the sweaty boy snarled.

"Or," said the man in khaki, "you and I are going to step outside and I'm going to ask you again."

The boy studied his opponent, perhaps noticing, as Lizzie did, that even though he wasn't particularly tall, he had broad shoulders and muscular forearms. "Screw it," the boy muttered, and lobbed the camera onto Lizzie's table. She grabbed it before it could fall, and managed to knock her malted onto the floor. The cup landed with a clang, and the boys burst out laughing. Lizzie knelt down to clean up the mess. On her knees, with cold ice cream soaking into the hem of her skirt, she felt her eyes burn. All she'd wanted was a little break, a little time by herself before she had to go home and deal with her sister's lectures, her brother-in-law's presence, and poor Milo, who'd probably had all his screen time for the summer taken away, thanks to Aunt Lizzie's vocabulary lesson. Why was it always like this for her? Why did it all go so wrong?

She squeezed her eyes shut, and when she opened them the troublemaking boys were filing out the door and Lizzie was looking into a pair of kind blue eyes behind wire-rimmed glasses. The man who'd saved her camera had square shoulders and a square jaw, like Dick Tracy or Clark Kent, like someone imagined by a comic-book artist instead of a real guy. "Hey," he said. "Are you okay? Can I give you a hand?"

Her throat felt thick. "I'm fine."

He got down on the floor to help her gather the sodden napkins. The ceiling fan stirred the air above them, lifting his hair from his brow as he stood up and lifted the camera, turning it in his hands. "Looks okay," he said, and gave it to Lizzie. Over her protests, the man behind the counter made her another malted, and the guy who'd helped her carried his banana split over to her table after asking, politely, whether it was okay for him to join her. "I'm Jeff Spencer," he said, and extended his hand.

"Lizzie," she answered, bunching her soaked skirt in one hand and shaking his with the other. He sat down, and as they ate their ice cream, he told her that he was twenty-eight, that he'd been in the army for six years before going to college, that he had a degree in environmental science and was earning his master's in recreation management at Temple while working as a ranger in the Independence Hall park in the daytime.

"So what brings you to Philadelphia?" he asked, after learning that Lizzie was from New York.

She'd given him a pared-down version of her story. She said that she was twenty-four, that she was working as a nanny for the summer, and that in the fall, she'd start a job as a photographer's assistant back in New York City. She left out the part about flunking out of Vassar and getting kicked out of NYU, and the stints in rehab in between. She didn't mention that her father was a senator and her sister was a doctor and she was the family's dirty little secret, its resident hot mess.

"How'd you get into photography?" he asked.

Lizzie could barely remember a time when she hadn't had a camera in her hand or her pocket or looped around her neck. Her first one must have been a birthday present from Marta, a little Instamatic, back when people still shot on film, and when her parents saw that she liked it, and that she could capture unexpected angles and surprising juxtapositions, they bought her nicer and nicer ones. At one point, they'd even offered to let her convert a walk-in closet into a darkroom. That was before she'd turned fourteen and decided she liked dope more than pictures.

"I've always been doing it," she told him. She considered the planes of his face, his square hands and his straight teeth, and thought she'd like to take his picture, in three-quarter profile, maybe with a cape billowing out behind him. It made her smile, which made him smile. Lizzie ducked her head, worried that he thought she was flirting, because she had no idea how to follow through if he got the wrong idea. She'd never hooked up with a guy when she wasn't drunk or high or otherwise altered, and she wasn't quite sure how it went. "Do you ever take pictures?"

He shrugged. "I've got a digital camera, but I'm not very good. Everyone comes out with red eyes, and I never know . . . I mean, I've read a little bit, but I don't know what makes one picture better than another. I guess you think that makes me a Philistine."

Lizzie watched the way his eyebrows lifted when he talked, the blond hair on his forearms. She didn't know what a Philistine was—some kind of religious thing, she figured—but she knew what made a good picture. "For me," she began slowly, "I guess it's about seeing something new. Or seeing regular things in a way you never thought about them before."

He frowned, thinking this over. "Look," she said, and raised her viewfinder so he could see it. While waiting for her malted, she'd leaned over the counter and snapped a close-up of two of the ice cream containers, a bin full of chocolate and one of mint chocolate chip. The way she'd framed the shot, with the lens practically touching the ice cream, they looked like gigantic vats of some extraterrestrial material, the terrain of another planet, with the ridges left by the scoop, the jutting shard of chocolate and the single feathery vein of ice crystals. "Whoa," he said, staring. "It's like . . . I don't know. Like looking at the moon or something."

She smiled, delighted. "That's exactly what I was going for." They looked at each other a minute before Lizzie dropped her eyes again. She liked him . . . or, at least, she liked the way he looked, his hands with their clean, clipped nails, his blue eyes, his voice, which was quiet but confident and reminded her of her father.

"How many kids are you watching?" Jeff asked.

"Just one. Milo's my nephew. He's a little weird, but he's a sweetheart."

"How's he weird?" Jeff looked at her expectantly, and Lizzie explained about Milo's thing with bugs—their identification and collection and eventual storage in the little plastic boxes he kept on his windowsill. She told him how Milo always wore a hat pulled down over his ears because, he said, sounds were too loud without it, and how she had to bribe him with television to get him to set one toe outside.

"Rough," Jeff said. "You should bring him to Independence Park sometime. I'll give you guys the VIP tour."

"That would be great," said Lizzie, taking one more look at those bright blue eyes. Jeff gave her his business card—it had a gold logo for the National Park Service embossed on its surface. Then he said, "Would you like to have dinner with me sometime?"

She looked at him and wondered what he saw when he looked at her—a girl with droopy blond hair and an ice-cream-soaked skirt; a damsel in distress, when the truth was that Lizzie was more like a Trojan horse. She might look okay, like the kind of fancy, pretty thing you'd welcome into your city or your home, but inside, she was trouble. Jeff seemed like a nice guy. He didn't deserve Lizzie.

"Or have you got a boyfriend?" Jeff asked, but not in a jerky way. She thought about telling him that she'd never had a boyfriend in her life, but instead she just said, "I work most nights, is the thing."

"Ah. Well, it was nice meeting you."

"Thank you for . . ." She stood, pushed her chair in,

and straightened the mess of her skirt. "Thanks for saving my camera."

"You bet." He waved at her cheerfully. The bells on the door jingled as he left. She walked home slowly, listening to her iPod, the Be Good Tanyas singing about how the littlest birds sing the prettiest songs, thinking about whether, at some point in her future, she could ever be with a guy like that.

The next day, while she was setting the table for dinner, Diana said. "You've got mail."

"Oh?" Sure enough, her sister handed her an envelope with her name—Lizzie—on the front. She opened it, and a newspaper clipping and a card fell out. The clipping was a review of an Italian restaurant that had excellent gnocchi and good Caesar salad. The notecard, with a pen-and-ink drawing of a red robin on the front, read, "In case you change your mind," and was signed "Jeff Spencer," with an e-mail address and a phone number underneath.

She must have stared at the card for five minutes, turning it over in her hands, before she locked herself in the powder room and dialed the number. "How'd you know where I lived?"

"I followed you home. Don't freak out," he said quickly, as if he could tell that Lizzie was getting ready to do that very thing. "It wasn't like a stalker thing. I just wanted to ask you about dinner again. And I didn't have your last name or your number, so . . ."

Lizzie leaned against Diana's perfectly arrayed hand towels and wondered whether the guy was a stalker, or if he was crazy, or if this was just the way normal men behaved when they were interested. She wished that she had someone other than her sister to ask.

"Okay," she finally said. "Dinner sounds nice."

"Tomorrow?"

"Okay."

The next night Jeff picked her up at eight o'clock. Milo was in bed, Diana was still at work, and Gary, as usual, was parked in front of the boob tube with his laptop on his lap. "You look very nice," Jeff had said. She'd worn another one of her mother's old skirts, this one denim, with patches of paisley and plaid (a little big, but a belt had helped), with a sheer long-sleeved tunic, ropes of beads, and feathered earrings. As they strolled south along the sidewalks, she thought they made an odd couple—her in her bohemian getup, him in his pressed pants and button-down shirt—but he didn't seem to notice, or, at least, he didn't seem to mind.

The restaurant had rough stucco walls painted white, red tiles on the floor, and a tiny open kitchen where two men in cook's whites sweated in front of a wood-burning oven. At a wobbly table so small that she could feel his knees brushing hers, they ordered the gnocchi and Caesar salad, stuffed chicken breasts and the special fettuccine, and split a tiramisu for dessert. He'd brought a bottle of red wine in a brown paper bag and asked if she wanted any. "Oh, it's so hot. I think I'll stick to iced tea," she said, and felt, when he'd nodded, that she'd passed some kind of test.

He asked about her day, and she told him that she'd let Milo watch an entire hour of *WordGirl* in exchange for a visit to the paint-your-own pottery place on Bainbridge Street, where Milo painted a ceramic dinosaur and Lizzie decorated a spoon rest for Diana's kitchen. Jeff told her about spending the day directing people to the restrooms and listening to terrible jokes about the Liberty Bell. "If I had a dollar for every time someone says, 'Hey, it's broken,' I could retire right now," he said.

"So where are you from?" she asked.

The answer was Philadelphia—not Center City, where Diana lived, but what he called the Far Northeast. He'd grown up with an older brother. Their father worked for the school district—Jeff didn't say exactly what he did, and Lizzie didn't ask. "What about your mom?"

His face tightened. "She's had some problems," he said, and for the first time that night looked past her, over her head, toward the restaurant's door.

"Like health problems?" Lizzie asked.

"A drinking problem, actually," said Jeff.

Lizzie swallowed hard. "Oh."

He turned to look at her again, his lips pressed together tightly. "She's been trying to deal with it for years. She'll do okay for a while, and then . . ."

Lizzie said softly, "That must have been hard for you and your brother." In her head, she was deciding that she wouldn't see him again. A guy with a drunk for a mother was not a guy who needed, or would choose, an addict for a girlfriend. She would walk home with him, thank him for a nice night out—and it had been a nice night out, one of the nicest she could remember—and then make herself scarce.

Lifting his water glass, Jeff drank, then shrugged. "We got out as soon as we could. Only thing we could do." He drained his glass, and, with a palpable effort, gave her a smile. "Anyhow. What about your parents?"

"My dad works for the government," she said, which was true. "He's away a lot. My mom did a lot of volunteer work. We had a nanny." His expression let Lizzie know how different this was from his own childhood, and listened when she talked about her private school (which she'd hated), her ice-skating lessons (which she'd hated even more), and how, honestly, she was still kind of trying to figure out what she wanted to be when she grew up.

After dinner, they'd walked to his apartment, in a high-rise building that overlooked Washington Square Park, ostensibly so he could show her a hilarious YouTube video of a cat who played the piano.

"This was my grandfather's place," he explained in the elevator, which was populated, like the lobby below, by senior citizens. Jeff lowered his voice as the doors slid open. "He died last winter. My dad put it on the market, but I'm staying here until it sells. It's kind of a mess," he apologized, leading her into the living room, which wasn't messy at all. Nor did Lizzie sense the presence of a departed elderly resident, either by sight or—she took a quick, surreptitious sniff—by smell. There were fishing magazines spread out on the coffee table, which Jeff quickly stacked in a pile, and a pair of running shoes, unlaced by the door. Framed family photographs—the grandfather's, she guessed—hung beside brightly colored vintage posters for Italian ocean liners and Orangina that were probably Jeff's. Lizzie had made her way to the window, drawn by the view of the park, with its richly green lawns bisected by wide slate paths, the fountain bubbling away in its center, underneath the starry night sky.

Then she'd walked into the bedroom. "Oh," she'd said, and looked around, delighted. The room was like a treehouse. She could hear the leaves rustle as the wind blew through them. Jeff's bed was set in a corner by the window, a king-size bed with a dark-blue comforter. There was a small bookshelf filled with textbooks and spy novels, and a small, old-fashioned TV against the wall. A guitar leaned in one corner, and the air smelled sweetly of cedar from the closet.

She pulled her camera out of her purse and pointed at the window. "Can you stand right there?"

"Really?" Jeff seemed somewhere between shy and flattered. "I'm not going to have to take any of my clothes off, am I?"

It took Lizzie a second to realize that he was teasing her. "I promise they'll be tasteful," she said, and got him to stand right where she wanted him, in profile, with his face silhouetted against the thickly leaved trees and the moon. Not Superman, but Batman, she thought, clicking away, a superhero with a painful past and an affinity for the darkness. She climbed onto his bed, without a thought of what signals that might be sending, to get a better angle, thinking that there was something so intimate about taking a picture, capturing someone's likeness and letting him see what you saw.

"These are really good," said Jeff when they sat on the couch and she clicked through the images. "Really interesting."

She looked at the clock, suddenly aware of the warmth of his leg against hers, and how he'd slipped his arm around her shoulders. "I should go."

"Or you'll turn into a pumpkin?" He was teasing her again, but it was without rancor, a kind, almost brotherly kind of ribbing. "Let me walk you down, Cinderella." At the sliding doors at the front of the apartment building, he kissed her—gently and quickly, his lips warm on hers. *Nice,* she thought. This evening ranked as among the best she'd had. She wanted to see him again, even though once he learned the truth he probably wouldn't want to see her. But maybe that could be postponed until they'd had a few more dinners, maybe a picnic in the park, or a night snuggled on his grandfather's couch, watching movies, the way she'd heard normal couples did.

By the night the story of her father and Joelle hit the news, she and Jeff had been seeing each other for weeks. They'd had their walks and their dinners and their picnics, and had made out once on Jeff's big bed. As soon as she left the hospital, holding Milo's hand, her telephone rang. "We still on?" Jeff asked. It took her a minute to remember that they'd made plans, the three of them: Jeff was going to come over with a movie. After dinner, they'd pop popcorn, she and Jeff and Milo, and watch it together.

"Hey, listen," she began, tugging Milo into the vestibule

of the 7-Eleven. Jeff waited patiently, wordlessly, for Lizzie to begin. "Did you watch TV today? About the senator who was having an affair?"

If he'd said something disparaging, something mocking, she would have found a way to cancel their plans and maybe even avoid him for the rest of the summer. But Jeff said merely, "Yeah, I think I heard something about it."

Lizzie gulped. "Well, the senator's kind of my dad."

Again, if he'd laughed, or joked, or said, "Kind of?" she would have hung up on him. But Jeff said calmly and kindly, "Wow. Are you doing okay? Do you still want to get together?" Lizzie thought about it, and realized that the answer was yes.

She was relieved that, so far at least, her revelation didn't seem to have changed the way Jeff felt about her. She'd seen that happen before. A classmate or a classmate's parent, a friend of a friend, or a nurse or an orderly would look at her face or read her last name, and there would be a click so clear it was practically audible. *Elizabeth Woodruff? Your father's not . . . ?* First came the recognition, which was quickly followed by the classmate or acquaintance trying to figure out how to capitalize on this new information. Lizzie was constantly astonished by the manner and magnitude of the requests strangers would make. She thought sometimes that there was nothing, absolutely nothing, to which the average American did not feel entitled.

Could you . . . would you . . . do you think that maybe . . . ? Sometimes the petitioners would feign interest in Lizzie in order to have a better shot at their prize: a handshake, a photograph, a bid on a government contract, or even just a moment with the great man, a chance to have a senator's attention for the length of a drink or a dance or a meal. When she was a sophomore in high school, a senior from Collegiate named Glenn Burkey had asked her out. She'd been thrilled until the moment that boy had shown up at their door, barely kissed her hello, and then gone to the living room, where he'd spent twenty minutes debating alternative energy sources with her father, in a naked attempt to secure one of the coveted summer internship slots.

Sometimes the petitioner would want nothing more than a small favor or a piece of information she could dispense. Help with a parking ticket, a dispute with a landlord, a Medicare claim? Dad could hook that up, or at least steer the request into the proper channels. But sometimes, especially after Lizzie had started her slide, things got dicey.

Last spring, when she and a bunch of friends had been trying to make a buy in the Village, the dealer had recognized her. This was a piece of bad luck: as Diana said, when she'd heard about it, usually there was very little overlap in the Venn diagrams of "people who watched enough CNN to recognize their senator's daughter" and "people who sold crystal meth out of apartments with holes in the floor." But that night she'd been spectacularly unlucky. "Holy shit," said the guy, a bug-eyed wraith in acid-washed jeans and a dingy wifebeater. "That's Senator Woodruff's kid!" Lizzie had gotten herself up off the floor, where she'd slumped when the rush had hit her, but she hadn't been moving very quickly. In fact, she'd barely been moving at all. The dealer and one of his buddies had tied her to a chair—with the dealer's girlfriend's ripped fishnet stockings, she recalled—and used her cell phone to call her parents and demand the immediate payment of ten thousand dollars, or else they'd send cell phone pictures to TMZ. Instead of sending the money, her parents sent the cops. The dealer and his girlfriend, who'd been smart enough to try to ransom Lizzie but not smart enough to hide their wares, fled into the bathroom to try to flush their stash down the toilet, while her drug buddies scattered. They'd all been arrested, Lizzie included, and it had been in the paper, a little squib in the Metro section of the *Times,* which had gotten picked up by Page Six and then a couple of the gossip blogs, and the next thing she knew, she and her dad were driving to Minnesota, on a road trip that had ended in rehab.

She gave Milo his bath and his dinner. Diana hurried out the door on her way out to a rare date with Gary, and by seven-thirty Jeff was there, with a bag of popcorn kernels and an edited-for-TV version of *Airplane!* He put the movie on, popped the popcorn, and brought it into the living room, along with a pitcher of iced tea.

"You doing all right?" he asked quietly, on the couch beside Lizzie, as Milo, lying on the floor in a fleece ski cap and his pajamas, howled with laughter at the opening scenes.

"I just never thought," she said, and then let her voice trail off, fidgeting with the painted glass beads at her throat. Jeff waited. Lizzie thought of what to say. If she talked too much about her father, she'd risk revealing things that Jeff didn't know and that Lizzie didn't want to tell him. Jeff still looked and thought and carried himself like someone in the army. He was so clean-cut, so upright, so moral, that she couldn't imagine how he'd feel if he learned about some of the things she'd done, and the people she'd done them with. When he looked at her, when he stroked her hair, when he told her she smelled like cinnamon sugar, she could tell he really liked her, that he was enchanted by her, and she didn't want to do anything to mess that up or reveal her true nature or remind him of his own mother.

Jeff pulled her close until her cheek rested on his shoulder. "Have you talked to him?" he asked. Lizzie shook her head. Diana had talked to him, and she could see from her Missed Calls log that her father had tried to reach her, but she hadn't called him back or even played his messages. What could he possibly have said? And what could she say to him? That she was disgusted by what he'd done? That she was disappointed? Couldn't he tell her the same thing, a hundred times over?

"Do you two get along? You and your dad?" Jeff asked.

Lizzie thought. Milo was lying on his side, breathing deeply and steadily, as, on TV, the air traffic controller announced that he'd picked a bad week to stop sniffing glue. She knew how he felt.

"We used to go get bagels," she finally said. When she was a girl, every Sunday morning she and her father would get up early and walk six blocks to buy a dozen bagels. He'd carried her on his shoulders until she turned five or so, and then she'd walk beside him. Standing in the steamy, dough-and-garlic-scented air of H&H, as people pushed all around her, calling out their orders, pointing at what they wanted and telling the fast-moving, sweaty men behind the counter to bag the everything bagels separately, Lizzie would hold her father's hand. Sometimes, she'd bury her face in his tweed overcoat and take a sniff, smelling the wool, and his aftershave. "Good morning, congressman!" the lady at the cash register would call, and people would turn to stare, to offer their own greetings, to ask questions about this vote or that bill and sometimes to offer dissenting opinions, to complain about traffic tickets or their taxes. Her father would listen for a moment or two, then say, "Excuse us. My little girl needs her breakfast," words that would defuse even the most irascible New Yorker. He would order a dozen bagels to bring home, plus a bialy for Lizzie to eat in the park.

She shut her eyes, remembering the warm roll in her hands, her father on the bench beside her, telling her the names of the trees, and in that instant she was six years old, Milo's age, in the park with her daddy, when nothing had gone wrong yet, and nothing ever would. *I want a pill*, she thought. *I want to smoke. I want to drink. I want to go to sleep.*

She must have done something—flinched, or made some noise—because Jeff, who'd been laughing at Striker trying to land the plane, turned and asked, "Are you okay?" In the darkness, Lizzie nodded, and forced herself to take a slow breath, remembering the mantra, which she'd learned in rehab that spring: HALT. When you were down and vulnerable, when you wanted to use, ask yourself: were you . . . Hungry? Angry? Lonely? Tired? Name the feelings instead of stuffing them down and hiding them away, her counselors had instructed. Address the feelings and move on.

She wasn't hungry—Jeff had made popcorn, and she'd nibbled at the fish sticks Milo hadn't eaten for dinner. She wasn't lonely. With Jeff, and Milo sleeping on the floor, she felt more connected and secure than she had in years. She wasn't tired: she'd been sleeping well in her sister's closet-sized guest room up on the third floor. That left angry. She supposed she was.

She remembered the trip she and her father had taken to Minnesota after the ill-fated ransom attempt and her arrest (had Joelle been in the picture then? Lizzie wondered, then decided she didn't want to know). Her dad had been home for the Senate's spring break, and neither of her parents trusted Lizzie to get herself on a plane and get herself off at the correct destination. Besides, she would have been spotted at an airport. Someone with a cell phone would have snapped her picture, and the whole thing would have been in the papers again. So her mother had packed her bags, and her father had rented a car, and as strained and odd as the circumstances had been, they'd had a pretty good time. The car he'd picked was a giant SUV that Lizzie had nicknamed Rapper's Delight. It was so high off the ground it came with its own step stool, and had spinning rims and a killer sound system and cream-colored leather seats with DVD players mounted into the headrests. Lizzie had draped herself across the backseat, pleasantly numbed by the Valium her primary-care physician had prescribed to get her from New York to Minnesota, with a plastic bag in her hands in case she got queasy as her body started to withdraw from the drugs she'd been feeding it for months.

As soon as they were out of the city, her father had pulled into a rest stop and gotten two bags full of junk food—chips and candy, pretzel nuggets stuffed with fake cheese, beef jerky and soda and iced chocolate cupcakes. In his jeans and sneakers and baseball cap, he could have been any middle-aged father, strongly built and still handsome, and she could have been any daughter, a student or a waitress or a nanny, on a road trip with her dad.

The two of them snacked their way across the country, listening to Lizzie's music: Lucinda Williams, the McGarrigle sisters, Shawn Colvin, k.d. lang, and Patsy Cline. Along the way, he told her stories. Lizzie heard all about the senator who was so cheap that he kept an inflatable mattress in his office instead of paying to rent an apartment. Her father filled her in on the three freshman representatives whose shared living quarters were so notoriously filthy there'd been a rat living in their kitchen for weeks, and the congressman from Colorado, a Democrat and a devout Catholic, who seemed to get his poor wife pregnant every time he went home to campaign. "They've got five kids," her father had said, "and I think he's met each of them once."

She'd had her camera, of course, and had managed to raise it to the window every hundred miles or so and snap a shot of the world blurring by. There was a picture of a rest stop, the weedy, trash-choked yards that backed onto the highway access road, a shot of the Golden Arches that she'd taken while lying flat on her back in the backseat, and a picture of the sani-band that girdled the hotel's toilet seat in the Best Western where they'd stopped for the night.

They'd gone to a diner for breakfast the next morning. Lizzie, still queasy, and starting to feel the beginnings of the familiar nausea and bone-deep ache, had huddled in her hooded sweatshirt, sipping a glass of ginger ale. While her legs twitched and jerked, doing a crazy dance under the table as she sweated through her shirt, her father ate an omelet and talked about the time in college when he'd gotten mono and fallen asleep during a haircut, right in the barber's chair. Finally, he dropped his napkin on his plate.

"So listen, Lizzie," he said, "what's this about, anyhow?"

She tensed her muscles, trying to get her legs to hold still. "Dunno."

"You gonna stop this time?"

She rattled her fingers on top of the table without answering. She'd promised him—promised them both—that she'd stop prior to both of her previous trips to rehab.

He sounded gentle as he asked, "Do you know why you started?"

She looked away. She knew what he was thinking, what anyone would think: how a girl who'd had every advantage, money and private schools and parents who loved her, should have ever been tempted by drugs, let alone hooked. What did she need to escape from? What pain did she need to dull? She could never explain, especially not to him, what it felt like knowing she was a disappointment. She wasn't smart like her sister or helpful like her mother or a leader like he was. She was just Lizzie, unremarkable, unexceptional Lizzie; a C student who couldn't make varsity and couldn't carry a tune, Lizzie, who'd never amount to much, Lizzie, whose eyes were shut and mouth was open in every portrait of the family at her father's inaugurations and victory celebrations. It was easier to hide in plain sight, which was what the Percocet and Vicodin (and, she supposed, her camera) let her do. She'd never answered, and her dad hadn't pushed.

He'd walked her to the bathroom, stood outside the door as she threw up, doled out the Valium and bought her celebrity magazines at the gas station where he'd filled the car's double tank. "Brief me," he'd call from the front seat, sounding as interested as he did in tort reform or Israel. "What's happening with

Spencer and Heidi?" She kept waiting for him to try to bring up the drugs again, to try to get to the bottom of why she was using, or maybe even to offer some pained and halting admission of how he and her mother had failed her, but he didn't try, and Lizzie was grateful. As the sky got dark, she imagined that the two of them were in a space capsule, traveling through a vast, empty world, sole survivors of some planet-ending disaster, a father and daughter, out on their own. It sounded weird—so weird that she didn't even try to explain it to Jeff—but those eighteen hours, when she had commanded her father's complete and undivided attention, were among the happiest she'd had.

"Hey." Jeff was looking down at her, smiling. Lizzie blinked. The end credits of *Airplane!* were rolling, and Milo was snoring on the floor. "You getting sleepy, too?"

She nodded. "A little bit." She hadn't expected to sleep at all that night, not with her mind churning, regurgitating the pictures she'd seen of her father and that Joelle, wondering how to square the man who'd lied and cheated with the father who'd driven her all the way to Minnesota and made himself fluent in the storylines of *The Hills* and, once, held her hair back when she'd puked.

Jeff took Milo up to his bedroom, then scooped Lizzie in his arms and carried her to the third floor. "My hero," she murmured as he settled her onto the bed, pulling the light cotton comforter up to her chin and sliding her sandals off her feet. He kissed her lightly, first her lips, then her forehead. She slipped his glasses off his face, folded them, set them on the little bedside table and stretched out her arms.

"Come here," she whispered. Diana and Gary would be gone for at least another hour, and Milo slept like the dead. She drew Jeff down onto the high, narrow bed, feeling none of the doubt and the hesitation that usually accompanied intimacy. The first time she'd been with a boy, it hadn't ended well, and ever since then, there was a fear that the guy would suddenly turn on her, grab her wrists, and force his mouth down on hers, too hard. But Jeff would never hurt her. Jeff liked her.

"Lizzie," he breathed. She ran her hands across his shoulders, then down the length of his back, delighting in the feel of him, the heat and the solidity, and his stillness, the way he kept himself perfectly immobile, holding her in his arms as if he could stay that way forever. Eagerly she worked at the buttons of his shirt, tossing her own tank top to the floor, until they were skin to skin.

She ran her fingertips over the muscles of his chest, the ridges of his abs, until he'd pressed himself against her, kissing her until she was dizzy. He pressed his erection against her belly. She spread her legs, pushing her hips toward him.

"Is it safe?" he murmured. Lizzie nodded without giving the question careful consideration—her periods had never been regular, and she couldn't exactly remember when she'd last had one—but this felt too good to stop.

"Sweetheart," Jeff murmured, sliding inside of her. "Beautiful Lizzie." She held him, burying her face in his neck, rocking against him, letting the terrible day slip away from her, thinking that maybe she didn't need drugs as long as she had this.

SYLVIE

The door to Richard's office swung open. Sylvie recognized everything there, every piece of furniture, Richard's diplomas, the painted cup that Diana had made him in kindergarten, where he kept his pens; everything down to the framed photograph of Lizzie's fifth birthday party, and the shot of the two of them dancing beside the president and first lady at the Inaugural Ball.

Her husband was on the couch, still in the blue suit she'd watched him put on in their hotel room that morning. ("All clear?" he'd asked, and she'd run a lint brush over his shoulders and lapels before sending him on his way.) He sat slumped, with his tie loosened, his hands hanging at his sides, and Joe Eido, his chief of staff, an unpleasant little rabbity man, bald and bite-sized with pale, red-rimmed eyes, beside him. Joe turned off the television set. Richard looked up at Sylvie, then wordlessly looked down at his lap.

Sylvie stared at him with that strange numbness still suffusing her. How did this go, she wondered, for husbands and wives who didn't have a chief of staff to act as witness and referee? What did they say when they knew there was no chance of the fallout happening in public, when it was just a man and a woman alone in a room? How did the conversation start? Was she supposed to yell at him, or throw something, or just wait?

She stared at her husband until finally Joe spoke up. "Let me leave you two alone," he said.

"No," said Sylvie. "Stay." She laughed, a strange, choked sound. "If the entire country gets to see me being humiliated, we might as well start with you."

At that, Richard opened his mouth. "Sylvie." His voice, normally full, almost booming, a voice for addressing an unruly crowd or a pack of reporters, was barely a whisper. She didn't respond. She just stood in the doorway, looking. Every part of him was so familiar to her—his big hands, his fingernails, the bald spot that, to his dismay, had gradually taken over the back of his head. She knew how he sounded, how he tasted, how his cheek felt when he'd just shaved it first thing in the morning, or the whiskery rasp of it against her own when he kissed her before they fell asleep. "I am sorry," he said. "I am so, so sorry."

After a long, squirmy silence, Joe got off the couch and stepped forward with his fingers interlaced. "We're planning a press conference for Monday morning," he announced in his wispy voice.

Sylvie ignored him. "How could you?" she asked her husband. There it was—her first line. She'd expected her voice to crack or wobble. After all, this was her life falling apart, the life she'd believed was a happy one, this was sadness mixed with visceral shame at not being enough of a woman for her man, because wasn't that, ultimately, what cheating meant? A man went looking for another woman when his own wife couldn't keep him happy. But the numbness kept her voice steady: she sounded as calm as she had when she'd addressed the ladies-who-lunch of Philadelphia in her two-thousand-dollar suit, her lips lined, her brow smooth, her hair just so, everything about her as perfect as if she'd been ordered from a catalog for politicians' wives.

Richard on the other hand, looked gratifyingly wretched, as bad as he did when he got the flu, which he did every spring. He would take to his bed in the townhouse in Georgetown, moaning and clutching his head, complaining about the aches and the fever. She'd take the train down and spend a week bringing him tea and chicken soup and the tissues with lotion that he liked. She'd turn off the telephone ringer and handle any pressing business that came up until he was better again.

"How could you?" she asked again, and again, he gave no sign of answering. Three quick steps brought her inches from him, his face at eye level with her belly. She lifted her hand, then brought it down hard, palm open, whapping him against the ear—*boxing* him, she thought, that was probably the proper term for what she was doing. She was boxing his ear.

"Hey, hey," said Joe Eido, who sounded alarmed but made no move to stop her. "Not the face, okay?"

She ignored Joe and hit Richard twice more, once on the left side, once on the right. There was no satisfaction in it other than the sound, the meaty slap of her palm against his ear and cheek, the cheek she'd cupped, the ear into which she'd whispered *I love you* and *deeper* and the names of their daughters, just after they were born. "You bastard!" she cried, and let her hands drop to her sides. She'd spoken her lines, she'd hit him. What now? Screaming? Throwing things? Telling him that she'd sue the socks off him, that she'd go first to a divorce lawyer and then to *60 Minutes,* that he was disgusting and a disgrace and a cliché, no better than the other cheating politicians, or that golfer, that fine upstanding young man she'd met at a White House luncheon for the Leaders of Tomorrow who'd turned out to have a dozen different girlfriends, porn stars and pancake-house waitresses and club promoters, whatever they were?

She stared at her husband. Had he really used his influence or done something improper to get her a job? Were there more Joelles? Would she and her daughters be subject to an endless stream of revelations, one surgically enhanced bimbo after another? Or was it worse than that? Was there just one other woman, not some beautiful bimbo but a lawyer, spunky and smart rather than sexy, a woman Richard was serious about? Would he leave her and their girls? And where would she be without him? She'd given herself to Richard as completely as any nun had ever pledged herself to God; she'd devoted her life to him, his wants, his needs. Everything she'd done, every piece of clothing she'd worn, every diet she'd undertaken and exercise class she'd endured, every time she'd sacrificed her own desires, and her daughters', it had all been for him, for his career, his future (and, of course, her certainty that she'd have a part in that future). What would she do if he replaced her? Where would she live, what would she do all day? Who would she be if she wasn't Mrs. Richard Woodruff, the senator's wife?

She stared at the shot of Hillary and Bill waltzing, looking perfectly in love. She felt herself trembling: her skin, her flesh, even her bones, echoing with the force of the slap, and the silence that filled the room Sylvie had vacuumed and dusted and straightened hundreds, maybe even thousands of times during their long life together.

Joe Eido shot a quick glance at his boss, then slipped out the door. Richard raised his head. "I'm sorry," he repeated.

"Why?" she asked, her voice raw.

He dropped his eyes. "I liked her."

"I figured that," Sylvie snapped.

"She was . . ." She waited for him to say *beautiful,* or *smart,* or *funny,* or *quick,* the endorsements he'd given her all those years ago. But Richard said none of those words. Instead, he said, "Helpful."

"Helpful?" Sylvie said. "Helpful?" She was no longer talking, she was shrieking. *Helpful* was the most terrible word she could imagine, far worse than *beautiful* or *sexy* or *smart* or *quick*, because *helpful* meant that this woman, this Joelle, had made herself valuable to Richard. Maybe she was the younger, D.C. version of Sylvie who would listen to his speeches and smooth out his schedules, confirm his Town Car pickups and his dry-cleaning drop-offs and make sure he knew the names of all his biggest donors' children, and even their dogs.

"You know what you give someone who's helpful? You give her a raise. You give her a job recommendation. You don't fucking fuck her, you stupid motherfucker!"

Richard dropped his head. "Sylvie."

"Fuck you," she said. Sylvie didn't curse. The Honorable Selma cursed like a longshoreman, Ceil had cursed plenty in college, when it was unusual and still titillating for a woman to have a dirty mouth. Her daughters sprinkled their conversations with the occasional dirty word, but Sylvie did not curse. She was badly out of practice, but maybe it was like riding a bike. Maybe you never really forgot how. "Fuck you, you stupid shit son of a bitch." Okay, maybe she needed some practice. She had a feeling she'd get plenty of chances to work on her new, old vocabulary in the days and weeks ahead.

She stood in front of her husband, his ears bright red and his eyes on his lap. "Listen," he finally said, scrubbing his fingers against his scalp. "We need to figure out what to do next."

She knew what he was talking about—after all their years together, how could she not? The official business of being a congressman or a senator might have been making laws, but the truth was, the real job was to raise money. You stockpiled cash to run for office, and, almost as soon as the election was over, you started gathering funds for the next round. A wife was an asset for such endeavors—a wife who could be counted on to organize the parties, to show up at the picnics and parades, to manage the guest list and cosset the big donors. A wife could deliver speeches and appear at your side or in your stead (and do all these things, of course, without benefit of job title or paycheck). If Sylvie wasn't going to be with Richard on the campaign trail, he and his handlers needed to know.

"We need to decide—"

Sylvie cut him off. "There is no 'we' here," she said. "Not anymore."

"I, then," said Richard. "I need to figure it out." He pulled in a breath, and his voice took on its familiar speechifying timbre. "The way I see it, it's a personal failing. A terrible transgression. I don't intend to minimize that, not for a minute, but this was not a public matter. It was a betrayal that has nothing to do with my service to the people of—"

"You got her a job," Sylvie said, each word bitten off, hard and distinct.

"Sylvie. Look. I know you don't want to hear this, but it isn't really that bad. This is going to be a one-day story, if that."

She gave a strange, hollow laugh. "And what a joyous day it's going to be for all of us."

"She was qualified," he said. "She's a Georgetown law grad. She volunteered in the D.C. office last year, and then she worked as a legislative aide."

"How civic-minded," Sylvie snapped. "Did you two have pillow talk about the single-payer plan?"

Richard winced. Health care reform was one of his passions. One of the ones she knew about, anyhow. "Stupid dumb fucker," she said, because she could, and because it felt good to say it, even though what should have been a shout was muted by the thick plaster walls of the apartment, and the heavy silk drapes and the rug that covered the office floor. The rug was the first nice thing she and Richard had bought together. They'd picked it out after he'd gotten his first annual bonus, back in 1983. Five hundred dollars. "We're rich!" he'd crowed, running up the three flights of stairs to their Brooklyn apartment, pulling the check out of his pocket and waving it over his head.

"How long has this been going on?"

Richard's face was crumpling. It was like watching one of those apple-head dolls in time-lapse photography, watching it shrink and shrivel and cave in on itself. "Sylvie . . . I swear I never wanted to hurt you or the girls. It's killing me that I'm hurting you."

"How long?" she yelled.

He dropped his head. "Six months. Maybe seven. It was never serious. It was just a fling." He stood, then, and took her elbow. He meant to guide her toward the armchair in the corner. This was where she sat during their strategy sessions, when they were discussing ad buys or campaign travel or, that one terrible night, trying to keep the news of Lizzie's arrest for possession with intent to distribute out of the papers. Except this time Sylvie refused to be guided and refused to be moved. She stood still, the pumps she'd slipped back on her bare feet planted on the rug, glaring at him. After a minute, Richard started to speak again, but haltingly. *Preliminary focus groups indicate . . . the mood of the electorate . . . crucial initiatives . . . that disabled-Americans rights bill in committee . . . work left undone . . .*

She stared at him, unable to believe what she was seeing. Her husband—her husband!—the man she'd promised to love and to cherish, the man who'd seen her pushing their daughters out into the world and defecating on the hospital bed in the process (and maybe that had been the problem? Maybe her mother's generation had had it right, leaving the men in the waiting room, never letting them see the blood and the shit and the tearing? Maybe then they wouldn't fuck young lawyers who'd never been torn?); her husband, a man of endless, boundless confidence, was stretching out one trembling hand, reaching for her like a dying man from his sickbed. "Sylvie," he said. She slapped his hand away. She wished that she could hit him again, could break his nose, could claw his eyes and blind him so that he'd never notice another woman again.

Do you love her? The words piled up in her mouth and stayed tangled there, a choking weight, because she couldn't ask him that.

"Don't touch me," she said instead. "Don't you ever touch me again." She walked away from him, toward the door, then turned with her hand on the knob.

"I will do that press conference, for our daughters' sake, not yours," she said. "Just me. Not the girls." She gave him a hard look, a look he'd never seen from her before. "Do not think of involving them in any way. Do not imagine for a minute that they'll stand onstage and endorse"—she sliced her hand through the air—"any of this." She would keep her daughters safe. That should have been her focus all along—her girls. Not this faithless, gutless man. Diana, she knew, would refuse to be part of such a show, but Lizzie would do it, out of loyalty and her eternal hunger for her father's love and his approval, her desperation to make things up to him, to blot out years of bad behavior and be his good girl again. Lizzie would do it, and Lizzie would not survive the pundits, the news anchors with their fake sweet smiles, the bloggers, the gossips, the twits with their Twitter accounts, every odious one of them just waiting to pounce and pass judgment. They'd stir up Lizzie's past (*Druggie Daughter Stands by Her Dad!*). They'd write that her hair was stringy and her skin was bad; they'd publish and post the least-flattering photographs; they'd embroider the truth, disgusting as it was, with smutty innuendo, and Lizzie, being Lizzie, would probably read every hateful, sickening word. And Lizzie wasn't strong.

"I'll do it," she repeated. "They won't." And then . . . *Call Jan for the keys,* her mother's voice said. It wasn't a bad idea. She needed to get out of here, and Connecticut was as good a place as any. "Monday morning at nine."

Already, her mind was working, coming up with a plan. She'd been quick once, in college and law school, smart and organized and never at a loss. She could be quick again; quick in her own service, not his. She'd go to the bedroom, pack a bag, change her clothes, and find a baseball cap—her husband had them from every team in the state—to tuck over her head. She'd slip out the back entrance, say "no comment" if any reporters saw her, and get herself to Ceil's place.

"I am sorry," he said, standing across the room from her. Looking at him, she could see the ghost of that barefoot boy in the narrow bed, the one who'd fallen through the ice and who'd wooed her with whiskey and sweet talk, who'd asked her, *Do you trust me?* "I still love you, Sylvie. I never stopped."

But what did love mean to Richard? That she, too, was helpful? That he wanted her to stay?

Never mind, she thought, as the numbness settled over her, encasing her like a girdle and control-top pantyhose. All of this—the apartment where she'd lived for years, the man she'd shared it with, the work they'd done, the life they'd built together—all of it was denied her, all of it was gone.

"E-mail Clarissa the details," she said. "And after that, I don't think I'll be seeing you again."

"Cookie!" Ceil had been waiting in the doorway of her Chelsea loft. She threw her arms around her friend as soon as Sylvie got off the elevator, pulling her through the metal door and into the welcome coolness of the high-ceilinged living room. Ceil smelled just the way she had in college, like almond soap and Coco by Chanel—from Paris, she'd told her new roommate, by way of Dillard's department store. She looked more or less the same, too, pink-cheeked and cheerful, short and solid in bare feet, black leggings, and a tunic that brushed the top of her thighs, even though her short cap of hair was more silver than blond these days, and there were wrinkles around her eyes. Sylvie hugged her friend, leaning against her wordlessly before following her into the kitchen. "What took you so long?"

"I took the subway."

"You did what?" Ceil stared at her, as if Sylvie had said she'd swum down the Hudson. Sylvie pulled off her Yankees cap and set her duffel bag down by the door. In their bedroom—*her ex-bedroom,* she thought—she had changed into yoga pants and sneakers and a zippered cashmere sweatshirt. She'd taken the elevator down to the lobby, and asked Juan to open the service entrance. The reporters and photographers would be out front, looking for a well-dressed lady getting into a car, or a cab. They wouldn't be looking for a woman walking, with a baseball cap on her head and a bag over her shoulder, heading toward the subway like she was late to a yoga class.

Ceil's loft was one giant rectangle, with a kitchen at one end and three bedrooms at the other, with soaring ceilings and bare, glossy floors made of some unpronounceable rare wood from Brazil (a native wood harvested by indigenous people, Ceil's husband, Larry, an architect, had explained, repeatedly and at length, at their housewarming). The furniture was all oversized, to accommodate Larry, a former defensive end. The white-painted walls were hung with challenging art: there were black squiggles and green blotches on stark-white oversized canvases with titles like *Divorce Song II* and *Truth and Beauty*, and one corner was dominated by a blown-glass sculpture that looked as if it had been squeezed from tubes of Aquafresh.

The loft was all Larry, but the kitchen was Ceil's, low-ceilinged and cozy, with copper pots and marble counters and a long trestle table that could have come straight out of a New England farmhouse. "Does Larry care that it doesn't really go with the rest of the place?" Sylvie had asked—this was at the housewarming, where Larry was out in the living room explaining that the indigenous people who harvested the rare Brazilian wood were paid a living wage, and also had health insurance, thanks to the largesse of microlenders. "Well, you know, the kitchen was always going to be mine. Larry doesn't really eat," Ceil had said, and Sylvie realized that it was true: Larry somehow maintained his football-player bulk on espresso extruded by the thousand-dollar machine in his study, supplemented by the protein bars he purchased at his gym and the egg-and-bagel sandwiches he grabbed at the deli down the block.

It was the kitchen where Ceil and Sylvie spent most of their time. There was a small couch and a TV set in one corner, along with shelves full of cookbooks and photos of Ceil and Larry and their children and their granddaughter. That night, Sylvie leaned against the counter, battered and numb and breathless, as Ceil put a mixing bowl and beaters into the sink.

"Are you all right?" Ceil asked, her voice as high and sweet and chirpy as (Richard had once observed) a cricket in a Disney film. "What can I get you? Coffee? Chocolate? Carbs? A drink? A gun?" Her eyes glittered. "Listen," she said. "You don't have to decide right now, but I looked up hit men on the Internet, and there's a very active community of men, and possibly some women, and for what I have to say is a surprisingly reasonable amount of money, they'll take care of whatever problem you're having, on a permanent basis."

"Ceil." Sylvie slumped onto a barstool. "Don't you think they'd know it was me?"

"Yes, well, I thought of that, and if I was the one making the call, and I was the one spending the money . . ."

"Then they'd figure out it was my best friend."

Ceil considered this. "Shoot. Maybe I'll get Larry to do it. That's, what, two degrees of separation? That's plausible deniability right there." She tilted her round face and gave Sylvie a smile.

Sylvie rested her head on her hands. The kitchen counters were, as usual, glittering with a dusting of bright yellow powder. Ceil was addicted to Crystal Light—she'd called it Crystal Meth until her granddaughter, Lincoln, started saying it, too—but she drank it by the glass, not the pitcher, while refusing to spring for the individual packets, which were, she pointed out, almost twice as expensive by volume as the canisters. Each time she made a serving, she would painstakingly tap powder from the canister into her glass, inevitably leaving a sprinkling of mouth-puckeringly sweet yellow powder on the countertop.

Ceil turned on her bare feet, bent, and opened the oven. A puff of warm, delicious-smelling air filled the kitchen. "Pecan-cinnamon rolls," she announced, pouring them each a mug of coffee and grabbing cream from the refrigerator.

Sylvie wrapped her hands around the heavy mug. Ceil's laptop was on the counter. Sylvie eyed it uneasily. The flickering screen saver reminded her of a snake's tongue, darting lazily in and out. Ceil saw where her eyes were going and snapped the screen shut. "Oh, no," she said. "Don't even think about it."

She swallowed hard. "What . . . what are they saying?"

"The usual nonsense, I'm sure." Ceil poured the cream into a cow-shaped pitcher—the cow's tail formed a handle, and the milk came spilling out of its mouth—and used a spatula to slide rolls onto a white-and-blue china plate. She put the plate in front of Sylvie, then took the barstool across the counter. "Just tell me," she said, "that we get to hurt him. Just a little bit. Nothing permanent."

Sylvie sipped her coffee, stifling a smile at the thought of four-foot-eleven-inch Ceil hurting anyone. She'd probably do it with her immersion blender. Ceil was a great believer in the restorative powers of soup, and used her blender nonstop from September through May, pummeling a variety of meats and vegetables into liquid submission. She served cappuccino at all her dinner parties, and would offer to refroth them midway through dessert. "I bet the press is doing a pretty good job of that."

"Okay, but I hate him!"

Sylvie nodded. She expected nothing less from her dramatic friend, and, at that moment, she hated him, too, but it was more complicated than that: hate and love and loyalty and embarrassment and loneliness, loneliness at the thought of a life without Richard, all of it sloshing around in her head and her guts like a toxic stew. She imagined that Ceil, who'd been her maid of honor and had known Richard almost as long as she had, felt the same way. She nibbled a bit of the roll, then asked the question she'd come here to ask, face-to-face: "Did you have any idea? Did you know that this was going on?"

"Absolutely not." Ceil answered instantly, and her blue eyes were guileless. She poked at her own roll with her fork. "Although, honestly, if I had known I'm not sure I would have told you. It wouldn't have been my place."

Sylvie stared at her. "You're my best friend!"

"But he's your husband. And marriages are mysteries." She raised her hands in the air, palms toward the heavens. "It wouldn't have been my place," she repeated. "But I'm here for you. However you want to handle this. Whatever you want to do."

"I can't stay with him," Sylvie said, and as soon as she'd spoken the words, she knew that they were true.

Ceil nodded, unsurprised. "Should we call a lawyer?" She tapped her pad. "I made a list." Ceil flipped the notebook open. "Actually, *People* magazine made a list on its website. There's the lawyer Charlie Sheen's wife used, when he went after her with a knife in Colorado, and the one that woman with the eight kids had, when her husband was cheating on her with some girl he met in a bar . . ."

Sylvie swallowed hard, feeling dizzy. "No lawyer," she managed, and sipped from her mug again, trying to steady herself. "Right now I just want to not see him." She took another sip of coffee. "I hit him."

"You did?" Ceil's eyes gleamed. "Well, good for you! Closed fist or open?"

"It was most like a slap. Side of his head. His ears . . ." Her voice trailed off. She was thinking of Richard's ears, the sweet pink curl of them. He had little-boy ears, she'd thought more than once. The rest of him had grown up, had grayed and wrinkled and slackened and spread, but his ears were as tender as they'd been when she'd met him, as sweet as they must have been when he'd been a boy, and, thank God, they'd never sprouted those nasty tufts of hair so many men his age got. She loved his ears. How could she hate him, when she still felt so tenderly toward his body parts?

She rested her head on the counter, and, after a minute, she felt Ceil's small hand on her back. "You can stay here for as long as you want." Sylvie suppressed a shudder as she thought of the guest bedroom, Larry's showplace. The bed was made of unvarnished birch branches, formed roughly in the shape of a nest. You had to clamber over the sharp sticks that stuck out in every direction to get to the mattress. On the wall was a truly disturbing piece of art, a white-on-white oil-paint oval with a single drop of red at its center, titled *Afterbirth*.

"Maybe for a few nights," she said. "Then I'm going somewhere else. You can't tell Richard where."

"I'm not speaking to Richard unless you tell me it's okay. At which point I will have a few choice remarks." She patted Sylvie's back again. "So where do you think? Canyon Ranch? Lake Austin? Rancho La Puerta? Do you want company? I could pick a fight with Larry and come with you." She thought, drumming her fingers on the marble. "Wherever you decide, you should have Clarissa call ahead and explain the situation." More drumming. "Although probably people know the situation by now."

Sylvie thought of the laptop, its flickering screen. She remembered a Leonard Cohen song that Lizzie used to play, over and over, in the middle of the night, which honestly, in retrospect, should have been a sign: "Everybody Knows," the song was called. When Eliot Spitzer had had his troubles, out of some mixture of sympathy and schadenfreude, she'd Googled Silda Spitzer's name, and been horrified (and, a little titillated) by what she'd read. *What Was She Thinking? Silda Joins Democrats' First Wives Club.* "What's more disgusting than a lyin', no good, cheatin, hypocritical, political man?" one indignant blogger had asked. "Their wives who stand by looking dumbfounded as their unfaithful husbands apologize to the public. Do these women have no pride?"

No pride, she thought. But what was pride compared to a life she'd loved? What would she do now, alone at her age? How could she start again, with no husband, no job, no place in the world? She let Ceil lead her toward the bathroom (more white marble, white towels, and a giant white Jacuzzi), and undressed without looking at her body, because considering her bulges and wrinkles, her stretch marks and scars, would have her, inevitably, comparing herself to Joelle, whose flesh was probably smooth and unblemished as a rose's petals. With her eyes squeezed shut, she got into the tub, and soaked until the water went cold. Then she wrapped herself in one of Ceil's bath sheets and padded into the horrible guest room. Ceil had made up the bed with flowered flannel sheets that Sylvie doubted Larry had ever slept on or even knew about. There was a cup of tea steaming on the bedside table, another cinnamon roll beside it, and a stack of well-worn novels, some of them dating back to their college years.

She settled herself gingerly on top of the mattress. Her lower back was throbbing, her legs ached. So did her chest, like she'd been punched there over and over. She crossed her hands, age-spotted, the nails neatly kept, over her heart, and pushed down, trying to ease the pain, lying motionless on her back until her friend slipped into the room to turn out the lights.

DIANA

Gary had been late. Trust her husband to be late on a night like this, to leave her sitting alone in her little black dress and strappy, high-heeled sandals, staring through the windows that had been flung open to the soft summer night and feeling, or imagining that she could feel, every eye in the room upon her.

If you'd asked her friends and neighbors—not that anyone had, or ever would—Diana assumed they would have said she and Gary appeared reasonably happy. True, over their seven years together, their sex life never got past perfunctory, but the neighbors wouldn't know about that, and Diana could deal with perfunctory, telling herself that maybe she just didn't have a very strong sex drive, and that the hot stuff faded away for everyone else anyhow.

She loved the day-to-dayness of her life, the balance she'd struck between work in the ER and days at home with her boy. Milo had been an easy baby, placid and good-natured, always happy to go down for a nap in the sunny nursery Diana had furnished and painted herself, always delighted to see her when she lifted him out of his crib. She adored their cozy brick row house, even if it was still mostly empty. She worked twelve-hour shifts, three days a week, and on her days off she would take Milo to the playground, to music class and tumbling class and on errands to the dry cleaner's or the grocery store. After lunch, she would sing him to sleep and spend a few hours cleaning the house, paying the bills, or folding the laundry while he napped. Then, just as boredom set in, just when she was sure she couldn't read *Red Fish Blue Fish* one more time, or sing "Tingalayo" again, or play another game of Sorry, it was time to go to work, back to the frenzy and demands and adrenaline rush of a big-city emergency room, where you never knew what was going to come through the door. It all suited Diana just fine.

They lived in a wonderful neighborhood—it wasn't New York, but it had plenty to offer. Within a twelve-block walk there were bars and French cafés and Vietnamese noodle shops, bakeries and gelaterias, the requisite coffee shop on each corner, plus a craft brewery that served the best veggie burgers she'd ever tasted. On Sundays she and Gary would try different places for brunch, sampling the breakfast pizza at Café Estelle and the stuffed French toast at Sabrina's, pushing Milo in his stroller or, when he got older, holding his hands, walking along and admiring the windowboxes, peeking through people's blinds to see how they'd decorated their living rooms, and stopping at the little neighborhood park for a few trips down the slide on the way home. With neighbors calling hellos and a pleasant afternoon awaiting her—Milo would nap, or read, or play with his Legos, and Gary would zone out in front of the television set with his laptop, leaving Diana with a few hours for a long run and a soak in the tub—she would think, happily, even a little smugly, that she'd gotten exactly the life she'd wanted: the husband, the child, the nest that she was in the process of feathering. On the best days, it would be enough to quiet the teasing, drawling voice in her head, the voice that sounded a lot like her sister saying that Gary was the tiniest bit stupid and boring to boot, that Gary, with his love for video games and YouTube videos, wasn't the right man for her; that he was maybe not much of a man at all.

When Diana was in college she'd read about arranged marriages, and how they lasted longer than so-called love marriages did, because the people who were in them knew they wouldn't have romance or passion to carry them along. They went in knowing that their marriage was a thing they'd have to create from scratch and work hard to maintain. That sounded sensible to Diana, who, in deciding on Gary, had in effect arranged her own marriage, choosing a man who was acceptable on every front and then building a marriage with the same will and concentration she'd once brought to her college papers and grade-school dioramas. But the older she got, the more she worried that passion, chemistry, attraction, whatever you wanted to call it, was like a kind of frosting that could be smoothed over the cracks and lumps of a badly baked cake. Passion mattered . . . and she'd never really had much with Gary.

The sex, which had never been great, had gotten worse, and much more sporadic, in the post-Milo years. Even if she wasn't constantly exhausted, even if she came home from the hospital or a day at the playground to find the bed made, the laundry folded, a tasty and nutritious dinner prepared and the table set, even if there'd been someone there to spirit Milo away to a playground or the library or the children's museum for an edifying hour or two, Diana just wasn't interested. Most nights she'd lie beside Gary until he fell asleep, fretting over how close she'd come to resembling the women's-magazine cliché, the wife who no longer wanted her husband. When she was with Hal, she'd read those articles with a lofty sense of superiority, thinking how silly those new mommies sounded. How hard was it to endure a few kisses, to spread your legs and offer up a few token moans for the five (or three) minutes it would take the man to finish his business?

The truth she learned when she became a mother herself was that she found the kind of sex her friend Lynette called the "charity ball" unendurable. After a day of tending to her patients, who'd show up at the ER with everything from a splinter to a rare and hard-to-diagnose parasite, and a night spent minding her son, she couldn't stand another set of hands or lips on her, another set of demands.

Still, she tried. On Saturday night she would shave her legs, brush and floss with extra care, and if Gary smiled at her from the depths of the couch, if he folded up his laptop and asked, in his good-natured teasing tone, whether she was prepared to fulfill her marital obligations, she'd make herself smile back at him, and let him take her hand and lead her to the bedroom. Sometimes it would be over almost immediately. ("Sorry," her husband would gasp, spent and wilting against the side of her thigh. "Sorry, Diana, but it's been a while.") That, sadly, was the best-case scenario. The worst times were when it took forever. Diana would lie underneath her husband, hands on his scrawny shoulders, face buried in his neck, while he'd pump and huff and pant and sweat. Sometimes she'd give a few tentative moans to speed things along, and sometimes, that would work . . . but sometimes Gary would roll off her without having finished.

"You're so wet," he'd say, in a tone just short of accusatory. He'd sigh up at the ceiling, then take his slick penis in his hand and start pumping, with the burdened expression of a man who'd been forced to shovel the driveway just when the game was getting interesting. Diana would lie beside him, wondering about the etiquette: Should she help? If so, how? She'd roll onto her side and rest her cheek on his chest, feeling the rapid rise and fall of his breath, waiting for his final gasp and shudder and the explosion of bleach-smelling sticky stuff.

"Grab me a towel, would you?" he'd ask, still breathing hard, and she'd hurry out of bed, glad for the excuse to leave his side.

He was a good guy, pleasant enough, but the things he enjoyed and wanted to talk about—professional sports, the mashups he made on his computer, the various online role-playing games that he found more engrossing than real life—were not things that interested her. But what could she do? She'd made a promise, she'd taken vows, she'd had a baby. She'd gone into marriage as an adult, with her eyes wide open. She had, as the saying went, made her bed, and if she found it hard or lumpy, it was no one's fault but her own. Love was a choice. She'd read that once, in a novel one of the patients had discarded in the waiting room. Love was a choice, and she was determined to make it, determined to make her marriage work, determined not to fail.

Tell him. For months, for years, in spite of her resolve, the words beat like a drum in Diana's head. *Tell him,* she would think, checking her e-mail, folding her husband's underpants while a police procedural blared on the TV. *Tell him how you feel. It isn't fair to stay married to him, just going along, pretending everything's fine, pretending you're feeling something you're not.*

In the shower, brushing her teeth, retrieving the paper from the front step, she'd rehearse it in her head. *Gary, there's something we need to talk about. Something I need to tell you. I've been feeling . . .* And this was where she stopped. What were the words for what she needed to say? The ones that came to mind were *I'm just not that into you,* but that wouldn't work. No way could she dismiss her husband, take the first steps toward ending their marriage, breaking up their family, breaking his heart and maybe her son's, with something that glib. But what was better?

She sat in the restaurant, staring out into the darkness, legs crossed beneath her black dress, sipping her wine, until finally her husband appeared, sweaty and disheveled, with the tiniest bit of shirttail sticking out through his fly.

"Hi, honey," he'd said, reaching for her hand. "Sorry I'm late. Bad traffic." Her heart sank as he touched her. There was no spark, no connection, nothing but annoyance and a wish to be left alone or, better yet, to be back home, counting out Milo's chocolate chips, talking about where he'd sat at lunch and whether he'd ever get picked to be Pet Helper at school. ("I'm always snack cleanup!" he complained. "It just isn't right!")

Sensing her discomfort, Gary peered at her across the candlelit table. "Are you okay?"

"I'm fine," she said, and emptied her glass. The waiter approached, pad and pen in hand, prompting Gary to begin his typical dining-out process of talking to the menu.

"You, or you?" he asked, pointing at the various items. "Who's it gonna be? Cassoulet? Coq au vin? You? You?"

"Gary," Diana said softly but firmly. "It's been a long day. Please just pick something." Left alone long enough, he'd spend ten minutes interrogating the entrées in his Al Pacino voice, demanding that one of them speak up.

"Well, I told you we didn't have to go out," he said. Diana closed her eyes and waited until Gary finally settled on the steak frites. Diana asked for broiled sole, sauce on the side, and more wine. Then Gary got to his feet. "Gotta go drain the dragon," he said. This was another one of her husband's quirks. He was incapable of going to the bathroom without announcing his destination, in addition to what he intended to do once he was there. *Gotta bleed the lizard. Gotta break the seal. Gotta air out the snake.*

She sat at the table, a basket of bread and a crock of butter and her empty wineglass before her. *This is it,* she thought. She would never leave him for her lover—not that Doug would ever want her to. Which left her with Gary, draining the dragon, Gary, with his mash-ups, Gary and his nasty Kleenexes next to the bottle of hand lotion by the computer that he left for Diana to pick up and put away; Gary for the rest of her life.

Before she knew it she was on her feet, her wrap around her shoulders, moving quickly toward the host stand, and the tall oak-and-glass doors beyond it. She was almost there when the waiter, who looked to be all of eighteen, hurried over. "Ma'am? Is everything all right?"

"Just getting a little fresh air." Diana's voice sounded as if it was coming from outer space. She hooked her purse over her shoulder and stepped out into the night.

She walked around Rittenhouse Square park, then down Chestnut Street all the way to Independence Mall, when her ankles that had chafed from the sandals' skinny straps wouldn't let her go any farther. She sat on a wooden bench with her purse in her lap. When she found herself crying, she wasn't sure whom her tears were for—her father, who'd cheated, her mother, who'd been betrayed, or herself, a cheater and a betrayer who was stuck, stuck with a man she did not love.

This cannot go on, she thought. In her purse, her telephone buzzed. Doug. U OK? She smiled. She couldn't help herself. How could she resist him? OK, she typed back. Seconds later, her screen flashed. COME OVER?

She jumped to her feet and hailed a cab. *I deserve this,* she told herself. Just for an hour. Sixty minutes of something sweet after this awful, awful day. Ten minutes later, her shoes in her hand, she stood on a stoop on a narrow street in South Philadelphia, knocking on her lover's door.

She and Doug Vance actually had met in the emergency room. "What've we got?" Diana had asked her intern that rainy Friday morning. Already the waiting room was filling with the lame, the halt, and the blind, the diabetic, the old folks with congestive heart failure, the kids with fevers who would sit for hours staring at the television set bolted to the ceiling or leafing through limp, six-month-old magazines.

"Eddie Taylor's back," said Karen, who was brisk and efficient and reminded Diana of herself, if she'd been five feet tall and Asian. She handed Diana his chart. Diana glanced at it, rolling her eyes. Under "reason for visit," Eddie, a well-known denizen of the ER, had written "dick is driping." The spelling mistake wouldn't have been so galling, Diana thought, if Eddie hadn't visited the ER the month before for precisely the same dripe. She flipped through a half-dozen folders: an old dude with diarrhea, a teenager who'd been vomiting all night long, an earache, a headache, and . . .

Diana peered at the chart. "Foot run over by Mummers?"

"He's a surgical intern," Karen said tartly. "Out partying last night. Probably slept it off and didn't remember until he woke up and saw the damage."

Diana picked up the charts, pushed through the door of Exam Room Three, and found Doug Vance, a muscular, ruddy-cheeked, thick-shouldered fellow with a halo of dark curls, sitting on the exam table. He wore a dark-blue sweatshirt and exercise pants with snaps running up the sides of the legs. One foot was clad in a white sock and a running shoe. The other was bare, propped on a bag of ice.

He grinned at her ruefully. "Morning, Doc."

"Good morning yourself." She stared at his ankle, spectacularly discolored, grotesquely swollen. "Yowza."

"Is that a medical term?"

"From the Latin." Doug Vance looked familiar. She looked at his face—the round cheeks, the broad features, the nose that was squashed slightly sideways—then back down at his ankle, which was a riot of purple and yellow and black. She pulled on gloves and touched the skin gently, watching for a flinch, listening for a hissed intake of breath. Doug Vance smelled, not unpleasantly, of sweat and beer, which meant that his reactions were, perhaps, not to be trusted. "You're an intern?"

"First year. Which you'd think would mean I'd know better."

She grasped his toes. "What happened? Should I see the other guy?"

"Guys, plural. A bunch of them, in sequins. Well, technically, the other guy is a Firestone tire." Doug sighed. "Can we just say it's a rugby injury?" He looked at his ankle sadly. "This is very undignified." Diana took notes as he told her what happened. The story involved a late-night pub crawl and an eventual altercation with some Mummers getting in an early-morning rehearsal under the I-95 overpass near Reed Street. "I mean, they were wearing dresses. How were we supposed to know we weren't supposed to whistle?" Doug asked, aggrieved. "We're not from here."

"Ah." If Doug had asked, he would have learned that the Mummers were, at least publicly, hard-core heterosexuals from South Philadelphia who rehearsed all year long and then, every New Year's, went parading down Broad Street dressed in gaudy skirts trimmed with feathers and sequins. Some played stringed instruments, and others did dance routines. Almost all of them got ferociously drunk and several invariably wound up in the ER, where they'd celebrate the first day of a new year hooked up to IVs, vomiting into the kidney-shaped bedpans and praying for divine intervention. "So I take it there was a fight?"

"Words were exchanged." Doug considered. "You think I'm going to get in trouble?"

"For fighting with Mummers? If it was up to me, I'd give you a medal." She rotated the ankle, first to the left, then right, holding his toes and flexing and then pronating the foot. His skin was warm, and there was a dusting of hair, light brown and crisply curling, on his ankles and his calves. "How's the pain? One to ten."

"Five . . . ooh, that's a six," he said, as she manipulated his ankle. "Seven. Ow."

"I think it's probably just bruising. I'm going to send you for an X-ray, but I think you're okay. For now, I'd keep icing it."

"Will do," he said . . . and unless she was crazy, he was giving her the kind of appreciative look that men gave to women when they found them interesting. But that wasn't happening . . . was it?

"A nurse will give you an Ace bandage, and one of the PAs will hook you up with crutches." She patted his good leg—professionally, she told herself; she'd touch any of her patients that way. "Sorry about this."

"Hey, it's not your fault." He grinned sweetly. Diana wondered whether he was still drunk, and wondered, also, how old he was—twenty-five? Twenty-six? She could sneak a look at his intake form . . .

Stop this, she told herself, *stop this right now.* But she couldn't stop looking at him—the pink in his cheeks, the way his chest lifted and fell as he spoke, the way he smelled like cut grass and malt and hops and, underneath it, something sweeter, something irresistible. She saw Doug Vance—really saw him, in a way she hadn't seen, hadn't permitted herself to see another man since the day she'd said *I do.*

Forget it, she thought. Tell him goodbye, close the door, wash your hands, go back to Eddie and his gonorrhea.

So she did . . . but, three hours later, after a morning of dispensing penicillin and Tylenol and bad news, she stepped into the waiting room and found Doug Vance again. His crutches were propped against the wall, and his bandaged foot was on top of a coffee table next to a stack of pamphlets on "The Facts of Lice."

"Nothing's broken," he said, smiling and hopping up onto his good foot. "Good diagnosis. Can I buy you a cup of coffee?"

She didn't answer right away. Maybe he didn't know that she was married. She never wore her rings when she was on duty. They were just one more thing to worry about keeping clean.

"You can protect me," he said, already hopping toward the door. "In case the Mummers come back."

She followed him. "You think they might?"

"They are a vengeful lot, the Mummers. I can tell." Even on crutches, he held the door open for her, and she felt herself responding as she passed him, almost close enough for her hair to brush his cheek.

I should say something, she thought, as she sat across from him and sipped her latte. She'd work in some reference to "my son" or "my husband," she'd casually drop her recent thirtieth birthday into the conversation. Except that never happened. They chatted easily, talking about med school and restaurants and running routes, about whether she liked her work. (Diana explained, putting as positive a spin on it as she could, that she didn't have the kind of patience for seeing patients regularly and dealing with a lifetime's accretion of illnesses and complaints, that she much preferred treating acute cases, then sending them on their way.) Somehow, an hour had sped by, and Doug was asking, "Do you ever go out and listen to music?"

"Sure," she lied.

"There's this band playing tonight at the Khyber. Screaming Ophelia?" By the way he said the name she could tell that this band was some kind of big deal, so she nodded, even though she'd never heard the name and had only the vaguest idea of where to find the Khyber, a club that even she knew was infamous for its cheap beer and its bouncers' willingness to admit the bearers of some of the world's least-competently faked IDs. Needless to say, she'd never been. It wasn't the place where married mothers in their thirties hung out.

He grinned, exposing an adorable chipped front tooth. "You should come."

"Maybe," she said. Her mouth was dry. Lizzie could take care of Milo—or, if Lizzie had plans, Gary could do it. He'd sigh, and complain, but he could, for once in his life, read Milo his Lemony Snicket, make sure that he'd brushed his teeth, and lay out clean clothes for the morning . . . and she could go to a bar with this intriguing new guy.

She'd thought she'd forget about the show, and about Doug, as soon as she was home again, but he stayed on her mind. Once the dinner table was cleared, she'd said to Gary, "I need to go back to the hospital for a few hours." He grumbled, the way she'd known he would—Lizzie had her meeting, which meant that Gary would be responsible for Milo—but Diana had ignored him, hurrying through the dishes while he sat in the recliner, reading *Sports Illustrated* while Milo read to himself.

In the bedroom, she'd slipped on her tightest jeans and a lacy white blouse she'd bought on sale, thinking it was romantic, with its square-cut neckline and long, billowy sleeves. She'd never had a chance to wear it, never had a place where it would be appropriate. With Milo downstairs, negotiating for fifteen more minutes of reading time, Diana pulled on her raincoat, then knelt in the coat closet and dug out her old cowgirl boots, the ones she'd had since high school, that had spent the last fifteen years crammed into a shoebox in the back of a series of closets. While Gary made a noisy show of putting Milo to bed ("Just you and me tonight, little buddy!" he said, a veneer of mock cheer in his voice that barely managed to disguise his irritation), she'd shoved her makeup bag into her purse. "Back by midnight!" she called and hurried out the door.

Nothing's going to happen, she told herself as she ducked into a Starbucks, locked herself in the bathroom, and pulled out her makeup bag. She'd stroked perfume behind her ears and between her breasts, then brushed bronze shadow onto her lids and painted her lips a glossy red. *I'm not doing anything wrong, I'm just going to hear some music. I'm having a night out.*

She made it to the club just after nine-thirty. Gary, she knew, would probably be sacked out on the couch watching *Law & Order* reruns, and Milo, please, God, would be asleep in his bed, lying on his back with his sheets pulled to his chin and dreaming innocent dreams.

"Ten bucks," said the guy on a barstool by the door. She handed it over and slipped into the dark, narrow room.

Screaming Ophelia was midway through a cover of Better than Ezra's "Good." She leaned against the wall, listening, and finally Doug found her, and hopped over briskly on his crutches. "Hey!" he shouted, leaning so close that she could feel his breath tickle her ear. "You want a beer?"

She'd nodded. Once he'd headed off, Diana slunk into the corner, her back pressed against the wall by the crowd (so many screaming girls! Who knew Philadelphia was so full of them!). The band, she thought, was just okay, making up in volume what they lacked in skill. But Doug was another story. She watched him hop over to the bar, in jeans and a short-sleeved T-shirt that rose when he lifted his arms, revealing a tantalizing inch of flesh between its hem and his waistband. His arms flexed and bulged as he worked the crutches. Diana couldn't stop staring as the band swung into a cover of a Richard Thompson song. "Oh, mascara tears, bitter and black / Spent bullet drilled a hole in my back / Salt for the memory, black for the years / Black is forever, mascara tears." Diana closed her eyes, telling herself that she wasn't doing anything wrong, and that it still wasn't too late to leave.

When she opened her eyes, Doug was standing in front of her, two plastic cups of beer in his hand.

"You actually came," he said.

"*Grey's Anatomy* was a rerun," she said.

He grinned, looking her up and down in a manner she would have normally found insulting. She licked her lips and tossed her hair over her shoulders, a Lizzie move if ever there was one. "I like your shirt," he said. Diana felt her entire body flush. *I like your shirt.* Had more erotic words ever been spoken?

He handed her one of the beers. "Okay?" he yelled. Onstage, another band was doing unspeakable things to "Smells Like Teen Spirit," crimes that poor dead Kurt Cobain did not deserve. *With the lights out, it's less dangerous.* Indeed. Did Doug remember Nirvana, or had that been before his time?

Instead of thanking him for the refreshments and the entertainment, dashing back to the street, grabbing a cab, and going home, Diana took the cup and lifted her mouth toward the irresistible pink curve of his cheek. She breathed in deep, thinking that his scent—nutmeg, pine needles, lit matches—was as sweet a rush as crack or crystal meth was supposed to be. Not that she knew. Maybe her sister could tell her. "Thanks," she shouted.

His eyes moved over her again. "You look good." His mouth was hovering in the vicinity of her neck—a practical matter, she thought, just a question of making sure she heard him—but she felt his voice moving inside of her, rippling through her skin and muscles, illuminating every inch of her like a careening ball lit up the surface of a pinball machine. *Oh, I can't stand this,* she thought. *I can't.*

Then Doug leaned into her, one arm on either side of her head, and just like that, his lips were on hers, hot and demanding, and she was kissing him back, pressing one hand on the soft bristle of hair at the nape of his neck, fitting herself against him as her knees went weak, thinking that it had never been like this, never with Gary, maybe not even with Hal.

"Ooh," she breathed as he pressed her against the wall and pressed himself against her, and God, she could feel every inch of him, every delicious muscular inch of him, solid shoulders, the muscles underneath the skin of his chest and his belly . . .

She made herself turn her head and take a breath. What was

she doing? He was a med student, she was a doctor, a university employee. She was married, she was a mother, and besides all of that she was in a room full of people, any one of whom could see her and tell. Tell someone. Gary, or the dean, or the hospital's chief, mean-mouthed Hank Stavers, who was visibly uncomfortable with the lady docs on staff and would probably delight in the chance to make trouble for her. "No," she gasped. "Doug. I can't . . . I'm . . ." *Married,* she'd started to say when he covered her lips with his own.

They kissed and kissed. She couldn't get enough of it, his lips, hot against hers, his tongue slipping deliciously in and out of her mouth, his hands cupping her ass, holding her against him, squeezing her so hard she gave a squeak of pain and pleasure. He lifted his head and looked at her, breathing hard, eyes slitted.

"Outside," he said, in a tone more command than request. Diana felt his voice stirring inside of her, in her belly, between her legs, tugging her like a leash. He turned on his crutches, and she followed him through the crowd, out into the darkness, down the street and into a parking garage and the entirely inadequate backseat of what she later learned was his mother's Honda Civic, on loan to Doug for the semester. There, with Diana on her back, her boots pressed against the window and her wedding ring on her hand, they consummated their love, or whatever it was. Diana sobbed as her orgasm burst through her, kicking at the windowpane so hard she thought her boot heel would crack it. She was thinking of the ocean, imagining salt water closing over her head, icy gulps filling her nose, her mouth, her eyes, her lungs, and she welcomed the water even as it cut off her breath, because at least, finally, she was feeling something.

SYLVIE

On Monday morning at just after nine o'clock, Sylvie stood on the podium in her Spanx and her best suit (blue, not teal) for six excruciating minutes, looking out at the sea of reporters as her husband mouthed his act of contrition. The press conference was in the Grand Hyatt's Regency Room, an utterly bland, perfectly nonspecific space that could have been anywhere, or nowhere at all. It was almost biblical, she thought, half listening to the words that rolled across the teleprompter screen at the foot of the stage, then, magically, out of her husband's mouth as he stood at a lectern beside the American flag. He had sinned. He was arrogant. He was full of pride. "I foolishly convinced myself that the rules didn't apply." Sylvie shifted her weight, thinking that he was always better when he had her as an editor.

The speech went on. Richard admitted to hurting his family. He had betrayed his wife's trust. Here, Richard turned to Sylvie with a look of grief on his face that struck her as stagy and rehearsed. She stared at him coolly until he turned back to the script, and reminded herself that it could be worse. Poor Dina McGreevey, wife of the governor of New Jersey, had had to stand on a podium much like this one, listening to her husband admit not only that he'd cheated on her with a staffer, but also that he was—surprise!—a "gay American."

"I know I do not deserve the forgiveness of the ones I have wronged, or the indulgence of the people of the great state of New York," Richard intoned. "But my mistakes were personal, not political." Sylvie swallowed a sigh. At six that morning, Larry had brought her an egg sandwich, kissed her cheek, and wished her good luck. She'd caught a cab uptown and was back in the apartment by seven, which left her enough time to shower and change and pack everything she'd planned on taking.

When she couldn't stall any longer she walked down the hallway and knocked on the door of Richard's office. He was sitting behind his desk, in his good suit, one knee bouncing up and down. A pinprick of shaving cream clung to his jaw, and she found herself automatically reaching for a tissue before making herself stop. *Maybe his girlfriend can wipe it off,* she thought.

"Sylvie," he said.

"I need the car keys."

He nodded, as if this was what he expected. "I'll have Joe get them for you." He paused. She was about to leave when he said, "I could never tell you how sorry I am."

She considered this. "Probably not."

"It was stupid," he said.

That she didn't bother answering.

"It was just . . ." He raised his hands in the air. "It was just that she was . . ."

There? Sylvie wondered. Pretty? Hot? Available? But no. It was none of that. The woman had been helpful, in the way Sylvie herself had once been, helpful to the detriment of her own dreams, and she didn't want to hear about the details. "Not interested," she said. She'd slept soundly the night before, with the help of the green-and-yellow capsules that Ceil gave her, but now, suddenly, she was exhausted, wanting nothing more than to curl up on her bed—formerly their bed—and close her eyes and let this day pass without her participation.

"It was stupid," he said again. "She was . . ." His voice trailed off. Sylvie looked at him hard with the glare that was usually reserved for Lizzie when she knew that Lizzie was lying.

"She was what?"

He stilled his bobbing knee, lifted his shoulders, and raised his hands. "Tell you the truth, Syl, she reminded me of you."

"Except twenty years younger," Sylvie said archly. "If you really wanted to distinguish yourself, you should have taken up with a sixty-year-old." Richard managed a smile, and Sylvie felt her own mouth rising in response. It was so easy, seductively easy, to slip into her old, familiar banter with him. She'd known him so long, all the rhythms of his speech, all the things that would make him smile. "Or you could have just been faithful," she said, her voice flinty. "That was always an option."

He reached for her hand. She stepped backward so that he couldn't touch her, but he leaned in, grabbing her hand, pulling her close. "I want you to forgive me," he murmured. "I don't want this to be the end of us. We're a family, Sylvie."

She thought about that—about Diana, her brilliant but humorless eldest, and Lizzie, her dreamy, wandering lost girl. "We're a photo op," she said. *We are props who exist for your pleasure,* she thought . . . and she had let it happen. She had let her family, her daughters, become those things.

"That's not true."

She looked at him, letting her silence be its own reply. The numbness had lifted, and she could feel it now, the pain and the shame she'd probably be feeling every day until she died. Richard's Adam's apple bobbed as he swallowed, and at that moment she could see him as he'd been, a student sprawled on his back on the ice, a drunk boy on a neatly made bed, telling her he wanted to be president.

She forced herself to look away as he said, "I know I don't deserve to even ask, but can you ever forgive me?"

"I don't know," she said. After a minute, he dropped his eyes, letting go of her hand. A minute after that, Joe Eido came marching down the hallway to tell them it was time. At no point over the weekend, or during the morning, or during the car ride to the hotel, with Derek sitting stoically behind the wheel, had it occurred to her to ask what it was, exactly, that her husband planned on saying. *Personal, not political?* The hubris, she thought. The pride of it! Did he expect congratulations, high-fives and way-to-gos because, in spite of all the speculation, he hadn't misappropriated money to pay the girl and she turned out to be qualified for the job he'd helped her find? Was this a triumph because he hadn't raped anyone, because he hadn't given some foolish answer about hiking, because no money had changed hands and there wasn't a sex tape and nobody had died?

"I have considered resignation," he continued. The flashes were firing, so many of them, so bright and so fast that Sylvie couldn't see anything but light. She squinted until the lights turned into a blur. *I'm going to be single again,* she'd told Ceil the night before, and Ceil had said, *You know, the problem with that is the maintenance. A man who's never seen you naked before . . .* Her voice had trailed off, but Sylvie took her meaning. There, on the stage, she started doing Kegel exercises, squeezing her pelvic floor as tightly as she could for a count of five, then slowly releasing. Probably it was locking the barn door after the horse had gotten out, or, more specifically, after the horse had had two kids, but it couldn't hurt.

The noise from the crowd rose as the reporters, three dozen of them, shifted in their seats and the cameramen jostled for their close-ups, a concussive murmur that threatened to drown out Richard's voice. He leaned close to the microphone to compensate. "But resigning would be the easy way out. While I have hurt those who loved me, I have committed no financial improprieties, broken no laws. And I will stay the course. I believe that

I can still effectively represent the interests of the people of this state in the Senate, and I will continue to do so."

Richard bowed his head. "I made a terrible mistake. I betrayed my daughters. I betrayed . . ." His voice choked up. *He practiced that*, thought Sylvie. "The woman who knows me best, who's known me and loved me for thirty-two years. But I did not"—and here, he looked up, shoulders squared, jaw set, tall and solid in his expensive blue suit—"and I will not, betray the people I serve, the people of the great state of New York."

When Richard stopped talking she stood beside him, her left shoulder brushing his right one, while the flashbulbs fired. She had no idea how she looked, what expression she wore. The numbness was back, in full force, leaving her so frozen that she could no longer feel her face. Reporters shouted questions. Richard turned away. "That's all," he said, and reached for her hand. She let him take it, but as soon as they were through the bunting that separated the stage from the drafty corridor behind it she jerked it back.

"Excuse me," she said to Joe Eido, who stood at Richard's side with a watchful look, his pale eyes narrowed, as if Sylvie had turned into a strange dog, one that might bite. Her bag was where she'd left it, tucked under a table loaded with bagels and coffee urns. In the ladies' room, she pulled leggings and a loose sweater out of her bag, shucked off her suit, her hose, her Spanx and underwire bra, and shoved all of it into the capacious purse she'd brought along for the very reason that it could hold a change of clothes.

She slipped on her comfortable outfit and pulled the car keys out of the zippered pocket of her purse. When she opened the door the hallway was empty. Someone had wheeled the bagels and coffee away. That was too bad. She'd picked at her meals all weekend long, even as Ceil had tempted her with creamed chicken and biscuits, cinnamon rolls and chocolate layer cake, and had, once again, offered to give Sylvie cooking lessons. In the early days of her marriage, Sylvie had cooked. She'd made the simple foods that Richard had liked—casseroles with ground beef and Campbell's cream soups as their main ingredients; battered chicken dipped in breadcrumbs, a decent meatloaf. But then they'd moved to Manhattan, where you could get a dozen different kinds of takeout delivered to your door in minutes . . . and when your husband came home late and one of your daughters subsisted on buttered boiled noodles and peanut-butter sandwiches and the other had gone vegetarian at ten, delivery became the only sensible option. By the time the girls left home, Richard was spending the workweek in Washington while Sylvie took care of things in New York City, and saw him on the weekends. She ate most of her lunches out, with Ceil or at fund-raisers for the women's shelter or the library, and the easiest thing to do at night after a day spent in the car or in meetings or with Richard was to order in soup or pick up a salad. Her mother cooked only on holidays, so there was no long-standing tradition of home cooking. Sylvie had come to think of her lack of skills in the kitchen as something she was powerless to change.

Over the weekend, Ceil had coaxed her with poetically written cookbooks, with glossy photographs of boar prosciutto, oily olives on rustic pottery, and glistening, crisp-skinned roast duck with figs—pornography, Sylvie thought, for women of a certain age. Not that she'd been tempted. She would taste, she told Ceil. She would set the table and pour the wine, she would wash every pot and pan her friend used making beef tenderloin with a red-wine reduction and fresh-baked popovers and a salad of baby spinach greens slicked with walnut oil, but, she told Ceil, she just wasn't interested in learning something new. Still, she wished she'd tucked a muffin in her bag, or even one of Larry's horrible protein bars that tasted like strips of chocolate-flavored rubber, because now she was starving, and there was nothing left to eat.

Joe and Richard stood a ways down the hall in front of a television set tuned to one of the cable news free-for-alls. Sylvie hadn't intended to watch, but a flash of blue caught her eye. Her blue suit. She paused as the familiar, expected strains of "Stand By Your Man" filled the air, and she saw herself on that stage, live from fifteen minutes ago, looking busty and beaky and fat and old, hands folded awkwardly at her waist, the tweed fabric of her skirt straining over her hips, those extra inches, that bit of flab she'd devoted the past decade of her life to trying to eradicate, when she should have been . . . what? Servicing her husband, according to the leathery, turtlenecked crone currently being interviewed.

"That's exactly what I'm saying," the woman said, in response to a question Sylvie had missed. "Wives, submit to your husbands as the church submits to God. That's the Bible, and the Bible doesn't lie. If Sylvie Woodruff had been taking care of business on the home front . . ." The woman gave the camera a broad, knowing smirk.

"Now, Jane," the avuncular host began. His name was Greg Saunders. Sylvie knew him; she and Richard had had him to dinner at the Georgetown apartment. "Are we talking just traditional intercourse here, or what?"

Sylvie forced herself to breathe deeply, to try to forget the image of herself, wrinkled and dewlapped and old, in her too-tight suit, standing by a man who'd shamed her and broken her heart, standing there as if he hadn't dishonored her, as if she still loved him, to try to forget that there were people, probably lots of them, who thought this was her fault.

She stared at Richard's back. He and Joe, standing beside him like a leashed capuchin, would watch the shows, they'd monitor the online chatter. Later, they would commission a poll, accurate to plus or minus 5 percent, starting with the magic words: *If the election were held tomorrow . . .*

I'm done with this, she thought. Then she said it out loud. "Done with it." Richard turned, his face softening as he saw her. He held out his hand, as if she'd take it, as if all the bad times were behind them now.

"Sylvie?"

She ignored him. Head held high, shoulders back, she walked right past his outstretched hand, his familiar face, without saying a word.

PART TWO

Not Waving but Drowning

SYLVIE

"Shh!" On the stage of an overheated South Florida ballroom, a woman in a pink mesh and satin hat that looked like an ambitious Easter bonnet was hissing into a microphone. "Ladies. Ladies! SHH!" Flecks of spittle sprayed from her mouth and pattered onto the podium. Sylvie winced and hoped she'd be able to wipe it off discreetly before her speech began. She inhaled, but not too deeply. The room smelled of the floral centerpieces and a dozen competing perfumes and, faintly, of the eye-watering undertone of animal urine. That was what you got, Sylvie supposed, for holding your event in the Monkey Jungle.

Beside her, Selma squeezed her knee. "You doing okay?" Selma asked. Sylvie nodded, even though it wasn't true. It was five days after Richard's press conference, and she was a long way from home and a long way from okay.

After the press conference, Sylvie had gone back to Ceil's. Clarissa had e-mailed Sylvie her schedule for the next six months, her speaking engagements and board meetings, the luncheons she'd promised to attend and silent auctions she'd pledged to organize. After several deep cleansing breaths and two glasses of wine, Sylvie and Ceil had worked their way through the list, calling various presidents and chairs and telling them that Sylvie was to take a leave of absence. Almost everyone had been understanding, from the chair of the library luncheon to the organizer of the ballet ball. The synagogue's silent auction committee chair had balked—"we were really counting on you and the senator to be there," she said plaintively—but Ceil had donated a weekend at her house on Shelter Island, plus a session with her daughter, Clemmie, who taught what *New York* magazine had judged the city's best Pilates class, and the woman had grumpily agreed to take Sylvie's name off the host committee.

Everyone had let her off the hook except for the head of the South Florida chapter of Women for Women, a charity devoted to raising money for the formerly homeless making the transition from shelters back into the workforce. Sylvie had sat on their national board for years, and would occasionally attend events at local chapters, to give speeches, to hand out awards, to remind wealthy ladies of their obligations to their less fortunate sisters and their children.

"You praw-mised!" the group's president, one Wendy Silver, had said when Sylvie had called. Wendy lived in Boca, but had a Long Island whine so pronounced that it made Fran Drescher sound sedate and refined.

"Of course," Sylvie had said, struggling to keep her temper. "But I'm sure you understand that my circumstances have changed."

Wendy Silver was unmoved. "I've got five hundred women"—rendered as *foive hundrit wimmin*—"who paid a hundred and eighteen dollars apiece to see you."

"I understand that—"

"And," Wendy continued as if Sylvie hadn't spoken, "our angels, who pay one thousand dollars a year to sponsor a child in need, and our silver angels and our Golden Halo circle." She detailed the level of financial support each group gave, then added emphatically, "You can't back out now!" Sylvie suspected that prior to the news of her husband's infidelity, the women who'd paid to see her would have been perfectly happy with the substitute she'd volunteered to arrange. Now they probably were eager to see her—the disgraced wife, up close and in person. They were excited about the chance to look at her face and her figure and try to determine whether or not Richard had been justified in cheating. "You signed a CAWN-tract," Wendy Silver shrilled triumphantly, "and we already paid you."

This was true. She'd signed a contract; they'd already paid her, and Sylvie, as usual, had given her honorarium to a halfway house for pregnant teenagers here in New York. So here she was, in the suit she'd worn at the press conference, with her entirely-too-amused mother at her side. ("The bitches of Boca Raton," Selma had called them after checking out Wendy Silver, a predictably emaciated woman who could have been any age from thirty-five to sixty, with stiff, dyed hair and a face full of fillers. Wendy had worn Prada pumps, major diamonds, and a Missoni dress that Sylvie recognized from Saks and knew cost enough to support a formerly homeless mother and two of her kids for a month.)

"I'd like to thank our sponsors, BMW of Boca, Jay Green Jewelers . . . ladies! Please! Shh!" Onstage, the hat lady was still hissing, and the women in the audience were continuing to ignore her. Sylvie had been to enough luncheons like these, as a speaker and as a guest, to know that the ladies weren't there to listen to speeches, or even necessarily to support women making the journey from welfare to gainful employment. Their hundred-and-eighteen-dollar price of admission gave them the privilege to see and be seen, to sport four-figure outfits and four-inch heels, to show off their Botox and their spray tans, their diamonds and their gold, to pick at their lunches and ignore their dessert and gossip about who was getting a divorce, who was having an affair, who'd lost weight and who'd gained it, and feel good—even righteous—while they did it. The hat lady would have as good a chance of silencing the five hundred chattering ladies-who-lunch as she would herding cats.

Sylvie lifted her fork and poked at the slimy rectangle of salmon on her plate, which would have been unpalatable even if the room didn't smell like monkey pee. The good news was, she wasn't the headliner—they'd hired a stand-up comedian for that. Sylvie's job was to introduce the group's Mother of the Year. Five minutes, she told herself, and sipped her too-sweet iced tea. Five minutes on stage, then she'd slip out the back door, where her car and driver would be waiting to take her to the airport, where she'd fly back to New York.

She had the keys to the Connecticut house, but after leaving the press conference, she'd gone to Palm Beach, to her mother's condo. Selma, normally in New York through Thanksgiving, had flown to join her, and Sylvie had spent the next three days shadowing her mother. She'd have a hard-boiled egg and a slice of toast for breakfast, go to an eighty-and-over water aerobics class, have tuna salad and a tomato for lunch, then nap—or, really, lie on the guest-room bed, stare up at the ceiling fan, and think of how angry she was and how betrayed. Dinner was at five o'clock, in one of the delis or Italian restaurants that Selma frequented—places where they knew her and greeted her not just by name but by title. "Good evening, Judge," they'd say, setting her pasta on the table. Sylvie would pick at a salad or a slice of garlic bread while her mother kept up a steady monologue about everything from the state of the European Union to the state of Sylvie's own. "Are you talking to him?" she'd ask, and Sylvie would shake her head. "Are the girls all right?" she'd continue, and Sylvie would nod. They'd be home by seven o'clock, eight at the latest. Selma would read—even in retirement, she kept up with the papers and the legal journals. Sylvie would try to read, but she'd find herself stuck on the same page of her novel.

"And now," said the hat lady, "I'd like to call to the stage, to introduce our mother of the year, Sylvie Woodruff." Sylvie got to her feet as the woman recited her resume: Barnard and Yale, lawyer, national board member, mother of two, "and wife—of course—of Senator Richard Woodruff." Thankfully the woman left it at that, but Sylvie could hear the whispers getting louder as she mounted the stage, could feel five hundred pairs of eyes on her, measuring and judging and probably finding her wanting.

"Good afternoon," she began, setting her notes on the podium. "I don't need to tell any of you of the vital importance of the work your volunteers, and your dollars, are doing." She gave them the statistics: how many women lived in poverty; how hard it was for them to improve their circumstances without help above and beyond what the government could provide; how it was the obligation of women—Jewish women in particular—to do the work the Talmud commanded, the work Tikkun Olam, repairing the broken world. *A broken world,* she thought, as the women applauded for themselves. That was what she had.

Swallowing hard, she turned back to her notes and introduced the mother of the year, a full-figured foster mother of three in a black dress who hugged her warmly and whispered, "Good luck to you," in Sylvie's ear.

Back at the table, her mother squeezed her hand. "Very nice, dear," she said. Sylvie nodded numbly, still feeling all of those eyes on her. She kissed her mother goodbye and promised to call when she landed. Then she slid her bag out from underneath her seat where she'd tucked it and escaped to the bathroom. Pulling down her pantyhose in the stall, she heard the door open and shut, and recognized Wendy Silver's unmistakable voice.

"I thawt she'd be thinner," said Wendy before starting to pee. "She looked thinner on TV."

Sylvie was surprised to find that her feelings weren't hurt, the way they'd normally have been by this bitchy little critique. Maybe this was the benefit of what she'd lived through—have your husband admit to infidelity, be humiliated coast-to-coast, and you would no longer care about what your peers had to say about your body. She found herself biting back laughter. For someone so tiny, Wendy Silver urinated as noisily as a three-hundred-pound linebacker. It was the kind of thing she'd once have told Richard, when the event was over and she was home, barefoot, with a cup of tea, and he was on the couch beside her.

"And what about that suit?" demanded Wendy's friend. "You think they don't have irons in New York?"

Sylvie looked down at herself, thinking ruefully that she could have had her suit pressed and her nails done. Then again, Wendy could have been decent and let her off the hook.

"Well, I'm going to complain," announced Wendy over the sound of the toilet's flush. "There's an evaluation form. I'm going to tell them that her clothes weren't appropriate."

Sylvie opened the door of her stall and saw Wendy, at the sink, catch sight of her in the mirror. Wendy's already-mostly-frozen face got even more frozen as Sylvie gave her one of her well-practiced pleasant smiles. "Sorry you were disappointed," she said.

Wendy's mouth opened and closed like a fish tossed on a dock. "I . . . I'm . . ."

"Have a good day," said Sylvie, and breezed past her. It was evil, she knew, but there was a certain satisfaction in the stunned, stupid look on her face. Let them complain, she thought. Let them tell her fellow national board members that her suit was wrinkled and her nails unpolished. Given the circumstances, she was sure they'd understand.

Outside, the humidity and the stink of monkeys hit her like a slap in the face. Her car was waiting for her. So was a young woman, standing on the sidewalk in jeans and a blazer, with her brown hair in a ponytail. She had a notebook in one hand and a camera in the other. Sylvie's heart sank. The event was private, but it had been written up in the paper, which meant that people—and reporters—knew she'd be in town.

"Ms. Woodruff?" the young woman asked pleasantly. "I'm Mandy Miller from the *Miami Herald*."

Sylvie shook her hand. "It's nice to meet you, but I'm not doing interviews right now."

"Just a few quick questions?"

She shook her head again, her hand on the car's hot chrome door handle. She'd gotten the door open when the woman blurted out, "Why?"

Without meaning to, Sylvie turned.

"I just want to know," said the woman. Her notebook was closed, and beads of sweat dotted her hairline and her upper lip. "I mean, as a woman. What were you doing up there onstage with him? You didn't have to be there."

Sylvie opened her mouth. She thought about explaining, or trying to—that if it wasn't her up there, it would have been her daughters, that she loved her husband, loved him in spite of it all, in a way that a woman as young as the one in front of her would never be able to understand. The life they'd built together, the history they shared—that meant something. But she knew whatever answer she could give wouldn't satisfy her inquisitor. To Mandy Miller from the *Miami Herald*, Sylvie was a symbol, a feminist heroine who'd failed her, and no explanation or amount of rationalizing would change that.

"I'm sorry I disappointed you," she said. Then she got into the car and bowed her head and cried silently all the way to the airport, where she wiped her eyes and checked her bag and boarded a flight back home.

Two weeks later she woke up to the sound of pounding surf and the shrill crying of birds. In her dream, the girls had been young again, and they'd been at the beach. Diana, tall and lean and already with a teenager's disdainful attitude, lay on a towel on the sand, while Sylvie bobbed in the shallows with Lizzie in her arms. In her dream, Lizzie was little, plump and tow-headed, dressed not in a swimsuit, like she should have been, but in the pale pink leotard she'd worn for ballet class, the one that, somehow, always left an inch or two of underwear drooping out underneath the leg bands. Sylvie turned toward the horizon and saw a wave swelling in the distance. Heart pounding, mouth dry, she held her daughter in her arms and started swimming for the shore, but the sand was sucked backward underneath her feet, and she couldn't move. The wave crested, breaking over her head, yanking her down. She struggled toward the surface, managing to get her head, and Lizzie's, above water. *Save her,* she thought. *I have to save her.* But her feet kept going out from under her, and the water kept crashing and pounding, and when she finally managed to thrust her head into the air again she saw, high on the bluff, not the Connecticut house, but her New York City apartment building, and it was on fire. Flames leapt out from every window, and, before the waves took her down, she saw the western-facing wall crumble down to the street.

She jerked upright in her bed, dry-mouthed and gasping. It took her a minute to remember the specifics of her life: that she was in Connecticut, that Richard had cheated on her, that she was alone.

Except she wasn't.

"Hello, missus," called a voice from downstairs. Quickly, Sylvie got out of bed, wincing at the ache in her back. She scrambled into her clothes and hurried her stiff legs down the stairs as fast as they'd go to meet Mel, the caretaker, who'd been calling since she'd arrived, trying to set up a time when he could stop by and see how she was getting on.

Mel was tall, and painfully thin, bent like a string bean someone had tried to snap. "Hello, missus," he said, sneaking a quick look at her face before dropping his eyes. Sylvie turned away. She'd have to get used to this: people looking at her, and then turning their heads. They had television in Connecticut, the same channels featuring the same rogue's gallery of pundits pulling back the covers of her marital bed and speculating about what was, or was not, happening beneath them.

She put on a pleasant half-smile. After her plane had landed at LaGuardia, she'd driven up to Connecticut, and spent the drive flipping through the talk-radio stations, where the hosts and callers blathered on about biblical judgment and the sanctity of marriage and whether a senator sleeping with another woman really mattered in this day and age. By far the number one topic, the one they came back to over and over again, was why his wife would choose to stand up on a stage beside a man who had disgraced her. Sylvie would force herself to listen calmly for a minute or two. Then she'd start arguing in her head with the callers. Soon she'd be arguing out loud. "For your information, Suzanne from Falls Church, I have children. Better I was the one standing up there on that podium than my daughters, don't you think?" she demanded. "Well, Fred from Dallas," she said, after a man had called in to read Bible verses in a thick Southern accent, "let he who is without sin cast the first stone. You ever heard that one?" She flipped until she recognized the voice of the brittle redhead, the one who laughed at her own jokes and salted her Sunday columns with the boldfaced names of politicians and Washington insiders she inevitably identified as "my close friend." (Richard had once been one of them.) "If I were Sylvie Woodruff, I'd just be grateful that it wasn't a live boy or a dead girl," she said. "Plagiarist!" Sylvie hollered, thumping the leather-wrapped wheel with her hand. "That's Edwin Edwards's line!"

She'd made it to Fairview at just after five o'clock on a bright blue afternoon. Downtown was as pretty as she'd remembered it: neatly kept buildings of clapboard and brick lining sidewalks so pristine it looked as if they'd been swept. There were boutiques and bakeries and coffee shops to go along with the places she remembered, the library and town hall and the emerald square of the town green behind it. The corner store, Simmons Grocery, was now a yarn shop, but Violet's ice cream parlor was there, its painted sign advertising sixteen flavors faded, but otherwise the same as Sylvie remembered it. A brisk wind rattled the leaves. It had been hot and humid when she'd left the airport, but there was always a breeze by the ocean, and fall had made some inroads here. She was north, away from home, feeling hollow and empty, sick with sorrow, and utterly unlike herself.

"I see you got things in shape," Mel said, looking around. Sylvie nodded. As miserable and furious as she'd been on the drive up from the city, her heart had lifted a bit as she'd steered the car up the long driveway and parked in front of the rambling white Colonial that hunkered on top of the bluff. She'd always been happy to come here, as a child and as a bride and a young mother, excited for the promise of summer, and all the things she'd loved: the swims in the bracing ocean water, the barbecues and the picnics they'd pack to watch the Little League games on the town green, riding her bicycle, or napping on the daybed on the porch with a novel and a glass of iced tea waiting on the coffee table.

The house had looked good, the porch freshly painted and the lawn newly mowed. Jan had told her that the house had been empty all summer. None of the cousins had wanted or, Sylvie guessed, been able to afford to come. When Sylvie had wiped her feet on the YOU ARE WELCOME HERE mat and turned the key in the weathered oak door, a puff of warm, stale air hit her face, a smell of mold and mouse. Breathing through her mouth, she dropped her purse on the kitchen counter and walked toward the windows, drawn by the view—the crescent of dark-gold sand, the gently churning gray-green water. She stood, entranced, listening to the sound of the waves until she realized that she'd left the front door wide open, and that she needed to unpack.

She walked back through the big room that ran the length of the first floor. In the living room section there was a pair of overstuffed couches, their upholstery clawed by long-dead cats, and another table for playing cards or board games. The bookshelves were full of law journals and stained, water-bloated paperbacks—the romances and Agatha Christie books her grandmother had favored, the westerns and mysteries her grandfather had loved—and a mounted deer's head hung over the fireplace in the middle. Past the great room was a porch that stood under a deep awning and was lined with lounge chairs, a glider for two, and little wicker tables. Out past the porch was the sea, with white-curdled waves rolling gently over the sand.

Selma and Dave, together with Selma's sister, Ruth, and her husband, Freddie, had bought the place forty years ago, with the idea that they'd spend summers there, and that Sylvie and her daughters would visit, along with Selma's parents, Freddie and Ruth's children, kooky cousin Jan and her brother, George, now a dentist in Reno. With its mismatched furniture, hodgepodge of castoff coffee tables and plates and dishes purchased at tag sales or donated from the cousins' homes, the house was far from fancy, but there were five bedrooms: room enough, Sylvie remembered her mother saying, for everyone to be together, to have a place at the table and a bed to sleep in.

Sylvie closed the front door. It was so quiet here. No cabs zipping down the street, no buses belching toxic clouds, no businesspeople chattering into their earpieces; just the sound of the water, and the occasional seagull squawking into the waves. She could smell dust and mildew and decaying paper and the bracing scent of the salt water, and found herself unexpectedly filled with a buoyant sensation that it took her a minute to recognize as excitement. She'd gotten through the press conference, and the terrible weeks that followed. She had driven herself here (and how long had it been since she'd driven herself anywhere, since it wasn't Richard or Derek behind the wheel? She thought it was the long weekend three or four years ago when she and Ceil had gone to Canyon Ranch in Lenox and, in spite of the GPS that came with the rental car, gotten themselves hopelessly lost). Standing in the house, which needed her love and attention in a way that nothing had in years, she felt, on top of her sadness, a bit of that old first-day-of-school lightness, when the world was brighter than normal, and filled with possibilities. Never mind that all she'd done during her stay so far was sleep, drink whiskey from an old bottle she'd found in the kitchen, eat peanut-butter-on-Wonder-bread sandwiches (she'd bought the peanut butter and the Wonder bread at the gas station where she'd stopped to fill the car), take long, aimless walks on the beach, and sleep some more.

Mel led her through the living room, telling her that the oil tank had been filled, the plumbing lines flushed, and the gas bill paid, that if she planned on staying through the winter (here, he chanced a quick look at her face), she had only to let him know.

"You seen any critters?" he asked.

"Not live ones," Sylvie said. Ten minutes after she'd brought her luggage—what there was of it—into the kitchen, she'd gone looking for the source of the bad smell and found a desiccated mouse corpse, caught in a snap trap in a corner of the pantry.

She'd stared at it for a moment, wondering what to do. They'd had mice in Brooklyn. Sylvie had vivid memories of being home with baby Diana and spying a furry little visitor scurrying along the floorboards of the kitchen. She'd screamed an extremely clichéd "eek!" and jumped up on one of the kitchen chairs with the telephone in her hand and the baby in her arms, and stayed there, terrified, until Richard came running up the stairs to their third-floor apartment. He'd gone to the hardware store and paved their floor with snap traps, and convinced Sylvie that he would keep her safe, that mice didn't bite or carry diseases, and that they did not need, nor could they afford, to decamp to a hotel. Every morning he'd bring the baby into bed, and she'd sit up, nursing, while he went to check the traps to see if they'd caught anything. "Home is the hunter, home from the sea," he'd proclaim, thumping his bare chest and dropping the dead mouse into one of the paper bags they'd started collecting just for that purpose. "Don't show me," she'd begged, with her eyes squeezed shut, and Richard never had.

Sylvie had lifted the trap by its edges, and then, feeling queasy and sick with the memory of a younger Richard who'd once loved and cared for her and kept her and their baby safe, she dropped it into a trash bag, tied the top shut and set it on the porch, where, presumably, it still was. She hoped Mel hadn't noticed it. She hoped it didn't smell.

Mel hitched up his pants and led her back to the kitchen. "You haven't been in here in a while."

"Twelve years," said Sylvie. She could hardly believe it had been so long. From the time she was a baby until she'd left for college, she'd spent three weeks every August at this house, along with her Aunt Ruth and Uncle Freddie and their children, her cousins Jan and George. They were the happiest times: building sandcastles, roasting hot dogs over the fire in the sandy pit that her Uncle Freddie would dig, complaining bitterly with each turn of the shovel; braving the icy water in her one-piece Jantzens and, later, as a teenager, wearing bikinis, basting her body with baby oil and dousing her hair with lemon juice and barely touching a toe to the surf. There had been bikes in the garage, and one was always just the right size for her every summer she came. Best of all, she'd gotten to be part of a tribe. They'd play tricks on the grown-ups: telling Aunt Ruth that Jan was missing was a perennial hit; hiding Uncle Freddie's Budweiser was another, and moving her mother's legal pads had been Sylvie's favorite of all. "Goddamnit, I've got work to do!" Selma would holler. With a streak of white zinc on her nose, in her flowered, skirted bathing suit, she looked like a cross between an alien and an angry couch. Dave, with a mesh fisherman's hat over his bald head and his cigar clamped between his teeth, would pat her shoulder. "Selma, relax! You're on vacation!" "I've got a deadline!" she'd yell. The cousins would stay up late scaring one another with ghost stories, and wake up to the smell of French toast. Once every summer, on the last Friday before school, she and Jan and George would take sleeping bags and blankets down the rickety wooden steps that led to the water and spend the night camped out on the beach.

She and Richard had come up with the girls every summer, but when Richard started commuting to Washington, it was clear that he couldn't afford to spend two or three prime summer weeks cloistered in an out-of-the-way town in Connecticut. Although trophy homes had blossomed along the coastline, Fairview was too far away to become fashionable with New York's smart set. The people with summer homes here were from Connecticut and Massachusetts; a lot of the money was still old money, Republican money that did Richard no good. The last time up, twelve years ago, Richard had gotten in a fight with Uncle Freddie about gay marriage that had almost come to blows. Uncle Freddie and his family had left two days early. Richard spent the remainder of the visit in their bedroom on the telephone, sneezing and complaining about the mold, while Sylvie stayed downstairs, sitting at the dining room table, pounding out press releases on the Mac Classic she'd brought up from New York.

Mel was still talking, demonstrating the improvements: the electric baseboard heating on the second floor; the powder room that had been added onto the kitchen five years ago—"shipshape," said Mel, through a pair of bright white dentures, except that the toilet handle needed a jiggle in order to flush.

Following his plaid-shirted back up the staircase, Sylvie remembered what a wonder this house had been when she was a bookish girl with a vivid imagination. It had been her enchanted castle, her Narnia, her attic garret and her secret garden. When she was a girl here she'd slept next to her cousin Jan, beneath faded cotton comforters, whispering secrets until one parent or another would make the trip to the third floor and tell them to quiet down and go to sleep, that tomorrow would be another beautiful day at the beach.

"You gonna be all right?" Mel asked, after he'd shown her the thermometers and the closet where the extra lightbulbs were stored.

She nodded. Mel looked down, shuffling his feet. "I'm sorry for your troubles," he finally said, and Sylvie, surprised, said, "Thank you," before walking him out to the porch.

The plastic bag with the dead mouse was still next to the door, where she'd left it, and she was, she knew, out of food. She'd scraped the last bit of peanut butter out of the jar the night before.

Time to deal with it. Time to deal with all of it.

She walked through the living room, past the television set, which she'd refused to turn on since she'd arrived. She could imagine what they were saying. She'd heard it all before, about every other politician's wife (and there were so many of them, such an unhappy sorority to have joined). Better to try to ignore it, to pretend it wasn't happening, to hope that, in the intervening days and weeks, some public figure, some politician or professional athlete had made a bigger fool of himself than her Richard. She swallowed hard, letting the familiar mix of sorrow and rage and shame fill her as she imagined herself like an ostrich, its big behind waving in the air and its head stuck firmly in the sand. *Ladybug, ladybug, fly away home, your house is on fire, your children are gone.* Even though she could try to ignore it, to stick her head in the sand or jam her fingers in her ears and not listen, it didn't stop what was happening out there, the things they were saying about Richard, the names they were calling him, and her, and their daughters.

Never mind. She'd faced Mel, and it had gone all right. She'd get some food, diversify her diet. Then, eventually, she'd worry about the rest of it.

Simmons Grocery had once been a glorified convenience store with sandy wooden floors and a single cash register and a smell of sour milk, a place where vacationers would stop on their way back from the beach to pick up a package of hot dogs, canned soup, or disposable diapers. There'd been a cooler full of ice cream sandwiches and popsicles by the door, and dirty magazines high on a shelf that the boys would dare one another to look at.

Simmons was enormous now, housed in a red brick building on the edge of town, with lots of glass windows, tiled floors and fluorescent lights, a bank of a dozen conveyer belts and cash registers, and an entire section devoted to organic foods. Had all supermarkets swollen in this steroidal manner? Sylvie had no idea. For the past five years, she'd had her groceries delivered from a service where one (or, in her case, one's nutritionist) could plug in a shopping list, and, each week at a predetermined time, your groceries would be delivered right to your kitchen.

She shoved the bagged mouse into a trash can at the store's entrance, then spent thirty minutes pushing her cart up and down the aisles, marveling first at the selection, then at the prices (five dollars for a gallon of milk! When had *that* happened?). She piled a few low-cal frozen dinners into her cart, then wandered around, picking up items—a box of crackers, a can of soup, a bundle of rosemary—before setting them down again.

She wanted everything: chocolate chip cookies, coffee cake with crumbly, buttery topping, lamb chops with crisp, crinkled fat around their bones. She shook her head and slid two apples into a plastic bag. Then she snatched a half-dozen fat sweet potatoes from the neighboring bin and had them bagged and in the cart almost before she could stop herself. She grabbed onions and garlic and celery, staples she recognized from Ceil's kitchen, and then, wheeling her cart to the meat case, she pointed first to a rib roast and then to a turkey big enough to feed a small village. "Fuck it," she muttered under her breath, before noticing the pair of young women with tight bodies and tighter faces staring at her. She hoped it was because of the cursing and not because they knew who she was. In the glimpse she'd gotten of herself in the rearview mirror, with her hair loose, in a sweater and flats instead of a suit and heels, with no makeup, she hoped she wasn't immediately identifiable as the latest woman scorned; that maybe the news hadn't trailed her to Connecticut.

But that was silly. What did she have to be ashamed of, anyhow, she thought, pushing her cart faster and faster. She was the one who'd been sinned against. She wasn't the sinner. She looked up, reading the sign of the aisle she'd stopped at: Baking Needs. "Yes," she murmured, "I have a Baking Need." Into the cart went chocolate chips and coconut flakes, brown and white sugar, two bags of flour, corn syrup and molasses and a large tin of Crisco. *If your grandmother wouldn't recognize it, don't eat it,* her nutritionist had said. Well, too bad, nutritionist, because Selma's grandma would have recognized Crisco just fine. She'd used it in her pie crusts. She'd fried chicken in melted Crisco.

Fried chicken, Sylvie thought. She remembered her grandmother marinating chicken overnight, in a green ceramic bowl filled with buttermilk seasoned with salt and cayenne pepper. She went back to the meat aisle for chicken. Then there was bacon (she'd loved bacon, and hadn't tasted the stuff in all the years she'd been placing slices on Richard's breakfast plates). And hot dogs (hot dogs! Sizzling on the grill as the sun went down and the Red Sox game played on the radio!). Of course, if you had hot dogs, you needed hamburgers, too. That was practically a law. Sylvie added a container of burgers and one of plump white bratwurst.

She steered the cart back to the bread aisle, past a mother bribing a toddler into silence with a bagel, grabbing buns and English muffins and pita pockets. Then she turned to Dressing and Condiments. Into the cart went salad dressing and bottles of ketchup and mustard and relish. She added barbecue and sour-cream-and-onion-flavored potato chips, then reached past an elderly gentleman hovering indecisively in front of the seltzer to pick up a two-liter bottle of Coke. Not New Coke, not Diet Coke, just plain old-fashioned Coke, one of her favorites during those teenage summers, when she'd allow herself a single bottle each afternoon. Back to the snack-food aisle for pretzels and cheese puffs and crackers, and, because it was only civilized to offer guests cheese with their crackers, she tracked down a wedge of Stilton, a chunk of Jarlsberg, a half-wheel of triple-crème Brie.

She went to the deli for sliced ham and cheese and turkey,

fresh garlicky pickles that she scooped from a brine-filled barrel, and a pound of dill-flecked potato salad before heading back to Produce. More potatoes, white ones this time. She lifted a can of chicken noodle soup before setting it down. Why have canned soup when she could make soup from scratch? She had time. For the first time in as long as she could remember, Sylvie Serfer Woodruff had nothing but time.

Back to the meat aisle for another whole chicken, and then a box of egg noodles. Over to the bakery for corn muffins and cinnamon rolls—not as good as Ceil's, but they looked okay, and an okay corn muffin was still good. Wasn't that what men said about sex, or was it pizza? That even bad pizza's still good? Bad pizza. Probably that was what she was to Richard, the cheap, freezer-burned stuff you'd pull out from the back of the shelf when you were ravenous and desperate enough not to care. Maybe that girl, that Joelle, had been fresh-baked, right out of the oven, the cheese hot and stretchy, the dough soft and yielding. Sylvie grabbed a long loaf of French bread and a small round loaf of raisin challah, and had put on her glasses to peer at a price tag when she noticed that a young woman in a Nike visor and fancy running shoes on her feet was staring at her.

Sylvie dropped her eyes. She thought she might start crying. Then she raised her chin, her jaw set defiantly. "Can I help you?"

"Excuse me," she began. "I was wondering—"

Sylvie cut her off. "Yes," she said. "That's right. I am."

The woman stared. Sylvie decided that some amplification was necessary.

"I'm Sylvie Woodruff. Richard Woodruff's wife. And no, I didn't know he was sleeping with that girl, and no, I haven't decided if I'm divorcing him yet. And in case you were wondering, we still had what I considered to be a perfectly acceptable sex life, and we loved each other . . ." Her eyes were filling with tears. She blinked them away. "We have two beautiful girls, Diana and

Lizzie. Diana's a doctor, she's married, she's got a little boy, and Lizzie, well, Lizzie had some problems but I think she's doing better now, unless this completely derails her, which I worry about. I do. I worry about it a lot. And I'm furious at my husband, for jeopardizing her . . ." She swallowed the word *recovery,* squeezed the challah under her arm, and swiped at her cheek with her sleeve. "I guess what I have to figure out is, can I ever forgive him? Can I ever trust him again? Can we be a family? And I don't know. After something like this, I just don't."

"I'm sorry," the woman whispered.

Sylvie held her round challah tightly, the way she'd held her daughters when they were babies. "Sorry," she repeated. "I'm sorry, too. I'm sorry that I didn't see it coming. I thought I had a happy marriage. I thought that. I did. We said 'I love you' every night. We never went to sleep angry. But you don't know . . . it's like it could happen to anyone. Like getting struck by lightning. It could happen to anyone." Her voice was hoarse, and loud, and she could feel herself sweating as her fingertips sank through the plastic and into the bread. "Nobody likes to think it, but it could happen to anyone." This was not technically true—she supposed it happened more frequently with powerful men who had ample opportunity—but at that moment, with her heart thundering in her ears and sweat rolling down her back, it felt true. Like a natural disaster, an earthquake, a tsunami, and her only mistake was that she'd been in the way. "Anyone," she repeated.

The woman finally opened her mouth. "I just . . . I wanted to ask . . . I parked next to a Camry with its lights on, and I wondered if that was your car."

Oh. "Well, that could happen to anyone, too," Sylvie said, feeling her face burn as the woman backed away.

"I'm sorry for your troubles," the woman whispered. "Can I help you at all? Get someone for you, or . . . ?"

"Oh, no," said Sylvie, her old social graces taking over, her knack, honed over the years, of putting others at ease. "No, I . . . I'm not myself right now." She tried to give a my-isn't-this-an-amusing-misunderstanding laugh, but it sounded like a sob instead. "Really, I'm fine." The woman nodded, managed a weak smile, then fled in the direction of Ethnic Foods. Sylvie stood for a minute, her hands resting on the shopping cart. That hadn't gone well.

Leaving her two brimming carts behind, she went out into the parking lot, which had filled up with minivans and SUVs, young mothers on their way to meet the buses or pick up little kids at nursery school. *Just do what you can,* she told herself. Breathe. Finish shopping. Go home. Unpack the groceries. Eat some lunch. Take a bath. Take a nap. Keep breathing.

She dug her keys out of her purse, unlocked the Camry, and turned off the lights. She thought, for a moment, of just getting behind the wheel and driving back home, leaving the groceries sitting in the carts . . . but she couldn't. She imagined the frozen foods thawing, the milk and meat going bad, and how long it would take for someone to put it all back. She'd never been the kind of person to make work for others, and she wasn't going to turn into that kind of person now.

Sylvie plodded back through the parking lot, head down, eyes on her shoes. Her brimming carts had been moved to one of the conveyor belts, and there was a man with gray hair and a white shirt and a tie standing behind them, obviously waiting for her.

"Are these yours?" he asked. Sylvie stifled a groan, but she made herself nod and answer the man pleasantly.

"They're mine. I'm having a party. I just moved up here, and I'm stocking the house. I stepped out for a moment because I'd left my lights on." Sylvie closed her mouth. She lifted the poor mangled loaf of challah out of the cart and set it on the conveyor belt, then began unloading the rest: the chickens and potatoes, the cold cuts, the olives and the stuff from Baking Needs.

When she looked up, she saw that the man—he had a rectangular plastic nametag clipped to the side of his shirt—was staring at her. *Here we go again,* she thought. Was this how it was going to be, every place she went, where every time someone looked at her she'd worry that they knew about Richard, and that they were thinking the worst?

The man was still staring, his gray eyes cool and somehow amused. "Sylvie?" he asked. "Sylvie Serfer?"

She stared at him, startled at hearing her old name, her maiden name. For so long, she'd been Sylvie Woodruff, Mrs. Senator Woodruff, wife of. The tag on the man's shirt read TIM SIMMONS, MANAGER. "Tim Simmons," she said, and finally it clicked. He'd been Timmy when she'd known him, when she was a kid and then a teenager. His hair had been emphatically red then, and one Labor Day, at a bonfire on the beach when she was sixteen, he'd said, *Come with me,* and walked her through the sharp-edged sea grass and into the dunes. The sand had been damp and cool beneath her bare feet, and his lips had been warm. "Timmy?"

"Sylvie! My God!" He took a step forward, as if he meant to hug her or take her hands, then stepped backward—remembering, Sylvie bet herself, who she was now. "I haven't seen you in . . . my God, how long has it been?"

"Years."

"So what have you been up to? You went to Barnard, right?"

She studied him and thought, or imagined, that she could see the ghost of the boy she remembered hiding behind the gray hair and the wrinkles. Was he teasing her, or did he honestly not know?

"I live in New York City," she said. If he'd heard about the scandal, Tim would be too polite to say so. He'd always been polite, he'd held the door for Sylvie, and stood whenever Selma entered the room, much to her mother's amusement. "I went to law school after college."

"Barnard," he said again, and she nodded.

"Barnard, then Yale."

His eyebrows lifted, and he pursed his lips in a silent whistle of admiration, which she waved away, embarrassed.

"But I only practiced for a few years. I had two daughters—Diana's a doctor in Philadelphia. She's married, with a little boy, and Lizzie's a student." This was not exactly true, but maybe Lizzie would go back to school someday. For now, she was a student of life. "And . . ." Here was the problem, the blank she would have to fill in, the years where she'd done nothing but tend to Richard and watch every morsel she put in her mouth. "Well. Maybe you've heard the news." Her hands wanted to tremble, to gesture wildly, to find the challah, now safely in a plastic Simmons shopping bag, and start squeezing it again. She bent over the second cart and started unloading. "And now I'm here. How about you?"

The corners of Tim's eyes crinkled. His reddish hair had thinned, and there were furrows in his forehead, but she could still see him at sixteen. That night on the dunes, his mouth had tasted of beer and cigarettes and, touchingly, of the spearmint gum he'd chewed and then, she supposed, spit out before he'd kissed her. "I went to Cornell for hotel administration. Ran restaurants in upstate New York," Tim was saying. "Then my dad got sick, and I came back down eight years ago, and . . ." He gestured down the wide, well-lit aisle. "We've expanded. As you can see."

"I noticed. The organic section! It's very . . ."

"Impressive?" He took the rib roast out of her hands and gave it to the checker. "Bag this separately, okay?"

The girl behind the register nodded. Was Tim flirting with her? Was that even possible? Or did he treat anyone who'd buy two carts' worth of groceries that way?

"I was going to say 'confusing,'" Sylvie confessed. "I don't know what half those things are. Gluten-free beer?" she said, and borrowed a phrase she'd heard Lizzie say. "What's that about?"

He shrugged, still smiling. His hair was much more gray than red, and he seemed a little subdued. But maybe that was just because she was used to Richard, whose every movement, every gesture, had been larger than life. "It's about fourteen dollars for a six-pack, so it's good business."

She glanced at his left hand, hardly believing she was doing it. No ring. But that might not mean anything. Lots of men didn't wear them, men who worked with their hands. Did Tim work with his hands? His nametag said *MANAGER*, but what did that mean? She pictured him running a sponge over the gleaming edges of the meat slicer, pushing a mop over the floors at the end of the day.

"Do you have children?" she ventured.

He nodded. "Three boys. All grown. Frankie's in New York, actually. He's a banker. Ollie's in grad school in Boston, and Tim Junior, my oldest, he and his wife have a baby girl, but he's all the way in Seattle. My ex-wife moved out there. She helps with the baby."

She nodded again, registering the *ex* in front of *wife* even as she made sympathetic noises about the distance to the West Coast. "Would you like to come to dinner? Help me eat some of this?" she blurted, gesturing toward the mountain of groceries. Heat rose in her cheeks as she realized what she'd done—had she just asked a man on a date? Not even three weeks after leaving her husband?

"Sure," said Tim. He stuck his hands in his pockets, rocking back on his heels. "I think I remember the way."

They agreed that they would meet at seven, that he could pick up a bottle of wine. Together, they unloaded the second cart. "Take care of Sylvie," Tim said to the girl behind the cash register, and patted Sylvie, once, on her shoulder. "She's a friend."

It took Sylvie almost an hour to haul everything out of her car and put the food away. She worked carefully, using her legs, not her back, carrying the bags in one at a time, thinking all the while about what had happened in the grocery store—her challah-squeezing breakdown, her reunion with Tim. Once the food was crammed into the refrigerator or loaded onto the shelves, she peeled sweaty strands of hair off her cheeks and realized that she had absolutely no idea what to make Tim for dinner, or how to cook the majority of the things she'd purchased. Worse—much worse—she was going to be alone with a man who was not her husband or a relative, alone with a man she'd once kissed, for the first time in more years, more decades, than she cared to consider.

She stared at the rib roast, which was big as a baby under its white cap of fat, glistening and somehow reproachful, on the countertop. Scowling, Sylvie thought how much easier this would have been if she'd been a different kind of woman, a different kind of wife. There had been men, over the years, with whom she could have spent a few discreet hours or evenings while Richard was away. She'd had opportunities. Oh yes she had. There'd been a friend of Larry's, an architect in town for a conference on sustainable design who'd was separated from his wife and stayed with Larry and Ceil. He'd told charming stories over Ceil's veal and then taken her hand in the kitchen (she'd been washing, he'd been drying) and kissed her almost before she knew what was happening. *Please,* she'd said quietly, so as not to alarm Ceil, setting her wet hands on his chest and pushing him away. He'd given her a sheepish shrug and said, *Can't blame a guy for trying.* Then, once, at a fund-raiser in their apartment, she'd found herself talking with a man about her age. He wore a beautifully cut suit (after years of picking out Richard's clothes, she had learned to recognize and appreciate the weight and drape of certain fabrics and even the work of certain designers) and an expression, as he gazed around the room, that looked a lot like contempt.

"I'm with her," the man had said, tilting his chin toward his wife. Elizabeth Cunningham, known professionally as Bitsy, was a spectacularly groomed woman with a narrow, horsey face, a prominent nose, and a braying voice. Bitsy wore a patterned wrap dress, black tights and high black leather boots. Her hair was elaborately streaked with copper and gold, the kind of hair that announced to the world that Bitsy could afford to spend four hours and five hundred dollars in a high-end salon every four weeks. Her fingers were freighted with rings, diamonds twinkled in her earlobes, and she was, of course, enviably thin, with hip bones that protruded through the jersey and a sternum as articulated as an anatomy chart, but none of it added up to beauty, thanks to Bitsy Cunningham's perpetually sour expression. She looked, Ceil thought, like the kind of woman who'd as soon bite you as say hello.

Sylvie knew her story, which had been retold in more than one of the women's magazines, and in the *Wall Street Journal* as well. Bitsy, married and bored, with round-the-clock nannies caring for the twins she'd paid a surrogate to carry, had made her fortune designing hundred-dollar hand-embroidered bibs and burp cloths that sold, Sylvie assumed, to women who had no idea what it was like to try to get spit-up stains out of Irish linen . . . or, more likely, to young mothers who, like Sylvie, had nannies and cleaning ladies to do it for them. Bitsy's Bibs had spawned a successful line of children's clothing, everything from miniature tutus to teeny tiny tuxedos that were now sold in fine department stores around the world. Bitsy probably earned ten times what her high-powered husband made at his investment firm each year. She collected politicians like other women collected handbags, or porcelain figurines. As Sylvie watched, Bitsy tilted her face and honked her laugh at Richard, who smiled back so warmly you'd never know he'd told Sylvie that they should put out a bowl of sugar cubes and maybe a carrot or two along with the rest of the appetizers. ("Don't be mean," Sylvie had said, swatting him.)

"You know what my job is?" Mr. Bitsy had murmured in the vicinity of Sylvie's ear. He was, she knew, the CFO of Bitsy's company, having left a job at a hedge fund to manage his wife's business. "It's the same as yours. We carry their purses. We hand them their mints, and their Purell."

"Oh, no," Sylvie demurred, even though she had both of those items in her purse at that very moment. Nor did she want to tally the times Richard had nonchalantly given her something, a folder or a coat or a briefcase, to hold while he shook hands with someone more important, or the times she'd slipped a tin of Altoids into his pocket, or run the lint brush over his shoulders. This wasn't servitude, nor was it degrading, it was simply what married people did for each other. But then a troubling thought surfaced: Had Richard ever once returned the favor? Had he ever offered her a mint, or the lint brush? As she wondered, Mr. Bitsy slipped his card into her hand. "Call me," he said, his face so close to hers that she could feel his whiskers against her cheek. "I think we'd have a lot to talk about."

Of course, she'd never called. She'd thrown out his card, and, when the party was over, she'd asked Richard what he and Bitsy had been laughing about. "Oh, she was telling me all about how she got bumped out of the big dressing room on the *Today* show because the teenage track star they interviewed showed up with her six brothers and sisters," Richard had said, helping her clear the bowls of nuts and olive pits and carry them into the kitchen, where Marta would wash them the next morning. "I told her I'd get right on it. Call my friends at Amnesty International. Get some 'Justice for Bitsy' T-shirts made up." Sylvie had smiled, and hadn't told him about Mr. Bitsy and his business card. The poor man was just bitter, as any man would be, living in the shadow of a woman who was so entitled and so obviously unpleasant. Her life wasn't like his at all. She and Richard had a partnership. Well. Look how much she had to be smug about. Look how that had turned out.

She poked at the meat with one finger, then flipped open her laptop. Thankfully, Ceil was home. "Rib roast," her friend coached, with her face looking out, disconcertingly, from the screen (Skyping was another trick Diana had taught her, one she'd actually mastered). "It's the easiest thing in the world." Ceil had a fabric flower clipped in her hair, and a smear of pink lipstick on her lips—her going-to-town look, Sylvie knew, which meant she'd been at music class that morning, and maybe even that Suri Cruise had shown up.

"Also the most expensive," Sylvie murmured.

"Spend his money," Ceil said. "It's the least you can do. Do you have butcher's twine? Never mind. Just get your floss. I know you've got that." Sylvie managed a smile—she and Ceil shared a periodontist, who was practically evangelical on the subject of flossing. Ceil talked Sylvie through slicing the meat off the bones, then tying it back on with floss. "What's the point of this?" Sylvie asked, and Ceil, who'd been reading aloud from *Us Weekly* while Sylvie worked, said, "Don't know, but it's just how it's done."

"Now you salt and pepper it, sear it in a hot pan until

it's brown, stick it in the oven at three hundred degrees, and you're set."

"That's it?"

"That's it. And it'll be spectacular."

For a side dish, Sylvie was going to make mashed potatoes. Ceil had assured her that even she couldn't screw that up: boil them in salted water until they were soft, mash them, add salt and pepper and butter and half-and-half until they tasted right. And she'd caramelize carrots and parsnips, which involved putting them into a cast-iron pan, sprinkling them with sea salt and rosemary, pouring a little olive oil on top, and putting the pan in the oven along with the meat. "It's Home Cooking 101," said Ceil. She paused—up until now they'd confined their conversation to the logistics of getting dinner on the table ("ask him to carve" had been Ceil's last word on that subject).

"You-know-who called again this morning," Ceil finally said.

Sylvie sighed. "Again?" Richard, she knew, had been calling her friend daily, leaving messages asking if she'd heard from Sylvie, and if Sylvie was ready to talk.

"He's nothing if not reliable. But don't worry. He's still just talking to my voice mail."

"Thank you," Sylvie murmured. She felt . . . oh, she didn't know how she felt! Furious and betrayed and worried about Richard all on his own, and touched that they were still connected; still, in the face of such terrible betrayal, such endless humiliation, husband and wife. "How did he . . ." How did he sound? What had he said? Was he broken, a changed man? Had he cried? What was he eating for dinner, and whom was he having it with? Would Joelle bring him pizza or a sandwich? Did she know he had to watch his cholesterol? Her head was swirling, and she had dinner to deal with, dinner and Tim Simmons.

"I'm not taking his calls, but if I had to guess, I'd say he wants you back," said Ceil.

"Because I'm useful to him." The word *useful* came out with a spiteful, bitter twist.

"Oh, cookie," said Ceil. "It isn't just that. He loves you. And you have such history together."

Sylvie laughed. Such history. Of course, Richard had ensured that the part of their history the world would remember was the bit where he had fucked a legislative aide. Not the parent-teacher conferences they'd attended (Richard would always rearrange his schedule so that he could be there), not the birthday parties for the girls they'd hosted, not the twenty-fifth-anniversary trip they'd taken to Paris, where they'd eaten at three Michelin-starred restaurants and he'd given her a diamond bracelet as they walked along the Seine. "I should go," she said to the screen.

"Enjoy your meat," said Ceil, with a saucy grin. "And call me later. I want a report."

Sylvie tied one of her grandmother's old aprons around her waist. She seasoned the meat and set it carefully into the sizzling oil in the cast-iron skillet, turning it with tongs until each side was brown and crisp. She put it in the oven, seasoned the vegetables, and put them in, too. She set the table, locating a tablecloth and good napkins, silverware and wineglasses, washing what needed to be washed, arranging a bouquet of gerbera daisies, bright orange and hot-pink, that she barely remembered buying in a blue glass vase, and setting that in the center of the table.

Just before seven o'clock, headlights washed over the kitchen. A car door slammed. Sylvie wiped her hands on her apron and made sure the matches were out for the candles. As Tim climbed out of the car, she felt her heart sink—by now he'd probably Googled her to fill in the blanks; by now it was 100 percent guaranteed that he knew what had brought her back to Fairview.

"Hello there," he called, jogging up the porch's three sagging steps. There was a bottle of wine tucked under one arm, a

Simmons tote bag in the other, and he looked so boyish, so vital, so different from Richard, who was always in a suit and whose skin always retained a certain indoor pallor and who never ran anywhere, except on the treadmill after his doctor said he had to. Sylvie raised her hand. "Hello to you," she said, and nudged the door with her hip, letting the light and the warmth and the good smells of dinner brighten and scent the night air.

LIZZIE

"So can we talk about it?" Lizzie asked her sister. It was a Wednesday morning, two weeks since the press conference where their father had announced that he would not be leaving the Senate.

"Talk about what?" Diana asked. Her tone was neutral, but Lizzie could tell her guard was up.

Lizzie sat cross-legged in one of the kitchen chairs. Diana stood at the counter, pulling clean silverware from the dishwasher basket and placing it in the drawer, a task that went quickly because Diana always loaded forks with forks and spoons with spoons before she washed them.

The whole time Lizzie had been in Philadelphia, her sister's morning routine never varied. Diana would get up at five-thirty for her run and come home forty-five minutes later, drenched in sweat, or rain if it was raining. She'd gulp down a protein shake, start a pot of coffee, take a shower, and dry her hair. By the time Milo and Lizzie and Gary came downstairs at seven, Diana would have the dishwasher emptied, the counters wiped, toast in the toaster, cereal and juice on the table, and her commuter mug filled with black coffee.

"Dad," Lizzie said, a little impatiently. "I want to talk about Dad." She also wanted to talk about Diana's frequent absences from the house on Spruce Street, and why her sister had been sleeping on the couch in the living room instead of in bed with her husband, but she'd decided to start with the elephant in the room.

That morning, Lizzie had set her alarm for six-thirty, intending to catch her sister post-run, pre-breakfast. Since that first night, she and Diana had barely discussed the situation at all . . . and every time Lizzie brought it up, Diana would find a way to avoid the topic. She'd point her chin at Milo and say, "Little pitchers have big ears," or she'd tell Lizzie that she had to go to the gym, or back to work, where she'd forgotten something. Maybe that was where her stress was showing. Diana had never been forgetful, but lately, she'd been running back to the hospital after dinner every night or two to retrieve her purse or her cell phone or her cell-phone charger. Lizzie wondered if she was using the time away from home to talk to someone—a friend, assuming Diana had one, or a therapist. Maybe she was just walking alone by herself trying to make sense of it. Maybe she was crying.

"What about Dad?" Diana grabbed a handful of knives out of the basket and put them, with a noisy rattle, into the drawer. Lizzie sighed. Diana had always treated her like a waste of space with nothing useful to say. It had gotten worse after Lizzie's first trip to rehab, and Diana's attitude had not improved during the time Lizzie had been in her sister's employ. Any fantasy she'd had about forging a new and deep connection with her sister during her summer in Philadelphia had been dashed her first night in the row house. "I have an amends to make," she'd announced, approaching Diana in the living room after Milo had fallen asleep, and Diana, who'd been reading a medical journal while texting on her BlackBerry, had laughed at her, and then said, "Whatever it is, I'll forgive you if you'll wipe the toilet off after Milo uses it in the morning."

"Have you talked to them?" Lizzie asked. Diana shrugged. Lizzie continued, "Maybe we could go see Dad. See how he's doing. And then we can go see Mom in Connecticut."

Diana shrugged again, her hands still full of dishes, an exasperated look on her face.

"We could bring Milo. Do, like, a road trip. It could be fun."

At the word *fun,* Diana rolled her eyes. She set down the plates and took a long swallow from her coffee mug. "I don't have time for a road trip right now."

Lizzie nodded. This was what she had expected. She watched as Diana bent and began emptying the top rack of the dishwasher, lining up mugs and glasses on the counter. Scandal seemed to agree with her sister: Diana's skin was clear, her hair shiny, and her body, already lean from running, seemed more graceful than usual. Instead of squatting to retrieve the basket of silverware, Diana bent from the waist, letting her hair sweep down, obscuring her face. Her breasts pressed against the front of her white blouse, which was dazzling against her tan skin. Lizzie wondered whether Sniffling Gary appreciated her sister, and bet herself that he didn't. She wondered, again, about Diana's early mornings and late nights, how she'd been sleeping on the couch and the way she kept forgetting things at the hospital.

"Maybe you're right," Lizzie said, thinking out loud. "Maybe we should just let them be." She helped herself to a cup of coffee, adding cream and sugar that she'd had to buy with her own money because Diana didn't keep anything besides skim milk and agave nectar in the house. "I don't know. The whole thing's just gross. Entitlement," she said, hoisting herself onto the counter, parroting one of the words she'd heard someone on TV use. "Do you think that's what it was? Like, powerful men just think they can take what they want, and who cares if it hurts anyone?"

A shadow moved across Diana's face. "Maybe he was unhappy."

That was surprising. Lizzie had never known her sister to care about anyone else's unhappiness, or even to notice it. Certainly, Diana had never paid much attention to Lizzie's unhappiness. "Why would Dad be unhappy? He had a wife who devoted her entire life to him."

Diana shrugged. "Maybe they grew apart. Maybe they weren't in love anymore. How can we know?"

This was even more surprising. Diana generally claimed to know everything about everyone, or to at least be able to give an educated guess. "But if you've been married that long, don't you owe it to the marriage to stay faithful? Not to mention your kids."

"We aren't kids," Diana said. A glass slipped from her hand onto the countertop, and would have shattered on the floor if Diana hadn't managed to grab it. "We're grown-ups. We're adult women, and it shouldn't matter to us."

"Of course it matters!" Lizzie said. "No matter how old we are, they're our parents, and I think—"

"We were his props," Diana said, her voice uncharacteristically sharp. "You know that, right?" She lowered her chin, approximating their father's tone and stance. " 'My daughter, the doctor, the emergency-room physician, stands on the front lines of the health care crisis facing this nation.' " Lizzie nodded. She'd heard her father deliver that line more than once, usually with Diana standing beside him or behind him, tall and formidable in her suit and high heels. Diana was the daughter he used at press appearances and rallies. Lizzie herself was rarely spoken of. "A student," her father would say when anyone asked. Hardly anyone did. Lizzie had been more useful when she was a cute little girl with curly blond hair who'd worn pretty dresses and had been schooled in how to stand on a stage and listen, or look as if she was listening, attentively.

"Let's be honest." Diana slid the last glass into the cabinet, then closed the cabinet door and turned toward Lizzie. "They weren't exactly going to win any parent of the year prizes." She gave Lizzie a meaningful look. Lizzie swallowed hard.

"Dad was a good father," she said, even though, deep down, Lizzie suspected it was not entirely true. "And maybe he needs us," she ventured.

Her sister began wiping a counter that looked spotless already. "And when we needed them," she asked, "where were they?" She raised her eyes, staring straight into Lizzie's own. Lizzie felt goose bumps prickle her skin. Clearly, Diana had figured this was the one card in her hand that she could play against her sister, and she'd keep playing it until Lizzie gave up.

She couldn't sit still a second longer. She slid off the counter, hurried out of the kitchen, and took the stairs two at a time until she was up in her room, which was already stifling in the summer heat. Flopping facedown on her bed, she squeezed her eyes shut, with her sister's words echoing in her head.

When she was twelve she'd looked sixteen, especially if she wore eyeliner and a blouse that showed off her top. There'd been a boy, a prep school junior who'd lived in her building and smiled at her in the elevator when he came home for breaks. She got a job babysitting for the boy's half sister, and one night the boy came home from a party smelling of beer and cigarettes, a little sloppy, wiping his wet lips on the back of his oxford shirtsleeve and grinning when he saw her on the couch. "When's the missus coming back?" he'd asked—the missus was what he called his stepmother, who was only twenty-nine years old. "Eleven," Lizzie told him—it was just after nine o'clock then. He'd given Lizzie her first drink, a vodka and cranberry juice, and after she'd had two of them, he'd given her her first kiss. And then . . .

She sprang off the bed, but she could still picture herself, with her eyes darkened with Mrs. Ritson's eyeliner and mascara (she'd been trying it on before his arrival), her blouse unbuttoned, her lips swollen from his kisses and her cheeks and chin abraded by his stubble. *Come on,* he'd told her. *Don't be a tease. You know you want it, too.* Then he'd grabbed her wrist, yanking her back down beside him, and somehow his fly was open, his penis sticking out from his white boxer shorts like some kind of ridiculous pink jack-in-the-box, a bald, featureless head on a thick, veined neck. *No,* Lizzie had whispered, but she hadn't said it very loud, and when the boy put his hand on the back of her neck she'd bent down willingly enough, telling herself it would be over fast. She could wash her face and rebraid her hair and go back to being a girl.

She hadn't counted on the memories: his fingers digging into the flesh of her neck, the way he'd talked to her, the disgusting things he'd said, the lazy smile he'd given her as he tucked his wilted penis back into his pants. *Not bad. Maybe I'll see you around.* She'd gone straight to the bathroom and barfed and then she'd run upstairs, not even waiting for the elevator, and told her sister everything. Diana had told her parents. And her parents had . . .

Lizzie rolled off the bed. It was seven o'clock, the start of her workday. Downstairs, Diana was still in the kitchen, smiling at her BlackBerry. She looked up as Lizzie walked in.

"You okay?"

Lizzie gathered herself, smoothing her hair and putting on a smile. "Fine." Diana tucked her BlackBerry into her pocket. Lizzie wasn't positive, but she thought her sister's face looked flushed. Or maybe it was just a by-product of her morning run. Even this early, the air outside was steamy and thick as soup.

"Gotta go," said Diana, grabbing her keys and her sunglasses and shoulder bag and giving her hair a quick flip in the mirror beside the front door. Lizzie had seen her do the grab-and-flip a hundred times over the summer, but today her sister seemed . . . she stared, trying to think of the right word, finally arriving at *glowing*. Diana was glowing. Lizzie wondered, briefly, whether she could possibly be pregnant before dismissing the thought instantly. Diana had told everyone who'd asked, and probably plenty of people who didn't, that she wanted only one child, that she couldn't afford to take the time off a baby would require at this point in her career. Any fetus foolish enough to take up residence in her sister's uterus would be dealt with swiftly and harshly, Lizzie figured. That was if she and Gary were still having sex, which Lizzie seriously doubted. As far as she could tell, Gary reserved most of his passion for his laptop and the Phillies, and Diana couldn't get knocked up if she was sleeping on the couch.

"Can you give Milo breakfast?"

"Sure." Giving Milo his breakfast entailed either toasting a slice of Ezekiel bread or pouring him a bowl of high-fiber Kashi. Lizzie could handle it. Gary probably could, too, if it had ever occurred to him to feed his son, although, from what Lizzie had seen, Gary had enough trouble just getting himself dressed and out the door each morning.

Once her sister was striding along the sidewalk, her hair loose and bouncing over her shoulders as she walked, Lizzie went to the living room and began picking up the mess Gary left behind each night—the pair of beer bottles and crumpled Kleenexes on the side table, his shoes and his inside-out socks in front of the couch, an empty cereal bowl with the spoon milk-glued to the bottom that sat like a sculpture on the coffee table. She carried the shoes to the closet, dropped the socks in the laundry basket, and put the dishes in the dishwasher. She plumped the pillows, then sat on the couch, waiting for Milo to wake up so that her workday could begin.

Finally, at seven-thirty, Milo followed his father down the

stairs, hair uncombed, dressed in what had become his summer uniform: a pair of khaki shorts, a dark-blue short-sleeved T-shirt, boat-sized sneakers (Milo was of average height but his feet were enormous), and one of his dozens of hats—this morning, it was a tweed plaid newsboy's cap, tugged down low. "Good morning!" Lizzie said, as Milo rubbed at his eyes. Gary grunted a hello, picked up his work bag, and walked out the door. Lizzie served Milo toast on one of the salad plates Diana insisted on (a smaller plate made portions look larger, she said), and poured him a bowl of Kashi. "What should we do today?"

"Can we go see Jeff?" he asked, sounding surprisingly eager to leave the house.

She told him that they could, and, when he was done with breakfast and had consented to comb his hair, they walked together to Independence Hall. Jeff was speaking to a group of tourists, crisp and handsome in his khaki uniform and wide-brimmed hat. "Hey, guy!" he greeted Milo, who greeted him with a shy "hello" and a smile. They lined up for the Liberty Bell, Lizzie snapping pictures, not of the bell itself but of the tourists' faces, some avid and some bored, as they came close enough to see it. Then they joined Jeff's tour as he led them into Independence Hall, telling the story of the signing of the Declaration of Independence, explaining to the tourists that this—this building, this room where they were standing—was the place where the United States of America had become a free land.

They went to Whole Foods for Jeff's lunch break, sharing a Diana-approved meal of organic hummus, carrots, and whole-wheat pita. For dessert, Milo asked for, and received, a gluten-free carob brownie. Jeff took a bite and then spat it out into his recycled-paper napkin. "You like this?" he asked, wiping his lips over and over, as if to eradicate the taste, and Milo, giggling, had shrugged and said, "It's okay."

"Dude, I've got to buy you an ice cream," Jeff said. Milo had looked at him and said, "I'm only allowed to have ice cream at birthday parties."

Jeff had taken Lizzie's hand under the table and squeezed so hard she knew he was trying to keep from laughing.

"Is he for real?" he asked, murmuring into her ear while Milo diligently sorted their trash into the six different bins the store provided.

"Yup," she whispered, and Jeff had said, "I think we should go out for cheeseburgers and malteds tomorrow night. Just thinking about that poor kid is making me hungry," and Lizzie said that cheeseburgers sounded very nice.

She and Milo were back home by five o'clock. Gary arrived half an hour later to take his son to the Phillies game, which Lizzie knew for a fact Milo did not want to attend. "Do I have to go?" he whined as she smeared his face with the PABA-free sunscreen Diana had left out and made sure his aluminum water bottle was full. "You'll have a good time," Lizzie said. Milo looked dubious, so Lizzie had lowered her voice and whispered, "I bet your dad will buy you a hot dog." Milo brightened at the prospect of processed meat and a bun made with white flour, and trotted down the stairs, where his father was whacking his fist into the cup of his baseball glove. "C'mon, champ," he said. Milo, his head filled with hot dog visions, waved at Lizzie, then followed his father out the door.

Lizzie ate leftover pad thai for dinner, then went to a meeting in the church on Walnut Street, where, as usual, she sat quietly in a folding chair in the back of the room.

Once the Serenity Prayer had been read, instead of lingering for cookies and coffee and the small talk people made after the meeting, Lizzie decided to use the guest pass her sister had given her to try out a spinning class at Diana's boutique gym on Sansom Street. They'd been big on exercise in rehab, about how it released endorphins, the same chemical reactions in the brain that using did, and that it really was possible to jog or hike or spin oneself into an approximation of a high. She thought of her sister's happy, flushed face that morning. Exercise worked for Diana, so maybe it could help her, too.

Sixty minutes later, drenched in sweat, with her thighs and calves quivering and aching between her legs, she'd staggered out of the darkened spinning room, down the flight of concrete stairs, and the eight blocks home, promising herself that she'd buy padded shorts or a gel seat before attempting spinning again.

Gary was, as ever, in the living room, the remote in his hand and his laptop in his lap. "Milo's sleeping," he said, without taking his eyes from the screen. Upstairs, Lizzie took a long, cool shower, then, wincing, pulled on a pair of cotton boxers and a tank top, and settled into her bed. She talked to Jeff, who'd had class that night. "Sleep tight, sweetheart," he'd said. Lizzie, beaming, had said, "You, too." Sweetheart. She could get used to that.

A minute later, her telephone rang again.

"Hi, Mom," Lizzie said.

"Hi there, Lizzie," said Sylvie, miles away in Connecticut. She said the thing she said every night. "I just wanted to see how you were doing today."

"I'm doing fine." Maybe they'd gotten a bad connection, but unless she was mistaken, her mother's voice sounded a little slurry. Was Sylvie drinking, up there in that big old beach house?

"How's Milo?" Sylvie asked.

"Milo's good. He's getting out more." She told her mother about their trip to Independence Hall, and how Milo had gone to a ball game with his dad, and painted pottery with her, and how she'd convinced him, a few times, to swap his ski cap for a Phillies hat.

"And you went to your meeting?"

"Yep." She turned onto her side, wincing at the pain between her legs, cursing the bicycle seat and thinking that all her mother's interest in Lizzie's meetings and Lizzie's job was a classic case of too little, too late. Sylvie also sounded as if she was reading from a script. How to Handle Your Addicted Child. *You should think about having a real conversation with your mom,* her Minnesota counselor had said, with her eyes soft behind her glasses. Well, maybe someday she would. But definitely not now.

"Take care of yourself, Lizzie," her mother said, and Lizzie, as always, promised that she would.

She turned out the lights and closed her eyes, wishing her mother had called before Jeff had, so that Jeff's voice saying *sweetheart* in her ear would be the last thing she'd heard. Two hours later she was still awake, unable to find a comfortable position. If she'd known that class would leave her in such agony, she never would have given it a try. She slipped out of bed and down to the second-floor bathroom, where she stared for a long moment at a bottle of Advil PM. *Don't take anything,* they'd counseled her in Minnesota. *Even an aspirin can start you down the road again.* But everything below her waist was in agony. And did Advil even count as an actual drug?

What the hell, she decided, and shook two pills into her hand, considered for a moment, added a third, and swallowed them with a mouthful of water from the sink. Then she walked through the silent house to her bedroom tucked under the roof and lay down, eyes closed, until sleep finally arrived.

She woke up the next morning to the sound of her alarm clock blaring. Diana was shaking her, with two of her fingers pressed against Lizzie's neck, searching for a pulse.

"Whah?" Her tongue felt heavy and furry, her head as heavy as a bowling ball.

"What did you take?" asked Diana, giving her another shake.

"I didn't . . ." Lizzie sat up, blinking. Gary was standing at the doorway in his pajama bottoms, getting an eyeful of Lizzie in her tank top, which was sheer, in spots, from sweat. "I went to a spinning class last night, and I was really sore, so I took some of your Advil . . ."

"Oh, sure," Diana said. "Oh, right. Advil. Absolutely. For your information," she said, her voice dripping scorn, "Advil does not cause you to pass out and sleep through your alarm . . ."

"Advil PM!" Lizzie shouted. "It was in the bathroom downstairs!"

Diana ignored her. Her lips were set in a grim line, and her hair was still wet. She snatched Lizzie's embroidered, sequined purse off the bookshelf and dumped it out onto the bed.

"What are you doing?" There was a pack of cigarettes in the purse. Sometimes Lizzie would have one at the end of the day, curled in the narrow space in front of the dormer window, blowing smoke out into the night. Diana snatched the cigarettes and tossed them at Lizzie's chest.

"I told you no smoking! Milo's allergic! And you're asthmatic!"

"I never smoked around him," Lizzie said, scrambling to restuff her purse. "I'm not doing drugs . . ."

"Hey," said Gary. "Hey, ladies. Let's all just calm down, okay?"

"Calm down?" Diana shouted. Her hands were balled into fists. "Calm down? She's been watching our son high! Probably driving our car high!"

"I was not," Lizzie protested, clutching her purse. She was beginning to realize that her protests weren't doing any good, even though, for once, she had truth on her side.

"I think you'd better leave," said Diana, turning away from her.

"What about Milo?" Lizzie managed.

"Milo can do computer camp."

"I don't want to do computer camp!" yelled Milo, who was standing behind his father, listening to the whole thing. He launched himself onto Lizzie's bed, and threw himself against her. "I don't want you to go!" he said, and started to cry. "You and Jeff said you'd take me for ice cream!"

Diana crossed the room in two quick strides and yanked Milo off Lizzie as if she were pinching a tick off a dog. "You can stay in day care at the hospital today," she said to Milo, who started crying. "Start packing," she said to Lizzie. She turned, with Milo still in her arms, and stalked out of the room.

"Fine!" Lizzie muttered, and added a "bitch" under her breath. She sat on the bed, still holding her purse, stunned and shaking. She couldn't believe how quickly things had happened, how fast everything had changed.

Diana clomped down the stairs. "And I'm telling Mom and Dad!"

"Fine!" Lizzie shouted. "Tell them I took your Advil. I'm sure that's exactly what they need, something else to deal with!"

Diana didn't answer. Lizzie pulled on last night's skirt with trembling hands and, after two failed attempts, got her bra hooked. Her hands were sweating, her heart pounding in her ears. She braced her hands on either side of her dresser and looked at her face in the mirror, trying to make herself be still. No more Milo. No more Jeff. What would she tell him? *My sister thought I took drugs and kicked me out?* And where would she go?

Don't do anything hasty, a voice in her head—her counselor's voice, she thought—told her. But her mind had gone directly to the liquor in the cabinet next to Diana's sink. Back in June, when she'd arrived, Diana had asked if she should get rid of the booze, and Lizzie had said, *Oh no, no problem.* The world was full of beer and Baileys, and she might as well learn to deal with it. But now she thought of exactly what might be in that cabinet. She thought about the bottle of vodka in the freezer. She thought that maybe Gary had painkillers, somewhere, God knew he was always bitching about his back and his tendinitis. She could wait, pack up her things, biding her time in the bedroom until Diana left with Milo and Gary went to work. She could find pills, she'd always been able to find pills, the world was as full of pills as it was of liquor, and if she couldn't find them she could buy them somewhere. There was a bar around the corner, and where there was a bar there were drunks, and where there were drunks there was, more often than not, someone who had pills to sell or pills to trade. She could comb her hair, put her shoes on, figure out how much cash she had in her wallet. She could . . .

It was at that moment, staring at herself in the mirror, that a voice in her head spoke up, and what the voice said was, *Halt*. Lizzie knew, instantly, that the voice wasn't referring to the mnemonic of Hungry, Angry, Lonely, or Tired . . . that what the voice meant was, simply, *Stop*.

She looked in the mirror, cheeks red, blue-gray eyes wide and shocked, blond hair sticking up like a bad wig around her head. *You can do this,* the voice said calmly. It was a female voice, possibly even her own voice, although it sounded a little like her mother and a little like Grandma Selma, a little like that counselor in Minnesota, and even, she had to admit, a little bit like Diana, when Diana wasn't yelling or accusing her of driving Milo while high. Maybe it was God, she thought; God as she understood Him, her Higher Power. Maybe God actually spoke to twenty-four-year-old junkies in recovery who'd been tied to chairs with fishnet stockings and shipped off to rehab in Minnesota, and consoled them when they lost their jobs.

So she'd go home early, she thought, pulling her suitcase and duffel bags out from underneath the bed where she'd stashed them back in June. She would tell Jeff what had happened, or at least an edited version of the events. She would say goodbye to Milo as best she could. Then she'd take a train up to New York City. She still had the keys to her parents' apartment. Maybe, for once, instead of showing up needing help, instead of being the hurricane that tore through the family, Lizzie the permanent disaster, maybe she could help.

In New York City, she punched the button for the elevator in her parents' building, unconsciously closing her eyes and holding her breath, as always, as it ascended past the eighth floor, where that boy had messed with her. She'd expected to find the apartment empty, had planned on a little private nap in her old bedroom, but she was surprised to find her father in the small, cluttered kitchen, a low-ceilinged room that was always dark and that her mother had always complained about. Barefoot, unshaven, in sweatpants and a stained white undershirt, he smelled stale, but he brightened when he saw her.

"Hey, Lizzie-Bee," he said.

He's falling apart, she thought, glancing over his shoulder at the pizza boxes and takeout containers on the kitchen table, the stacks of newspapers cluttering the living room beyond it. "How you doing?" he asked, still holding her.

"Fine," she said, trying not to be too obvious about wiggling out of his grasp. He did not smell good at all. She wondered whether he was depressed, and tried to remember the symptoms as they'd been taught in Minnesota. *Change of appetite, change in sleeping habits, lack of interest in things you once enjoyed.*

"Diana good?" her father asked. She followed him into his office in time to see him sit down on top of his laptop, which was sitting on the couch, next to a blanket and a pillow.

"Dad . . ."

"Shit." He got to his feet, shaking his head. He flipped the laptop open and shook it gingerly, as if it were a Magic 8 Ball. "You think it's broken?"

Lizzie looked over his shoulder at the darkened screen. She pressed the power button, and the screen flared to life.

"Thank God," her father exclaimed, then looked at her,

shamefaced. "I broke one of these guys already." As Lizzie stared, her father gave an unhappy chuckle. "I guess I'm not doing so well on my own."

"Well, listen," she said casually—if Diana had, in fact, ratted her out, she'd find out in a few seconds. "I've got a little time before my job starts. Maybe I could, you know, help out."

He looked at her, eager as a puppy dog who's just heard the rattle of a leash. "That would be great, Lizzie. I've got some ADL dinner to go to tomorrow night, and I'm . . ." He swept his arm out, indicating the cluttered living room. "I've got documents I'm supposed to read, I've got a schedule, somewhere, but I don't know where it went, and I know I'm supposed to sit down with the corn lobbyist sometime this week, but I'm not sure when. I think I forgot Grandma Cindy's birthday . . ." He stopped talking and looked at his feet, seeming startled to realize that they were bare. "Thing is, Lizzie, your mom took care of a lot of this stuff. And Marta's off for August."

She nodded, feeling relief as sweet as the rush of a drug hitting her bloodstream. She could be useful again. She could help. "Let me clean up in here," she said. "Maybe you can go take a shower, and then we'll figure out what to do next."

He nodded—not the single firm up-and-down that she was used to, but a little boy's rapid head-bob. Again she glimpsed that eagerness, a gratitude that struck her as more than a little pathetic, which was never a word she could have even imagined applying to her father. He'd always been the strong one, decisive, in command, in his suit and cologne, looking and smelling the part of the head of the house and a leader of men. And now . . . she watched him shuffle down the hall, his bald spot gleaming, picking at the drooping seat of his sweatpants, and felt an enveloping sadness as she saw, for the first time in her life, her father looking old.

She dropped her clothes in the bedroom she'd once shared

with Diana, locating trash bags underneath the kitchen sink and filling four of them with old newspapers and magazines (if her father hadn't read them, she reasoned, he could find the articles he needed online), the pizza boxes and grease-stained paper plates and paper napkins that littered the kitchen table and the coffee table, the soda cans and beer bottles and bottles of Smartwater.

By the time her father returned to his office, still barefoot but in a clean Columbia T-shirt and jeans, Lizzie had restored the room to order and was wiping the screen of the sat-upon laptop with a square of paper towel she'd squirted with Windex.

"Oh," said her father, watching her. "So that's how you clean it off."

"I think so," said Lizzie. Her father had always had her mother to clean up after him, and Lizzie had spent much of what should have been her adulthood in a fog. On drugs, you didn't care much about clean clothes or hot meals, and in rehab, they'd been provided. A snatch of something she'd read during her first, aborted trip through college popped into her head: *faithful Penelope, always spinning.* Substitute *cleaning* and *shopping* and *straightening up* for *spinning,* and you had Sylvie Woodruff.

You can do this, she reminded herself. "Are you hungry?" she asked.

"A little, I guess," he said.

"I'll make us something," she said.

In the kitchen, Lizzie pulled on a pair of rubber gloves and attacked the refrigerator, where the vegetables her mother must have purchased before she'd left were liquefying in the crisper bin, and there were dozens of half-eaten containers of hardened pad thai noodles and General Tso's chicken. When she was through, all that was left in the fridge was a crumpled half-loaf of bread, a tub of butter, a wilted cucumber, and some lox. The vegetable crisper was empty, and the cold-cut drawers were both full of beer.

That wasn't promising. Lizzie located a can of chicken noodle soup and heated it up, and toasted four slices of the bread. She set the table and served her father, then poured herself soup in a mug from the teacher's union—they'd endorsed her dad—and sat down to eat with him.

"So," he said, and tried to smile. "You're home early."

"Milo decided to do computer camp after all," she said, leaving out, for the time being, the conditions under which Milo had made this decision. She rested her toes on the frayed wicker bottom of the chair where her mother always sat and asked, "How are you doing?"

He pushed his spoon through his bowl. "I'm ashamed of myself. I love your mother. I love you girls. I never meant to do anything to jeopardize that."

"Then why?" she asked.

He stared at his soup as if he was going to find the answer spelled out in the noodles.

"I don't know if I have an answer for you."

"She wasn't even that pretty!" The words burst out of her mouth.

A ghost of a smile lifted the corners of her dad's lips. "You would have liked her," he said. "Under different circumstances."

Lizzie shook her head. She'd heard enough about the woman—the good schools, the law degree—to know that she'd have nothing in common with her father's ladyfriend.

Her father dropped his head, the smile gone. "She reminded me of . . ." His voice trailed off. "It doesn't matter."

She wondered how much any woman mattered to any man, whether they were all disposable. But Jeff hadn't treated her as if she were a take-and-toss girl, she thought, feeling shyly proud.

Jeff had acted as if she'd mattered. Of course, she assumed that would change as soon as he heard about what she'd done and why she'd left. She remembered the way he'd looked, the way his lips had tightened when he'd talked about his mother, and imagined he'd feel a similar disdain toward her.

"It wasn't about her." Now her dad was practically groaning, rubbing at his eyes with the heels of his hands. "She made me feel . . . important."

"Is it over?" Lizzie asked, and again, he nodded.

"It was never going to last. It was never about your mom and me. It was just . . ." He raised his hands, palms up, then let them fall to the table.

"Did you do this before?"

His answer came immediately. "No. Never."

"So why?" she asked. "I thought you and mom loved each other!"

"We do, Lizzie. Of course we do. We love each other, we love you girls. It was just . . ."

Meaningless, Lizzie imagined him saying. She lifted a spoonful of noodles and broth, then set it back in the bowl, untasted. *Just some girl.* It was, perhaps, the same reason a man would attempt any number of stupid, dangerous undertakings: because it was there. Because he could. Because he saw something and wanted it, and was used to getting everything he wanted. She remembered accompanying Diana and Milo to Nuts to You, the candy and dried fruit store on Walnut Street in Philadelphia, when Milo was a little guy, three or maybe four. Diana had been after flaxseed to put in her morning oatmeal, but as soon as Milo saw the bins and bags and boxes crammed with every manner of treat, he'd started grabbing at everything he saw. Licorice ropes, chocolate-covered macadamia nuts, raspberry jelly rings, foil-wrapped kisses, pillowy marshmallows, lollipops, taffy, gumdrops, wrapped hard candies. *I want! I want! I want!* he'd wailed, until Lizzie had gotten him out of the door. If you were a man like her father, the world was a kind of candy store, where anything you wanted was yours for the asking.

"Your mother and I," her father began. She looked at him—his pallor, the slack flesh of his cheeks, a streak of stubble on his chin that he'd missed while shaving—and braced herself, praying that he wasn't going to launch into some confession about their sex life. But instead of talking about how they didn't sleep together anymore, or how Sylvie was frigid or he was impotent with any woman who didn't dress up in black vinyl or a Smurf costume, her father said, "We've known each other a very long time. With . . . with her, it was a little like being young again. Before . . ." Before kids? she wondered. Before her? But instead, her father said, "Before anything went wrong."

She wondered what he was talking about. Was she the thing that had gone wrong, or was there something else, something she didn't know about and couldn't guess?

Her father got up from the table, taking his bowl with him. "I'm going to take a nap. I haven't been sleeping too well these days." She sat at the table, in front of her soup. Behind her, she could hear the water running, hear the click of a bottle cap landing on the granite counter and the glug-glug noise of beer being poured into a glass. Beer had never been her thing, but her father still wouldn't drink one in front of her, which was a little insulting but kind of sweet, too.

She washed their dishes and put them in the dishwasher and thought. What would happen for Thanksgiving? They had all these traditions: dinner at Grandma Selma's, which tasted awful but was, at least, traditional. They'd go to Chinatown Friday night, and out to a Broadway show afterward, and walk around Rockefeller Center on Saturday, looking in the shop windows, having tea at Takashimaya. On Saturday, Marta would come over, bundled in a down coat and a fur-trimmed hat, and she and the girls would always spend Saturday afternoon baking Christmas cookies, tray after tray of pfeffernussen and gingerbread men. Lizzie would have her camera, and she'd snap candid black-and-white shots of them in the kitchen, shots of the Christmas tree and the ice-skating, the turtles and the sea lions in the Central Park Zoo, and, sometimes, homeless men on grates, even though it made Diana roll her eyes and her mother look worried. One of her counselors in Minnesota—the same one, now that she thought about it, who'd said that both of her parents owned the decisions they'd made with regard to Lizzie—said maybe her picture-taking was a distancing strategy. "If you're taking pictures, it takes you out of the story," she'd said. "It turns you into an observer instead of a participant." Lizzie had disagreed. She thought her camera gave her something to do, a role to fill: the family historian, which was a lot better than being the family disgrace. But now she wondered whether there was something to it, whether having a lens between herself and her family, their apartment, their world, wasn't her unconscious way of keeping herself apart from them, and safe.

Lizzie kicked the dishwasher shut, the way Diana did, and decided not to worry about November now. For now, there was the empty refrigerator to contend with. She'd make a shopping list, ask her father for a credit card. After her summer with Milo, she could cook some basic stuff: organic chicken broth with noodles and cut-up bits of carrot, organic chicken nuggets and sweet-potato fries, oatmeal and fresh fruit.

"Hey, Dad," she called. "What's up with the laundry?"

He came into the kitchen, looking embarrassed. "That's been kind of piling up."

Kind of piling up turned out to be a sorry understatement. The wicker hamper in the master bedroom was overflowing with gamy sweatpants, socks, ripe-smelling T-shirts, button-down shirts and ties spotted with sauces, inside-out suit pants with boxer shorts still inside them . . . one pair of pants even had a shoe stuck in one of the legs. He stared at the pile helplessly. "I guess usually your mom takes care of this. Or gets someone to come in for August to help."

Lizzie pulled two pillowcases off the pillows on the bed and began sorting the laundry into piles of machine-washables and dry clean only. She sat cross-legged on the bed with her back against the headboard and her father standing beside her, holding up items for her inspection.

"So," her dad asked, when they were about halfway through the mountain of soiled clothes, "heard from your mom much?"

"A little bit," she said carefully.

"I worry about her," Richard said. "Up in that big house all by herself."

"You should go up there and tell her you're sorry," Lizzie counseled . . . and wasn't this rich? Her, giving advice to an actual grown-up, her dad, a senator. She wished, for a minute, that Diana could be there to bear witness . . . but Diana thought she was still the same irresponsible junkie, and that she'd put Milo in danger.

From the living room, the telephone trilled. "Lemme grab that," her father said. From the way he hurried to pick up the phone she guessed he hoped it was Sylvie. Lizzie gathered the laundry in her arms. Normally she'd use the machines in the apartment, but there was so much of it she thought maybe she should just take it to the wash-and-fold place around the corner. She'd drop off the dirty clothes and buy the things she'd cooked at Diana's house. That, at least, would be a start.

For three weeks, Lizzie took over her mother's duties, shopping and straightening, cooking simple meals, extracting her father's schedule from his Outlook Express, printing it out each morning and leaving it in a folder on the kitchen counter. She went to a meeting first thing in the morning, then collected the daily briefing binder that Joe Eido dropped off each morning and made sure her father read it. She kept track of his phone calls and appointments, his meetings with lobbyists and staffers, and kept the reporters who still occasionally called the house phone at bay. "I'm sorry," she would say in a coolly adult voice that sounded like her sister's, "the senator is unavailable." When she wasn't cleaning and cooking, she noodled around, editing the pictures she'd taken in Philadelphia. There was Milo, grinning and bare-chested in a spray of rainbow-sparkling droplets, after she'd coaxed him into going down the waterslide at Dutch Wonderland, and Milo riding the carousel at Franklin Square, standing on tiptoe in the wooden horse's stirrups, stretching one arm up to grab the brass ring while Jeff stood behind him. She put together a booklet of her best shots, had it printed on heavy, high-gloss paper, and sent a copy to Diana in Philadelphia. No note, but she thought her sister would know it was a peace offering. At night she talked briefly to her mother, and at length to Jeff. "Miss you," he said. "When are you coming back here?"

"Soon," she said, lying on her childhood bed with her camera balanced on her chest, feeling peaceful at the sound of his voice in her ear, and proud of the way she was helping her father. "I miss you, too, but right now, my dad really needs me."

At the start of the third week, with her father packing to start the congressional session, he called her into the office, sounding excited.

"Look what I found!" he said. Instead of using the sat-upon laptop, he had the desktop computer up and humming—a feat in itself, given that he was practically computer-illiterate—and he was pointing at something on the screen. Lizzie slipped beside him and looked at the "Welcome!" banner for FreshDirect. "Her whole shopping list is on here!" her father crowed, thumping at the keyboard and getting several "error" messages before, indeed, Sylvie's grocery list appeared. "All we have to do is point and click, and everything she got every week is just going to show up at our door."

They scanned through the list, murmuring items out loud: cheeses and crackers; cranberry juice; green grapes, one pound; fabric softener sheets and Tide detergent. With the arrow hovering over the "health and beauty" button, her father cleared his throat. "Do you need any, um, feminine things?"

For a minute, Lizzie wasn't sure what he meant. Once she realized, she started to tell him no, when the voice, the one she'd heard while looking in the mirror at Diana's house, asked, *How long has it been?*

She thought back. How many weeks had it been since she'd bought, or, more likely, borrowed Diana's napkins and tampons? Rehab was a blur, Philadelphia wasn't much better, and her periods had never been regular, which made it hard to keep track. Had she gotten her period at all this summer? And if not . . .

Her father was staring at her. "Lizzie?"

"Don't worry," she mumbled, through lips that felt frozen. "I can take care of it myself."

DIANA

When she was in the thick of her residency, working thirty-six-hour shifts, then going home to a preschooler and a husband who was more inclined to complain about his own lack of sleep than to help Diana address hers, there was a patient, a repeater, whom she saw every few weeks in the ER. The patient's name was Crystal, and Diana remembered her because she was exactly her age.

Crystal was a diabetic and an addict. Her drug of choice was crystal meth—Diana had occasionally wondered whether Crystal was actually her name or if she'd renamed herself after her favorite substance—but she'd take whatever she could get, or steal, or trade sex for. Heroin, cocaine, pills, pot, glue . . . every few months too much of one or all of the above would send her to the ER, stuporous, her blood sugar dangerously low. She'd shoot up, nod off, forget to eat, never mind monitoring her blood sugar, and she'd pass out, sometimes in an apartment and sometimes in a park or on a street. The cops knew her places. They'd keep an eye out, and if they found her, they'd scoop her up and bring her in.

On her first visit, Diana had mentioned rehab. Crystal had just laughed. "Forget it," she said, her voice rough and slurred. She'd chipped one of her front teeth during the prelude to this last trip to the hospital, but she was still beautiful, with high cheekbones and lush lips. "You don't think I've tried?" She shook her head, presumably in sorrow at Diana's naivete. "And what is there for me, if I clean up? Some job?" Her voice soaked the last word in scorn. "Some man who's gonna make an honest woman of me? Or do you think I'd go to college like you?"

"Maybe you could," Diana answered. She was at the end of an eight-to-eight shift, so exhausted that the world had blurred and doubled in front of her eyes. She told herself that all she really wanted to do was get enough glucose into her patient that she'd stabilize, sober up, and be able to make her way to wherever she called home. "I don't know what you could do. But I know it's not going to end well if you keep doing drugs."

Crystal threw her head back and laughed, "Be seeing you," and waved a jaunty goodbye when Diana left her cubicle.

The next time Diana saw her, she'd been beaten badly, one of those high cheekbones shattered, a tooth knocked out, her lip split and requiring stitches. She wouldn't say who'd done it, or why, and when Diana wheeled up on a stool and said that her internal had shown recent sexual activity and asked, gently, if she'd been raped, Crystal had merely shrugged and turned her face away.

"We could do a rape kit," Diana offered, feeling sick and sad, knowing that it was her job to make the offer and knowing, even before she'd made it, that Crystal would refuse. She'd shaken her bandaged head, braids whispering against the pillow.

"Now what good's that gonna do?" she asked. "I don't know who I was with. How we gonna catch 'em?"

"The police," Diana began, and Crystal hooted her rough laughter.

"I bet they'd make me a real priority," she said, and shook her head some more. "They'd get those detectives working in shifts."

The last time Diana had seen Crystal, there was a scar bisecting her lip, and a puffy mass of scar tissue over the healed cheekbone. She wore thigh-high boots, a hot-pink miniskirt, and a white lace top, underneath which her belly bulged like a basketball.

Instead of using a curtained-off exam cubicle, Diana took Crystal into the break room, pointed at a chair, and closed the door behind them. "Now you listen to me," she said as Crystal looked at her with insolent eyes. "If you can't get cleaned up for yourself, you need to do it for your baby. If that baby's born addicted, I'm going to have to report it to social services . . ." At this, Crystal sucked her lips. "They are going to take your baby away," Diana said, naming the worst thing that she could think of. "Do you hear me? Do you understand? They'll take your baby."

"You think I want this damn baby?" Crystal shot back.

"Yeah, I guess you do, since you're still carrying it," said Diana.

"You don't know anything," Crystal said with great finality. "Not anything about anything."

"I know they're going to take your baby," Diana said again, and Crystal, laughing, slid around Diana and out the door, shouting across the room to the nurses' station that somebody better find her a damn doctor who could help her, a real doctor, not this worthless white bitch.

Diana hadn't been able to fathom it. Addiction had never made sense to her—not Lizzie's, not Crystal's, not the movie stars whose troubles she'd read about in the tabloids when she was getting her hair done; not the food addicts or the sex addicts, not any of it. How could a woman, a mother, continue to get high when her own child was at stake? What feeling could be so compelling that you'd risk your son or daughter to pursue it?

But now, at thirty, she had learned a shameful truth—that there were things in life you were simply powerless to say no to. For some people—her sister, she supposed—that thing was a substance, liquor or powder or pills. For Diana, it was Doug. He was the thing she was unable to resist or give up, even though she knew it was wrong, even though he knew she was married, even though he was her student, even though she was risking everything to be with him, she couldn't stop or tell him no.

They did it in her office. They did it in a locked exam room with two of his fellow interns chatting not ten feet away. They did it in the backseat of the Civic, which Doug would park in the farthest corner of the lowest level of a parking garage on Broad Street. They did it in the handicapped stall of the women's restroom at the Prince Theater. They did it—God help them—in a cemetery in Strawberry Mansion one hot afternoon, Diana leaning back on a tombstone, with her skirt hiked up around her waist, her panties (black lace ones she'd bought for thirty-eight dollars, which was more than she'd ever spent on underwear in her life) down around her ankles, and Doug kneeling in front of her, licking between her legs until she gasped and pleaded with him to stop.

In bed, sweaty and glowing, Doug would trace the line of her deltoids, her quads, her calves, licking the tender skin underneath her ear, whispering, "I love that you're so strong."

"I love you," she'd whisper too softly for him to hear, while inwardly thinking, *This is the last time. After this, no more. Tomorrow, I'll tell him goodbye.*

But that was a promise she'd been making to herself on a regular basis—say, every morning. Shaving her legs, blow-drying her hair, loading Milo's lunch into his backpack for computer camp while Gary readied himself for the day, leaving a trail of wet towels, whiskers, and dirty dishes in his wake, she would list the things that she could lose: her marriage, her job, possibly even Milo. She could imagine Gary, tall and formidable in a suit and tie, standing in a courtroom, making his case for custody: *Your Honor, this woman carried on a flagrant affair with a younger man: a med student. Her student. What kind of mother does that?*

What kind of mother, Diana would ask herself, and promise that she'd stop. At the bus stop, waiting with Milo, she'd chat about the weather and the homework assignments and set up playdates with the other moms, some of them in business suits, others in workout wear, all of them ready to begin blameless days that would not involve torrid sex with a twenty-five-year-old in the backseat of said twenty-five-year-old's mother's car. Sick with guilt, she'd talk to them, her face a smiling mask as she voiced expected complaints about the school's tuition and the bus driver's habitual tardiness, while in her head she'd be promising to change. She'd take up hot-room yoga or Pilates, like Samantha Dennis, who came to the corner every morning in Lycra tights and a hot-pink sports bra that barely restrained her implants. Or maybe she'd quit medicine, pick up an MBA, and go for the big bucks like Lisa Kelleher, who did something with the stock market, and wore a Rolex as big as the Ritz. Diana could make a different life, a better life, a life that did not involve breaking her vows and betraying her husband and sentencing her son to a Wednesday-night-and-Saturday-afternoon father. Her whole life had been scheduled and correct—college and med school and marriage and motherhood, the house, the car, the career. Now she was off the map, off the grid, behaving like someone she didn't recognize and of whom she would not approve.

Her resolve to give him up would last her until ten o'clock. That was usually when Doug would find a moment to text her. She'd be in one of the exam areas, scribbling down a history, taking a woman's blood pressure or listening to a man's lungs, when her BlackBerry would tremble in her pocket. She'd pull it out and read the words *HI PRETTY,* and she would melt, her pulse quickening, feeling hot and liquid between her legs. Had anyone ever called her "pretty"? The most Gary ever managed was a "you look nice." By the time Doug texted *can I c u?* her mind would be churning with possibilities. Her office? His car? A room at the Society Hill Sheraton, where the clerks always seemed to be smirking at her when she checked in under the name Becky Sharpe and slid cash across the counter?

Once they went to his apartment. Doug and three other students rented a place on Tasker Street in a neighborhood poised on the border between seedy and hip. That afternoon, after he'd texted *come 2 me,* Diana pulled her raincoat's hood over her hair, even though it was barely drizzling, and raced over and up two flights to his place. He opened the door and she threw herself into his arms, and, together, they tumbled through the living room (she caught glimpses of the expected beer bottles, and absurdly gigantic TV on the way) and onto Doug's bed, breathing hard, so turned on that she could barely take time to do more than pull down her pants. They'd done it fast first, just to take the edge off, and then Doug had undressed her, slowly, sliding off sleeves and straps, nipping at her shoulders, the curve of her elbow, the small of her back, lavishing kisses over every inch of skin he touched. He hadn't shaved, hadn't brushed his teeth, either, but Diana found the prickles of his beard against her skin, the slightly sour taste of his mouth, unbelievably arousing. She was so wet, she could feel the insides of her thighs getting slippery with it, so hot she couldn't keep from touching herself, her fingers gliding between her legs as Doug slid just the tip of his cock into her mouth, then pulled it out.

"Get on the bed," he said. It wasn't a request. Diana lay back on his rumpled sheets, spreading her legs as wide as she could.

"Please," she whispered.

"What?" he asked, his voice rough. "Tell me. Tell me what you need."

Diana could hardly believe the words coming from her mouth. She'd never been so aroused in her life, not with Hal, not with anyone. "Please fuck me, please fuck me, I need it so bad . . ."

"You want it?" he grunted, kneeling between her parted thighs, one hand sliding slowly up and down his cock.

Well, I think I made that clear, she thought . . . but the part of her brain that was thinking that, the part of her brain that still could think at all was a small part indeed. Doug placed his other hand between Diana's legs, slipping in one finger, then two, then three. "Please," she panted, raising her hips higher, rocking them back and forth, trying to get him to push harder, more deeply. "Oh. God. Please."

He pulled out his hand and slid his cock inside her. She made a high, whinnying sound and wrapped her legs around his waist, tilting her hips, squeezing her eyes shut, thinking that nothing mattered, nothing in the whole world mattered as much as this.

Twenty minutes later, she'd turned her panties back right-side-in, buttoned her skirt with trembling hands, and stood at the door, her mouth welded to Doug's. "Tonight?" he whispered when they finally stopped kissing. She nodded. "You're gorgeous," he said, tucking a lock of her hair behind her ear. She clung to him, unable to speak, practically unable to move, until he put his hands on her shoulders and turned her toward the street.

She spent every day in a fever, trembling and dry-mouthed as she went through the motions of normal life. She'd tend to her patients and her charting, sit through Wednesday meetings about how to handle a potential flu vaccine shortage and a looming nurses' strike with her thighs clamped together and her favorite scenes playing in her head. After work, she would push her cart through the grocery store, watching her hands pick up apples and milk and organic chicken as if she'd never seen such items, or even her hands, before. At home as she would unload the bags, restock the refrigerator, do the laundry, make the beds, and cut up apples for her son, she'd be overcome by a memory of Doug: she'd imagine the taste of his skin, the way he groaned "oh, baby," when she curled between his legs and took his cock in her mouth, the way he looked, kneeling above her, stroking himself, saying, "You want it?" looking down at her as if she was the most gorgeous, the most precious and desirable thing he'd ever seen. She was strong—Doug often praised her body, the muscles of her legs, the grace with which she moved—but he was stronger, she thought, both physically and emotionally. He was the one making the decisions, telling her when they'd meet, and where. When they were in bed together, he'd move her as if she were as dainty as a doll, and it felt good to her, so good she could barely believe it, and could not imagine living without it, to have the man be the strong one.

Doug knew that she was married—she'd blurted out that information, teary and breathless, after their first night in the backseat. "So what's your husband like?" Doug had asked. Diana had thought about how to answer that, about what anecdote or example she could give that would sum up the ways Gary had disappointed her. Finally, she came up with, "His fantasy football team is called Double Penetration." Doug had laughed, and she'd hit him playfully on his chest. "It's funny! I'm sorry," Doug had protested, so she'd never bothered mentioning that when Gary commented on YouTube videos, his screen name was ItBurnsWhenIPee, because, probably, he would have laughed at that, too, and she'd never told him about Milo at all.

Doug didn't know she was a mother, and she was a good mother, maybe better than she'd been before things had started. When Milo came home from school on Tuesdays and Thursdays, trudging through the door with his heavy backpack over his shoulders, she'd take him on mother-son adventures, the kinds of outings Lizzie had taken him on, although Diana tried not to think about her sister, and whether Lizzie might have been telling the truth about the Advil, and whether Diana had kicked her out not to keep Milo safe but to ensure that her inquisitive little sister wouldn't learn her secret. She'd let Milo leaf through the pages of one of the free weeklies (after she'd tossed the sex ads in the back) and pick out a place to visit, a museum or a gallery or a restaurant, or they'd go to his favorite, the Academy of Natural Sciences, where Milo would stare, entranced, at the dinosaur bones for as long as she'd let him. She'd loosened up a bit about his diet—she still made sure he got plenty of fresh, unprocessed fruits and vegetables, but she'd take him out for pizza once a week, and let him get the ice cream she knew Lizzie had given him after they stopped by Head House Books for the latest installment of the *Wimpy Kid* saga. At home, they'd put on their pajamas and watch DVR'd episodes of *American Idol,* sometimes even singing along. They'd play backgammon or Yahtzee, eating apple slices dipped in peanut butter, while Milo talked about his day. "Well, actually," he would begin his sentences, or "Well, basically." She suspected he had a crush on his teacher, Miss Pai, who was young and beautiful and wore gold bracelets and an alluring perfume, and they spent hours making her a card for her twenty-fifth birthday.

Milo was the only thing that could get her mind off Doug . . . but eventually, Milo went to bed, leaving Diana awake, moving restlessly through the house, refolding laundry, wiping down already-clean counters, running the half-filled dishwasher just to have something to do. The weekends were almost unendurable. Locked in the bathroom ("Diarrhea again?" Gary complained. "Seriously, Diana, can't you prescribe yourself something?"), she'd text Doug, and then wait, frantic as a teenager, until he responded. *Adore u. Miss u. Can't w8 2 C u.* If he went longer than a few minutes without answering, she was consumed with despair, and with jealousy, especially on Saturday nights, when she was stuck at home and he, she was sure, was out at parties, with beer and music and any number of young, pretty, available, appropriate girls who would love him and want him for all the reasons she did.

For weeks, she'd fall asleep with her head full of Doug, full of longing and fear, imagining what they'd done and what they'd do when they were together again. When Gary reached for her, as he still did once in a while, she'd make up an excuse: "I've got my period," she would say, thinking that she was lucky it would never occur to him to notice whether or not there were tampons visible in the bathroom. Or she'd tell him she had a headache, ostentatiously swallowing Advil when he was around to see it.

Nobody knew except her friend Lynette, one of the RNs who worked in the emergency room. Three weeks into the affair—if such a dignified word could be applied to what Diana realized was a tawdry situation—she and Lynette had been on their way to grab lunch at the falafel shop when Doug had walked past them on the street. They'd said hello, nothing more, but Lynette had given her a sly grin. "A friend?" she'd asked. Something on Diana's face must have given her away, because instead of staying in the shop with their salads, Lynette had tugged Diana back to the hospital and directly into the locker-lined break room, where she'd picked up a pen that read VALTREX, as if she was about to take notes, and said, "Tell me everything. Every single detail. I want to hear every single thing you're doing with that luscious boy."

"Nothing's going on," Diana had insisted . . . but she couldn't keep herself from smiling. *Luscious boy*. That was Doug.

"Come on," said Lynette, gathering her braids into a twist that she secured with the Valtrex pen. "I am forty-two years old and I don't think I've slept for more than five hours straight in the last twelve years. The highlight of my week is Kevin's poker night, when I can eat Chinese food and watch *Top Chef*. Throw an old lady a bone."

Diana had perched herself on the edge of the chair. "You know," she began, "that things with Gary aren't so great."

Lynette had nodded. "Yes, yes, you've lost that loving feeling; calls himself ItBurnsWhenIPee; go on, go on."

Diana's blush deepened. Was her marriage that predictable and sad, that easy to sum up? She made a mental note to limit herself to a single glass of wine the next time she joined the nurses for karaoke Fridays, and continued. "Well, the thing is, Doug . . . Doug and I . . ."

Lynette, meanwhile, was curving her fingers into cat's claws and making *mrraow! mrraow!* sounds—the universal mating call of the cougar.

Diana buried her face in her hands. "He's not that much younger," she said in a muffled voice. "And I know. It's awful. But I can't . . ." She peeked through her fingers to find Lynette staring at her.

"Oh my God," she said. "Are you in love?"

Diana wasn't sure if this was love or just a desperate infatuation. "It's pretty intense," she said. "Pretty . . ." She was remembering the time in the graveyard, the marble warm underneath her bare thighs, Doug's tongue quick and hot between her legs. "I've never felt like this before in my life," she blurted.

"Oh my God," Lynette said again—she was, Diana thought, turning out to be surprisingly devout. "Tell me about his body. Is he a good kisser? Ooh, I bet he's a good kisser. Where do you guys go?"

Diana curled up in her chair and told her—not the gory details, or the embarrassing ones, not about sitting next to her son in bed, reading to him while Doug's semen trickled out into her panties, but about the in-love feeling that had been absent for so long in her life. From the avid way Lynette listened, she thought maybe she wasn't the only woman quietly withering away in a marriage that looked all right from the outside—the house, the kids, the cars—but inside felt as arid as a locked room in an abandoned building.

"Well, I can't say I'm surprised," Lynette finally said. "It happens a lot."

Diana nodded glumly. She'd seen it, too: the distinguished cardiothoracic surgeon who had to be almost seventy and who took one of his fellows as a mistress every July and dumped her, firmly but courteously, the following June; the gastroenterologist so notorious for luring nurses into his office and asking them to take off their tops that he was now required to keep his door open at all times. Except in all the examples she could think of, it was always the male docs who treated the hospital as their personal harem, never the ladies.

She also knew what it could mean if someone found out she'd been messing with an intern. She'd get a reputation, not the kind any lady doctor wanted, and the plum assignments and promotions wouldn't come her way. Just add it to the pile, she thought bleakly. Add it to the list of things she was willing to sacrifice on the altar of love, or lust, or whatever it was she had for Doug Vance.

"Just be careful, Diana," Lynette said, with all the joking gone from her voice. "You're my friend, and I don't want to see you get hurt."

Diana nodded. She was, of course, being careful already. She deleted every text she sent and received, and erased Doug's number from her call log if they spoke on the phone. Theirs would not be an affair of love letters and long weekends and public displays of affection. They couldn't even share a meal—the times they'd tried to grab a burger or sushi or even takeout Chinese, they hadn't been able to keep their hands off each other long enough to take more than a bite or two. What they had—all they'd have—were snatched moments in semipublic places, afternoons in hotel rooms that smelled like the last person who'd stayed there, and texts that used abbreviations and emoticons to express the words they could not say. There was no future.

Diana decided her only hope was that this would burn itself out, that there would be some natural end to it. Passion like this couldn't last. They'd get caught, or they'd both starve to death. Already she'd lost six pounds, the inevitable by-product of having sex instead of lunch (the good news about that was, it gave some credence to her claim of chronic diarrhea). Doug would meet someone else, someone appropriate, maybe one of his fellow med students, and that would be that; he'd move on and she'd be brokenhearted, but eventually, the madness would loosen its grip and she'd be free once more to become the woman she'd always been.

LIZZIE

Before she started and stopped two colleges, before she was ransomed and sent away to rehab, before she moved to Philadelphia, before she met Jeff, Lizzie and her best friend Patrice had discovered a television program called *I Didn't Know I Was Pregnant.* The show, true to its title, featured a series of women, represented in dramatic reenactments, who did not, in fact, realize that they were pregnant until they went into labor, which they universally failed to recognize as labor, and surprised themselves and their loved ones and sometimes the paramedics by pushing out a baby.

Lizzie's memories of the past decade were patchy, a moth-eaten lace doily hanging together by threads, but she had an indelible recollection of the last time she and her friend had watched the show. "This is bullshit," Patrice had said, setting down her MegaGulp and picking up the bong. "*I didn't know I was pregnant.* I mean, excuse me, but how are you not gonna be knowing some shit like that?"

Lizzie had giggled. Lizzie was a great giggler and snorter even when she wasn't high—and, she'd learned in the years following her twelfth birthday, dope made almost everything funny.

"Bullshit," Patrice repeated, wrapping her lips around the glass pipe. "Bull. Shit." Patrice was eighteen and lived in the

Pembroke House apartment building, with her nephrologist mother and neurosurgeon dad, both of whom were constantly on call and neither of whom kept careful track of their prescription pads. Patrice had spent her summer vacation at the Wellspring Center, dealing with the eating disorder that had left her at seventy-eight pounds, with every ridge of her rib cage and bump of her kneecap or clavicle visible beneath the covering of fine blond fur that her body had grown to keep itself warm. Lizzie reasoned that Patrice's parents knew their daughter was a pothead—her clothes and hair always had that telltale skunky reek—but maybe they didn't mind. Pot equaled munchies, and Patrice's weight was back into the triple digits, so probably they figured it was an acceptable trade-off. Potheads didn't drop dead of heart attacks. They just watched dumb TV shows and laughed a lot, and okay, so maybe they weren't the most productive members of society, but she and Patrice weren't hurting themselves (at least not that much), and they definitely weren't hurting anyone else.

"My periods had never been regular, and I went on the pill, so I thought we'd be safe. One night, my stomach just started killing me, but I thought it was bad sushi," said the girl on the screen, holding her nine-month-old surprise visitor in her arms.

"Bad sushi," Patrice said, and passed the bong Lizzie's way. "Baaaad suuuushiiiii."

Lizzie laughed and laughed, choking on the smoke. Patrice smacked her leg. "Pay attention!" she cried. "The baby's coming!" Lizzie set the bong on the coffee table, and the two of them leaned forward as the actress portraying the episode's ignorant pregnant lady crouched on the toilet.

"I was trying to have a bowel movement," the real-life lady reported, in case there was any doubt about what all that straining and grunting were meant to convey. "I thought if I could just have a bowel movement I'd feel better and I'd be able to go to sleep."

Patrice squinted at the screen. "You know," she said, "that's actually kind of harsh. I mean, someday her kid's going to see this and know that his mom thought he was a bowel movement."

"Harsh," said Lizzie, who thought she knew a little bit about what it was like to feel like a less-than-wanted, less-than-ideal child. The actress sat on the toilet, bracing her arms against the walls, and pushed with all her might. "And then I heard a splash . . ." said the mother's voice-over.

"A splash!" Patrice and Lizzie cried.

". . . and a thunk," she continued.

"Oh, Jesus," Lizzie murmured. She hated this part. "Thunk!" Patrice was laughing so hard that she'd rolled herself into a hundred-pound ball on the floor. "Thunk!"

"I turned around, and I saw this cord . . ."

"Ew!" Patrice and Lizzie shrieked, as the actress, looking shocked, turned on the toilet and followed the swollen, purplish-blue cord down into the blood-spattered bowl and retrieved a slimy, white-streaked baby (Lizzie knew it was probably a doll, but it looked so real!).

"And that's another thing," said Patrice, catching her breath. "They shouldn't call this show *I Didn't Know I Was Pregnant.* They should call it *I Pooped a Baby.*"

"Patrice!" said Lizzie. She flopped back on the couch, accidentally knocking the bong to the floor. Bong water—the stinkiest liquid known to mankind—instantly soaked the carpet.

Patrice had scrambled to her feet and was standing on top of the couch, gazing down at the spreading, stinky brown puddle. "Oh," she said. "Oh shit. Hey, Lizzie, we should clean that up, right?"

They'd gone to the kitchen for rags and Comet, which, Lizzie reasoned, was what you wanted for a tough and smelly stain. They'd sprinkled the Comet on the rug, and laid the rags on top, and stood on top of them, sopping up the mess until another unsuspecting pregnant lady came on TV. This one thought she was too old to get pregnant, and figured that the growing bulge in her midriff meant she was eating too many carbs, so she'd gone on a diet, until the fateful day when she'd rushed to the hospital with crippling stomach pains, certain that she was dying of cancer, only to discover . . .

"Lizzie?" Lizzie looked up from the couch, where she'd fallen into a pleasant doze, to find her mother staring at the two of them. Sylvie wore a Chanel suit—black, with beige trim on the pockets, and matching beige pumps. A leather attaché case was under her arm, and she looked tired. Lizzie struggled to remember what she'd been doing—some luncheon, some speech, some something—as Sylvie sniffed the air. "What's going on?"

Quickly Lizzie used her foot to roll the bong underneath the couch, while Patrice, under the guise of helping herself to a handful of chips, grabbed the lighter.

"Nothing!" Lizzie said brightly. "We're just watching TV."

"No homework?" Her mother's nose wrinkled. Lizzie took a surreptitious sniff. It still smelled pretty bad in the living room. "Did you spill something?"

"Just a little soda," said Patrice.

"What's that smell?" Sylvie asked. She bent and took off one high-heeled shoe, then the other.

"Mother," Lizzie hissed, shooting Sylvie a stern look, one she hoped her mother would interpret as a cue not to ask too many questions about smells when Patrice was around. For a while, in the throes of her eating issues, she'd allowed herself nothing but kimchee, and her farts could clear rooms.

Sylvie looked at them for another long moment before walking, barefoot, down the hall, to Lizzie's dad's office, where she'd probably plan another party, a picnic or a parade or a Rotary Club sit-down, a street fair or a Jewish holiday where Diana, in her second year of med school, would be trotted around like

My Pretty Pony, and to which Lizzie would most likely not be invited.

"Close call," breathed Patrice, retrieving the bong, wrapping it in a towel, and tucking it into her bookbag. Lizzie thought of explaining that she could have been shooting heroin in front of her mother, her arm tied off with surgical tubing, the needle right there in her vein, and Sylvie would have chosen not to notice. *Oh, it's just vitamins,* Lizzie would say, and Sylvie would give a vague wave, then retreat to the office to do something else for Lizzie's dad.

Patrice scooped up the snacks, and shook her head once more at the screen, where yet another hapless mother was recounting giving birth on the toilet. "Tell you what," she said. "If I was pregnant, I'd be knowing that shit."

I'd be knowing that shit, Lizzie thought. At the Duane Reade on Seventy-second Street she pulled her baseball cap low over her forehead, on the off chance that someone would recognize a disgraced senator's daughter shopping for sundries at eleven o'clock in the morning. Grabbing a plastic basket from a stack by the door, she loaded it with shampoo and deodorant, lip balm and skin cream, ponytail holders and razors . . . and then, in the Feminine Needs aisle, she bought tampons, napkins, and two home pregnancy tests.

I'm wrong, she thought. *I've got to be wrong. We just did it that one time. No one can be so unlucky.* Up in the apartment, she walked through the entryway lined with family photographs: her father at his inauguration, her father with the president, her parents all dressed up, dancing at some ball. These were all pictures other people had taken. She'd taken shots of her parents over the years, getting ready for parties or returning from them, but they'd never hung her work. They'd thank her and lavish praise on the framed pictures, but Lizzie didn't know where they put them—only that she'd never seen them hung.

She dropped her purse on the table by the door and locked herself in the bathroom where she'd spent large swaths of her adolescence, rifling through the medicine cabinet, or puking, or under the influence, studying the fascinating topography of her face in the mirror. She read the instructions, then squatted over the toilet with first one indicator stick, then the other, beneath her, counting to five, then setting the sticks on the side of the sink and squeezing her eyes shut. One Mississippi, two Mississippi . . . after two minutes, she wiped, flushed, washed her hands, and looked at the sticks. One of them had two bright, distinct blue lines. The other had a plus sign. And even Lizzie, who'd nodded out in health class and skipped out on science, knew exactly what that meant.

Just tell him, Lizzie thought to herself, the way she'd been thinking for the two weeks since she found out she was pregnant. She got off the train at the 30th Street station and followed the crowd of passengers up the escalator and out to the street. Telling him was the right thing, the adult thing, to do. At least she was pretty sure that was the case. She would tell Jeff it was a mistake. God knows it was the truth, she thought, as she plodded along the sidewalk. She hadn't been trying to trap him or trick him. It had just happened . . . and she would take care of it herself.

Jeff had sounded happy to hear from her the night before when she'd told him she'd be in town to visit her nephew and her sister. She'd been avoiding his calls ever since the positive pregnancy test, certain that if she spoke to him she'd wind up blurting out the news. When she finally called he'd asked if she was mad at him; if he'd done something wrong. "No," she'd said, trying to sound as if she meant it. "No, I've just been busy. I'm not mad. Everything's fine."

"I've missed you," he said, his voice warming. "Are things okay with your sister?"

"I think so," she said.

He paused, then asked, "Do you want to stay over?" It was all Lizzie could do to keep from groaning out loud. If this hadn't happened, she would have loved to spend a night in his sweet-smelling treehouse of a bedroom, snug in bed with him, warm and happy. But now . . . "Let's play it by ear," she said, even though she was pretty sure that once she gave him her news, the last thing he'd want would be her company. Probably he'd be angry at her, she thought, remembering how his jaw had tightened when he'd talked about his mother . . . and here she was, another irresponsible female, messing up his life.

She'd packed a bag, just in case, and then, steeling herself, she'd called her sister, leaving the same message on her home phone and her cell phone and her e-mail and her pager: *I'm sorry for the misunderstanding* (not that the misunderstanding was her fault, but she could afford to be the bigger person here—she knew the voice that had told her *You can do this* would concur on this matter). *I'm coming to town. I would like to see you and Milo.* None of her messages had gotten a response.

She walked through the gathering clouds all the way to Washington Square, which took her almost forty minutes. It was a gloomy gray day with a brisk wind blowing, and she wished she'd brought a sweater, and worn jeans and actual shoes instead of billowy cotton pants that ended mid-shin and flip-flops. She took the elevator up to Jeff's apartment on the eleventh floor, making her way slowly down the hallway with her bag over her shoulder. She'd barely finished knocking when the door swung open, and there was Jeff, barefoot, in jeans and a collared shirt, with his hair still wet from the shower.

"Lizzie," he said, and pulled her into his arms for a hug. They stepped into the apartment, with its family photos on one wall, its bright posters on the other, and—she squinted, making sure—the photograph she'd taken of him, the first night she was over, in a frame on the kitchen table. She looked over his shoulder, through the big window. From eleven floors above the street, the park looked like a puzzle, with wedges of green and lines of gray and the round fountain splashing in its center. "You look great," said Jeff.

She doubted that this was true. Whether it was the hormones or the stress, she had a major zit on her chin, and her hair, in its customary bun, had gotten tangled on her way over. Holding her hand, Jeff walked her to the couch—she could see he'd fluffed the pillows and folded the blanket draped over its back. She wondered whether he'd planned on pulling her onto his big, soft bed for a predinner quickie. She could smell something cooking in the kitchen, the rich smells of garlic and onions and chicken, she thought, roasting in the oven, and all she wanted to do was take off her clothes and be with him on that big blue-quilted bed. Was this normal? Were pregnant ladies even supposed to get horny? Maybe there was something wrong with her.

Jeff leaned in for a kiss. Lizzie turned her head away. "Can I talk to you for a sec?" she asked.

Looking puzzled, Jeff shrugged and stepped aside, letting her walk past him. "Sure thing." Lizzie pulled her bag off her shoulder and pressed it against her midriff. Jeff sat on the couch while she stood by the window that looked out over the cloudy sky and the clean-angled lawns of the park, and spoke without turning to face him.

"So listen," she said. *Soonest begun, soonest done,* Grandma Selma always said. Lizzie's hands and knees were trembling, the muscles in her legs were twitching. She wanted to move, to hurry back out into the hallway, down the elevator, out onto the street, to run away from what she had to tell him.

"Whatever it is, you can tell me sitting down," he said, patting the cushion again, but Lizzie knew better. Start on the couch, and end up in the bed. She took a deep breath, trying to still her jittery body . . . but when she opened her mouth she found that she could barely speak. All her good intentions had evaporated; all her words were gone.

He was staring at her. "What is it?" he asked again.

"I'm . . ." She swallowed hard, then said, "I'm an addict."

Jeff's face was as shocked as if she'd slapped him. "What?"

Lizzie bent her head, not wanting to see the way his eyes had widened and his mouth had dropped open. "I was in rehab this spring, before I started working for Diana."

"So you're okay now?" Before she could answer, he gave an unhappy laugh. "Never mind. Stupid question. If I told you how many times I heard my mom . . ." He pressed his lips together hard.

"Heard her what?" Lizzie whispered. Jeff got to his feet and walked to the window.

"Heard her say that she was fine. That she was done drinking forever. Forever was usually a couple of months. Then it would all start again."

She was gripping the straps of her bag so hard that her knuckles were white. "I'm so sorry," she whispered. "I should have told you."

Jeff exhaled, shoving his hands in his pockets and finally turning toward her. "No. It's . . . I mean, you were going to tell me eventually, right?"

"Of course," said Lizzie, who actually wasn't sure. She'd never thought in terms of *eventually.* She'd never had a guy hang around that long.

He turned to look at her. "So are you okay? Do you think . . . ?" His voice trailed off. He stared at her hopefully and she knew, looking at his open face, that she couldn't go through with it, couldn't tell him the rest of it. He'd had a drunk for a mother, and she had failed him, that was clear. How could Lizzie tell him she was pregnant, pregnant and, in Jeff's mind, getting ready to start the same sad dance over again?

"I think I'm okay," she said. "I think I'm actually done with it. I think I'm going to be fine."

"Yeah?" Everything about him—the look on his face, the tone of his voice, the way his body had turned toward her—said that he wanted to believe it. *Time to go,* Lizzie thought. *Time to go before I tell him everything and break his heart.*

"What time is it?" she asked.

Jeff looked puzzled. "Five-thirty."

"Oh my God! I totally forgot! I told Diana I'd pick Milo up after his chess club . . ." She slung her bag over her shoulder. "I've got to run."

"Wait," he said. "Hang on. You just got here! What about dinner?"

"I'll come back," she said.

He still looked puzzled as he held the door open for her. "I'll walk you down."

"No, no, I'll be fine. I can just grab a cab on Walnut Street."

Poor Jeff looked astonished as he gestured toward the kitchen. "I can keep everything warm."

Lizzie felt her insides cramp. No boy had ever cooked dinner for her before. The guys she'd been with, she felt lucky if they had a few bucks for a slice of pizza. "I'll come right back," she promised . . . and then she stepped forward, stood on her tiptoes, and kissed his cheek, choking back a sob because she knew it would be the last time she touched him, the last time she was in these rooms, the last time she saw him. "You're a good guy," she whispered. *Find someone else,* she thought. *Be happy. You deserve it.*

"Thanks," he said . . . and then, before he could say anything else, she slipped past him, out the door.

• • •

Outside, it had started to drizzle. Rain spattered against her cheeks, mixing with her tears, and her sister still wasn't answering the phone. *Perfect,* she thought. Just perfect.

She knew she should go to a meeting. There was one at six o'clock, in the church on Walnut Street. Attending a meeting was the absolute most important thing, protecting her sobriety, there was the ticket, because if she started making bad decisions it would be like dominoes falling, one after another after another until she was worse off than she'd been before her parents exiled her to Minnesota. Go to a meeting . . . but first, she wanted dinner. In spite of what had happened in Jeff's apartment, in spite of her sorrow, Lizzie was starving. It didn't make sense. Or maybe it made perfect sense. Maybe it was because of the baby.

The baby. She thought of the words, then said them out loud. "The baby." The woman walking along the sidewalk next to Lizzie turned sideways and gave her a strange look. Lizzie shut her mouth. An actual baby, growing inside her. What a concept.

She walked through the rain, toward Diana's house, passing a sushi restaurant. Sushi sounded good, but she remembered reading somewhere that pregnant women weren't supposed to eat raw fish. Better to play it safe. The poor thing already had the deck stacked against it.

Burritos, read a sign that glowed orange in the drizzly twilight. She could do a burrito. She'd get one with chicken, with black beans and extra cheese and guacamole, and a big soda (was soda okay for pregnant ladies? Was there an app that could tell her?), and a brownie for dessert if they had brownies, and if they didn't she'd go find a place that did.

Ten minutes later, with a warm sack of food under her arm and her flip-flops squishy from the rain, Lizzie trotted down the sidewalk. Her sister's house was two blocks away and Lizzie still had her key. She only hoped that Diana and Gary hadn't been so disgusted with her that they'd changed the locks.

The rain was coming down steadily, and Lizzie was shivering, with her skirt pasted to her legs, as she pushed Diana's front door open. "Hello?" Lizzie called. "Diana? Milo? Anyone home?"

From the sound of it, nobody was. A BlackBerry—her sister's?—was plugged in and blinking on the little table by the front door. But the living room and kitchen were empty, the lights off. Gary's laptop was shuttered on the coffee table. The TV set was dark, the room was quiet and still.

Lizzie crept upstairs. If no one was home she'd just go up to the guest room on the third floor, have her dinner, and then take a little nap. Maybe she'd sleep straight through until morning without anyone even knowing she was there, and slip out when they'd all left for school and work. She was edging past the master bedroom on the second floor when she heard giggling, and then a deep, male voice, a voice that definitely did not belong to Gary, say, "Open your mouth. Do it now."

Lizzie froze. Oh, God. What if Diana was being raped? Except she'd been giggling, so maybe not. Except what if the rapist had told her to giggle, to act as if she was enjoying it, and Diana was, at this very moment, lying on the bed with a knife at her throat and some stranger doing horrible things to her?

Lizzie held her breath as her sister's voice rose in a croon that could have been pained or ecstatic. "Oh, God," Diana groaned. "Oh, God. Oh, God."

"You like that?" The man's voice was gloating, taunting. "Tell me you like it."

Pained, Lizzie decided. And what if the guy had Milo and Gary tied up somewhere? What if they were in the house, Diana's husband and her seven-year-old son, being forced to listen to this? The resounding smack of a slap made up her mind. She groped in her bag for a weapon. Finding only her burrito, she snatched the first thing she saw, which was an iron statue of the Buddha that Diana and Gary had gotten for their wedding from one of Gary's fraternity brothers who'd just returned from some kind of vision quest trip to Tibet. Diana had been completely nonplussed. Opening the box during the morning-after brunch, she'd scowled at the plump, cross-legged Buddha and said, "I don't think this was on the registry." "Lighten up, Diana," said Gary, who'd been hung over, and Diana had set the statue aside with a prissy little wince, mouthing *Get rid of it* to Lizzie, who instead had reboxed the Buddha and set it in a prime spot on the bookshelf when she and her mother were back at Diana and Gary's house unloading gifts.

Clutching the Buddha in her right hand, Lizzie grasped the doorknob with her left and threw the bedroom door open. There was her sister, naked, with her hands tied at the wrist with silk scarves to the bedposts and a man kneeling above her with his penis sandwiched between her breasts.

"Get out!" Diana shrieked, and wriggled sideways, forgetting that her hands were tied. The Buddha that Lizzie had meant to hurl as hard as she could thudded onto the comforter and bounced against her sister's hip. Diana hissed in pain as the man jumped off her and scrambled into his pants.

"Diana?" Lizzie said. Oh, God, this was horrible. Just horrible. She averted her eyes, but not before she noticed a livid hickey on the side of her sister's breast. Diana's hair was tangled, her pupils enormous, as if she'd been drugged. Maybe she had been drugged. Lizzie didn't know where to look or what to do. Untie Diana? Call the cops? Brain the guy with the Buddha?

"Lizzie, get out of here," Diana ordered.

"It's okay," Lizzie said bravely, figuring that Diana didn't want to be seen in this state. Keeping her eyes on the man as he struggled with his zipper, she flipped the covers up over her sister's torso. "Don't worry. I'll call the cops—"

"No!" said Diana and the guy, at the same time. Lizzie looked across the bed, where the guy had gotten his pants up and a button-down blue cotton shirt on. There was a nametag clipped to his shirt pocket. *DOUG VANCE.* What kind of idiot rapes a woman with his nametag on, Lizzie thought confusedly, before the guy started talking.

"It's okay," he said. His fingers flew over the row of shirt buttons. He had dark hair, flushed, ruddy skin, and the blocky build of a football player. "Diana and I know each other."

"You . . ." Lizzie stared at Doug Vance, then at her sister, still tied to the bed. Diana squeezed her eyes shut and rolled sideways, as far as the scarves around her wrists would let her.

"Could you excuse us for a minute?" Diana said.

Lizzie grabbed the Buddha off the bed and stepped outside the bedroom door. A few minutes later, her sister emerged, with her hair combed and her clothes on.

"Let's talk in the living room." There was a strange, pleading note in her voice. Lizzie followed Diana downstairs, where her sister, who rarely touched her, grabbed her hands. "You can't tell Gary," she blurted. "Please, Lizzie. You can't."

"Okay." Lizzie knew it was ridiculous, and that it probably meant she was a terrible person, but she found herself delighted with this new turn of events. No longer was she the family's number one fuck-up. Adultery. That was a bad one. So, of course, was pregnancy out of wedlock, but never mind that for now. Her perfect priss of a big sister, her married big sister, had a boyfriend! A kinky boyfriend!

"And don't tell Mom," Diana said.

"I think," said Lizzie loftily, "that Mom has enough to worry about right now." It was wrong, undoubtedly wrong to be tormenting Diana this way, but it was also an awful lot of fun.

Diana covered her eyes with her hands. "I feel like I'm losing my mind," she muttered. Then she looked at Lizzie. "What are you doing here?"

Lizzie rubbed her hands together, as the reason she'd come to Philadelphia came rushing back. "Just visiting a friend."

"That guy you were seeing?" Diana said. "Jeff?"

"Yep," said Lizzie . . . and then, because she couldn't resist, she said, "Maybe we can double date. Or would you have to bring Gary, too? Is that, like, a triple date?"

Diana balled her hands into fists, pressed them against her eyes and groaned out loud. The sound was thrilling and delicious. Without saying another word, Diana got off the couch and found her purse. As Lizzie watched, she started peeling off bills: twenty, forty, sixty, eighty dollars. "Here," she said, pushing the money at Lizzie. "Why don't you take yourself out to dinner?"

"I've got dinner," said Lizzie, remembering her burrito. "I thought maybe I'd say hi to Milo."

At the sound of her son's name, Diana groaned again, only more softly. "Milo's at the movies with Gary." She held out the money again. "Please, Lizzie. I really need to be alone right now."

"You're not alone," Lizzie pointed out, raising her eyes to the ceiling.

"Come on," Diana snapped.

Slowly Lizzie collected her things. She tightened the straps of her bag, folded the money neatly, and slipped it into her back pocket while Diana twitched beside her, in an agony of anticipation for her to be gone. "What was that about up there, anyhow?"

"It's none of your business."

"Well, yeah," Lizzie said. "I mean, under normal circumstances. But, given that I saw what was happening . . ."

Both women turned as Doug Vance, now fully clothed, came down the stairs. "I'll see you at work," he said to Diana, as casually as if they'd been having tea or playing badminton. He nodded at Lizzie—nodded! as if, not ten minutes ago, he hadn't been doing unspeakable things to her sister!—and gave Diana one more lingering look before letting himself out the door. As soon as he was gone Diana jumped to her feet. "I don't want to talk about it," she said, in case Lizzie had been confused, and she stood pointedly by the front door until Lizzie had no choice but to walk through it, back out into the cold, rainy night, back to the train station and then back up to New York, back home.

SYLVIE

There was a transistor radio in a cracked plastic case on the windowsill above the kitchen sink. Her grandmother had listened to Red Sox games on that radio, carrying it out on the porch and angling the antenna just so. She'd sit out there with whichever children and grandchildren cared to join her, sipping a beer and cheering at every home run as moths beat their wings against the porchlight.

On a cool day in October, with a white crescent of moon still visible in the blue morning sky, Sylvie stood in front of the sink, flipped past the all-news stations, and found Frank Sinatra singing "Summer Wind." Upstairs, the last of the sheets and down comforters clung to the barrel of the washing machine. Sylvie had made it a project over these past weeks, getting each of the bedrooms dusted and aired out, floors mopped and waxed, beds made with freshly laundered and ironed sheets and quilts. It kept her occupied during the days when she could have been, for example, listening to talk radio and crying, back when the Ballad of Joelle and Richard had still been news. It wasn't anymore, as far as she could tell. Richard had been right. His transgression had been a one-day story. The media had moved on to the pop singer accused of doing vile things to underage girls, and a basketball player who'd been caught fixing games. Richard's reputation and undoubtedly his approval ratings had sustained some damage, but he'd kept his job; that girl, Joelle, had presumably kept hers, too. What was it her daughters had said when they were young? *No biggie.* No biggie, she supposed, except to the people who were still living with it.

Sylvie kept her cell phone plugged in on her nightstand, and she'd check it every night before she went to sleep, counting the missed calls from Richard. Most days she got at least half a dozen. One Saturday there'd been ten. She never answered them. She wasn't ready for that yet. She would take off her clothes, pull on her nightgown, and stretch out on the sheets she'd washed and hung to dry in the sunshine. Her sleep was sound and dreamless. She saved her worrying for the daylight hours.

Worry Number One was Diana, whom Sylvie hadn't been able to reach for days. Diana's home phone just rang and rang—no surprise there, though; Sylvie knew that she and Gary hardly ever answered it, preferring to communicate by cell phone or e-mail or text—but Diana wasn't responding to any of those, either.

She talked to Lizzie regularly, but recent conversations with her youngest daughter had prompted Worry Number Two. Lizzie was back home, in their apartment, and she had started her job as a photographer's assistant. Both of those things were good, both promising, but Lizzie did not sound right. She didn't sound high or drunk, and that was a relief, but she sounded different in a way Sylvie couldn't name, except for the fleeting thought that Lizzie sounded more like her sister than like herself. Was she going to meetings? *Yes, Mom.* Was her job all right? *It's fine.* Was she taking care of herself? Eating well? Did she need someone to talk to? Was everything okay?

"Everything's fine, Ma," Lizzie said, in a tone that made it clear she had other things to do, other places to be.

"Have you talked to Diana?" Sylvie had finally asked the night before. "How is she doing?" She paused, then plunged ahead. "I haven't been able to reach her in days. I'm worried about her."

Lizzie gave a brief snort of laughter.

"What's going on?" Sylvie asked, feeling bewildered. "Is Diana okay?"

"Diana," said Lizzie, "is busy, I think."

"Busy with what?"

Lizzie paused. "Maybe you should ask Diana what she's busy with."

"Or you could just tell me." Sylvie tried to keep her voice pleasant, but it was a struggle. "For heaven's sake, Elizabeth, don't you think I've had enough surprises for one year?"

"Call her," Lizzie said.

"I do," Sylvie said. "She doesn't answer. Are you talking to her?"

"I haven't in a little while," Lizzie said.

"Well, if you happen to speak to her," said Sylvie, struggling with her temper, "would you mention that I've left her messages, and that I am concerned?"

"I'll tell her," Lizzie said. "I gotta go. I'm late."

"For what?" But instead of getting an answer, she got a dial tone. One daughter wasn't answering, and the other one was hanging up on her. That wasn't good at all.

Of course, she could always call Richard. Maybe he'd spoken with Diana. Sylvie thought it over, eventually deciding that she wasn't ready to brave a conversation with her husband . . . although at some point she'd have to. There was a sum just shy of ten thousand dollars in the joint checking account, which was the only account she could access. Ten thousand dollars could last her for a while, maybe as long as a year, if all she had to pay for were groceries and utilities and heating oil, but at some point, she'd need more money. She could try to get a job—but, realistically, who'd hire a fifty-seven-year-old attorney who'd been out of the workforce for decades? Her lawyering, she acknowledged, was more than a little bit rusty, and the skills she'd acquired during her years as a senator's wife were not, as they said, readily transferable. Not unless she could locate another powerful man who needed his life run for him.

She sighed, wiping the sink and squeezing out the sponge. The telephone burped. She let herself hope it was Diana, returning her messages, telling her she was all right, before seeing her mother's picture—her official portrait, in judicial robes and a lace collar—flash on the screen.

"Did you call a lawyer yet?" Selma said, in lieu of hello. Her New York accent made the word sound like *loy-uh.*

"Not yet," said Sylvie.

"Well, what are you waiting for?" Selma demanded. "You think he's getting any more faithful while you're up there ironing the sheets?"

Sylvie sighed. Telling her mother about her adventures in laundry had clearly been a mistake. "What can I do for you?"

"We should talk turkey," said Selma, her voice raspy and insistent. When Sylvie didn't respond, Selma said, "Thanksgiving? Hello? Happens every year?"

"Of course," Sylvie said. Her mother always hosted Thanksgiving, first in the big apartment she'd shared with her husband, then in her smaller but still impressive apartment at the Davidson Pavilion, the assisted-living place where she'd moved after Dave had had his first stroke. Diana and Gary and Milo and Lizzie and Richard and Sylvie would watch the Thanksgiving Day parade, choke down Selma's dry turkey and stuffing the consistency of spackle, and then adjourn to the living room for dessert: your choice of instant coffee along with pies from Sarabeth's, a homemade pumpkin pie that would be ignored by everyone but Richard, and a mixed-berry tart in a buttery crust. She remembered when the girls were little, combing their hair into ponytails, helping them into their Polly Flinders dresses and ribbed tights and Mary Janes. She recalled the year that Diana got tangled up in the curtain of beads her mother used to have hanging between the dining room and the kitchen, and the time Lizzie smoked some pre-parade pot and giggled nonstop while scooping pumpkin-pie innards directly from the pie plate into her mouth. She also had vivid recollections of the fellow Lizzie had brought with her that year. He was called Chuck or Chad, some name like that, a rich boy in a beautiful tie and a French-cuffed shirt who'd nodded off at her mother's table. "He's just tired!" Lizzie had insisted, and Diana, in her third year of medical school, had said, "If by 'tired' you mean 'high,' then yes, Lizzie, he's very tired."

Then there was the time Sylvie hated to think about, when she'd gotten back to the apartment—with a Tupperware container full of leftover turkey that she intended to toss immediately into the trash—to find the telephone ringing. "I don't want to alarm you, dear," Selma had said, "but I seem to be missing my pearls and my wedding ring." Sylvie had found the jewelry in her daughter's pocket, after Lizzie had tossed her jeans in the hamper and fallen asleep ("passed out," Diana said, with her hands on her sister's wrist, checking her pulse) in just her panties and a Barclay Prep T-shirt.

"Sylvie!" her mother was yelling. "Are you still there? Hello?"

"Yes, I'm here," she said.

"Well, are you coming?" her mother asked.

"I thought," said Sylvie, struck by a sudden inspiration, "that we could do Thanksgiving here."

Sylvie could practically hear her mother's canny brain turning. "No Richard?"

"No, no Richard." Maybe Tim, though. Tim was a possibility.

But how would she tell her mother, not to mention her daughters, that she'd been seeing someone? *Another man, Sylvie?* she could hear her mother sigh. *Really, do you think that's going to fix you? Is that the answer here?*

Tim wasn't an answer, she thought stubbornly. Tim was a reward, a reward for what she'd suffered. Listening to his stories about his sons, the trips they'd taken, the time they'd spent together, was like storytime at the library, where she'd taken the girls a few times when they were little. They'd sit cross-legged on the carpeted floor and listen, entranced by stories of magic beanstalks and houses made of candy. She listened the same way when Tim talked.

"If you really want to do it." Selma sounded dubious. "I'll bring the turkey."

"No!" The word burst out of Sylvie's mouth, a little more vehemently than she'd intended. "No. Just come. I'll take care of everything."

Selma sounded amused. "So now you're a cook?"

"I've made a few things." Driving aimlessly through Fairview's streets early one Saturday morning, she'd passed a tag sale, where there'd been a box full of dozens of old issues of cooking magazines, *Gourmet* and *Saveur* and *Bon Appétit*. "You can have them all for five bucks," said the woman, and Sylvie, who'd been prepared to offer twenty, eagerly handed over a five-dollar bill and loaded the box into her trunk. "They were my mom's," the woman said, and Sylvie knew without being told that the woman's mother had died . . . that her death might, in fact, have been what occasioned the tag sale, the boxes of cloth napkins and racks of blouses and coats; the piles of word-search and Sudoku books arrayed on the woman's lawn.

She'd taken the magazines home and spent much of the weekend, when she wasn't waxing the upstairs floors, poring over their stained and spotted pages. Some of the recipes had been dog-eared, and some had notes written in the margins: "needs more butter" beside a recipe for raspberry cobbler, "Bill likes" next to a chicken-and-sausage stew.

By Sunday night Sylvie had paper clipped a dozen things she thought would be good and, better, would be things she could make, if she got the right ingredients and followed the steps carefully.

Every morning, she'd wake up, feeling tiny and adrift, alone in a queen-size bed with the ache for the life she'd lost threatening to subsume her. The temptation would be to lie in bed all day, feeling sorry for herself. Instead, she'd force herself through her routines: up, out of bed, into her clothes, down to the kitchen. She'd drink coffee, brush her teeth, push her hair back from her face with a terrycloth headband that some cousin or tenant had left behind in the bathroom, loop her recycled shopping bags over her shoulder, and walk to Simmons's with her shopping list in her pocket. She'd buy her ingredients, maybe stop for tea and a muffin at the coffee shop downtown, then walk home and spend the afternoon in the kitchen, with the radio playing and the sunlight warming the linoleum. Most nights, Tim would come for dinner. It wasn't anywhere near as busy as the life she'd left behind, with eight A.M. board meetings and luncheons that stretched past three, sessions with the trainer and the daily barrage of e-mails and phone calls, but still, she filled the hours, she kept moving; and she tried as hard as she could not to think about Richard with Joelle, or about Richard alone, which was, somehow, worse.

The first Monday after she'd found the magazines she made soup, roasting butternut squash with sea salt, a slick of olive oil, and a drizzle of maple syrup, then scooping the flesh out of the shells and pureeing it with chicken stock and a bit of cream. Ceil had been thrilled to hear that Sylvie was continuing with her cooking and had offered ("threatened" was probably closer) to send Sylvie her immersion blender. "Picture Richard's face when you're whipping," she'd said. "Or maybe not his face." Sylvie had declined the offer. The next morning, she'd walked out onto the porch and bumped into a cardboard box from Federal Express, and opened it to find that Ceil had sent her one anyhow. *Every woman needs a room of her own,* the note with the box had said. *You've got room, so here's a blender.*

Since the blender's arrival, Sylvie had produced a credible lentil stew, cinnamon rolls from Ceil's recipe (lopsided, but still delicious), an approximation of her grandmother's fried chicken, and Indian pudding, after she'd woken up with an inexplicable craving for it one morning. She'd eaten two bowls of that, with heavy cream on top, and then scraped most of the remaining pudding into a Tupperware container and given it to Tim to take home, along with a half-gallon of French onion soup for which she'd made the stock, from beef bones, by herself. His sons, Frankie and Ollie, were coming for a weekend—they'd go camping, Tim said, the way they did every year. Normally Tim Junior came with them, but he was busy with the baby.

Cooking was a comfort. Making herself a good meal, food that would please her—not a trainer or a picky daughter or her husband—felt good, too. So did the rote work of cleaning up—the warm water on her hands as she washed her pots and pans, the satisfaction of spritzing a countertop with cleanser, then using a rag to wipe away all traces of her work. Arranging a bouquet she'd bought at the farmer's market that was held on the town green every Saturday, straightening the haphazard stack of cookbooks that had collected in the beach house over the years (including one that had to have been a gift to her Uncle Freddie and featured only recipes with beer), even the donkeywork of polishing the silver was satisfying.

But come Thanksgiving, Selma wouldn't be impressed by her daughter's adventures in the kitchen. Selma's generation had been born a little too late for *The Joy of Cooking,* and too early for Martha Stewart to reinvent the home as a laboratory-cum-art gallery in which a woman could exercise all of her creative energies and scientific impulses by whipping meringues and hanging her own wallpaper. Sylvie's mother saw the kitchen as a place of drudgery, a prison she couldn't escape fast enough, and, as a result, her dinners had fallen into two categories: reheated and frozen. Thanksgiving was the only meal she attempted to cook from scratch, and she could ruin even catered meals by sticking them in the oven and forgetting they were there.

On the telephone, Selma was still talking. "I'll send you my recipes," she said.

"Yes, Ma." Sylvie wondered whether the phrase *cook past the point of edible* figured prominently in the one for turkey.

Her mother's voice softened. "Are you doing all right? You're not lonely up there?"

"I'm fine," Sylvie said automatically. For the first time since she'd fled to Connecticut she found herself wondering about Clarissa and Derek. They worked for her but they were on Richard's payroll, Derek as a driver, Clarissa as a social secretary. She hoped that Richard had found them some other work, that he hadn't laid them off, that there weren't more people suffering because of what he'd done.

"I remember after your dad died, it took a long time before I stopped seeing him everywhere. I'd turn around and I'd catch a glimpse of him, out of the corner of my eye . . ." She paused. "Of course, Richard isn't dead," she rasped.

"True." Nor had Richard spent much time in the Connecticut house. Sylvie had never gotten used to seeing him there, coming in from the porch with the paper, or rounding the corner into the kitchen with an empty coffee mug in his hand, so she wasn't seeing him now. This was her house, her place, with her meals and her memories. She'd washed the curtains and waxed the floors, she'd made each bed and reorganized every closet. She'd thrown out the mouse's corpse, and that, more than anything else made this place hers. "Can I ask you something?"

"Ask," said the Honorable Selma.

"Do you think . . ." Sylvie tried to choose the right words. *Should I have seen it coming? Was it my fault?* In spite of the routines she'd strung together, in spite of Tim's company, she still felt unmoored and desperately lonely. She'd lost her husband, her best friend, her personal and professional identity, not to mention her job, all in the span of a few terrible hours, and her daughters, for better or worse, were grown women. Who was she now? What was her purpose? "Was I a good wife?" she finally asked.

"Sylvie," her mother said, her voice insistent and confiding. "You were a better wife than he deserved. You are a wonderful mother to your daughters."

Sylvie made some noise of negation. Tears filled her eyes and spilled down her cheeks. "You are," Selma insisted. "You did the best you could. That's all any mother can do. You've got two good girls. You're a good woman. And if Richard can't see that . . . if he can't treat you the way you deserve to be treated . . . if he's not even smart enough to keep it a secret . . ."

"Oh, Ma," Sylvie said. That wasn't what she wanted: a husband who fooled around and covered it up, even though she knew, or at least suspected, that there were a number of women in her circle who'd made that very arrangement, who were willing to carry on being Mrs. So-and-So because the perks were so enjoyable, even if they had to look the other way when their husband was seen at a restaurant or a bar or a beach resort with a woman who was not her.

"Well, I'm sorry!" Selma cried. "But every man I know with something on the side at least had enough respect for his wife to make sure she never found out about it. Or at least they wouldn't rub it in her face."

Sylvie thought about that. The numbness she'd felt that day on the drive home from Philadelphia was seeping back into her bones. She didn't want to ask, didn't want to know, but the question felt as if it was swelling in her mouth, a terrible tumor that would burst if she didn't say the word. "Daddy?"

Her mother answered instantly. "Oh, honey, no. Not him." A pause. "At least, not that I ever knew about." She paused again. "Although there was that Miriam Selkin. Remember her? With the bosoms?"

Sylvie didn't remember Mrs. Selkin, except as a friendly neighbor who'd always bought Girl Scout cookies from Diana, but she did remember her father, a swimmer and a crossword-puzzle enthusiast, a man she would always picture the way he'd been during his final years, round and bald and tanned the golden-brown of a roast chicken from ten years' worth of winters in Palm Beach, with a sun-spotted scalp and a familiar, comforting smell of cigars and Gold Bond Medicated Foot Powder. Her father would slip notes under her pillow signed "T. Fairy" when she lost her teeth (he'd written them without bothering to disguise his handwriting, on his monogrammed business stationery. Sylvie pointed this out as soon as she was old enough to read, and her dad had shrugged and said, "Maybe T. Fairy just borrowed a piece"). Selma had thanked her husband at a dozen awards dinners as "my biggest supporter and my number one fan," and Sylvie felt certain that he would never have done anything to disgrace his wife.

"When you get to be as old as I am, sex isn't as big a part of your life," Selma explained.

"Ma . . ."

"And your father, with his bad back . . ."

"Ma," she managed. "Please."

"I don't know. Maybe if Viagra had come on the market earlier, things would have been different," Selma mused. Sylvie held the phone pinched between two fingers. Somewhere in the world, there was surely a conversation taking place that she'd less enjoy hearing. Trouble was, she couldn't imagine what that conversation might be.

"I've got to go," she said, exactly the way Lizzie had said it to her. It was true—Tim was coming for dinner in half an hour, and the table wasn't set.

"How are the girls?" asked Selma.

"They're fine," she answered, again, automatically, knowing in her heart that it wasn't true, not with Lizzie sounding so strange and Diana not even taking her calls.

"I hope I didn't upset you," said Selma. "I just wanted you to know that you never know what's going on in someone else's marriage, behind someone else's bedroom door. Nobody's perfect," Selma continued. "Not even your mom and your dad."

After saying goodbye, Sylvie hung up the phone and hurried upstairs, into the shower, preparing herself for dinner with her . . . boyfriend? Was Tim her boyfriend? Could a woman her age, a woman who was still, technically, married, even have a boyfriend?

Whether he was her boyfriend or not, she'd been seeing a lot of Tim Simmons. In the mornings, while she did her shopping, there he'd be, conferring with the deli manager or going over an order with the organic produce guy, a young man who'd left Brooklyn in order to minimize his carbon footprint and consume only things he could make or grow himself. This had come to involve, Tim had told her, going toilet-paper free the year before, and making his wife use discarded athletic socks for her monthly cycle. "That poor girl!" said Sylvie, privately resolving to figure out where the young woman was living and anonymously deliver some tampons, the really bad kind, with nonbiodegradable plastic applicators.

Tim usually brought wine or dessert or something else he'd

picked up—a novel he'd read about that he thought she might like, a sauté pan he thought she could use, cookbooks for Indian food and Greek food, a soup kit for her slow cooker. Best of all, he would come with stories about his sons—the ski trip Frankie and Ollie had taken, and how they'd decided to rent snowboards, even though they'd never tried them, and how Frank had gotten to the top of a run and then frozen, too terrified to attempt it, and had to unstrap his snowboard and walk all the way down the mountain. Or the time when Ollie had just gotten his license and was taking a turn behind the wheel on the family's trip to Cape Cod, and had gotten stuck in a rotary and gone around and around and around it, the rest of the family screaming with laughter, until finally he'd worked up the courage to merge. Normally taciturn, low-key, and self-effacing (or maybe, Sylvie thought, any man would pale in contrast to charismatic Richard), Tim would become voluble and vivid when discussing his boys. His cheeks would gain color, his voice would rise, and his booming laugh would fill the kitchen. Tim had pictures, Tim had stories, and, best of all, Tim and his sons had all kinds of rituals and traditions. There was the fall kayaking and camping trip to Arcadia State Park, the rafting trips they were planning for the spring, and how they were already thinking about renting a big RV in a few years and visiting the state parks between Connecticut and Seattle.

Tim and Sylvie would talk about current events, the latest scandal with the latest starlet, keeping far away from politics and from sex (the sex-addicted golfer and the movie star's husband who'd fooled around with the tattooed white supremacist stripper were never discussed). Sylvie would finish cooking dinner, with Tim leaning easily against the counter, nursing a bottle of beer. They'd eat—Tim complimenting her cooking lavishly—and then they'd clear the table and do the dishes together. She'd make coffee; Tim would build a fire. Then they'd sit on the sofa, and he'd talk more about his boys . . . which, of course, made her think about her girls. Could she lure Lizzie and Diana, and Milo, of course, to Connecticut, with promises of kayaking or camping? Would those activities please her girls the way they'd pleased Tim's boys? Maybe, she thought sometimes, when she'd added a bit of brandy to her coffee, she would marry Tim, and they'd be one big blended family, happily hiking and camping the years away. Maybe Lizzie would even fall in love with one of Tim's sons!

Sylvie would listen to Tim, entertaining herself with these private reveries, for once not thinking of Richard. At the end of the night, usually by eleven, Tim would stand up and shove his hands awkwardly into his pockets. "Well, good night then," he'd say. The first night, he'd shaken her hand and pulled her into a half-hug. The hugs had gotten less awkward with each meal, and a few times he'd kissed her cheek and once, briefly, her lips, but it never went beyond that.

Sylvie wondered about those kisses. Did he want more? Did she? She was beginning to think she'd like being with him that way—she'd like the warmth, the comfort of another body in her bed, and she could imagine that once the loving was over, Tim would be even more relaxed and tell her even more about his boys. Maybe the problem was that Tim couldn't do more than kiss her—from friends and acquaintances, she'd heard that plenty of men their age couldn't have sex, because of a variety of medical conditions, or because of the drugs they were taking to address them. She knew that he'd been divorced for sixteen years. His ex-wife's name was Kathy. She'd worked as a school nurse in Rochester when they met. "It's not much of a story. We grew apart," he said the first time he'd come for dinner, sharpening her mother's old knife, then carving the meat into rosy slices.

She supposed that she and Tim were dating. She supposed, even, that he was courting her. Such an old-fashioned word, such an old-fashioned concept. Sylvie had never been courted. She and Richard had, in the parlance of her children, hooked up (although she would die before telling Lizzie and Diana that). They'd noticed each other; they'd talked at that party, they'd tumbled into bed, and then they'd been a couple, which was, in her defense, how many of the couples she knew, including Ceil and Larry, had gotten together.

But Tim took her out on proper dates. "Got any plans for Friday night?" he'd ask when he saw her at the grocery store on a Tuesday morning. When Sylvie told him no, he'd ask if she was interested in accompanying him to a movie at the old, ornate single-screen theater in town, or a chamber music concert, or a high school performance of *Our Town* (she was certain the last one would be excruciating and amateurish, having suffered through a number of Lizzie's high school shows and musicals, and was pleasantly surprised by the proficiency of the Fairview students. The girl who played Emily Webb was especially affecting). He'd always drive, and hold her door open before circling the car to climb in; he insisted on paying for dinner, at the French bistro or the wood-burning pizza place. "You're spending a fortune on groceries," he said, smiling his old, familiar smile, with his hands tucked into his pockets and his chin tucked into his chest. "It's the least I can do." But Sylvie wasn't sure if this made him her boyfriend or even if a word like that could apply to two people in their fifties.

Never mind, she thought, and got herself off the couch and up the stairs, smiling, knowing she'd need to hurry if she wanted dinner to be ready by the time he arrived that night.

DIANA

She'd been with Doug for more than four months when she'd finally taken him to her house on that rainy October night. Doug's mother had reclaimed her car, Diana was worried that they'd been spotted together once too often for anywhere in the hospital to be safe, and the Society Hill Sheraton, preferred hotel of all Philadelphia adulterers east of Broad Street, was vexingly completely occupied. He'd offered his apartment but she felt weird about going back there, where his roommates could see her and talk.

"Close your eyes," she'd whispered, looking up and down the street before pulling him through her front door.

"Why?" he'd asked. "Is it messy?"

It wasn't. During the length of their affair Diana had become a more obsessive housekeeper and a more devoted runner who'd shaved a minute and a half off her previous 10K personal best. She was even, she thought, taking better care of Milo, and Gary, too, now that she had a secret life, a secret self to nurture, which somehow gave her more energy to tend to her son and her husband. She didn't need Doug to shut his eyes because her house wasn't clean. She needed him to close them because she didn't want him to see the picture propped on the mantel that she'd taken the previous Christmas, of her and her husband and the son she'd never told him about, the three of them smiling for the camera and looking as if everything was fine.

When Lizzie had shown up and found them in bed, Diana had been convinced that it was the beginning of the end. What was it Benjamin Franklin had said? *Three can keep a secret if two are dead?* "Don't worry," said Doug, whose relationship with his own little sister was, it seemed, very different from Diana's with Lizzie. "What's she got to gain by ratting you out?"

Diana turned her face away. She couldn't explain it, couldn't tell him that she'd always been the family's straight arrow, the superstar, the senator's presentable daughter; that Lizzie had always been the failure and the fuck-up, and that the chance to reverse those roles, even temporarily, would be too much for her sister to resist. Diana had spent the next twenty-four hours in an agony of dread, convinced that Lizzie, either accidentally or on purpose, would say something to their parents. Either that or she'd go straight to Gary, and her world would come crashing down.

A week went by, then another, and Diana didn't hear from her sister. Not a phone call, not an e-mail . . . and, of course, she was too scared to try to contact Lizzie herself. She ducked her mother's calls and felt too guilty to exchange more than ninety seconds' worth of pleasantries with her dad, who, she knew, missed her. She was in no position to console him or censure him. All she could do, she thought unhappily, was compare notes. *Did you and Joelle ever do it in a parking garage? How'd you keep it a secret from Mom?*

She told herself that maybe it would be all right, that she and Doug could continue indefinitely, aided by her husband's extreme cluelessness. As long as they were careful, as long as Lizzie kept her mouth shut, maybe they'd be okay.

What finally happened wasn't Lizzie tattling, or anyone else from the hospital catching them together. What happened was, one perfectly autumnal Sunday morning, she and Gary and Milo went out to brunch.

They had decided on a place called Green Eggs in the Italian Market neighborhood. Milo had chosen it because he'd liked the name and Diana had agreed because they had quinoa porridge on the menu, and Gary had shrugged and said, "Sure, fine." They'd just rounded the corner onto Dickinson Street when Diana spotted Doug and two of his roommates walking toward them. The guys were dressed in jeans and sweatshirts and running shoes—play clothes for a day off. Doug carried a football, and one of the roommates had a white paper sack of bagels in his arm. Time seemed to slow down. Diana's legs trembled beneath her, and she felt her face turn red. It was as if a spotlight was aimed at her, as if the word GUILTY had appeared on her forehead, written in indelible red ink for everyone to see.

Would he speak to her? He wouldn't, she thought, as they approached each other. If he said hello she'd be forced to introduce him to Gary and Milo, to say, "This is Doug. He's an intern at the hospital." He wouldn't want that. He wouldn't do that to her.

Doug walked past her without a word, seemingly without a glance. Diana exhaled in a shaky rush. Milo looked at her strangely, and Diana forced herself to smile as she took his hand and tweaked the bill of his baseball cap. They walked the few remaining blocks to the restaurant and took their place in line. "Are you all right?" asked Gary, sounding somewhere between concerned and annoyed, when he noticed the beads of sweat on her face.

"I'm fine," said Diana, in a voice that barely sounded like her own. "Just a little dehydrated."

"Mom ran ten miles this morning," Milo said. This was true.

She'd run ten miles at a sub eight-minute-mile pace, and she'd finished her run on Tasker Street, breaking her own rule about Doug's apartment, ending her workout, sweaty and glowing and breathless, tangled in Doug's disreputable sheets, wrapped in Doug's arms.

They gave their name to the hostess and stood in the mild sunshine, waiting for a table to open up. Milo played his Leapster. Gary shifted his weight from foot to foot and remarked to the air that there were plenty of places in their neighborhood that served brunch. Diana stood, feeling as if she'd been carved from wood, until the hostess led them inside. They'd just placed their order—pancakes for Milo, the porridge for Diana, something called the Kitchen Sink, involving fried eggs and biscuits and sausage cream gravy, for Gary—when her BlackBerry thrummed in her pocket.

"Work," she said, and raised the screen to her eyes. It wasn't work. It was Doug, with the text she'd been waiting for since he'd glimpsed her walking with her husband and her son: *i don't think i can do this anymore.*

"Excuse me," she said.

Gary sighed noisily. "Mommy's got the poops again," he said as Diana walked to the bathroom, without bothering to tell him to watch his mouth. There, trembling, crouching on top of the toilet, she punched in Doug's number and pressed the phone to her ear.

He picked up on the third ring. "Hey, Diana."

"Can we talk about this?" she whispered. She knew what the problem was, or she thought she did—he'd seen her with Gary and assumed that he was breaking up a happy marriage, when, in fact, her marriage was anything but happy. She needed Doug. She couldn't imagine her life without him. He couldn't leave her. He loved her. She knew he did.

"I don't think there's much to say."

She pressed her arms tightly against her sides and jammed her quivering legs together. "Doug. Listen. I know what that looked like. But the truth is . . ."

"You've got a little boy," he said dully. "You never told me that."

"Look, things with us have nothing at all to do with him. I'm a good mother," Diana said. "It's not like I'm taking time away from Milo to see you."

She could hear him sigh. "I can't do this to a little kid." His voice dropped. "I'm sorry. But we should never have started. And we've got to stop now, before someone really gets hurt."

"Doug." What about her? What about her getting hurt? Diana dropped her head between her knees, she felt dizzy, and sick, and someone was knocking on the bathroom door, knocking and calling, sweetly, "Everything all right in there?"

"Doug?" she whispered desperately into the phone. "Doug!" There was no answer. He'd hung up.

She clutched her belly and groaned, a sorrowful sound that would have sent her running to the exam room if one of her patients had made it. She sounded like she'd been mortally wounded . . . which, she thought, was true enough. After a minute, she made herself get to her feet. She flushed the toilet and washed her hands and went back to the table, to smile at her son and swallow a few mouthfuls of porridge. Her shift started at two. She texted Doug before she left—*call me pls. Need 2 talk.* But by the time she arrived at the hospital he hadn't called, and she didn't think he ever would.

At her desk, she started frantically reviewing the charts that had piled up, scribbling orders. Coumadin for the lady who'd come in with a suspected stroke, insulin for the eight-year-old with type 1 diabetes, IV antibiotics for the girl whose infected labial piercing had resulted in a nasty case of sepsis.

Lynette stuck her head into Diana's office. "You okay?" she asked, and Diana had nodded, her mind whirling as she tried to rearrange the puzzle pieces of her life in a shape that made sense. Maybe she'd leave Gary and go to Doug a single woman. Maybe they could make it work. Maybe . . .

She ran through the scenarios of divorce and separation, and staggered through her day like a sleepwalker, checking on patients, taking temperatures and blood pressures, writing prescriptions, asking questions and writing down the answers without really hearing. She checked her BlackBerry every minute or two, but heard nothing from Doug. When she came back home after her shift ended at midnight, Milo was sleeping, Gary was in front of his computer, the television was blaring, and the kitchen was a mess. From the box on the counter, the grease-stained napkins and paper plates, Diana surmised that there'd been pizza for dinner, and even though she'd asked Gary to cook, and had made a point of showing him the tenderloin and the fresh zucchini she'd bought at the farmer's market.

She was folding the pizza box into the recycling bin when the telephone rang. Her heart leapt—maybe it was Doug, Doug calling on the home line to announce himself, to tell Gary that he didn't deserve her and that he, Doug, was on his way over to claim Diana and Milo as his own.

"Diana?" Gary, in sweatpants, entered the kitchen. The telephone was in his hand and there was a concerned look on his face. He coughed wetly into his fist, then said, "Hank Stavers for you."

Diana felt the blood rush out of her extremities. Hank Stavers was the chief of staff. She took the telephone in one cold hand.

"Dr. Stavers?"

"Dr. Woodruff." His tone was clipped, his voice as cool as

she'd ever heard it. "We need you back at the hospital immediately."

She could barely find the breath to say, "Of course."

"My office," he said. "Frank Greenfeldt will be waiting." Frank Greenfeldt, Diana knew, was the hospital's attorney. She knew him by reputation, but she'd never met him, never had a reason to meet him. With shaking hands she buttoned up her coat. Had Doug told them what was going on? Had he suggested that she'd behaved improperly somehow? Did she need her own lawyer? A sob caught in her throat as she grabbed her purse and her keys. At that moment, she missed her father desperately. He'd always been great in a crisis, assured and decisive. He could have told her exactly what to do.

"Hey," said Gary, sounding irritated. "Where are you going?"

"Emergency," she whispered, and bolted out the door.

They were waiting for her in Hank Stavers's immaculate mahogany-and-leather office up on the fifth floor, a world away from the blood and mess and noise of the ER. Diana bit her lip to keep it from trembling as Stavers said, "Please sit."

Late as it was, Frank Greenfeldt was wearing a suit, navy blue, with a lavender tie. Diana wondered whether he'd gotten dressed especially for this, or been called away from something else that night. He slid a folder across Hank's desk and tapped at a line with the tip of a silver Montblanc pen. "Read this, please."

Diana bent and read out loud the orders she'd written that night: "Insulin, 100 milligrams."

"Is that the correct dosage for a sixty-five-pound eight-year-old?" Greenfeldt's tone was neutral, but his jowly face was flushed.

"No. It should have been . . ." Diana's voice failed. She'd written down a dosage ten times what it should have been, and if the little girl had gotten 100 milligrams . . .

She looked up, her eyes wild. "Oh my God," she blurted. "Is she . . ."

"The drug was never administered," said the lawyer. "The nurse on duty, Lynette Arnold, noticed the error in time."

"Thank God," Diana whispered, hearing blood rush in her ears. "Oh, thank God." She should never have been working. Distracted as she'd been, her thoughts bouncing between her boyfriend and her husband, she had no business taking care of patients. No business at all.

Somewhere, far away, the hospital's lawyer was talking. Diana wiped her sweaty palms against her skirt and forced herself to focus. ". . . the seriousness of an error of this nature."

"I'm sorry," she blurted, her voice too loud, her face too hot, as if those words could make a difference, as if they could undo what she'd done. "I'm sorry. I'm so sorry. I can't . . . I just can't believe that I . . ."

"You've had a lot on your mind lately," said Hank Stavers, speaking for the first time. Diana found herself nodding. A lot on her mind. Yes indeed. That didn't begin to cover it. "Given your . . ." He paused. "Family situation?"

For a minute she thought he was talking about her and Doug. Then she realized he meant her father. She nodded again. "I'm sorry," she said. "I don't know what else to say except how very, very sorry I am."

"We got lucky," said the lawyer. "This time."

"I'm going to recommend that you take a leave of absence—paid, of course. Certainly, the administrators at Philadelphia Hospital understand that there are . . ."—Stavers paused again—"circumstances that arise that make it difficult to perform up to the best of one's abilities."

The best of one's abilities, she thought. Even an idiot, even a first-year medical student knew the difference between 10 and 100 milligrams. It was an unforgivable mistake. She sent up a quiet, fervent prayer to Lynette, who'd saved her life—hers and the little girl's. Then she straightened in her chair, squared her shoulders, and looked at the men on the other side of the desk. "For how long," she asked politely, for she had been raised with good manners, "would you like me to leave?"

Once the arrangements were made, the dates agreed to and the forms signed, Diana took the stairs down to the emergency room. Lynette was waiting behind the reception desk, looking haggard underneath the fluorescent lights. She got to her feet as soon as she saw Diana getting off the elevator.

"Thank you," said Diana, before Lynette could open her mouth. "I'm so sorry. I'm so grateful to you. I can never thank you enough—"

"Diana." Lynette cut her off. "I owe you an apology. I was going to try to, you know . . ." She glanced at the elevator, then lowered her voice. "Change the chart, but one of the attendings was breathing down my neck."

"Don't worry," said Diana, moved almost to tears at the idea of Lynette risking her own job that way.

"Did they fire you?"

Diana shook her head. "Paid leave."

Lynette exhaled, slumping onto the desk. "Oh, Di," she said. "Shit, I'm sorry."

"Oh, God. Don't be. You've got nothing to be sorry for. You saved that girl's life." Diana's eyes and throat were burning. "I had no business being anywhere near patients today." She took her own glance at the elevator doors. "Doug and I . . . I think it's over. He saw me with Gary and Milo, and I think . . . I mean, he knew I was married, but I think seeing me that way made it . . . you know. Real to him."

Lynette put her arm around Diana's shoulders and squeezed. "Is there anything I can do for you?"

Diana shook her head. After this long day and this terrible night, she just wanted to go home, put on her flannel pajamas, sit in the living room by herself, and cry over the mess she'd made of everything: her marriage, her job, even her friendship with Lynette. And Doug. She'd lost Doug. How could she go on without him?

In a supply closet she found a cardboard box that had once held syringes, and carried it back to her locker. There was a mug Milo had painted (*World's Best Mom!* it read), extra socks and a spare sweater, some sweaty, stale running gear, a bottle of Tylenol, the photograph of her husband and her son that she kept taped to the locker's metal door. She filled her box, tucked it tight under her arm, and started walking.

She knew she should be feeling lucky that a child hadn't been hurt or killed thanks to her idiocy; she'd gotten paid leave instead of a pink slip or a lawsuit. She'd dodged a marital bullet, too—instead of Lizzie's ratting her out or Gary's figuring it out, Doug had ended things, which left Diana free to go about the business of rebuilding her marriage, or even just pretending that none of it had happened.

The problem was, she didn't want to rebuild . . . and she didn't want to be with Gary, either. She wanted Doug . . . and Doug didn't want her, wouldn't want her even if she got a divorce, would not want a woman with a child who had cheated on that child's father.

I want my life to change, she thought as she walked. A block later, she amended it. *I want to change my life.* A bracing wind blew along Market Street, and a pack of girls scurried by with their hands in their coat pockets. Diana shivered but kept walking, with the box under her arm and her head held high. This was another part of her discipline, another habit she'd cultivated as a safeguard against sloth and laziness: Diana was a great maker of lists.

So she walked through the chilly October darkness, under the star-speckled sky, legs eating up block after block of sidewalk, down to the river, where she'd run that morning, making her list in her head. She'd tell Doug that she was leaving her husband and gauge his continued interest in her, if any. But first, she would have to tell Gary, poor, sad-faced Gary, who was probably at home, snoring in their bed. She'd tell him that she'd taken a leave of absence, and then she'd tell him, as gently and as kindly as she could, that, at some point, she had fallen out of love with him, that she no longer felt toward him the way a wife should feel toward her husband. She would say that she wanted a different kind of life. She wanted to go somewhere and live simply, to find a house that wasn't as expensive and a job that wasn't as hard. She wanted to live in a place where Milo could play outside, where not every parent was focused on getting his or her kid into the right elementary school, which would lead to the right magnet high school, which would be a conduit to the Ivy League.

Name what you want, name what you need, and be specific, some New Age guru she'd caught five minutes of on *Oprah* had said. Diana had absolutely no use for New Age gurus—or, for that matter, for Oprah—but the idea of naming what you wanted made perfect sense. When she thought she had it clear, when she had it memorized, she turned and started walking back toward home.

It was after two in the morning by the time she slipped her key into the lock. The block was dark, her virtuous neighbors tucked tight in their beds. Her own house was the only one still lit, the windows glowing warmly yellow. Gary was still awake, sitting in the living room, riding his recliner, his face bathed in the laptop's blue glow.

"Everything okay?" he asked.

She didn't answer as she set her box of belongings on the closet floor. Gary raised the remote and clicked the TV set off. "What happened?" He looked at her closely, really seeing her for the first time in weeks, maybe months—since Doug, anyhow—as she stood before him, numb fingers working at her coat buttons, shivering from the cold. "Diana, what's wrong?"

She opened her mouth to tell him everything: that she'd done something terrible, that she'd broken her vows, her promises, that she'd had an affair, that she didn't want to be married anymore, and that, oh, by the way, she'd almost killed a small child and had come within inches of losing her job. "I . . ." she started to say. Nothing came out except a sad little gust of air. Diana put her hand on her throat experimentally and tried to make a noise, any noise, an *Ah* or an *Ee* or an *Oh,* as in *Oh my God, I'm so sorry.* No sound came.

Gary's expression became sympathetic. "Lost your voice, huh? Hang on, I'll make you some sick tea." Gary's sick tea, which he insisted on brewing whenever anyone in the house had a cold or sore throat, was regular old Lipton, doctored with honey, lemon, and a generous slug of whiskey. It worked, too . . . and it sounded like just the thing, maybe the only thing, she could tolerate in her system at this particular moment.

"Go to bed," Gary called from the kitchen. He'd bring her the cup of tea. He would also leave the sticky, honey-coated spoon on the counter, and the teabag oozing in the sink . . . and did that matter so much? Spoons could be picked up, counters wiped off, teabags tossed in the trash. Her marriage would not be repaired so easily. When Gary found out—and Gary would find out, eventually—he wouldn't forgive her. They had one night left; one night together, in innocence, as man and wife.

"Diana?" Gary approached with a mug of tea steaming in his

hands. "Whoa, you look lousy. You want to call something in for yourself?"

Oh, Gary, I'm so sorry. Diana shook her head and let her husband lead her to the bedroom, where she took off her clothes, put on her flannel nightgown, drank her sick tea, and lay, for the last night of her life, in a bed beside him.

SYLVIE

If Tim knew the specifics of her story, if he had questions about what her husband had done, in all of their nights out and their meals together he'd never let on. They never talked about politics, and, while he'd asked her questions about Lizzie and Diana and their lives, he'd never once asked about Richard. Sylvie policed her own conversation carefully, and she didn't think she'd ever said Richard's name in front of Tim. *My husband,* she would say instead, relating some anecdote about moving Lizzie into the NYU dorms and how Richard had paid a pair of male students to haul her belongings onto the elevators, or how he'd believed that Diana's college boyfriend was going to grow up to be a psycho killer. To Tim, she was Sylvie Serfer, a grown-up version of the tan and laughing teenager she'd once been, the girl who had gotten her braces off the spring before he'd kissed her and had spent much of that summer with her teeth constantly bared in a grin, or running her tongue over their newly smooth surfaces, marveling at the feeling.

Up in the bedroom, she combed her wet hair with her fingers. The curl was coming back, along with the gray, but she found she didn't mind so much. It was an interesting look, an interesting change . . . and besides, who'd be taking her photograph up here, or commenting on the weight she'd gained? She pulled on a black cashmere sweater set and dark-brown wool slacks with an elastic waist (the way she'd been eating, she knew better than to even attempt any of her regular pants). When she hurried downstairs in her stocking feet she had ten minutes left to set the table and bring the sauce to a simmer. That afternoon she'd pan-roasted duck, which had yielded, just as the recipe promised, startling quantities of fat. She'd used some of it to make an outrageously rich side dish of rice, and the rest to sauté bok choy. The sauce was one of the five-ingredient specials Ceil had tried to tempt her with: brown sugar, star anise, honey, fresh ginger, and five-spice powder. Sylvie dipped in a finger and sucked it clean, eyes closed, humming happily. *Richard would love this,* she thought, and then pushed the thought away.

At six o'clock, when she opened the door, it was dark already, the clear night sky pricked with dozens of stars, the waves beating on the shore and a gentle wind stirring the treetops. Tim was dressed for the weather in a canvas jacket and a green sweater and plaid shirt, and there was a pleasing shyness about him, a stillness that Sylvie couldn't help contrasting with Richard's hale good humor, his incessant need to win over every person in every room. That night Tim brought her candles, a pair of elegant ivory tapers, and a jar of lavender honey, and something in a wax-paper bakery box. "Whatever you're making, it smells great."

"Roast duck with five-spice sauce," she said, uncorking the wine as he came over and kissed her cheek. In New York, Richard was always the one to open the bottles. Sylvie wasn't sure she'd even known how. But she'd surprised herself, she thought, fluffing the rice, then scooping a bed of it onto one of her grandmother's shallow serving dishes and arranging the pieces of duck on top.

Usually Tim stuck to a single glass of wine over dinner. That night, with the moon a heavy ball of gold sinking into the ocean, they polished off a bottle between them and opened another, and each had two portions of the rice and the duck. By eight o'clock, they'd pronounced the meal a success, stacked the dishes in the sink, and brewed coffee to accompany the cannoli that Tim had brought. In her hurry to get dinner on the table, Sylvie had forgotten about the candles. Now Tim stuck them into her grandmother's pewter candlesticks. He touched a lit match to their tips and said, "I want to talk to you about something."

At the sink, where she'd been rinsing her hands, Sylvie stiffened. He was going to tell her that he had, to use her mother's parlance, done a Google, and now he knew exactly who she was, and what her husband had done.

Instead, Tim found his wineglass and refilled it, and said, in a voice that was thicker than normal, "I wanted to tell you why I got divorced."

Well, thought Sylvie. This was unexpected. Tim picked up the candles, and she took the wine and their glasses, and together they walked to the living room and settled into their customary places on the sofa—Sylvie at the end near the kitchen, Tim closer to the fire.

He sipped his wine and said, "It wasn't that we grew apart. I mean, that was true, but there was more." He drained the glass, then rolled the wineglass between his palms. Tim's fair skin was flushed, his expression troubled. "Remember how I said we had three boys, that we'd always wanted a girl?" Without waiting for Sylvie's nod, he said, "We had one. Janette. She died."

"Oh, Tim." She reached for his hand, and Tim, who'd never been anything but gentle, jerked it away.

"It was an accident. A long time ago," he said, in a voice that was rougher than normal. "She was eighteen months old. She'd be twenty-three if she'd lived. But it wrecked us. Every time I looked at Kathy, and every time she looked at me, all we could see was . . ." He lifted his hands to his eyes.

"What happened?" Sylvie made herself ask.

One of Tim's hands worked at the back of the worn couch. The other twirled the wineglass, sending the dregs spinning. "She drowned."

"Oh. Oh, Tim, I'm so . . ." She reached out to touch his arm. He twisted away.

"No," he said, cutting her off. "I'm sorry, I just . . . everyone in town knows the whole story already, so I never have to tell it." He took another breath. "I think you just have to let me tell it."

She nodded, then whispered, "Okay." She wondered if it had happened at the beach where they'd swum as children and as teenagers, in the ocean that she could hear slapping at the sand beneath the house.

"Well, we had—have—the boys. Eight, six, and four, they were. Janette was a . . . surprise." He sighed unhappily. "Tell you the truth, I wasn't too happy when it happened. Four kids through college? I thought, *How are we ever going to do that?* Kathy and I talked about . . . you know. Ending the pregnancy. But in the end, we talked so long that it was too late to do anything, and we decided we didn't want to. Kathy was thirty-nine by then, and we figured, God gave us the baby, maybe there was a reason. And when Janette came, she was . . ." He swallowed hard. His hand made a rasping sound as he rubbed his cheek. "She was such a love. Just the sweetest girl, and so pretty, with big brown eyes, and these eyelashes." He held his hand out in front of his own face to demonstrate.

Sylvie put her wineglass on the coffee table and forced herself to be still, knowing that it didn't matter; that Tim was so lost in the story he might have actually forgotten she was there.

"Kathy was giving Janette a bath and she heard this crash downstairs, and then Ollie started screaming. Janette could sit up by herself by then—she was trying so hard to keep up with her brothers, she could do all that stuff, pulling up, crawling, walking, all of it, pretty early. Kath left her in the tub with her tub toys, and she ran downstairs. Turned out Ollie had pulled the television set down, and by the time Kath got the TV off him and made sure he was okay . . . it was two minutes, maybe three, but by the time she went back upstairs . . ."

They both were quiet. Sylvie shuddered as she pictured the scene—a little girl, facedown in the shallow water, with a rubber ducky drifting near one chubby hand.

"It happens," said Tim. His voice was flat. "That's what the coroner told us." He gathered himself. "He told us that it happens more than you'd think." He was quiet again. "That wasn't even the worst part. The worst part was the trial."

Sylvie interrupted, hardly believing what she'd heard. "The trial?"

Tim gave a thin smile. "The prosecutor had political ambitions. He was tough on crime. Especially child abuse."

"But it was an accident, not child abuse!" She felt her face flush, her body thrum with fury.

"That's what the judge said. He threw the case out, read the prosecutor the riot act. Said no jury, no jail, could punish us worse than we'd been punished already." He turned to her, still wearing that terrible smile. "He was right. Every time Kathy and I looked at each other, all we saw was our little girl. And every time anyone looked at us, there'd be this . . . sympathy, I guess, but also a kind of there-but-for-the-grace-of-God-go-I thing. I guess a lot of people take a chance sometimes—they'll leave a kid in the bathtub for a minute, or look away while a kid's on a swing, or run into the dry cleaner's with a baby in the car seat. Everyone's done something like that, and it's almost always fine. If you're lucky. Looking at us was like looking at their worst-case scenario."

Sylvie nodded, swallowing hard against the lump in her throat, aching for Tim. She knew what it was like to be a walking worst-case scenario; she'd grown familiar with looks that mixed sympathy and secret relief. On the couch beside her, Tim buried his face in his hands. His shoulders were shaking, but he made no sound. She couldn't imagine what he was feeling, couldn't imagine the pain of it. She'd come close, closer than any parent should have, with Lizzie's misadventures. But Lizzie had survived, almost in spite of herself, where Tim would never see his daughter start nursery school or kindergarten or get dressed for a dance or graduate from high school. His daughter would never grow up to break his heart, but he'd never get to hope for her, or see her dreams come true. Sylvie knelt down and took his hands in hers.

"Come with me," she said, pulling him gently to his feet. Tears were streaming down his face. She wiped them with her sleeve, then led him upstairs to her bedroom. By the light of the lamp by the bed she slipped his sweater over his head, unbuttoned his shirt, untied his shoes and pulled them off his feet. She worked at the clasp of his belt, pulled his pants off over his hips. When he stood before her in his T-shirt and boxers, she pulled back the covers, the fluffy down comforter she'd washed, the crisp cotton sheets that she'd dried in the salt and the sunshine. "Lie down," she whispered, and kissed his cheek . . . and then she lay down beside him, letting him gather her body in his arms, his chest warm through the fabric of his shirt, solid against her back.

"I'll bet you were a wonderful mother," he whispered. Sylvie lay in the darkness, with Tim's body warming the bed, the moon spilling silver light through the window, the wind sighing through the trees.

"No," she said. "I wasn't."

She'd never told anyone the story—not Ceil, although her best friend would have listened without judgment; not her mother, although Selma would have listened, too, then offered hardheaded advice. The story belonged to the four of them—Diana and Lizzie, Sylvie and Richard. Now, she supposed, it would belong to Tim, too.

"When Lizzie was in sixth grade, she got a job babysitting for the Ritsons. Carl and Amanda. They lived on eight, two floors down. We were friendly with them—maybe not friends, but acquaintances. The father ran a hedge fund, and he was a big political contributor. The mother was his second wife, and there was a seventeen-year-old son from the father's first marriage. But we never saw that boy. He was away, up in New Hampshire, at boarding school." She waited until she felt Tim's nod, then continued. "They had a little girl named Victoria. Tori. She adored Lizzie, and Lizzie loved her, too, so when Amanda asked Lizzie to babysit, we all thought it sounded fine. She'd be two floors away, and they never kept her past ten o'clock, and they paid her really well—ten dollars an hour, which was a lot back then for a twelve-year-old. Especially since most of the time Tori was asleep." Sylvie smoothed the pillowcase, remembering Lizzie at twelve, her silky blond hair in a French braid down her back, her cheeks and upper arms still plump with baby fat, with buds of breasts pushing at the front of her school uniforms. She'd been so excited, telling her parents about the job, and Sylvie had been thrilled for her, thinking that maybe this was something Lizzie could excel at. Already, she was struggling in school, doing work that was barely adequate in everything but her art classes. She wasn't going to be an athlete or a musician or a leader of student government, but maybe she had an aptitude for caring for small children, and maybe this would shape the rest of her life. She could be a teacher, a child psychologist, a nanny or a pediatric nurse or a mom. Lizzie and Sylvie had made lists of activities that Lizzie could do with Tori, and Lizzie had purchased, with her own allowance, something called *The Toddler's Busy Book,* which was full of simple games she could play with Tori and foods they could prepare.

"Richard and I were out at a party one night—a fund-raiser, a black-tie event for one of the museums. Lizzie was babysitting, but Diana was home, so we thought it would be fine. The man's son, Kendall, came home that night and found Lizzie there. He . . ." Sylvie's hands were clenched into fists, her short, unpolished fingernails digging into her palms. She and Richard had come home late, the tiniest bit tipsy. They'd been kissing in the elevator, and Sylvie had been flushed and giggling as they'd walked down the hall, hand in hand. She wanted to get out of her dress and her heels, she wanted to be in bed, naked, with her husband. When she'd unlocked the door and found Lizzie weeping on the couch next to her sister, her face flushed and tearstained, her sweater misbuttoned, her hair coming loose from its braid, her first reaction was one of impatience, of frustration. *Oh, God, what now?* she'd thought . . . and then, unforgivably, that of course it was Lizzie who'd need her, Lizzie, still babyish at twelve, who'd spoil her evening. Of course it was Lizzie, not Diana.

"The boy had done things to her," she told Tim. "Or, I guess, made her do things to him." That was almost as much as she knew. Lizzie had whispered the details of what had happened to Diana, and Diana was the one who'd told them, her voice clinical and cool, that there had been no penetration, but that the boy had made Lizzie do things to him.

"Richard and I talked it over, and in the end we decided not to go to the police. We—well, Richard, mostly—we thought it would be better for Lizzie to handle it quietly. Lizzie was always sensitive, and we thought that putting her through the process, having her make a statement, go to the police station, to have it end up in the papers, to have everyone know . . ." She took a shuddering breath, knowing that the truth was that she'd certainly considered what was best for Lizzie, but, as always, she had also given a great deal of thought to what was best for Richard. "I got her into a warm bath. Richard went down to talk to the family. We never even saw the boy. He wrote Lizzie an apology, and she hardly ever talked about it after that, but I wondered . . . I always wondered . . ." She shut her mouth, remembering the worst parts of that night: her first thought of *Oh, God, Lizzie, what now,* and then, later, the sight of her youngest daughter in the bathtub, strands of wet hair clinging to her cheeks, her eyes filled with a terrible, drowning hope as she'd wiped her tears and whispered to her mother, "Do you think he wants to be my boyfriend?" It was a long moment before she had her voice under control enough to speak again. "The husband had raised tens of thousands of dollars for Richard's first Senate campaign, and, after this all happened, he gave half a million dollars to the state Democratic party. Five hundred thousand dollars," she said. "That's how much I sold my daughter for."

Tim stroked her hair. He told her, in the same calm voice he'd used when he'd seen her in the grocery store, teetering on the edge of hysteria with her two carts crammed with food, that it wasn't her fault, that she'd made the best decision she could have with the information she had, that plenty of parents would have done the same. Sylvie listened, knowing he was wrong. At her age she knew that things were rarely clear-cut. Life was full of ambiguity, of compromise and shades of gray, but not in that case. In that case there had been a right thing to do and a wrong thing. She and Richard had chosen incorrectly, and now she would spend the rest of her life wondering whether if she'd done things differently, Lizzie would have grown up a different kind of girl.

Oh, she'd tried to make it better, tried to take back that first, terrible thought. For weeks, months, after the incident she'd made sure that she was there when Lizzie came home from school, that she was available and present if Lizzie ever wanted to talk. But Lizzie hadn't wanted to talk. For a while she'd gorged herself at night, in secret—Sylvie would wake up and find empty ice cream cartons or cookie boxes stuffed into the trash can every morning—but that hadn't lasted. Lizzie had simply drifted away. She was silent when she was home, an expressionless, mute, moon-faced girl who dyed her pretty blond hair crow's-wing black and styled it into matted, filthy dreadlocks, a girl who stole prescription drugs from her parents and jewelry from her grandmother, a girl who pierced her eyebrow and her nose and God only knew what else, a girl with a crowd of sullen, smoke-smelling friends who'd look at Sylvie with flat, incurious eyes, a girl who could not be trusted and was almost impossible to like. She and Richard had chosen the political over the personal; his ambition—and hers, too, she knew; at that point the two things were so intertwined it was impossible to tell them apart—over Lizzie's need. They'd been paying for it for years, with every late-night phone call from Lizzie, drunk or high or lost somewhere, in need of bail money or rehab or help. Sylvie had paid for it at that rest stop, standing in front of the television set as pictures of Richard and Joelle looped across the screen. She was paying for it now. She would, she supposed, be paying for it forever.

Eventually Tim fell asleep, curled on his side with his cheek pillowed on his hands. Sylvie lay stiffly beside him, watching the moon dip down to the sea. Slowly, the thought fluttered up in her mind, a thought that warmed her like the sunshine after a cold night alone in the dark. The thought that came to warm her was *Maybe it isn't too late.* Maybe she could rebuild things with her daughters, with Lizzie, and with Diana, who, she supposed, she'd also failed in a hundred ways, large and small. Maybe she could fix it. At least she could try.

Slowly, noiselessly, she worked herself out of the bed. In the bathroom, she took off the clothes she'd worn to dinner, put on a flannel nightgown, a bathrobe, and a pair of thick wool socks, and padded down the stairs to the living room, where she sat on the couch and wrapped herself in the afghan she kept draped over its back. Tim and Kathy had made a mistake and lost their daughter forever. She and Richard had made a mistake, but their girls were alive and well, and now she had time. She could try to fix things, try to repair some of what she'd done by always putting Richard first. She closed her eyes as she thought, *I want a second chance.*

When she woke up it was morning, and she was lying on the couch. Tim had tucked the blanket in around her feet and left her a note on the coffee table. *Sorry I had to leave so early, but duty calls. Thank you for everything.*

Sylvie stretched her arms over her head. The clock on the oven had it as just after six. She'd bake biscuits, and have one with her coffee. Then she'd go about trying for the second chance she wanted so desperately, figuring out how to set things right, how to get her daughters here, with her, so that she could try to make amends, so that she could care for them the way they needed to be cared for. They were grown, true, but even grown girls still needed their mother.

In her bathrobe, in the kitchen, she laid out her ingredients: flour and sugar, both kept in her grandmother's ceramic canisters; Crisco, baking soda, salt, the buttermilk she'd bought at the store the day before. She measured, then mixed them in a cold metal bowl, moving quickly, so as not to overwork the dough. She cut the biscuits into circles with a water glass, set them on a baking sheet, slid them into the oven, and picked up her telephone.

[illegible] the kingdom. [illegible]

[illegible]

[illegible]

[illegible]

PART THREE

Fly Away Home

LIZZIE

"Date of your last menstrual period?" asked the nurse.

"Third week of June," Lizzie said. Under better circumstances, she would have been proud that she'd been able, after long hours fretting over her calendar, to come up with an answer. But these circumstances were not good. These circumstances were terrible. That morning, Lizzie had woken up at seven, planning to get to an eight-thirty meeting before taking the subway to Queens . . . but, in the bathroom, she'd noticed blood, the kind that had once presaged her period, streaking the toilet paper.

She was definitely pregnant even though she didn't look that way or feel any different, except for an odd stiffness at the very base of her belly and a sudden aversion to eggs. She hadn't been to a doctor yet, hadn't even found one. It had been on her to-do list, but she'd kept putting it off until she made up her mind.

There was plenty for her to do alone in her parents' apartment, which she'd cleaned and where she cooked herself dinner each night. Three days a week she'd take the subway to a studio in Queens, where she'd work for a few hours creating a digital database of every photograph Warren Crispen had taken over the last thirty years. She'd pack her afternoons with meetings or trips to the swimming pool, and telephone calls with her mother in Connecticut and her dad down in D.C., and between all of that she'd postponed her decision quite nicely.

Only that morning, when she saw the blood, it seemed that she'd made up her mind. She wanted the baby; was in fact sick at the thought of losing it. In a panic, she'd called Dr. Metcalfe, her old pediatrician, telling the nurse who'd answered that she was an old patient having an emergency. Once she'd explained the nature of the emergency, the service had referred her to an obstetrician a few blocks away from her parents' apartment, in whose office she was now sitting, wearing a thin cotton gown open in the back, naked underneath it except for her socks.

"So!" Dr. Gutierrez was short and round, with perfect white teeth, walnut-colored skin, and glossy black hair that Lizzie suspected was a wig. "The spotting's been going on how long?"

"Just since this morning," Lizzie said. Her knee was bouncing up and down beneath her thin paper gown. She made herself be still and ran through her mnemonic—not hungry, not angry, not tired. Maybe a little lonely—Jeff had been calling and e-mailing, but she hadn't answered. He would be sweet, she knew, and his sweetness would only make her feel worse about the thing she hadn't told him; the lie of omission that lay between them. "Well, this morning was when I noticed it."

He asked her a bunch of other questions, his fingers warm on her wrist as he checked her pulse, then slid the gown off her shoulders so he could listen to her heart. Lizzie answered as best she could, admitting that she hadn't seen a doctor yet, nor had she had an internal exam in years. Then there was the matter of her history. With her cheeks burning and her eyes on the floor, she gave a bare-bones description of everything she'd swallowed or smoked or snorted over the past six years, ending with her stint in rehab that June. Maybe it was for the best that she hadn't told Jeff about the baby, she thought, now that it looked as if she was maybe going to lose it.

The doctor took notes. "You haven't used since you've been pregnant?"

"Just Advil PM. Just once. Before I knew."

He nodded. "Well, we need to start you on prenatal vitamins and folic acid, and you need to eat a healthy diet, but I think you should be fine," said the doctor.

She looked at him, hardly daring to believe it. "The human body is resilient," he said. "Drugs don't stay in your system forever. As long as you stay clean, and eat a sensible diet, and get some moderate exercise, you've got as good a chance at having a healthy baby as any other woman."

He washed his hands and pulled on a pair of rubber gloves. "We'll do a transvaginal ultrasound to hear the heartbeat and take a peek. My guess is that everything's fine, and I'll put you on modified bed rest."

"What's that mean?"

"Just what it sounds like." He pulled up Lizzie's gown. "You'll stay in bed. You'll be able to get up to use the bathroom, and you can go up and down stairs once per day, but mostly, I want you to lie down and rest, and we'll see if the spotting stops." He smiled, and his dark skin and white teeth gleamed under the room's bright lights. "Take it easy. Get some movies from Netflix. Order in. Have your husband take care of you."

"But . . . but . . ." Lizzie's mind whirled with the logistics. Her father was down in Washington, her mother was up in Connecticut. She was in the apartment all by herself, and while there were no stairs, and delivery services that could bring everything from groceries to DVDs, there was also no one to help her. "I don't have a husband."

"Boyfriend?" said the doctor.

Lizzie bit her lip. "It's complicated."

The doctor just nodded, then turned down the lights. "You shouldn't be alone," he told her. "Maybe a friend or a parent can come stay. Breathe deeply," he said, and slid something inside her. Lizzie looked up at the screen and saw nothing but shifting gray swirls, like the Doppler map of a storm. "There," said the doctor, pointing at something. "Nice, strong heartbeat. I don't see anything obvious that's causing the bleeding. Sometimes it just happens. So you'll go home, and we'll hope that it stops." He scribbled a prescription for prenatal vitamins, handed her a pamphlet on bed rest, and told her to make an appointment in two weeks.

Lizzie took a cab home instead of the subway. On the way she called Warren, the photographer in Queens, a willowy man with a high, sweet voice and quick, narrow hands, who didn't seem too surprised or disappointed when Lizzie explained that a health problem would keep her home from work for the next few weeks. Probably her parents, who'd gotten her the job in the first place, had filled him in on her history. Probably he expected her to be a flake.

Up in the apartment, lying on top of her girlhood bed staring at the neat rows of framed photographs—Diana at her wedding, her parents coming home from a party, Milo on the carousel—Lizzie considered her situation. She could call the counselor she'd liked in Minnesota, except Susan was married with two kids of her own and probably couldn't drop everything to tend to Lizzie. She could call Jeff, except she hadn't spoken to him in weeks and didn't think she should restart their relationship by saying, "Hey, I'm pregnant, want to come to New York to make me sandwiches and rub my feet?" She could try to find Patrice, her old high school friend, except the last she'd heard Patrice had become a fundamentalist Christian who lived in Maine and homeschooled her stepkids.

Her mother was at the beach, in that big old musty house at the edge of a cliff, a place Lizzie had hated since she was eight years old and Diana, posing on the porch in a striped sundress, had asked her to take her picture. "Back up! Back up!" Diana kept calling, as Lizzie held the Instamatic and tried to frame the shot. "You're not going to get the whole house unless you move back!" With the viewfinder held up to her eye, Lizzie had kept taking giant steps backward until suddenly her sister had screamed, "Stop!" Alarmed by the shrill sound of her sister's voice, Lizzie had frozen in place and looked over her shoulder. One more step would have taken her off the edge of the bluff, sent her tumbling down to the rocky beach, or maybe right into the water. The next time they'd come up to the beach there'd been a fence at the edge of the yard. The Lizzie Woodruff Is Stupid Memorial Picket Fence, Diana had called it.

Mom was up in Connecticut; Dad was down in D.C.—and besides, honestly, what would the two of them do? Send her off to some home for unwed mothers the same way they'd shipped her off to rehab? Get her out of town before she could embarrass them again? That left Diana, her prig of a big sister, who'd gotten her sequence correct—first comes love, then comes marriage, then comes baby in the baby carriage. Wincing, Lizzie picked up her cell phone and was about to dial her sister's number when the screen flashed her mother's face.

"Lizzie?"

"Hi, Mom."

"Lizzie!" Her mother sounded strangely hesitant, her voice soft and uncertain. "I wonder whether you'd like to come up to Connecticut for a visit. You can call Warren, I'm sure he'd give you a few days off. I thought maybe it would be nice . . . it's so pretty here, with the leaves changing, and there's a great flea market on the town green and this vintage clothing store I know you'd like . . ." Lizzie looked at the phone suspiciously. Was her mother psychic? Had that nice doctor called her the minute Lizzie was out of the office? Wasn't that illegal?

"I called Derek," her mother was saying. "He can give you a ride. Call him whenever you're ready. Just pack some gloves and sweaters, because it gets cold at night."

Derek decided it. Derek had always been nice to her, even after the time she'd thrown up all over his backseat. Lizzie said, "I can leave Tuesday." It was Friday now. That would give her a long weekend, three days for the bleeding, hopefully, to stop.

"I'll have him come get you whenever you want. Oh, Lizzie, I can't wait to see you. I think it'll be so good to be together." Lizzie, feeling stunned, as if the gift she'd been longing for had landed in her lap, said that being together sounded good to her, too.

DIANA

Diana woke up at just after seven o'clock. For a moment, she was happy, caught in the afterglow of a pleasant dream of swimming in the ocean, paddling lazily through the clear salt water as waves nudged her toward the shore. Then she lay sick and motionless as the memories of the day and night before flooded her body. She'd lost Doug. She'd left her job. Now she had to do the worst part: tell Gary.

She forced herself out of the empty bed. Gary had actually gotten up before her and was in the bathroom, where he'd be shedding wet towels and whiskers and leaving a crust of toothpaste and shaving cream in the sink. She pulled on leggings and a T-shirt, her bathrobe and her clogs, and hustled Milo out of bed and into his clothes. She fed him breakfast, handed him his backpack, pulled on a long, belted cardigan, and walked him down to the corner, where the other mothers, who'd never seen her without her hair combed and her makeup on, looked at her strangely.

"Sick," she rasped, and pointed to her throat. One of the other women, who lived in fear of illness, cringed away, using her body to shield her child, but she thought she saw Lisa Kelleher lift an eyebrow at one of the kindergarteners' mothers . . . which meant, she thought, that the word might be out.

She practically shoved Milo up the bus steps and racewalked home. Reflexively, she checked her cell phone, which she'd left charging in the clean, empty kitchen. Nothing from Doug. Her heart knotted. She'd known, from the first time they'd kissed, that there was no future, yet somehow she'd let herself hope for one: the two of them, plus Milo, and maybe a baby of their own. Waking up every morning in bed with someone she loved. Could it really be over? Hadn't Doug loved her at all?

Gary was in the bathroom, a towel wrapped around his scrawny midsection, shaving. "Hey," she said. He stared at her impatiently, all traces of the previous night's goodwill gone.

"You feeling better?" he said.

"Better," she croaked. The truth was, she felt awful. "We need to talk."

"What's up?" he asked. "I've got to get moving."

"It can't wait. We need to talk. Right now."

"Okay," he said. Shaving cream dotted his cheeks and chin, and his chest hair clung wetly to the slack flesh of his chest. "So talk."

She shuddered. How could she tell him? And how on earth had she married him in the first place?

"I," she began, and could go no further.

"You," Gary prompted. He frowned. "Don't you need to go to work?"

"I've been thinking . . ." Her voice trailed off. Gary picked up his razor.

"Look, I've got a meeting at nine o'clock sharp, and I—"

"I don't love you anymore," she blurted, then clapped one hand over her mouth, as if the words were a flock of birds that had exploded out of a tree.

Gary put his razor down next to the uncapped can of shaving cream and stared at her, openmouthed. "What?"

She drew a deep breath of the steamy air. "Gary, I've been feeling for a long time . . ."

"Are you kidding me?" he shouted. "You don't love me? And you're telling me this now?"

She dropped her eyes. He had a point. The timing was less than ideal. But maybe if she told Gary that their marriage was over . . . if she went to Doug and told him she was free . . . if he met Milo, spent time with him, got to know what an interesting little boy he was . . .

Gary was still staring at her, the towel drooping around his midsection, his eyes, and even, she thought, his nipples, all staring at her accusingly. "You don't love me?"

She lifted her face and said the only words that could possibly apply. "It's not your fault. Really, it's not. You didn't do anything wrong. It's not you, it's me."

"You're goddamn right it's you!" He grabbed his razor and raked it over his face. Three tiny spots of blood bloomed on his cheeks. He grabbed a tissue, tore off three pieces, and slapped them to the wounds. "Look," he said, sounding marginally calmer. "If you want to go into counseling, or whatever . . ." He dropped his razor next to his toothbrush, which lay on its side, dribbling white foam onto the countertop. "Is this about your father? What's going on? Are you on your period?"

"I've been unhappy," she whispered.

"And you couldn't maybe have mentioned this to me? How was I supposed to know? I'm not psychic! Jesus, Di, what'd I do?"

She dropped her head. She'd told him the truth. He hadn't really done anything. Gary had simply been himself, and that would have been enough, more than enough, even, for a different kind of woman, but it was no longer enough for her.

Gary, meanwhile, had started to cry. Tears ran down his face, threatening to dislodge the toilet paper. They cut through the shaving cream drying on half of his face and dripped off his jutting chin. God, thought Diana, feeling disgusted. He can't even cry neatly. "I can't believe this," he said. "I can't believe this is happening." He moved toward her. She stood, frozen, as he wrapped his arms around her, snuffling into her neck, soaking her shirt. "I'm sorry," he said. "Whatever I'm doing wrong, I can change. But I don't want to lose you."

Tell him, she thought. Take the medicine, swallow the pill. Get it over with, and you won't have to do it again. She pushed him away, holding his shoulders, and as he stared at her, open-mouthed and half-naked in his towel, Diana looked up into his eyes and said, "I'm in love with someone else."

Gary jerked back. "You're kidding," he said. Diana shook her head. "You . . . this other guy . . ." He took one step away from her, then another. "You had sex with him?" he yelled.

Her heart broke as she nodded. Gary didn't deserve this, she thought, as his eyes narrowed and his mouth twisted. Then his arm shot out and shoved her, not gently, in the chest, sending her staggering into the bathroom wall.

"Get out of here," he said.

"Oh, Gary," she said.

"Get out! I mean it! Go be with your boyfriend, if that's what you want!" His voice cracked on the word *boyfriend,* and he turned away, crying again, holding a hand towel over his eyes.

Diana stood there, her back throbbing from where she'd hit the towel bar. This wasn't how she'd imagined things happening. When she'd tried to picture it, Gary was the one to leave, manfully packing a bag, giving her a look that was equal parts love and regret before driving off into the sunset, or maybe just to the Sheraton. But at the moment it didn't seem as though Gary was planning on going anywhere. "Get out! Get out! Get out!" he was shouting, still with the towel pressed to his face like a blindfold. "Go be with your boyfriend!"

Struggling with her temper, she said, "Gary. I'm not leaving."

"Well, one of us is," he said, a truculent note creeping into his voice. "And I'm not the one who's been cheating."

"Gary." Am I insane? she wondered. Didn't the mother and the children, or child, always stay in the house? Wasn't it always the father who left? "I was thinking that I'd stay here with Milo, and that you'd find another place."

"Forget it." He crossed his arms over his bare chest, dropped the hand towel, and glared at her with reddened, puffy eyes. "I didn't do anything wrong. I'm not going anywhere." He glared at her a moment longer, then dropped his face and muttered, "Except I actually have to go to work." With Diana staring at him in shock, he put his hands on her shoulders, pushed her out of the bathroom, then closed the door and locked it.

She walked down to the kitchen, rage starting to build inside her. She pictured the meals she'd cooked, the snacks she'd prepared, the games of Sorry and Monopoly she'd played with Milo at the kitchen table while Gary hunkered down in the den, too busy watching the game to tend to his son. Fury simmered in her veins as she considered how she'd found this house, convinced Gary to come see it, how the bulk of the down payment had been the money Grandma Selma had given her. Now it was going to be his? Where would she and Milo go?

Never mind. She pulled her hair back into a ponytail, shoved her feet into her clogs, and her arms into the sleeves of her cardigan, grabbed her purse and her phone, and hurried to the parking lot where she kept her car. It was almost eight. If she hurried she could probably catch Doug at his apartment. She reached for her phone—there were three missed calls, all from her mother. Diana ignored them and tapped out a text message: *Nd 2 C U.* Then she deleted it. Better to surprise him, to let him see her in person, to make him reject her, if that's what he was going to do, right to her face.

• • •

One of Doug's roommates, yawning in shorts and a T-shirt that read COLLGE, opened the door. "Is Doug here?" she asked, trying to sound sunny and upbeat and normal. The roommate squinted at her, rubbing one hand over his stubbly cheek.

"Yeah, he's upstairs."

Diana walked past him into the living room, which smelled like hot wings, and headed up the stairs. Doug's doorway was at the end of the hall. She lifted her hand to knock, decided against it, and pushed the door open.

He was sitting at his desk, looking pale and wan and miserable. He hadn't shaved, or combed his hair, and was barefoot in sweatpants and a plaid shirt. Seeing him tore her heart open. It was all she could do not to rush to him, to tell him how right they were together and beg for another chance.

He looked up. It took her brain a minute to make the cross-connection, to process what she was seeing and tie it in to a memory, years ago, of Hal's face. It was a look that said that things were over, that he'd given her his final answer and that wasn't going to change.

She slumped against the doorway, feeling dowdy and ridiculous in her leggings and her ponytail, like an old crone trying to look like a teenager. Her whole body cramped as she looked at him. *Oh, no,* she thought, in words that sounded as if they were coming from the bottom of a very deep, very cold well.

"Diana," Doug said. He crossed the room and reached for her hand.

"I left him," she blurted. "I left Gary. I told him about us."

Doug sighed. "I wish you hadn't."

She looked at him through her tear-blurred eyes. "We're not going to . . ." Her voice trailed off. Doug, too, looked as if he was struggling not to cry.

"It's not that I don't want kids. I do. It's just . . ." In the silence, she imagined she heard what he couldn't bring himself to say. *I want my own kids, not someone else's.*

She didn't answer. What could she have said? No words, no amount of pleading, nothing could make him take her back. He'd told her the truth, not with words but with his sigh. There was no future in which they'd be together. She could possibly manage to leave with a few shreds of dignity, but she would not be leaving with Doug.

"Are you going to be all right?" he asked.

She looked at him coolly, considering handsome Doug Vance, his dark hair and ruddy cheeks, his smooth skin and perfectly formed body, with the curiosity she might extend to a patient in her exam room who'd presented with a symptom she'd never seen before—an interesting rash, perhaps, or persistent bad dreams. Was she going to be all right? That was a good question. She felt awful. She had, after all, lost everything. Except she hadn't. Not quite. She might have lost her job, her husband, her boyfriend, even possibly her house, but she hadn't lost Milo. And so . . .

"Of course I'm going to be all right," she said, in a tone suggesting that she was well practiced in this kind of affair—its beginning, its care and management, its inevitable end.

"Well." Doug reached for her hand again. Diana pulled her arm away. "Well, listen. I guess I'll see you around."

She shrugged—of course he wouldn't see her at the hospital, but she wouldn't be the one to tell him that—and let herself out of his room, head held high, moving down the stairs like a teenage girl showing off her prom dress. Outside, she blinked in the sunshine. There was a park a few blocks away—she'd been there once with Milo. She managed to find it, and sat on a bench, unable to move, barely able to breathe. Time passed. Mothers came with children, dog walkers with dogs. Diana couldn't think of what to do, of where to go.

Finally, she pulled her phone out of her pocket and called the place where they had to take you in, the place you went when all other options were closed.

"Mom?"

"Diana!" Her mother's voice was high and happy, as if she didn't have a care in the world. "Where have you been? I've been trying to reach you for weeks!"

"Sorry." She started plodding down the street, back toward her car. "I've been busy."

"Well." Now her mother sounded shy and oddly formal. "I've been calling to invite you and Gary and Milo up to Connecticut. It's beautiful here. We can drive around and look at the leaves . . . or there's a big antiques market in Litchfield . . . and the beach, of course . . . and Lizzie's going to come."

"Gary's busy." The lie slid off her tongue as if it had been greased. Ignoring her troublesome sister's presence for the moment, she continued, "But I bet Milo would love to see you. And I could use a little break."

Sylvie paused, and when she spoke she sounded as if she could hardly believe it. "You're not working?"

"Nope." The heartbreak was still there, manifesting itself as a miserable twitchiness, as if she could leap right out of her skin. Thinking of the future without Doug was like imagining life without sunshine, without oxygen, but there was also a strange recklessness that went along, Diana supposed, with having absolutely nothing left to lose. "I'm taking a little time off, actually, I'm rethinking my priorities."

"Well, that's . . . that's wonderful," her mother said, although Diana didn't know how Sylvie could think it was wonderful at all. "When can you come?"

"How about tomorrow?"

"Wonderful," Sylvie said again. "I'll get your rooms ready. I'll be waiting."

Diana drove home and double-parked in front of her house, which already looked strange to her, as if strangers had bought it and furnished it, had eaten breakfasts at the kitchen table and sat on the couch watching TV at night. Moving fast, she threw her clothes into a suitcase, then spent fifteen minutes packing for Milo: pajamas and jeans and underpants, a week's worth of school clothes, his favorite books, his chess set, his insect collection bottles, the photograph album her sister had sent, and Mister Buttons, the threadbare teddy he'd had since he was a baby. She grabbed her coat and scarf, her sunglasses, her cell phone and charger, her wallet and her car keys, and wrote Gary a note: *Milo and I are going to Connecticut to see my mom. I'll call you when I'm there.* Then she threw her bags into the trunk and drove to Milo's school.

"He's in gym class," said the girl behind the reception desk. Dismissal wasn't for another twenty minutes, so Diana scribbled an excuse about a dentist's appointment onto the sign-out sheet, and went to collect her boy.

The first grade was playing volleyball. Kids in red pinneys stood on one side of the net; kids in yellow on the other. Milo, pale and solid in his shorts, was on the sidelines, holding an ice pack against his nose. They'd made him take his hat off. She saw its pom-pom peeking out from his pocket.

She hurried over. "Mom?" Milo looked up at her, blinking, relief spreading over his face (relief and confusion, most likely, because he'd never seen her out of the house without her hair done and her face made up).

"What happened?" she asked, bending down to hug him.

"I got hit by a ball." He paused. "It was an accident." Diana guessed that it probably wasn't an accident, that one of those little pinney-wearing fucks had done it on purpose. "Come on," she said to Milo, who was staring at her wide-eyed. "Let's go."

She waved at the gym teacher, a Nazi in a tracksuit with a silver whistle dangling from his beefy neck. Grabbing Milo's hand, she hurried him down the hall and out into the car, which she'd double-parked, hazard lights blinking, on the side of the street where the school buses lined up.

"Where are we going?" he asked, after Diana drove past the street that would have taken them home. Diana steadied herself, with her hands tight on the wheel. Ideally, she supposed, she and Gary would be doing this together . . . but the situation was a long way from ideal.

"Your dad and I are having some problems, and we're going to spend some time apart. I thought that you and I would take a little vacation."

"Problems?" asked Milo. His voice was small and frightened. "What problems?"

She waited for a red light and thought carefully about her answer. "Grown-up problems. None of it is your fault at all. We both love you." She swallowed hard. "We love you very, very much."

In the rearview mirror his face relaxed, but his voice was still wavery. "What's going to happen? Where are we going right now?"

She pulled into a gas station, put the car in Park, and patted the empty passenger's seat. Milo unfastened his seat belt and scrambled clumsily over the gearshift into the seat beside her.

"I'm not sure what's going to happen," she said, even though that wasn't true, she was almost entirely certain what came next, and it started with a *D* and ended with *ivorce.* "But what's happening right now is that you and I are going to stay in a hotel." Milo's face lit up. He loved everything about hotels, from the miniature bottles of shampoo and body gel to the room-service menus and pay-per-view movies. "Tomorrow we're going to drive to Connecticut to visit Grandma Sylvie for a while. Sound good?"

"Sounds good," he said, and when she squeezed his hand he squeezed back.

When she'd been making her grand descent down Doug's stairs, Diana had decided that she and her son would spend the night at the St. Regis in New York City, a place she'd walked by dozens of times on shopping trips to Saks, or visits to the Elizabeth Arden salon with her mother. She'd once had drinks with Hal in the King Cole Bar, but she'd never spent the night. Staying in a place like that, as opposed to a cheaper hotel or her parents' apartment, would make Milo feel, correctly or not, that they were on a kind of adventure.

In that spirit, Diana had treated Milo to lunch at McDonald's. He'd almost fainted in delight when she'd said he could have a cheeseburger and fries. They'd stopped at a Target on Route 1 for toiletries and a DVD of *Monsters, Inc.* It was close to five o'clock by the time they arrived in New York City.

"One key?" asked the woman behind the high marble counter, and Milo, who'd been staring, entranced, at the bellmen in their green-and-gold overcoats, had dashed up to Diana, whispering, "Two, please." (Among the hotel amenities that Milo especially loved were hotel key cards.) Diana slid her American Express onto the leather blotter. For one terrible moment she was convinced that Gary had canceled their credit cards, that he'd frozen their bank accounts, that maybe he'd even called the cops and told them Milo had been kidnapped. But the card went through. The woman handed Diana two room keys, and came out from behind the desk to escort them to the elevator.

"Your butler will show you to your room."

"Butler?" Milo whispered, his eyes wide beneath the brim

of the hat he'd worn to school, and Diana smiled as he slid his hand in hers. No matter what else she'd lost, she hadn't lost her son.

The butler who met them on the eighth floor turned out to be a woman, a woman in a tuxedo who showed them how to control the temperature, how to open the curtains, and how to use the remote to get the television set, which was concealed in the bed's footboard, to rise up. "I would be happy to bring you complimentary coffee or tea, and press any items of clothing," she said.

"Hot chocolate?" asked Milo, and the butler said she thought that would be all right.

Milo spent the next ten minutes making the set go up and down while Diana called Gary's cell phone.

"Are you doing okay?"

"Oh, I'm great," he said, in his clogged foghorn voice. "I'm just fan-fucking-tastic."

"Milo's fine." She paused, unsure of what to say to him, how much she should try to comfort him. "We're in New York. I thought we'd go to Connecticut for a few days and visit my mother." Gary sighed and said nothing. "Do you want to talk to him?"

She could picture her husband, slumped in front of his laptop, trying to pull it together. He'd minimize the screens filled with YouTube videos and sports news and gossip, he'd sit up straight and roll up his sleeves. "Of course I want to talk to Milo." Diana handed over the phone, then sat on the blue satin couch, sipped at her cup of tea, and thought that at least she had this tiny piece of her future planned out and under control.

Later, after they'd shared a room-service dinner of pizza and ice cream and watched *Finding Nemo* on the pay-per-view, Diana fired up her laptop, and pointed and clicked until she found what she was looking for. "Hey, Milo," she said—he was lying under the covers, thumbing through one of his insect books. "Want to see where we're going?"

Milo propped his chin on his hands and studied the photographs she'd found on the town of Fairview's website, which displayed a single shot of the big white house on a bluff overlooking the ocean. His finger traced the edge of the water. "It's probably too cold to go swimming."

She stifled a sigh—was the glass always half-empty with this kid?—and said, "Yes, but I bet it's cozy. There's fireplaces. And Grandma Sylvie's up there. She's excited to see you."

Milo's face brightened at the thought of his grandmother, who'd been considerably more liberal with her entertainment and snack options than Diana herself was, and was known to carry chocolate-covered pretzels in her purse. "Why is she there? Is it because of Grandpa's mistress?" he asked.

Jesus. "Where did you hear about that?"

"Dylan Berkowitz." Milo settled himself onto his pillow with a very Gary-like grunt.

But of course. Dylan's mom was a spray-tanned gym-bunny who lived on gossip and rye flatbread. "Do you know what a mistress is?"

He yawned and closed his eyes. "Like a girlfriend, only when you're married already. So it's bad."

Diana considered giving a little more explanation and context to the subject of mistresses, but decided that it had been a long day and he'd already heard enough. "I love you miles and miles," she said instead.

"Miles and miles," he agreed. She kissed his cheek, pulled up the covers, turned out the light, and sat cross-legged on the bed beside her serious, dark-haired boy until she knew he was sleeping. She was certain that she wouldn't be able to sleep—there were so many things she needed to plan for, like finding a lawyer and figuring out whether she wanted her old job back, and where she and Milo would live, and how she would live without Doug. She pulled off her clogs and slipped under the covers next to her son's warm body. *Just for a minute,* she thought, and closed her eyes, and when she opened them again it was morning, Saturday morning, with Milo frowning at the weather report on TV and the housekeeper knocking gently at the door.

"Is this Grandma's house?" Milo had asked as she'd cruised up the crushed-shell driveway to the house she hadn't visited in over a decade.

Diana nodded, and put the car in Park. "I used to come here when I was a girl."

Milo looked the house up and down—the sloping lawn, the wide wooden porch with the glider where Diana loved to sit and read. The leaves had turned from green to fiery orange and crimson, and the ones that were fallen had been raked into drifts at the base of the trees. Six pumpkins marched up the steps, and there was a basket full of apples and gourds by the front door. "It looks like the Haunted Mansion," he said, sounding thrilled, which was no surprise. She and Gary and Milo had made the obligatory family pilgrimage to Disney World for Milo's last birthday, and Milo had liked the Haunted Mansion better than any other ride, squealing in delight when their car spun around in front of the mirror and the special effects made it look as if there was a ghost in the backseat. Although, to be fair, Diana remembered as she climbed up the porch steps, Milo hadn't actually gone on many other rides. He'd nixed Space Mountain once he read in the guidebook that it was "too intense for young children," and, after forty-five minutes spent studying the faces of the people coming down the log flume, he'd announced that the ride also looked too intense. Gary, who'd planned on doing all the roller coasters with his son, had pouted for the rest of the day, and when Milo had asked to go on the spinning teacups on their way back to the car, Gary had said, "You're too old for the baby rides." Milo, hot and tired, had started to cry, and Gary had muttered, "Oh, great. That's just great," as Diana had thumbed through her guidebook, trying desperately to figure out where in the Magic Kingdom one could obtain an adult beverage.

She knocked. A minute later, the door swung open, and there was Sylvie, wearing a bathrobe and socks and a startled expression. "Diana?" she said. Diana wondered how she looked. She was wearing the clothes she'd left home in, the sweater Gary had wept upon, the leggings she'd pulled on to tell her husband they were through (and had her lover tell her the same thing). Her hair was uncombed, her face unwashed; and she hadn't put on makeup since before her ill-fated Sunday brunch, before she'd almost killed a little girl, before everything had fallen apart.

Maybe she could change her life up here. Maybe she could treat the Connecticut house like one of those spas she was always meaning to visit, if she could ever find the time, the places that had workshops on managing your stress and improving your diet and finding balance and joy in your life. Aside from Doug—and that hadn't turned out well—and Milo, there wasn't much joy in Diana's life. She worked so hard, and every penny she earned was spent almost before she'd finished earning it, gone to pay for the mortgage and the insurance and the property taxes, the private-school tuition, her dry-cleaning bill and the highlights for her hair, manicures and pedicures, the Internet and the cell phones and the cable. Maybe she could simplify; *simplifying* was a big theme at the spas that charged you three thousand dollars for a four-day retreat where experts would tell you about all the things you didn't need. She could find another job, one with normal hours. She could try meditation. She could learn to throw pottery or strip floors or hang wallpaper or do découpage. She could finally make her house the cozy, safe nest she'd always dreamed of. She could . . .

"Diana?" Her mother was staring at her. Diana cleared her throat.

"Hi, Mom." Her voice was still a little husky. She forced herself to stand up straight and tried out a smile. "We're here!"

LIZZIE

Lizzie had had the foresight to take a heating pad from the bathroom cabinet in New York so when she showed up in Connecticut and explained to her mother that she'd hurt her back and had been ordered by a doctor to stay in bed and rest, there'd be a prop. In the bathroom, she found that the spotting had stopped, and she didn't feel crampy or achy or any of the other ways the doctor had warned her she might feel. She spent the weekend visualizing herself walking slowly, with a bit of a limp, one hand clutching the affected area. On Tuesday morning, the intercom buzzed and Derek told her that he was downstairs waiting.

She listened to music for most of the drive, and woke as they were cruising up the steep driveway. She got out of the car, taking a deep breath of the cool air, then knocked on the door and stood waiting under the bright blue sky for someone to let her in.

Someone turned out to be Milo . . . and Milo meant Diana. Lizzie felt unease settle in her guts. Why hadn't her mother mentioned that Diana would be there, too?

"Auntie Lizzie!" Milo cried, his pale face breaking into a smile at the sight of her. He threw himself into her arms, with the bill of his baseball cap bumping her midsection. She hugged him hard, then stepped back, remembering what the doctor had told her about lifting anything.

"Hey, big guy. Take it easy, okay? I hurt my back."

Milo nodded, but he looked so forlorn that she bent over and gave him another squeeze. "What are you doing here?" she asked, as Derek carried her bags into the foyer.

"My mom and dad are having grown-up problems," he said.

Lizzie nodded, thinking that the grown-up problem was very likely named Doug Vance. Only why was Diana up here, and not in Philadelphia with her boyfriend? From what she'd glimpsed, it sure seemed as if they were getting along.

"It's so good to see you," she said, as Milo, grunting, heaved her duffel bag into his arms and tottered toward the staircase. "Are you having fun?"

"It's boring," he said and dropped her bag with a thud. "All the books are grown-up books, and the water's too cold for swimming."

"True," said Lizzie. "But I can show you how to play Frisbee for one."

"I don't know that game."

"Of course you don't. I invented it. You throw your Frisbee into the water, and if you time it just right then the waves bring it back to you."

Milo sighed. "My mom just stays in bed all the time."

Lizzie was surprised. Diana in bed? She'd never known her sister to sleep past six in the morning. She pictured herself and Diana, bedridden. She'd wait to make sure that the bleeding had stopped, and Diana would wait for . . . whatever she was waiting for. She left her bags where Milo had dropped them and walked slowly into the house, looking for her mother.

Sylvie was at the kitchen table, with a mug of tea beside her and a magazine with pictures of food spread open in front of her. Lizzie stared, blinking, until she confirmed that her impeccably groomed, meticulously dressed mother was, in fact, wearing yoga pants and a zippered hooded sweatshirt, and that there was a stretchy terry-cloth headband, the kind never intended for an outside-of-the-bathroom appearance, holding her hair, which was softly curling and streaked with gray, off her forehead.

"Hi, Mom."

Sylvie jumped up and hurried to hug her. "Lizzie!" With her mother's arms around her, her mother's familiar scent of perfume and Camay soap in her nose, Lizzie found herself on the verge of tears. She held her body stiffly, hoping Sylvie wouldn't notice anything different. She'd gained just five pounds, but her shape had changed, along with her center of gravity. She made herself grimace as Sylvie pulled away, hissing and grabbing at her back.

"What is it?" asked Sylvie. "What's wrong?"

"I slipped on the sidewalk a few days ago, and I hurt my back. It's no big deal," she added quickly as alarm spread over her mother's face. "It's just a strained muscle, but they want me to stay in bed for like a week. Maybe two." Sylvie hurried to usher her into a chair at the kitchen table, to get a pillow from the living room, to ask if she wanted tea or Tylenol, if hot baths or ice packs were recommended, if there was anything she could do.

"I'm okay," said Lizzie. "I'm really fine. I just need to rest."

Sylvie insisted on holding one of Lizzie's elbows and helping her up the stairs and into the bed in the bedroom closest to the landing. "Diana's down the hall," she said, pointing to a closed door behind which, presumably, Lizzie's big sister was hiding. Lizzie wondered again what she was hiding from. Had Gary walked in on her and Doug together? She smiled, then ducked her head to hide it, trying to imagine what her brother-in-law would do in such a situation.

The bedroom was clean and spare—a single bed, an oval braided rag rug with strands of red and blue and gold on the floor, a white-painted dresser, and a wooden desk by the window. Sylvie went downstairs, then came back up with a vase of daisies, a pot of tea, and a plate of butter cookies for the little table by the bed. Lizzie winced and grunted in what she hoped was an appropriate manner as she got under the covers and curled up on her side. Her mother pulled the covers up to her chin and smoothed her hair off her brow. "It's good to have you here," she said, and Lizzie smiled, then closed her eyes. Her heart was beating too fast—anxiety about the bleeding, fear of being found out—but otherwise, she felt exhausted, wanting to do nothing more than curl up and sleep.

She opened her eyes and looked at the ceiling, knowing that she needed a plan. First, she would wait to see if the bleeding had really stopped. If she had a miscarriage, she'd handle it herself, and her mother would never need to find out . . . and would Lizzie really be disappointed if the pregnancy ended? She decided that the answer was yes. Her whole life she'd been drifting, in and out of schools and jobs and rehab. A baby would anchor her. It would mean she'd have to stay in one place, it would give her a job—mother—from which she could never be fired. Over the weeks since she'd discovered her pregnancy, Lizzie had found those things increasingly appealing.

Her mother was still looking at her. Even with her eyes shut, Lizzie could feel her watching. "Are you all right?" Sylvie asked. "Do you need anything else?" She sounded sincere, which was new. Normally, Sylvie sounded as if Lizzie was an unpleasant task to be gotten through, a duty to be discharged.

"I'm fine," Lizzie repeated, opening her eyes. "Just sleepy." She yawned to prove her point, and shut her eyes again, and when she opened them it was dark outside her window, silent except for the sound of the waves. Her mother was bustling into the room, carrying a tray. Lizzie smelled chicken, which made her stomach roll over, her mouth flood with saliva, and her eyes spill over with tears. *I can keep everything warm*, Jeff had said, with that sweetly hopeful look on his face. *You'll come back, right?*

"Hi," she managed. Sylvie set the tray down, then sat on the edge of Lizzie's bed. "I want to talk to you about something."

Lizzie pushed herself upright. She wiggled her toes—the only part of herself that she could move without arousing suspicion—and wondered what was coming.

"That young man who . . . who bothered you while you were babysitting," Sylvie began.

Lizzie sat up straighter. "What? What about it?"

Sylvie was twisting her hands together, her fingers knotting and unknotting in her lap. "I've been feeling for the longest time that we—your father and I—that we let you down. That if we'd done something more, we might have . . ."

"Might have what?" Lizzie asked, her tone sharp. She could see chicken and mashed potatoes and carrots on the plate, and felt both queasy and ravenous as she wondered who had cooked it.

Sylvie looked at her hands, knotted at her waist. "I don't know," she said. "That we could have spared you a lot of pain."

Lizzie didn't know how to answer. She didn't want to answer. She wanted to be anywhere but the place she was, trapped in the soft bed in the cozy room with her mother talking about something she didn't want to discuss or even remember. She flung the covers back and gingerly swung her feet to the floor.

"Get back in bed," said Sylvie.

"I have to go to the bathroom!"

"Lizzie . . ." Sylvie put her hand on Lizzie's shoulder. Lizzie wriggled away.

"Look. I appreciate what you're saying. But it was a really long time ago. And I'm fine. I'm okay now. Really." Lizzie made her way slowly across the room. What she really wanted to do was go to the bathroom to see if there was any more spotting, then go down to the kitchen and find something to scrub, a dishwasher to empty, a floor to mop. She wanted to walk along the beach for hours while the waves licked against her boots. She wanted to move, and she couldn't. The doctor had said so. For the baby's sake, for the baby's safety, for once in her life of running and hiding, of ducking for cover underneath the candy cloud of painkillers, she had been well and truly halted. *You can do this,* she told herself. She took a breath, exhaled, then walked slowly to the bathroom, where she was heartened to see that the bleeding appeared to have stopped.

She washed her face and hands, brushed her teeth with one of the new brushes, still in its wrapper, that her mother had left out, and climbed back into bed. She tried a mouthful of potatoes, a single circle of carrot, chewing carefully, making sure each bite stayed down before attempting another. After a minute, Sylvie sat down beside her again. A minute later, Lizzie felt her mother's hand on her hair, stroking gently. "I'm so sorry," Sylvie whispered, in a soft voice Lizzie had never heard. Lizzie said nothing, holding her fork, concentrating on the baby inside of her, the size, maybe, of a raisin, a pencil eraser, a grain of rice.

DIANA

In the single yoga class that Diana had once endured, on a rainy day when all the treadmills were taken, the instructor, a dippy girl with tattooed hip bones, led them through an hour of twists and poses, until they'd ended up flat on their backs, legs spread to the edges of their mats. "Savasana—corpse pose—is the hardest pose of all. You would think, 'What could be hard about lying on the floor?' But the truth is that we, as humans, are not wired to be still and do nothing."

"Tell that to my husband!" one of the women on the mats had cracked, and everyone had laughed, but Diana knew exactly what the instructor was talking about—to simply be still, to listen to her breath, was for her, by far, the most difficult part of the class.

Before she'd had Milo, she'd trained for a marathon. She'd loved it—not just the running, but planning her workouts, arranging her days and weeks to get her miles in, entering data in her computer and plotting graphs of her distance and her speed. She'd had a heart-rate monitor and a special watch that calculated pace. She'd been able to figure out how long the twenty-six miles should take her and was pleased that she finished within twenty seconds of her predicted time. *Right on schedule,* she'd thought, crossing the finish line.

Now, eight years later, she woke up in the mornings with her heart racing, her flesh clammy, as if she'd been sweating all night. Always, there would be a few seconds of confusion as whatever nightmare had had her in its grip faded away: Where was she? How had she gotten there? Then it would all come slamming back: not Philadelphia, but Connecticut; no marriage, no job.

She'd get out of bed and pull on her socks and her sneakers, all she needed, because she'd started sleeping in her running bra, a T-shirt, and tights. On her way down the stairs, she'd throw on a long-sleeved shirt, or a fleece vest, or a raincoat if it was raining. She'd gulp juice straight from the carton, grab a PowerBar from her stash in the pantry, gallop down the stairs to the beach, and run. In her marathon-training days she'd vary her workouts. She'd do long, slow runs and short, quick ones; she'd do intervals and tempo runs, careful to keep her heart rate in its appropriate zone. Now she just ran as if something was chasing her, the way she'd run that steamy summer day in Philadelphia when she'd gotten the news about her father and Joelle—all out, as fast as she could, until her breath burned in her throat and stitches tore at her sides, until she tasted blood, until she couldn't go any farther. Her heels would send spumes of sand kicking out behind her, her arms would pump, her shadow would race ahead of her and Diana would try to catch it. Three miles, four miles, five miles she'd run, to the jetty that marked the end of the town of Fairview. When the tide was out she could run around it, but sometimes she'd have to plow through water up to her shins to skirt the rocks that stretched out into the Sound. Past the jetty, she'd keep on running, salt water squishing in the soles of her shoes, sweat stinging her eyes. Six miles, seven miles, eight, so fast that there was no room in her brain for thought, no room for anything but inhalation and exhalation and her body moving across the sand.

Eventually she'd stop, bent over, hands on her thighs, red-faced and gasping. She'd straighten up, lifting her arms over her head, do a few side bends, then touch her toes, and when her breath came a little more easily, when she didn't feel as if she was going to hurl, she'd turn around and start running back home. She'd take a shower and collapse back into bed, sleeping like the dead until Milo woke her. Sometimes one run would be enough, but sometimes she'd need to go out again before dinner. Her second runs were on the street—for variety's sake, she told herself, but really, it was because she was worried about people noticing her and talking, the way the moms at Milo's bus stop had whispered about the obviously anorexic racewalker who'd pump her bony arms and pipe-stem legs for hours along the sidewalks. She'd race down the shell-covered driveway, pounding along Fairview's narrow streets. It was three miles to the high school. She'd do sprints around the track until it got dark, then jog back home, jumping off the road if she saw a car approaching.

She was losing weight. Her running pants hung loosely on her hips, and she could see her ribs through her skin. Sylvie was worried. She'd cook all day—her mother, in an apron! In front of a stove! Diana wouldn't have believed it if she hadn't seen it with her own eyes. At the dinner table each night there'd be bowls of mashed potatoes, plates of pasta, then, later, popcorn and hot chocolate, when Sylvie and Lizzie would sit together on Lizzie's bed and watch movies on Lizzie's little laptop.

"Are you all right?" Sylvie asked, with Milo standing behind her, staring at his mother with his eyes dark and huge in his pale face.

Diana answered lightly, saying that she was thinking about doing another marathon in the spring, maybe even trying to qualify for Boston. Secretly, she thought there might be other races in her future, ultramarathons that went for fifty or even a hundred miles, twenty-four-hour time trials where you'd run all day and all night. How far would she have to go before she could outrun the mess she'd made, the way she'd laid waste to her own life? Would fifty miles stop the nightmares? Would a hundred miles bring Doug back?

A few terrible times each week, she'd have her hospital dream. In the dream, she would wheel her stool to the bedside of the girl whose face she could barely remember, the eight-year-old who'd come in semiconscious, with her insulin levels dipping dangerously low. She scribbled down the same incorrect dosage, only in the dream nobody caught the mistake, and she answered the phone in her kitchen to hear Hank Stavers telling her that the little girl had died. Then she'd wake up, covered in sweat, gasping for air, in the chilly gray of dawn, shove her feet into her sneakers, and go back to the beach.

She knew she was only postponing the inevitable. There were things that needed doing, tasks that required her attention. Gary was getting impatient with just talking to his son. He wanted to see Milo; he wanted Diana to bring him home, and, he'd said he'd hire a lawyer to make it happen if he had to. But somehow she was always either running or asleep. The living room couch loomed, as inviting as a lover's arms, with that cashmere throw draped seductively over its back, and she'd think, *Just for a minute,* and wake up three hours later in a puddle of drool, with her mother, this strange, new, solicitous version of Sylvie beside her, asking if she wanted some lunch, if there was anything she could do. She'd eat half a sandwich, drink a glass of milk—little-kid food, the kind she'd had for school lunches when she was Milo's age—and then, with barely a sentence spoken all day, she'd go running again.

She'd managed to take care of a few truly important things. The day after she'd arrived she called Milo's school to let them know he'd be absent indefinitely. The secretary had faxed his records and mailed his textbooks to the house in Fairview, so that at least she'd have the option of enrolling him in school in Connecticut, if it came to that. For now, she'd assigned him homework—a chapter in each of his textbooks, plus independent reading and writing each day. Lizzie had elected herself his art teacher. She'd given him her digital camera and assigned him twenty minutes outside, taking pictures of the leaves, the water, the crushed-shell driveway. When he came back they loaded the pictures onto her laptop and talked about cropping and composition, shadows and light. In the afternoons, when his work was done, Milo would go down to the beach to stand at the edge of the water and throw his Frisbee into the waves until it got dark and Sylvie called him in to help set the table for dinner. Diana managed to rouse herself enough to read him a chapter of *Harry Potter* every night before he fell asleep. Then most nights she'd join her mother and sister in Lizzie's bed. They would watch movies, she'd fall asleep.

She'd been desperately worried about her son—away from his house, his school, and his father. But as October slipped toward its end, Milo had proved surprisingly resilient. He loved Lizzie and his grandmother, and the truth that she'd never really wanted to acknowledge was that he'd never really liked school or the other kids there all that much. For him, Connecticut was a vacation. He could walk on the beach and look for sea glass and feathers and interesting pieces of driftwood. There were board games to play and books to read and marshmallows that his grandmother let him roast in front of the fireplace. Every night he'd talk to his father, carrying the portable phone into his bedroom and closing the door behind him.

The days blurred together—the gulped juice, the protein bars, the running, the sleeping, waking to nightmares and running again. Losing Doug was like going through withdrawal. She felt, she imagined, the same way an addict must feel when you cut off her supply. The only thing that kept her sane, that kept her from flying down the highway, back to Philadelphia, and begging Doug to take her back, was that tiny ember that had kindled in her heart when he'd not only rejected her but rejected, implicitly, her son. Milo was not expendable. Crazy in love as she might have been, she would never have foisted him on a man who didn't want him.

One sunny afternoon, with the crisp tang of autumn leaves and apple cider in the wind, she sat at the living room window, looking down at the beach, watching her son as he tossed the white disk of the Frisbee into the foaming waves. Her whole body hurt. Shin splints, she thought. Plantar fasciitis. A sore hip. A sore heart. She wandered upstairs to her sister's bedroom, where Lizzie was fussing with a tray Sylvie must have just brought up.

"Hey, Diana. Want some tea?" Lizzie lowered her voice. "It's Constant Comment. I hate that stuff. Mom made me a smoothie, too."

Diana sat on the edge of Lizzie's bed. She picked up the mug of tea and wrapped her hands around it. Her wedding ring hung loosely on her finger. Lizzie, in contrast, was plump and curvy, glowing with good health in spite of her back pain.

"I'm sorry about what happened this summer," Diana muttered. She knew she owed her sister an apology, and this seemed as good a time as any to deliver it.

"It's okay," said Lizzie. "Probably I would have thought the exact same thing if I were you. But just so you know, I wasn't using anything when I was taking care of Milo. I would never have gotten in a car with him if I wasn't safe to drive."

"I know," said Diana, realizing, as she spoke, that she'd known it all along. Lizzie, even at her worst, would not have put a child's life in danger. No, she thought, that was what she did. "I screwed something up at work."

Lizzie got very still. "What happened?"

"Nothing. Thank God. One of the nurses caught it. I wrote down the wrong dosage for a little girl—a diabetic. She needed insulin, and if they'd given her the dose I'd prescribed . . ." She stopped talking, unwilling to even speak the words *she could have died*. Down on the beach, Milo's Frisbee had gotten away from him. It bobbed in the waves, a tiny white dot, Milo stood at the water's edge, shoulders slumped, looking as defeated as his mother felt. "I took a leave from the hospital. I'm on leave from everything, I guess."

Instead of gloating, instead of sneering, Lizzie rolled over and patted her sister's knee, as tentatively as if she was checking to see whether a pan of Jell-O had set. "It happens. People make mistakes." She gave Diana a wobbly smile. "I guess I'm, like, exhibit A of that." They were quiet for a minute. Then Lizzie asked, "What about that guy I saw?"

"That's over," Diana said. No need to go into detail on that front.

"And what about Gary?" Lizzie's voice was so kind, so far away from the needling, sarcastic tone she usually used when the subject was Diana's husband.

"I think probably we'll get divorced," said Diana. "I think I kind of lost my mind."

"You and Dad," Lizzie murmured.

Diana wrapped her hands tightly around her mug. "It wasn't like Dad. Or at least, it wasn't like my understanding of how things were with Dad. It wasn't like, 'Ooh, there's a cute guy, let's hook up.' It wasn't about feeling entitled, or being tempted all the time." She took another sip. "I was lonely." She set the cup down on Lizzie's nightstand. "And I was tired. Tired of working so hard, tired of pretending everything was okay when it wasn't, tired of being unhappy with Gary, and disappointed with what the marriage turned out to be, tired of being the one who took care of the house and the shopping, and Milo, and . . ." She closed her eyes and flopped back onto her sister's bed, feeling so exhausted, so enervated, that she couldn't imagine ever running again, could barely imagine moving her body to the dinner table. "Everything." Lizzie nodded. Diana went on, "I think Gary's going to give me a hard time about the house. He thinks if I'm the one who was cheating and if I'm the one who wants out of the marriage, then I should be the one to leave. So I did. I just left."

Her sister's reaction was gratifyingly swift. "What? That's crazy! That's Milo's house! He's going to kick out his own kid?"

"I don't know." The house, she thought, seemed like the least of her problems. Her own broken heart, Milo's having to survive his parents' divorce, her having to find a new job, a new place to live, a new life for herself . . . she shut her eyes. It was all too much.

"What can we do?" Lizzie was asking—Lizzie, who'd never done much of anything in the years that passed for her adult life, Lizzie, who'd always needed someone to do things for her. "We can't let this happen. That's your house! Yours and Milo's."

"It'll be okay," Diana mumbled. The only thing she wanted was to close her eyes and sleep.

"And you don't think . . ." Lizzie spoke carefully. "There's no chance you and Gary can work it out?"

Diana shook her head. She couldn't imagine loving him again. At this point, from where she stood (or, more accurately, from where she lay, curled up and probably fragrant in the running clothes she hadn't changed out of), the thing to do was to acknowledge that, between them, they'd produced a remarkable, if socially awkward, little boy, and to move on as best they could.

"Then you need a lawyer," said Lizzie, reaching for the laptop next to her bed, and Diana, who no longer had the energy to form words, nodded her assent, then shut her eyes.

It felt like only a few seconds had passed when she woke up

to Lizzie shaking her shoulder. "Wake up!" she singsonged. "I got you a lawyer!"

Diana sat up, blinking, feeling a little bit rested. At least she hadn't had her dream again. "You did what?"

"I e-mailed Grandma Selma. Don't worry, I just said you were a friend."

Diana winced. Grandma Selma was a smart cookie, and what kind of friends did Lizzie have who came even close to fitting Diana's description? What friends, she thought with a sad pang, did Lizzie have at all? "What'd she say?"

"That the . . . hang on . . ." Lizzie paused, fiddling with her computer. "The presumptive standard is still that children do best with the primary caretaker. Which is you. That probably Gary will have to pay you alimony and child support, if you're awarded primary physical custody. And probably you'll get the house."

Diana narrowed her eyes, trying to suss out what had happened to Lizzie. "Are you okay?" she asked.

Lizzie toyed with her ponytail. "What do you mean?"

"Your back," Diana prompted. Her sister's back was the least of the changes she'd noticed, but it was a decent place to start.

Lizzie brightened. "Oh, yeah! That's fine! It doesn't even hurt anymore."

"You don't have to go in for a follow-up?"

Her sister fidgeted with a thread trailing from her sleeve. "I did. I saw someone in town last week. My doctor gave me a referral. Mom drove me. You and Milo were on the beach, I think. It's all good." She consulted her computer again. "Grandma gave me three names. I e-mailed two of them, and the third one's going to call me back, but here's the one I liked best." She tilted the screen so Diana could see a man's face, bald and avuncular, with a list of degrees earned, honors conferred, and articles published beneath it. Diana knew, from the first moment Doug had taken her hand in that grotty bar, that it could come to this—to lawyers and court dates and custody arrangements, the unraveling of her marriage, the end of everything—but, now that she'd actually arrived at the place she'd been at once dreading and longing for, she was terrified. What would life be like without Gary? As a husband, he'd disappointed her, but he'd been there, another body in the house (or, at least, another body on the couch), someone who thought of her fondly . . . or, at least, someone who had once. Gary probably didn't think of her fondly anymore.

She made herself breathe through the wave of dizziness that rolled over her, and put her bare feet on the floor. Baby steps, she told herself. She'd take a shower, get dressed, call the lawyer.

"Hey, Diana?"

Diana turned, one hand on the door frame. Her sister was fiddling with her hair, a gesture Diana remembered from when she was little and had ringlets—she'd pull one curl straight, then let it boing back into position. "People do this, you know?" said Lizzie. "People do this every day, and nobody dies of it."

Diana stared at her sister, wondering, once more, when the aliens had taken over her body. "Thank you," she said. *What happened?* she was thinking. *Lizzie, what happened to you?*

She found a towel and a washcloth, a toothbrush and toothpaste, and got herself cleaned up. After she took a shower, she made her way back to the bedroom, where her bed had been made, the pillows plumped, her cell phone plugged into its charger in the wall, and the lawyer's information and telephone number on the printout placed at the center of the bed. Diana hung up her towel, got into her clothes, picked up her cell phone, and walked out to the porch and sat with her legs crossed on the glider that looked out over the sea. "Diana Woodruff calling for David Bascomb," she said. When the receptionist said that Mr. Bascomb wasn't in, but could she take a message, Diana spelled her name and recited the digits of her cell phone number, and when the woman asked, "What is this regarding?" she found that it was, if not easy, then at least not impossible for her to say the words, "A divorce."

Once that was done, she put the phone in her pocket. She had hoped, she realized, as she walked down the lawn, breathing in the brisk fall air, that simply calling a lawyer, simply speaking the word *divorce* out loud, would be enough to cause some kind of transformation to take place. Magical thinking, she decided, kicking through a drift of bright, sweet-smelling leaves. Making the call, saying the words, telling her sister what had happened was a start, but it was far from the end.

Diana pulled out her cell phone again. Once, at summer camp, she'd climbed to the top of the ten-meter board because one of the boys had dared her to jump off. From the water, with the big kids doing jackknives and half gainers into the deep end, the high board didn't seem that high at all, but after you'd climbed the ladder and were standing at the edge, the concrete rough underneath your feet, looking down into the blue depths of the water, it seemed as if you were perched on top of the world, and that voluntarily stepping off the edge was nothing short of madness.

Still, Diana had made herself do it. *One, two, three,* she'd chanted in her head, forcing herself to the edge of the board and then off into space for the plummet that seemed to leave her stomach hovering ten meters above the rest of her before she plunged into the water. *One, two, three,* she chanted once more as she stood on the lawn and punched in the button that would connect her to Gary.

He picked up on the first ring. "Diana?" His voice was its usual wet rattle, which always made him sound as if he was on the verge of hocking up something horrible. *I never liked his voice,* Diana thought. There was a measure of relief—small, but present—in that realization, in being able to think it, even just to herself, and not have to hurry to suppress it, to tamp it down or paper it over or counter it with the ten things that she did like about him.

"I just wanted to check in . . ." She paused. What did she want to tell him? "We're still in Connecticut. Milo's fine."

"I know." Gary paused, then said a little reluctantly, "He sounds good." Another pause while he blew his nose. "When are you planning on bringing him home?"

"Do I have a home to come to?" Diana asked, and Gary sighed.

"Of course you do. Look. What I said about staying here . . . if we can't live together, we'll work something out."

Diana felt as if she'd been bracing for some blow, a punch to the gut, and she'd been hit with a pillow instead. Gary sounded as if he was suffering from the same kind of heartsickness that had afflicted her. "Just come home," he said. "We can talk about it. You probably didn't even get a chance to say goodbye to your boyfriend." He gave the last word a nasty spin.

"That's over," she said. When Gary didn't answer, she said, "I knew that it was wrong—of course I did—but . . . but I was very lonely."

"Right," he said. "Lonely. With me sitting right there."

Diana didn't take the bait. There would be plenty of time for accusations, plenty of blame to go around, plenty of time to tell him, if she decided it was wise, that it was entirely possible to be lonely with someone else in the room.

"Whatever happens," she said, "I want you to see Milo. You're his father, and I want you in his life."

Now Gary sounded offended. "Of course I'm going to be in his life. You think I'd dump him because of what you did?" He sighed. "I wish you'd come home so we could talk about it."

"For now, I want to stay up here."

"How long's for now?" he asked. She could hear that old needling tone back in his voice, what she'd come to think of as Gary's where-are-my-keys whine.

"Through Thanksgiving," she said.

"Jesus, Diana! What about school?"

"I'm homeschooling him."

"What about work?"

"I'm on leave," she answered

"Come home," he said again, and Diana thought, *I am home.* She did close her eyes then, and let herself imagine where the two of them might be in a year or two. Gary would find someone, of course. She could picture the woman, the kind of woman he probably should have been with from the start—a little younger than he was, short and round-faced, a laughing, bouncing, cheerful girl with none of the moodiness and melancholy that could afflict Diana. Gary's girlfriend would be a pediatric nurse, or a preschool teacher, some kind of job that made use of her eternal good cheer. Diana could picture her smiling and joking with a small, frightened child as she bent to administer a test or a shot, dispensing Band-Aids and lollipops or stickers, once the damage had been done.

This girl, Gary's girl, would love Disney World with unfeigned, unironic enthusiasm, and would be able to coax Milo onto the scary rides. She'd keep bowls of Hershey's Kisses on the coffee table, and she'd decorate the house for all the big holidays and most of the small ones. Probably she'd be class mother, and PTA president, and she'd deliver meals to the elderly once a month. In bed, she'd be willing and exuberant, and would take it as an endorsement when Gary sweated all over her. She'd have one of those names that ended in an "e" sound—Meggie, Carly, Kylie. She'd sign her letters "xo" and salt her e-mails with emoticons, and adjust her settings so that her signature appeared in pink. To her, Gary would never look stupid. She'd load his mashups onto her iPod. She'd sit beside him on the couch, watching football, cheering for interceptions and touchdowns.

Maybe she'd even come to love Milo—she'd be the kind of girl who would find it easy to love. She'd have some nickname for Diana's son—*pal* or *buddy*, a word that Milo would claim to detest but would maybe secretly like a little bit. *C'mon, pal,* Kylie or Meggie would say, helping Milo hop into her minivan with the THIS CAR CLIMBED MOUNT WASHINGTON bumper sticker—God, Diana could picture it, its maroon paint, a well-worn booster seat in the back, a can of Diet Coke, because Meggie/Carly/Kylie would always be on a diet, in the cup holder up front. *Don't call me that,* Milo would grumble, but he'd be smiling, the corners of his mouth turned up just enough so the girl would know he didn't really mean it.

"I just wish . . ." said Gary.

"I only wanted . . ." said Diana.

They paused again. "I'll bring him home this weekend," she said to her husband—her ex-husband, her soon-to-be ex-husband. She would have to get used to saying that, have to get used to thinking of herself as a woman who had an *ex* instead of a *husband*. But she could do it. It was like Lizzie had said. People did, every day. People did it, and nobody died. Diana leaned back against a tree trunk, feeling the sunshine on her face and arms, as she and her husband started tentatively making plans for the weekends, plans for Gary to see his son.

SYLVIE

"Wake up!" Sylvie said, knocking first on Diana's door, then on Lizzie's. "Come on, girls, rise and shine!" A faint groan issued from Diana's bed. Sylvie heard nothing at all from Lizzie's room. She knocked again, then flung the door open. Lizzie was curled on her side, covered in blankets except for a tuft of blond hair. "Come on," she said, opening the curtains, then the window, and letting the salty air scour the room. The sky and the ocean were both an undistinguished gray, and all of the trees were bare. "I've got plans."

Lizzie peeked out from under the blankets. "Plans?"

"Yes." She waited until Lizzie was sitting up, yawning and rubbing at her eyes. "Milo's going fishing with Tim, and now that you're feeling better, you and I and Diana are going on an adventure."

"What's up with you and Tim?" Lizzie asked.

Sylvie fussed with the curtains, stalling for time. Tim had come to dinner a few times in the weeks since the girls' arrival, bringing flowers and desserts. Lizzie and Diana had been polite, but not terribly curious. Then again, they seemed to have enough of their own problems to keep them occupied, although God knew she hadn't heard any details—not about Lizzie's bad back, not about Diana's job or Diana's husband. After she'd been in Connecticut for two weeks, Lizzie had locked her bedroom door and talked to her doctor in New York, the one who'd put her on bed rest. The next day, she'd asked for a ride into town. "I got a referral," she said, with the pride of someone announcing that she'd found a winning lottery ticket, and Sylvie had been so touched by this belated show of responsibility that she'd offered to take Lizzie clothes shopping afterwards . . . only Lizzie had given her a mysterious smile and said, "No thanks."

Meanwhile, Diana had loaded Milo into her car last Friday afternoon, taking him to meet his father back in Philadelphia. They'd come back on Sunday, thoughtful and quiet, but when Sylvie asked how Gary was doing and how the visit had been, all her daughter and grandson would say was "It was okay" and "Everything's fine."

"Get dressed," Sylvie told Lizzie, pulling the covers off her body.

"Are you and Tim dating or what?" Lizzie persisted, sitting up in bed (she wore a vintage slip as a nightgown, and there were pillow marks creasing her cheek).

"Tim and I are friends," Sylvie said. That was her story and she was sticking to it. She reached into her pocket and handed Lizzie the flyer she'd picked up at the Fairview Library.

"Unraveling: A Memoir of Midlife," Lizzie read aloud, making a face—whether at the title, the photograph of the lithe lady author, or the entire concept of leaving the house and going out with her mother in public, Sylvie wasn't sure. "I don't know. I think my back's still a little stiff."

Sylvie stifled her frustration. "You've been doing nothing but lying around for weeks. I'm not running a sanitarium."

"I was supposed to rest," Lizzie protested.

"Well, now you're fine, right?" She waited for Lizzie's reluctant nod before saying, "I'm sure fresh air is the best thing for you. You could probably use some exercise, too," she said, because Lizzie had definitely gained a few pounds after all of the popcorn and lounging around in bed.

Diana charged into the room in her running gear. "What's going on?"

"Mom's making us go to a reading," Lizzie said, handing her sister the flyer, which Diana studied as if she'd be quizzed on it later.

"Unraveling? Are you trying to tell us something?"

"I thought it would be interesting," Sylvie said, keeping her voice neutral while Diana read from the flyer.

"At forty-two, Drea Danziger had it all—a loving husband, a handsome son, a beautiful farmhouse in Litchfield. But still, she felt a nagging emptiness, a hole in the center of her life." Diana studied the author's photograph. "I think she was probably just hungry."

"Let me see." Lizzie giggled.

"Seriously," said Diana, handing over the flyer. "The hole in her life could have been filled with a corned-beef sandwich."

Sylvie struggled not to tell Diana that she, too, could use a sandwich or three. In contrast to Lizzie, her eldest was getting positively gaunt. "Both of you, behave. I'm sure that woman worked a long time on her book."

"Oh, barf," said Lizzie, rolling her eyes. "Some rich married lady with her own farm talking about how yoga solved her spiritual crisis is supposed to make us feel better?"

"Flake," Diana muttered.

"If you'd tell me what's wrong—" Sylvie began, but Diana cut her off.

"Why don't we just go running?"

"I hurt my back," Lizzie said.

"I'm old," said Sylvie.

Diana considered this. "Jogging? We could start off slow."

Sylvie didn't bother being insulted that neither of her girls had insisted that she wasn't old and that, in fact, all her best years were ahead of her. Maybe she should join Diana on her next trip to civilization and get her hair touched up.

"Maybe we could find a yoga class?" Sylvie suggested.

Lizzie bounced out of bed (Sylvie took a moment to appreciate how completely her back had healed, and to marvel at the resiliency of youth). "How about walking?" she offered. "We can walk on the beach and have a picnic. I can take some pictures."

They gazed dubiously out the window. At that instant, as if decreed by God, the clouds parted, and a beam of golden October light slipped through to sparkle on the water. A bird sang, a high, piercing note. In unison, the three of them sighed.

"I'll pack lunch," Sylvie said.

"I'll lend you a good bra," Diana said to her sister. Lizzie rolled her eyes again but managed a civil "Thanks," and Sylvie left them, driving into town to buy a picnic for their day at the beach.

Half an hour later, they assembled at the door. Diana had her hair gathered into a high ponytail. She smelled of sunscreen and was dressed in her workout clothing, with reflective piping and breathable panels that were made, she'd told them, from recycled bamboo. Sylvie wondered how that was possible—could you actually turn trees into textiles?—before deciding she didn't want to ask. Lizzie was her usual sweetly disheveled self, in droopy blue sweatpants and a hooded orange sweatshirt, with a knitted wool scarf looped around her neck and her camera on top of it. Sylvie wore her regular walking clothes—yoga pants, sneakers, a long-sleeved T-shirt she'd gotten on her birthday trip to Canyon Ranch with Ceil.

Tim arrived at ten-thirty, wearing jeans, a plaid shirt, hiking boots, and a many-pocketed fishing vest. Milo, wearing the hook-decorated fisherman's hat that Sylvie had bought for him, held his mother's hand as he approached the door, but ran out to Tim's truck when he saw the canoe loaded in the back. "Got a life jacket just his size," Tim said. "We'll be home by five." Sylvie slipped her backpack, containing the picnic lunch, over her shoulders, and ushered her girls down the rickety wooden steps and down to the water.

For the first ten minutes they walked in silence. Diana pumped her arms, bouncing off the balls of her expensive padded sneakers, clearly eager to break into a run and leave the two of them behind her. Lizzie loped along, wandering toward the water, then up toward the high-tide line, stopping to pick up shells and bits of seaglass or driftwood and put them in her sweatshirt's pouch, or to snap a photo of the water, or the seagulls wheeling in the sky. Sylvie walked between them. Part of her was enjoying the moment, the gentle sunshine on her head, the cool sand beneath her shoes, and the joy of being with her daughters, somewhere private, where there was nothing but time. The day stretched out ahead of them, the hours until Tim would bring Milo home, and they had no plans or obligations, nothing to do except spread their blanket on a promising patch of sand and eat lunch . . . and talk. Today was the day that she'd get to the bottom of things. She'd figure out what was wrong with her daughters, and once she knew she'd figure out how to fix it. She walked, keeping a comfortable pace, aware of her breath filling her lungs and the rhythm of her heartbeat. She looked ahead at Diana's bobbing ponytail, or back at Lizzie's meanderings, holding back her question, the same one for each of them: *Girls, what's wrong?*

Diana finally cracked. "Okay if I run for a little while?"

"Go ahead," Sylvie called. "We'll have lunch set up when you get back."

Diana was off like a shot, her sneakers leaving miniature tornadoes of sand behind them. Sylvie and Lizzie walked another few minutes before spreading the blanket on the golden sand. Lizzie sat down with a sigh, and Sylvie unloaded the picnic. That morning, she'd stopped at one of the little shops in town, a place called Village Cheese. She'd strolled past it a dozen times, always impressed with its pretty appearance, its white-painted walls and blue door and white-and-yellow-striped curtains. Inside, there were wide, planked wooden floors and urns of vinegars and olive oil, jars of jams and honey, and perhaps a hundred different kinds of cheese behind the curving glass case.

"Can I help you?" asked the girl behind the counter, whose striped apron matched the curtains. Sylvie picked out a slab of salty Gruyère, a creamy wedge of Brie, and a goat cheese studded with cranberries. She bought a baguette, a jar of fig jam, three perfect green apples, a half-pound of duck mousse, and a quart of raspberries, then added a bag of salted caramels and another of dark chocolate–covered pretzels. "Anything to drink?" asked the girl at the cash register, and Sylvie added a bottle of water and one of lemonade, then helped herself to plastic knives and a handful of paper napkins.

Lizzie poured herself some lemonade and sipped it, staring out at the shifting blues and greens and grays of the water.

"So," said Sylvie, "how have you been?" It was a ridiculous cocktail-party question, but she'd been thinking as she walked and she hadn't come up with a better way to get the conversation started.

"Okay," Lizzie said; strands of hair had come free from her headband and blew around her rosy cheeks. She wrapped her arms around her knees.

"Your back's all better?"

"It's fine," Lizzie said, still watching the water.

"Do you miss New York?" Sylvie ventured. "Your job or your friends?"

Lizzie made a face. "The job was kind of a make-work thing. And I haven't really had friends in years."

Sylvie winced at this—was it true? She thought. "That girl Patrice . . ."

"Patrice was in high school," Lizzie said. "I haven't talked to her in ages."

"Oh, Lizzie," Sylvie said.

Lizzie shrugged and looked at her mother sideways. "I've got you, right? You and Dad and Diana. Even though Diana doesn't really want me."

"Your sister loves you," Sylvie said reflexively.

"Oh, please," Lizzie mumbled. She lowered her chin toward her knees, then lifted her head and started fiddling with her camera. "I'm just another mess she has to clean up."

"That's not true," said Sylvie.

"Sure it is. That's what I am, really. Just a mess for you guys to take care of. I'm not . . ." She took a deep breath, and when she spoke again her voice was trembling. "Responsible."

Tentatively, Sylvie put her hand on her daughter's back, high, between her shoulder blades, not where it hurt. "I know your father and I weren't always there for you the way we should have been."

Instead of answering, Lizzie lifted her camera and put the viewfinder to her eye, pointing the lens out at the ocean.

"Put that down," Sylvie said. "You don't have to hide."

"Sometimes," said Lizzie, "it's good to have something to hide behind." The camera clicked. "Like you always stood behind Dad."

Treading carefully, Sylvie said, "That thing that happened. When you were babysitting. I've been thinking . . ."

She could see the dimples flash in Lizzie's cheeks beneath the camera's body as she smiled. "You still think that's why I was a junkie? Because some guy made me give him a blow job?"

"Well, I always thought . . . I mean, the timing . . ." Sylvie stopped talking, her face flaming at the words *blow job,* and also at her embarrassment at having been so wrong. If she'd been wrong. Had she?

"It wasn't just that," said Lizzie. "It was a lot of things." She set down her camera and picked up her glass of lemonade. "School was hard for me. Everyone thought I'd be just like Diana."

"But that boy . . ."

"It wasn't a big deal!" Lizzie jumped to her feet. Her face was flushed.

Sylvie grabbed her hand. "Just let me finish!" she said, and Lizzie, unused to hearing her mother raise her voice, stared at Sylvie, wide-eyed. "I've been thinking that we failed you," Sylvie said. "Your father and I." She waited, then said, "Actually, me more than him. Maybe just me. I wanted to call the police. I wanted to file charges. I thought that boy should have gone to jail." She twisted her hands together, then confessed. "I let your father talk me out of it, and I don't think there's a day that's gone by that I haven't felt guilty."

Lizzie lifted her camera again. "I don't think they send people to jail for doing what he did. Not if the girl was willing. And I was. Mostly. At least at first. He was cute, remember?"

"That doesn't matter!"

"It did to me," said Lizzie. "When I was twelve." Sylvie heard the shutter click. "So Dad didn't want to go to the police, and you did?"

"That's right." She felt guilty for betraying Richard this way, but it was time Lizzie knew the truth; knew that at least one of her parents had wanted to do the right thing, even if she'd lacked the guts to follow through. "I'm sorry, Lizzie. I'm sorry I didn't try harder."

"It's okay." Lizzie let the camera drop again, and squinted up into the brightening sky. "Believe me, I've got bigger things to worry about now."

"Like what?" Sylvie asked. "You can talk to me. I'm here for you now. We've got time . . ." But it was at that moment that they spotted Diana pounding down the beach, face red, feet churning through the sand, her ponytail flashing behind her like a banner.

"Incoming," Lizzie muttered, and lifted her camera to take pictures of her sister as she ran.

DIANA

Since talking to Lizzie, and her lawyer, Diana had made some headway toward getting her life back on track. She'd driven her son back home for a visit. Gary took Milo to the science museum and the zoo while she stayed behind, wandering from room to room of the row house, which had remained unchanged (and, she suspected, uncleaned) since the morning she'd left. She picked things up—the framed wedding photo on their dresser, the painted ceramic pitcher she'd bought on spring break in Mexico, the iron Buddha one of Gary's friends had given them as a wedding gift—and held them, weighing them in her hands before setting them down again.

In the mornings, after a more reasonable run, she'd go upstairs, shower, dress, and help Milo with his lessons, listening to him read out loud, coaching him through a few pages in his math workbook, watching as he wrote stories, and postcards to his dad. In the afternoons, she'd take him to the library, or to the town green, where he'd made friends with a girl who wore her curly blond hair in braided pigtails and taught Milo how to hula hoop with the pink glittery hoop that her mother carried to the park, looped over the handlebars of her little sister's stroller.

Still, by four or five most afternoons she found herself in bed again, a cup of chamomile tea steaming on the bedside table, a light down comforter pulled up to her neck, the window open a crack so that the crisp, salt-scented air could come through. She'd lie there and think about Doug. Did he miss her? Had he moved on? Was he bringing some other girl to the Khyber, or the parking lot, doing the things to her that had pleased Diana so well? Would she ever see him again? She would consider these questions until she dozed off, sleeping until the sun went down and someone came to wake her up for dinner, which she never helped prepare. Sylvie, who had somehow, miraculously, learned how to cook, would make soups and stews and homemade breads, chicken pot pies, casseroles and roast turkey breasts. Milo would help set the table, and Diana and Lizzie would do the dishes, and wipe the counters and sweep the floors. *Regression*, she thought . . . although could it really be regression if she and her sister were retreating to a life they'd never had, an idyllic childhood they'd never enjoyed?

Usually Lizzie delivered the late-afternoon wake-up knock, but one Friday she woke to Milo's husky voice outside her bedroom door. "Trick or treat!"

Trick or treat? Diana bolted upright in bed, her heart pounding the way it had at the end of one of her epic runs. Was it Halloween? Could that be? She'd noticed some decorations in stores and around town, and the curly-haired girl had told Milo how she planned on going out dressed as a football player (the little girl's mother, who'd never said more than "hello" and "see you later" to Diana, had rolled her eyes at this), but Diana had figured it meant that the holiday was approaching, not that it was here already. *I am,* she thought, swinging her legs out of bed and steeling herself to face her son, *the worst mother ever, the worst mother in the entire world.* She'd cheated on her husband, she'd torpedoed her marriage, she'd yanked Milo out of school and away from his home and everything that was familiar and dragged him up to Connecticut, and now she'd forgotten what she well knew was one of the most important nights in a child's year. Could he ever forgive her, and, if so, how many years of therapy would it take?

"Milo, I'm . . ." She started to say *sorry,* but the word died on her lips, because there was her son, dressed in a costume. He wore—she blinked—a shiny black sphere that extended from his neck to just above his knees, leaving his arms and legs free, and seemed to be unpeeling in sections, like an orange. Underneath it, he wore black pants and a black turtleneck.

"I'm a Bakugan!"

"A what?"

"It's some kind of toy," said Lizzie, who was standing behind him. "He said all the kids in school had them. They're, like, balls that unroll and turn into something else."

"Ah." Diana peered at her son, who spun proudly, then thrust a pumpkin-shaped plastic bucket at her.

"Trick or treat!" Milo said again. She felt her heart sink again.

"Oh, honey, we don't have any candy."

"Right here," said Lizzie, who had a witch's hat perched on her head. Underneath it she wore a loose black sweater, a long, tattered black skirt, black patterned hose, and ankle-high black boots. She handed Diana a bag of Hershey's Kisses and Diana, still in shock, took out two and dropped them in Milo's bucket.

"Oh my God," Diana whispered, as Milo thundered downstairs to show Sylvie the night's first plunder. "I totally forgot . . . I had no idea . . ." She sank back down on her bed. "Can he even go trick-or-treating?" Most of the other beach houses had been closed up for the season. Besides, Milo had never liked knocking on strangers' doors and asking for candy. Every year that he'd been verbal enough to articulate a request, he'd ask to stay home with Diana, sitting on their front step in Philadelphia, handing out the raisins and pretzels she bought. This, of course, drove

Gary crazy—in part, Diana suspected, because if Milo didn't trick-or-treat there was no in-house candy to poach from.

"Where'd he get the costume?" she asked.

"I made it."

She blinked at her sister. "You did? When did you learn how to sew?"

Lizzie shrugged. "There wasn't much sewing. It's mostly Velcro. I ordered this kit online."

Diana blinked and rubbed her eyes. "Thank you. He would have been destroyed if we'd forgotten."

"No worries," said Lizzie. She adjusted her hat, peering at her reflection in the window. "Mom's downstairs. She's got a costume, too."

Diana looked at herself, her corduroys and black boatneck sweater. Lizzie grinned. "Just say you're a psycho killer. They look like everyone else."

Lizzie led her downstairs, where they found Milo perched on the edge of the kitchen table and eating a bowl of soup. "I told him he had to eat something before we went into town," said Sylvie. Diana looked at her mother, who was dressed as she'd seen her a thousand times before, in an unremarkable, expensive blue skirt and matching jacket, in hose and heels, with her hair tucked behind her ears. Diamond studs sparkled at her earlobes, her Tank watch encircled her right wrist . . . and, her lips were curved into a perfectly polite and meaningless smile.

"Who are you?" Diana asked.

"I haven't decided," Sylvie said. "I'm either Elizabeth Edwards or Silda Spitzer. Or maybe just Generic Politician's Wife."

"Scary," Lizzie murmured.

"The funny thing is," said Sylvie, smoothing her hands over her hips, "it actually does feel like a costume now. Like I was in disguise for all those years." She fiddled with the waistband, sighed, then said, "I think I'm going to change."

"Don't change too much," said Lizzie, which was what Richard typically said when any other family member announced her intention to change. Sylvie gave them a wave and walked upstairs. Milo set his spoon and bowl into the sink with a clatter, then turned to his mom.

"Are you ready?"

"Where are we going?" Diana asked.

"To the town green," said Milo, as if this was obvious. "They're having a festival, with music and a puppet show. Lucy's going to be there." Lucy, Diana presumed, was the hula hoop girl. "Come on, come on, come on!" said Milo, who was dancing by the front door as if he had to pee. Diana thought for a minute, wondering whether he could pee in his costume, and if she should make him use the bathroom before they left.

"Ready?" asked Sylvie, coming down the stairs in her yoga pants and sweater . . . and before Diana could tell Milo to wash his hands or use the bathroom or take a sweater, they were in the car, backing down the steep driveway, on their way to the town green, where, as promised, there were merchants (her mother's friend Tim Simmons was among them) handing out candy and cookies and cups of apple juice, and the high school jazz quartet tootling away in the bandshell. Costumed kids carrying flashlights and buckets of candy chased one another over the lawns, while parents with conspirators' grins sipped wine poured into plastic cups from bottles tucked into purses or paper bags. Lucy's mother waved Diana and Lizzie over and offered them cups of red wine. "No thank you," Lizzie said, and the woman, who seemed a little tipsy, said, "Oh, that's right, you don't have kids. You don't need any of the mommy happy juice."

Lizzie smiled faintly—she was still sensitive about drinking, Diana figured. Impulsively, she reached out and gave her sister a hug. "Thank you," she said. "Thank you for not forgetting."

"You're welcome," Lizzie said, then bent to pick up her

witch's hat, which had gotten knocked off during the embrace. She's grown up, Diana thought, feeling a mixture of pride and sorrow . . . because if Lizzie was an adult, no longer in need of attention and rescue, where did that leave her? How much of her identity, her role as wife and responsible big sister, could be stripped away before she no longer knew who she was anymore, before there was nothing left at all?

Ah, well, she thought. Maybe she could convince Lizzie to come back to Philadelphia with her, after Thanksgiving. Gary had already found a place to rent, a two-bedroom apartment a few blocks away from their house. Maybe Diana and Lizzie could live in the row house together. They could tend to Milo, and Lizzie, of course, would find some kind of job eventually, and the three of them could keep one another from being too lonely.

"You okay?" Lizzie asked.

"I'm fine," said Diana. She sipped her wine and watched her son race to the top of a hill, then roll down, with his costume gathering leaves and dirt as he went. She imagined the four of them, together like this, every year—Milo getting bigger, Lizzie maybe going back to school, and Sylvie, she thought, going back to Richard . . . but maybe every Halloween they would come back to sit on the town green and sip wine and eat candy, bundled in sweaters and blankets as the moon rose overhead. Maybe it could be that way. Maybe someday she and her boy would be fine.

LIZZIE

The house on the hill, the house she'd never liked, was a three-mile walk from Fairview's downtown, where the town's single AA meeting was held in the basement of a Catholic church, and where the town's obstetrician kept an office three doors down. Lizzie would leave the house at eleven in the morning, once she was done supervising Milo's lessons, and walk briskly into town. She'd have a cup of tea and a scone at the coffee shop, go to her meeting at noon, pick up whatever her mother needed—groceries, a book she'd put on hold at the library, envelopes from the general store or stamps from the post office—and, depending on her load, either walk back home or wait for her mother or Diana to come fetch her. *Moderate exercise is fine,* the Fairview doctor had told her. *In fact, I'd encourage it.* So, five days a week, she walked. With her arms swinging and the music pounding in her ears, she could keep herself from thinking about the swell of her belly underneath her layers of T-shirts and sweaters, and how she was going to have to make some kind of announcement, and soon. Already, her excuses about too much time in bed and too much starchy food were feeling a little threadbare.

Each morning she'd bring her camera with her and take pictures: a crow perched on a power line, a group of girls laughing into their mittened hands in front of the empty fountain, a woman yawning as she stroked mascara onto her lashes while stopped at Fairview's single red light.

On Tuesday morning, two days before Thanksgiving, Lizzie set off under a bright blue sky, with her empty shopping bags, and her wallet and her grocery list and her iPod to keep her company. The air was crisp, so cold that she could see her breath in puffs in front of her. She looped a knitted red scarf around her neck and started walking. She'd rounded the corner from the driveway onto the street when she saw a gray car idling at the corner. There was a man behind the wheel . . . and, as Lizzie watched, the driver's-side door swung open, as if the man had been waiting for the moment when she'd come along. As he climbed out and turned toward her, Lizzie saw, with her heartbeat quickening, and a taste of old pennies in her mouth, that it was Jeff. He wore a crisp white shirt and khakis and silvery sunglasses. Beneath his short hair, the tips of his ears were red in the cold.

She tucked her hand into the pocket of her down vest until her fingers brushed her house key. She thought about running, trying to sprint back up the hill to the house, but what would that accomplish? If he'd followed her this far, refusing to take the hint of the way she'd ignored his e-mails and calls, what would stop him from chasing her to the door? And it wasn't as if she could outrun him. Not in her condition.

"Jeff," she said, trying to sound calm.

"Hey, Lizzie." His voice was friendly enough, but Lizzie couldn't see his eyes behind his sunglasses, only his neatly combed hair and his lips pressed in a straight line. She wondered whether he'd noticed her weight gain; whether he suspected, or just thought she was getting fat.

"What are you doing here?" she asked, trying to keep her voice calm.

"You took off." He was sounding less friendly now, a little annoyed. "I've been trying to reach you for weeks. Did you stop checking your e-mail or something?" When Lizzie didn't answer, Jeff said, "I thought we could talk."

She shrank back toward the driveway. "How did you find me?"

"I called your dad." His lips twisted. "Took me a while to get him on the phone, but I was persistent."

"How did you get his number?"

Jeff pulled off his glasses and folded them into his pocket. "From when you called me, remember?" He squinted at her through the sunshine, and she tried to read the expression on his face. Was he angry? "Your dad gave me the phone number up here, but I decided it'd be better if I came in person."

"And how'd you know which house?"

"Reverse directory." Finally, he smiled. "It's not that hard, really."

She smiled back, feeling uneasy as she tried to figure out her next move. "This isn't a great time. I've actually got an appointment." She thought about telling him her appointment was an AA meeting, but decided not to.

"Can I give you a ride?"

She shook her head. "I'm walking."

"I'll walk with you," he said. "Maybe we can get some lunch, after your appointment."

Walking into town with Jeff Spencer was the last thing she wanted to do, but she didn't see how she could refuse. "Okay," she said. She did need to eat, and he seemed to be set on the idea that they needed to talk, so maybe it wouldn't be so terrible to have a meal with him. Lunch sounded civilized. Better, lunch was public. There was no way he could start shouting at her in the middle of the Fairview Diner. At least she didn't think he would.

Jeff fell into step beside her, and they walked toward town. For a few minutes, Lizzie let herself enjoy the feeling of being half of a couple, the way they'd been that summer, when she'd walk beside him on the sidewalk or hold his hand at dinner and think of what a normal picture they made; how no one who saw them would guess how far from typical her life had been. "So how's Independence Hall?" she asked. He told her that the week before, a Japanese tourist had gotten stuck in the bathroom and they'd had to call the fire department, and the week before that a Boy Scout troop had lost one of its members, but it had turned out that the kid was safe and sound and asleep on a bench in front of the Betsy Ross House. "How's Milo?" he asked, and she told him that Milo was actually up here, that she had him taking pictures, and playing Frisbee, too. A few times, Jeff seemed on the verge of asking her something, but he didn't, so that in between their chatter about his classes and her photographs, the only sounds in the still fall air were their footfalls on the road, and their breath.

When they were paused at the town's single traffic light, Jeff took her arm. His coat felt nice under her hand. She wondered if it was wool or cashmere or something like that. She suddenly felt ashamed of her wardrobe. The sweaters and the down vest were fine for the eighteen-year-old freshman she'd been when her problems had gotten serious, but maybe not quite the thing she should be wearing at her age, even though the layers did a fair job of disguising her belly. She thought maybe for once she could skip her meeting. It might be nice to have lunch with him, to sit somewhere warm and look at him and listen to his stories, dispatches from the real world.

"Are you hungry for anything special?" he asked when she

told him that her appointment could wait. "Do you have a favorite place?"

She directed him to the Fairview Diner, which made a decent turkey club sandwich and good soups from scratch.

The waitress led them to a booth. Jeff set his glasses on the table and hung his jacket and Lizzie's vest on a hook on the wall. Underneath the fake Tiffany lamp that hung over the table, they sipped ice water and studied the specials.

"So what are you doing here?" she blurted, once they'd ordered their lunches—a turkey club for Lizzie, grilled cheese and tomato soup for Jeff.

"I want to apologize."

She stared at him, surprised. "For what?"

"I think I reacted badly in my apartment, when you told me about your . . ." He paused. She waited. "Your problem. I know that it's not always like it was for my mom. People get better. I know they do." The waitress set his soup down, and Jeff offered Lizzie a spoonful and, when she refused, the Saltines that came with it. "I'm sorry if I scared you away."

"It wasn't just that," Lizzie said. "I was going through some things . . . with my dad and all. My mom needed me, and my sister, and my nephew. It's not a very good time for me to be . . ." She bent her head, mumbling, "You know. In a relationship right now."

Jeff set down his spoon neatly next to his bowl. "I never stopped thinking about you."

Lizzie stared at him with her heart in her throat. During her lost years, she'd had drug buddies and fuck buddies, but no real boyfriend and, thus, very little idea about how to handle a potential suitor . . . particularly one who didn't know that he was the father of her child. She struggled to remember a movie or a television show in which a girl had dumped a boy and it had gone smoothly, but regretting the years she'd spent comfortably numb. If she'd been paying attention she'd know how to handle this. If she'd been Diana, for example, who'd moved through her teenage years and into adulthood with her eyes wide open, she would know how to send him away. "Look, you're a really nice guy . . ." *Good start,* she congratulated herself. "But I'm really busy. And you're down in Philadelphia, and I'm in Connecticut . . ." *Excellent work,* she was thinking, until Jeff started talking.

"It's not that far. And there's Amtrak," he said. "And I like you." Lizzie stared at him and wondered. "I liked being with you," Jeff continued. "I thought we got along. Didn't we have a nice time this summer?"

She found herself nodding, almost unconsciously, before her napkin brushed the bulge of her belly, and she remembered her secret. The problem was, she did like him. She could imagine a whole calendar's worth of dates—the two of them snuggled by a fire, ice-skating, walking through Washington Square Park in the springtime, when the dogwood and cherry trees were heavy with sweet-smelling blossoms. She could imagine her baby having a father, a solid, upstanding, hardworking guy. She made herself stop thinking about it, telling herself that it would never happen—not to a girl like her. "I just don't think it'll work," she said, and groped through snippets of sitcoms she'd watched and books she remembered until she arrived at, "I'm not looking for anything serious right now."

He looked at her soberly. "Are you seeing someone else?"

Lizzie burst into startled laughter. Seeing someone else! That was a good one! She grabbed two napkins from the metal dispenser and started pleating them with her fingertips. "No," she said. "There's no one else."

"So what, then?" He didn't look alarmed, just curious. He had such a nice face, open and calm, and there was a patience about him, in the way he carried himself, his stance and the set of his shoulders, the way he sat in the booth, alert and relaxed, waiting for her to answer. Maybe these were the things that had drawn her to him in the first place, on that summer night in the ice cream shop. Maybe she hadn't made such a bad choice.

She drummed her fingers on the table and shuffled her feet on the floor. A line from rehab rose up in her mind: *You're only as sick as your secrets*. Little lies, social lies were okay, but not telling the truth about something as big as this? Besides, if she kept the baby, he'd know. If he'd found her here there was no way she could keep a baby a secret.

He was looking at her intently, his pleasant face serious. "So what is it?" he asked.

"I'm actually kind of pregnant," she said.

His face collapsed into the same shocked expression he'd worn when she told him about her past. It was almost funny, she thought, as his blue eyes widened behind his glasses. Almost, but not quite.

"I know," she said unhappily. "I know every time you see me it's some big thing. Addict, pregnant. Probably you think that the next time we talk I'm going to tell you I used to be a dude."

Jeff choked on the sip of water he'd taken. Lizzie felt a flash of pride.

"I wasn't, though." Her cheeks were pink. "But I am. Actually."

He blinked. "What, a guy?"

"No. Pregnant."

"And it's mine? I mean, ours?"

She nodded, not even bothering to be offended by what his question implied, and Jeff didn't press her.

The waitress slid their sandwiches in front of them and asked if they needed anything else. "We're fine," said Jeff. When the waitress was gone, he looked at Lizzie and asked, in a low voice, "You're sure?"

Lizzie nodded again.

"And you're better now? You're not using?"

"Just prenatal vitamins." She pulled the toothpicks out of her sandwich and continued. "You don't have to be involved. My parents will—"

"What if I want to be involved?" he asked. He leaned forward, hands planted on the table, staring into her eyes. "If you're pregnant with my child . . ." The words *my child* seemed to linger in the air that smelled like French fries and strong coffee. For an instant, the low chatter that filled the restaurant ceased. Lizzie swallowed hard, marveling, for maybe the first time, at the enormity of what had happened; realizing, again, what the sickness and the spotting, the doctor's appointments and the clothes that didn't fit actually meant. A baby. Someday a child. "If I'm going to be a father . . . it's a big thing, right?"

Who said anything about him being a father? she wondered. Was it even up to him? Did he get a say? What were the rules here, and why, at her age, didn't she know them? "So you want to . . ." She stopped talking, because she honestly wasn't sure what he wanted, or what to offer him, or how to negotiate this situation.

"Are you taking care of yourself?" Jeff was asking. "Have you been to a doctor?"

She nodded.

"And what did the doctor say?"

"That I've got as good a chance of having a healthy baby as any other woman," she recited. The words struck her with fresh power. *Any other woman.* She thought maybe that was part of the appeal of pregnancy, a chance to belong to a group that did not have Anonymous as part of its name and was not made up of people who'd hit rock bottom and clawed their way back up, who met in overheated rooms to talk about the terrible things they'd done when they were drunk or high. She could sign up for prenatal yoga, she could chat with the mothers she'd seen in the park and the supermarket, and nobody would give her a funny look or treat her like she didn't belong. Her belly and, eventually, her baby would be all the passport she needed. She wouldn't be Lizzie the addict, or Senator Woodruff's daughter, or the little sister or the fuck-up. She'd just be another mom. Except probably not a very good one. With her history, what made her think she had any business being responsible for a baby?

"So what is it, then?" asked Jeff. "What's the problem?"

She looked down at the paper napkin she'd torn into shreds, the sandwich she hadn't touched. "I've never had a boyfriend," she said. Somehow that was more painful to admit than that she'd been an addict and that she'd gotten pregnant.

"Well, you've never had a baby, either," Jeff pointed out.

Head still bent, Lizzie sighed.

"Can I see you?" he asked.

"I don't know," she mumbled. "I don't know where I'll be living, or what I'll do for work . . ."

"We'll figure it out," said Jeff. His blue eyes were wide and serious. "We would talk on the phone. I would visit you up here, or in New York, and you could visit me in Philadelphia. We'd go out to dinner. Possibly to movies. There could be Broadway shows. Do you like Broadway shows?"

"Musicals," said Lizzie. At least, she'd liked them when she was a kid and, over the long Thanksgiving weekends, she'd been taken to see *Dreamgirls* and *West Side Story* and *The Sound of Music*.

"We would learn about each other. We'd see if we really got along, which I bet we will." He raised his hands. "And, honestly, the idea that there's a kid who's out there, a kid who's mine, and I don't have anything to do with him, or his mom, that I don't know him . . ."

"Or her," Lizzie said.

He nodded. "Or her. Whatever happens." He breathed in, looking her right in the eyes. "I want to be part of the kid's life. And I want us to have a chance."

Lizzie studied him, wishing, again, that she'd led a normal life like her sister, because if she had, she'd have a better sense of people, a better idea of whether this guy was lying to her or whether he was sincere; whether this was about getting to know her and being a father or he had ulterior motives regarding money, or her father, or something else, something worse, something she hadn't even thought of yet. Maybe he wanted her to have the baby so he could sell it on the black market. That had happened in a book she'd taken out of the lending library in Minnesota, only in the book the pregnant women had been mail-order brides lured over from Russia with promises of riches and American husbands. The people doing the selling had included a corrupt lawyer and a psychotic former child star, one of whom had ended up dead, the other of whom had told her story on *Oprah.* So maybe not.

"Do you think . . ." She swallowed hard, feeling that sensation of wings beating inside her, a tiny bird trapped in an attic, an unfamiliar hopefulness. "Do you think we'd be good parents?"

Jeff considered. "I don't see why we wouldn't be." He took a spoonful of soup, a sip of water. "I also think you can learn from people's mistakes. My mom wasn't the greatest, and I know that whatever I do wrong, it won't be what she did."

Lizzie nodded. Learning from mistakes. That sounded good. It meant that she could practically be a genius.

"Eat something," Jeff told her, picking up his sandwich. "You need extra calories now, right?"

They ate quietly for a few minutes, and when the check came, Jeff paid it.

"I have to get some groceries," Lizzie said.

"I'll come with you," he offered.

"Don't you have work?"

"It's Thanksgiving. I took the week off." He managed a smile. "And even if I left right now it's five hours back to Philadelphia. Come on, Lizzie," he said, and held out his hand. "I can carry your bags. I can do that for you, at least."

They walked down the street to Simmons Grocery. Lizzie pushed the shopping cart, and Jeff followed behind her as she filled it. For a moment, she allowed herself the fantasy that this could work, that the two of them could be a normal couple, mother and father and the baby they raised together. Unlikely, she decided, putting milk and butter into the cart . . . but maybe it was possible. It happened to other people. Why not her, too?

He insisted on paying for the groceries, and on carrying everything but a small bag of onions up to the house. "So," he said, in the driveway. "Do I get to meet your parents?"

She looked at him, shifting the mesh bag in her hands. "It's just my mom."

"That's another part of it, too," he told her. "The boyfriend-girlfriend thing. Meeting the parents."

Lizzie nodded, thinking that as she made her belated, one-step-forward, two-steps-back journey into adulthood, a trip that had recently been hastened by her pregnancy, at some point she would have to trust her instincts. And she'd also have to trust other people, too. She set her hand on the brass handle of the door and swung it open. Inside, the sunshine made rectangular patterns on the hardwood floor, and she could smell bread baking in the kitchen.

"They don't know about . . ." Her voice trailed off as she gestured toward her belly. Jeff's eyebrows rose, but all he said was "Okay."

Lizzie swung the door open and took his hand. "Come on in."

SYLVIE

On Thanksgiving morning, Sylvie stood with her hands on her hips, looking over the table. The blue-and-white dishes and crystal glasses sparkled, the creamy linen napkins that she'd ironed the night before looked just right. Except for the fire crackling in the living room and the drip and hiss of the coffeepot, the house was quiet. Diana, still troublingly thin, but not as gaunt as she'd been in October, had gone down to the beach for a run, with Milo trailing behind her. Lizzie and her young man were still upstairs, asleep. Sylvie had given Jeff his own bedroom, but she suspected that he was sneaking into Lizzie's at night.

Sylvie had been surprised—really, she'd been astonished—when, two days earlier, Lizzie had breezed through the door with a handsome young man carrying her groceries behind her. At first she'd wondered whether Lizzie had picked Jeff up at the supermarket. Her daughter had pulled stunts like that before. "This is Jeff. He's a friend of mine from this summer," she'd said, which didn't help Sylvie at all: "summer" could have meant Philadelphia, or could have meant rehab. She looked him over—his short hair, his glasses, his neatly pressed shirt, his handsome face and friendly manner. Philadelphia, she decided. Unless he'd been in rehab, too, and the clean-cut appearance and the small talk were just overcompensation.

"Will you be joining us for Thanksgiving?" she'd asked, and Jeff said, "Oh, no, I don't want to impose," but it turned out he had no plans—his parents were divorced, his mother in New Mexico, celebrating with friends, and his father in Arizona with his new wife and her family. "If it's all right with Lizzie," he'd finally said, and Lizzie, her voice oddly formal, had said, "That would be lovely."

Standing at the sink, looking out over the lawn that she and her daughters had raked over the weekend, Sylvie washed her hands and ran through her menu. She'd cook turkey and stuffing, of course. Lizzie, who'd displayed an awesome affinity for bread, rolls, and anything flour-based, was preparing corn bread, a cranberry loaf, buttermilk-cheddar biscuits, and Parker House rolls, a miracle four times over, because in years past Sylvie barely trusted her younger daughter to carry the butter to the table. There'd be Brussels sprouts in a balsamic vinegar glaze and a sweet-potato casserole. The Honorable Selma, who would arrive later that morning, was bringing an assortment of cheeses and pâtés, smoked fish and fancy crackers. Ceil and Larry were also on their way, with wine and mulled cider, and Tim was bringing pies for dessert.

When Lizzie and Jeff came down the stairs, Jeff dressed and Lizzie in a bathrobe, Sylvie slid the cheddar-and-sausage strata she'd prepared the night before out of the oven. Jeff set the kitchen table, and Lizzie poured juice, and, eventually, Diana, glowing and sweaty, came up from the beach with Milo trailing behind her, carrying his Frisbee. Sylvie had just taken her seat when a black Town Car came crunching up the driveway. "Grandma!" Lizzie cried, and in that moment, with her eyes sparkling and her round cheeks flushed, Sylvie could see, with heartbreaking clarity, the little girl that Lizzie had been. She watched through the window as her mother climbed out of the backseat, wrapped in an ancient mink that made her look like a small, Botoxed bear.

"Oh, Lord," she murmured, noticing the writing on the car door.

"What?" asked Lizzie.

"That's the car from her apartment complex," Sylvie said, pointing at the words DAVIDSON PAVILION stenciled on its side. "It's supposed to take her anywhere she wants to go within a five-mile radius."

Diana smiled faintly. Lizzie hooted, clapping her hands together. "Way to go. Grandma hijacked the Hebrew Home car!" Selma tottered out onto the crushed shells, pressed a bill (probably a five, if Sylvie knew her mother) into the driver's hand, and made her way up the porch steps.

Milo ran to open the door. Selma handed him her mink, revealing a black velour tracksuit and orthopedic shoes underneath it, and bent to kiss his forehead, which was the only part of him visible between his ski cap and the armload of fur. "My number one great-grandson!" she said, and handed him a lollipop she'd pulled from her purse, the kind Sylvie knew that they gave away free at her bank. "Sylvie," she said, and kissed her daughter's cheek. Then she looked at the girls, her gaze seeming to linger on Lizzie's midriff. Sylvie's heart sank—over the years, her mother had passed the occasional critical remark about Lizzie's weight, and Lizzie was, she had to admit, significantly rounder than she'd been at the start of the summer. She hoped her mother would keep her mouth shut; would recognize that a few extra pounds were better than a drug problem.

"Well, well, well," Selma said. She looked the way she always did, from her bright red lipstick and carefully curled hair to the bags beneath her eyes and the wrinkles that grooved her face. "What have we here?"

"I'm just visiting," Lizzie said. "I hurt my back, and I was on bed rest for a while, but now I'm okay." She took Jeff's arm and pulled him beside her. "This is my friend Jeff Spencer from Philadelphia." Selma lifted her penciled eyebrows as Jeff offered his hand. Sylvie could tell that Lizzie wanted to add something more: *No, really, it's really just a visit, I'm okay*—but instead she said, "Want some coffee?"

"How about a Bloody Mary? Heavy on the horseradish."

"Oh, Mom," Sylvie murmured, and Selma turned her gimlet eye on her daughter.

"I am eighty-six years old," she announced, in case her family had forgotten. "I am no longer employed, thanks to the antiquated mandatory-retirement laws of the state of New York. If I want to enjoy a little vodka in my tomato juice, I believe I have earned that privilege." She turned back to Lizzie. "Unless it's going to bother you."

"Oh, no!" Lizzie said. "I'm fine."

"Heavy on the horseradish," Selma said again. Lizzie retreated into the kitchen. "Finish up your breakfast," Diana told her son, "then start your independent reading." Milo rolled his eyes and, with the sigh of a dwarf setting off for the coal mines, ate a slice of toast, then trudged up the stairs. Grandma Selma watched him go, then turned her gaze to Diana.

"That boy needs a tonic."

"A tonic?" Diana was trying, and failing, to sound amused. "I think they went out with the mustard poultice."

Selma's driver had hauled the last of her luggage and bags from Zabar's onto the porch. Sylvie slipped outside to give him two twenties. "Your mother's a pip," the man said. As if Sylvie didn't know. When she got back to the foyer Selma was rummaging through one of her bags and continuing with her inquiries.

"Don't tell me you're on vacation," she said to Diana, who was twisting the drawstring of her running pants around her index finger. "You don't take vacations. Especially not when your son should be in school. What are you doing here?"

"Um," Diana murmured.

"Speak up!" said Selma, who wore hearing aids in both ears and could hear just fine.

"She's taking a break," Sylvie said, hoping that would end the conversation. Selma ignored her, staring expectantly at Diana, who let go of her drawstring and let her hands hang by her sides.

"I left my husband," she said.

"Good." Selma seemed neither surprised nor perturbed. "I never liked the cut of his jib."

"You didn't?" Diana seemed surprised to hear it.

Selma turned and started rooting through her bag some more, eventually producing a pair of reading glasses that hung on a brightly colored beaded lariat. "I thought he was a big baby. I tell you, Diana, that marriage was very hard on me."

"He's going to be here," Diana said. "For Thanksgiving."

"In that case, I will keep my opinions to myself." Selma pulled her glasses' chain over her head, lifted the tote bag, and marched into the kitchen, where Lizzie was standing at the counter stirring a dollop of horseradish into a juice glass brimming with tomato juice and ice and, presumably, vodka. "So are you getting a divorce?" Selma called over her shoulder.

Diana's voice trembled minutely as she said, "I think that's the plan."

"And you?" Grandma Selma asked, pointing at Sylvie. "My friend David could give you a two-for-one deal."

"That's very tempting, but I'm not sure what I want," Sylvie said. She turned away, cutting herself a piece of the strata, then sat at the table and said, "Actually, there's something I need to tell you." She waited until she had her mother's attention, then said, "I've been seeing someone."

"Wait," said Diana, who'd been pouring herself a cup of coffee. "Who? Tim? You and Tim are seeing each other? Seeing-seeing each other?"

"Yes," said Sylvie, who wondered what Diana thought they'd been doing.

"Seeing each other like dating?" asked Lizzie. She made *dating* sound as if it was some kind of unnatural act, as if she and Tim were picking nits off each other's scalps instead of sharing dinner and the occasional movie and, just once, her bed.

"Your mother has every right," Selma said . . . and then, in a lower tone, added, "I'd think she'd have had enough of men for a while, but it's her choice." She sat at the kitchen table across from Sylvie with her drink and a plate, served herself strata, and pulled the *New York Times* out of her tote bag. "What's his name?"

"Tim Simmons. He'll be at dinner tonight."

"Not Timmy Simmons who molested you out on the dunes?" Sylvie felt her jaw clench as her mother grinned, wondering if she was doomed to spend the rest of her life as a punch line, because her husband had cheated and because she'd dared, at her age, to go looking for love.

"He didn't molest me," she told her mother. "We kissed. And why were you watching?"

"Because I'd finished reading *Peyton Place,*" said Selma.

"So you guys were, like, summer lovers?" Diana asked. "Was he your boyfriend?"

"Not exactly," Sylvie said.

"Could have fooled me!" said her mother. "That boy was sweet on you. He's probably been sweet on you for the last . . ." She paused, counting, before making a face. "Never mind. It's only going to depress me."

Sylvie turned back to her breakfast, hoping no one would see her blush.

"Um," said Lizzie. She'd lifted herself onto the counter and was swinging her legs, with Jeff standing beside her, munching a slice of toast.

"What?" asked Sylvie.

Lizzie swung her legs faster and fiddled with her hair. "This is awkward."

"What's awkward?" Selma demanded.

Her voice was barely a whisper. "I kind of invited Dad."

"For Thanksgiving?" Sylvie was as startled as if she'd been slapped. "Lizzie!"

"I thought it would be a nice surprise." Her daughter's words came out in a breathless tumble. "I miss him, and you do too."

"How do you know what I'm feeling?" Sylvie asked sharply. *Especially*, she thought, *since I barely know myself?*

Lizzie was scowling at her. "How can you not miss him? You guys were married so long, you're like each other's . . ." Her voice trailed off. "I mean, how can you even imagine the holidays without him?"

Sylvie answered coolly, "I believe I was doing just fine."

Lizzie's face reddened, and her chin quivered. "Well, I miss him," she said.

So invite him to your house, Sylvie thought—an uncharacteristically uncharitable thought, and one she would never give voice to.

"He's falling apart," Lizzie continued. "And I thought that other guy was just an old friend."

Sylvie cleared her plate and held her tongue. From what she'd seen in the papers, Richard hadn't fallen apart . . . his career had, in fact, been enjoying a small renaissance. He'd championed a House bill—something to do with taxes on soft drinks—that had been written up favorably in the *Times* piece. He'd given a terse "no comment" when the reporter had asked about his marriage. Joelle Stabinow, contacted at her law office in Washington, had said merely that Senator Woodruff was "a fine man and a dear friend." Richard had continued calling Sylvie, too, every morning and every night, but she hadn't talked to him once. She tamped down her anger at Lizzie's presumptuousness and tried to consider the practicalities. How would she handle Richard in her kitchen, in her house? Would he want to stay over? Would he expect to sleep in her bed?

"Dad's an adult," said Diana, pulling off her sweatshirt and tying it around her waist. "He can handle his business."

"No, he can't, Diana!" Lizzie said. "You should have seen him. The house was a mess, and he sat on his laptop twice while I was there. He can barely open his in-box."

"Learned helplessness," said Selma, without looking up from the bridge column. "That's all that is. You get enough women to take care of you—do your laundry, manage your campaigns, wait for your eggs . . ."

"Mother," Sylvie murmured.

". . . then why should you bother learning how to do things for yourself? He's falling apart like a fox, is what I think."

"I told him to bring dessert," Lizzie said.

"Tim's bringing dessert," Sylvie said, wringing her hands.

"Milo and I don't eat sugar," said Diana, standing up to clear her juice glass. Selma cackled.

"Are you sorry we didn't do Thanksgiving at my place?" she asked her daughter, and Sylvie, standing at the sink, had no answer.

By six o'clock the turkey, which she'd filled with a sage-and-sausage stuffing and had been basting since the morning, had turned a lovely golden-brown. The sugar-free cranberry-orange chutney that Diana had contributed glowed like rubies in an antique cut-glass dish. Lizzie's breads and rolls were cooling on the counter, next to the casserole of sweet potatoes with a puffy marshmallow crown. Selma stayed out of the kitchen, but set out a gorgeous array of cheeses and spreads and crackers on the sideboard in the dining room, along with the bottles of wine she'd brought up from New York. Sylvie had just put the metal mixing bowl and the beaters into the freezer to chill for the whipped cream she'd serve with the pies when the doorbell rang. Tim was standing on the porch, beneath a sky already deepening toward twilight, smiling at her shyly, in khaki pants and a green wool sweater with two bakery boxes in his arms.

She wiped her hands on her apron and gave him a hug. "I need to tell you something," she whispered, feeling his cool cheek against her warm one.

"What's that?" he asked, following her into the kitchen and setting the bakery boxes he'd brought on the counter.

Sylvie turned away from him to peek under the tinfoil tent to inspect the turkey, which, per her recipe's instructions, was resting before it was carved. She wished that she could rest, too, just sit somewhere warm, hidden from sight, and stew in her own juices. "My husband is coming. I had no idea—Lizzie invited him without telling me." She glanced at him, worried that Tim would be scowling or, worse, that he'd rezip his jacket, pick up his pies, and tell her that he'd come for turkey, not drama. He'd been patient with her so far, letting Sylvie spend her time with her daughters, cooking for them, watching bad reality TV with them, offering to play Scrabble (so far, no takers) or to walk on the beach with them, making herself available for whatever they wanted.

"That should be interesting," he said.

"Interesting," she repeated.

"Does he know about . . ." He paused, eyebrows lifted. "Us?"

She shook her head. "Richard and I . . ." Her voice trailed off. Had she ever told Tim Richard's name? He'd asked once how she felt about her husband, and she'd said, with more venom than she'd intended, "I don't want to talk about it. I'm not ready yet," and that had been that. "Richard and I haven't been talking since I've been up here," she said, pulling a handful of silverware from the dishwasher.

"We're all grown-ups. I'm sure it'll be fine," Tim said mildly. He went into the living room to greet her daughters and meet her mother. Just then the doorbell rang again, and there was Ceil, in fur-trimmed boots and a puffy down coat, with her arms full of bottles and Larry standing behind her, beaming the way he frequently did around his wife, as if he still couldn't quite believe that he'd won such a prize. Sylvie rushed to hug her. "I'm so glad you're here!" she said. Ceil kissed her cheek.

"Richard's coming," Sylvie whispered, taking her friend's coat and leading her into the kitchen as Larry headed inside to greet her daughters.

"He is?"

"Lizzie invited him without telling me."

Ceil's eyes widened. "Did you smack her? Are you okay?"

"I didn't smack her . . . and honestly, I'm not sure."

"Well, you let me know what I can do. Smack him. Short-sheet his bed. Poison his food. Ooh, is that Tim?" Ceil snuck a look into the living room, then took a pinch of stuffing from the platter and gave Tim an approving once-over. "Huh. Cute." She popped the stuffing in her mouth, chewed and swallowed, then stared at her friend. "Did you make that? It's delicious. And are you guys dating now or what?"

"Tim's . . ." She stopped talking before she'd have to think of what, exactly, Tim was. "I made the stuffing. I made almost everything."

Ceil looked impressed—whether at Tim's good looks or Sylvie's culinary prowess, Sylvie wasn't sure.

Ceil helped herself to another bite of stuffing. "I just need to know how to behave. Do we hate him now, or are we in forgiveness mode or what?"

Sylvie stared at her helplessly. "I honestly don't know."

Ceil wiped her hands and studied her friend. "You look good."

Sylvie nodded, smoothing her hair, which was longer than it had been since she'd gotten married, and fled back to the Brussels sprouts that needed glazing, to the butter dish that needed washing, to problems she could solve.

She checked to make sure that there were platters and dishes and serving spoons and forks for everything she'd cooked. Milo had made placecards, handwritten in his laborious printing and taped onto the miniature pumpkins he and his mother had bought at a farmstand a few miles outside town. Sylvie was at the head of the table, with Selma on one side and Tim on the other, and Richard was all the way at the foot, with no pumpkin to mark his place. *Keep your distance,* Sylvie thought, running her fingers around the rim of his wineglass. But did she want him to keep his distance, or to come through the door, take her in his arms, and make everything the way it used to be? Did she want things to be the way they'd been before Joelle? Could she go back to that time, even if it were possible, even if she wanted to?

She straightened a fork and surveyed her table again. "Everything all right?" asked Selma, who had her cane in one hand and a platter she'd refilled with grapes and cheese in the other.

"Everything's fine," Sylvie answered. Tim squeezed her hand as he followed Selma back into the living room.

"Mom, you remember Tim Simmons, right?"

"How could I forget?" Selma asked.

Sylvie went back to the kitchen, where Lizzie was lining a wicker basket with a printed cloth napkin for the breads and rolls, and Diana was filling a pitcher with ice water. Back in the living room, Selma was handing around plates of appetizers—cheese-stuffed olives, truffled pâté, Champagne grapes and quince paste, sesame crackers and a raisin-studded baguette—and talking with Tim about where she'd bought them, and whether such items would do well at a grocery store in Connecticut. Ceil stood in front of the fire. When she saw Sylvie, she handed over her glass of wine.

"Drink this," she whispered. "You'll need it." She glanced at the door. "When's the Big He coming?"

"Don't know," Sylvie whispered back. *Don't know and don't care,* she wanted to say, but it was a lie. She cared, still, she cared desperately. She was nervous as a schoolgirl on her first date. She wondered how she would look to him, and if he'd try to kiss her; then stopped herself before her mind could wander off on a Richard-fueled reverie. He'd wronged her, he'd hurt her. More important, her girls needed her, maybe more than her husband ever had . . . and the three of them, plus Milo, had done just fine for themselves up here without him.

Still, her heart leapt when the doorbell rang. "Open it," she whispered to Ceil.

"You open it!" Ceil whispered back. Sylvie put one of her pleasant smiles on her face and opened the door . . . but it was just Gary, with a bouquet of flowers tucked under his arm and a large cardboard box in his hands.

"Hi, Sylvie," he said, handing her the flowers and brushing her cheeks with his lips. "Hello, Diana," he said to his wife. The two of them looked at each other unhappily, until, with a cry of "Daddy!," Milo hurled himself at his father's legs. The box turned out to contain a computer gaming system, which Tim and Gary and Milo spent the next forty-five minutes trying to hook up to the house's ancient TV set.

After an hour of snacking and fussing with the table and listening to Selma bad-mouth the president's Supreme Court nominee, Sylvie decided not to wait any longer. Big He or not, her guests were hungry, and her turkey was getting cold. "I think we should get started," she said, and called everyone to the table.

Tim carved the turkey, deftly separating the drumsticks from the thighs, explaining to Milo how a sharp knife was the most important tool for the job. Diana and Lizzie carried side dishes to the table, and Milo poured grape juice for himself and Lizzie and red wine for everyone else.

"Should we say grace?" Lizzie asked. She'd done her fine blond hair in elaborate braids that wrapped around her head like a crown, and she hadn't had even a sip of wine. At Selma's, they always said a brief prayer of thanks for the food and the fellowship. Sylvie nodded and bowed her head, but it was Lizzie who spoke.

"Lord, we give you thanks that we're all here, and healthy and together. Please bless this meal, and bless all of us."

Sylvie's eyes filled with tears. Her Lizzie, in spite of everything that had happened, seemed to be doing all right. It was nothing short of a miracle. Milo seemed thrilled to have his father there. Diana looked uneasy, pale and guarded and still, in her sweater-dress, too thin, but so far she and Gary were managing to be polite to each other. Sylvie looked at the door, then looked away as Tim lifted the platter of turkey, and across the table, Ceil said, "Who wants Brussels sprouts?" and Milo said, "I hate Brussels sprouts," and Diana said, "That isn't a word we use in this family," and Lizzie said, "What, Brussels sprouts?" Sylvie had just helped herself to a roll and some white meat when Selma turned to Jeff and said, "I do hope you two are planning to get married before the baby comes."

"Grandma!" Lizzie gasped.

Milo looked mystified. "A baby? What baby?"

Sylvie stared at her daughter . . . at her midriff, in particular, which, come to think of it, Lizzie had been keeping swathed in sweaters and pullovers and which did seem distinctly rounder than she remembered. But Lizzie was rounder all over, with all of the stuff she'd been eating, the snacking and the late-night sandwiches... although Lizzie never seemed hungry in the morning, when she'd just sip a cup of chamomile tea. Was it true? Was this what Lizzie had been on the verge of telling her that afternoon on the beach?

"You're pregnant?" she whispered.

"For God's sake, Sylvie," her mother snapped. "She was on bed rest."

"She hurt her back," Sylvie said, still unable to believe what she was hearing ... and unable to believe that she hadn't guessed. Add it to her list of the ways she'd failed Lizzie, the things she hadn't noticed, the steps she didn't take. Was Lizzie seeing a doctor? Could she have a healthy baby after everything she'd done?

"If you believe that, I've got a bridge in Brooklyn I could sell you," Selma said.

Sylvie looked around the table. Diana seemed to be just as shocked as she was. Jeff was fiddling with his glasses, looking somewhere between embarrassed and proud. Milo looked confused, and Tim looked bewildered, and Gary, true to form, was blowing his nose in a rumpled tissue he'd produced from his pocket, looking more or less oblivious.

"So do I congratulate you two?" Diana asked her sister.

"I don't want to talk about it," Lizzie murmured, tugging at her hair.

"Eat," Selma instructed, returning to her own plate, which she'd piled high with turkey and gravy and sweet potatoes. "You need the calories for the baby."

"Where's the baby?" asked Milo.

For a long moment no one answered until Lizzie said, quietly, "It's inside me."

"How did it get there?" Milo asked, peering at Lizzie.

Diana straightened in her chair. "Milo," she began. "When a man and a woman love each other very much, and, usually, when they're married . . ."

"Oh, great," Lizzie muttered. "Here we go with the judgment."

"The man will give the woman a special seed . . ."

"Like a pumpkin seed?" asked Milo.

"He'll plant it in the woman's belly, and a baby will grow."

"How does it get out?" Milo asked.

Selma cackled. Ceil made a strangled sound and bent over, wiping her eyes. Sylvie shot her mother a stern look that Selma, of course, ignored.

"I can get you a book and show you pictures," said Diana. "The important thing to remember is that you don't have to worry about any of this until you're much, much older."

Lizzie helped herself to one of the biscuits she'd baked. "Can we move on to someone else's life?"

"Absolutely!" said Selma, and pointed one gnarled finger across the table. "Diana, honey, what's new with you?"

Gary, who'd just taken a gigantic bite of turkey, started coughing, and Milo thumped him on his back.

"Are you two getting divorced?" Selma asked.

"Grandma!" Lizzie hissed, and cut her eyes toward Milo.

"What?" Selma asked. "Divorce isn't such a tragedy. A tragedy's staying in an unhappy marriage, teaching your children the wrong things about love. Nobody ever died of divorce."

"Sunny von Bülow?" Ceil piped up.

"They never got divorced," Selma said. Sylvie glared at her mother, and Selma lowered her voice incrementally. "Claus just tried to kill her. See, if they'd gotten divorced, it could have worked out better for both of them."

That, of course, was when the doorbell rang. Diana sank back into her seat. Gary, who'd finally stopped coughing, stared miserably, longingly, at his wife. "Can I get anybody anything?" asked Jeff, who was probably wishing he'd made the trip to Arizona.

Sylvie walked to the door . . . and there was Richard, hair combed, freshly shaved, in a sports coat and tie, with a bakery box in his hand; Richard, tall and commanding, familiar and dear. She felt, as she supposed she always would, the atmosphere change when he was near her, as if every cell in her body had subtly shifted, trying to get closer to him. It took a conscious act of will to keep from leaning against him or reaching for his hand. All she wanted to do was throw herself into his arms, close her eyes, and say, *Fix this. Make this right.* Instead she said, "Hello, Richard," and allowed him to kiss her cheek.

Sylvie led him into the kitchen, feeling him look at her. She wondered what he was seeing, what he was thinking. Instead of her usual suit and heels, she'd chosen loose cashmere pants and a cowl-necked black cotton top, with wool socks and a pair of Lizzie's embroidered clogs. She'd pulled her hair, now streaked with gray, back in a headband made of cranberry-colored velvet. The only jewelry she wore was a simple gold cuff bracelet that she'd bought at the craft fair on the village green two weeks before, with Tim. Her fingernails were unpolished and clipped short, and her wedding and engagement rings were, presumably, in her jewelry box back in New York, where she'd left them.

Richard looked at her, his eyes warm, before straightening and launching into a speech. "Sylvie," he said. "I can't thank you enough for letting me come. I missed you . . ." He swallowed hard. "More than I can say." He thrust the box into her hands. Sylvie was unsurprised to see that it was from Simmons's. "I hope it's all right," Richard said. "I stopped at the place in town."

Wordlessly, she set the box on the counter, next to the two Simmons boxes Tim had brought. She was trembling all over, her knees shaking, her lips quivering. She hoped he couldn't see it.

"You look beautiful," he said, and reached to touch her hair before pulling his hand back with a rueful smile. "If I'm allowed to say that." He took an appreciative sniff. "Smells great. That's a nice change. Where'd you get the food?"

"We cooked," she said. "The girls and I."

He stared at her again, this time in shock. She turned, serenely (she hoped), and led him into the dining room. Everyone at the table looked up at him, everyone except for Gary, whose gaze was still fixed on his plate. Tim Simmons got to his feet.

"Senator," he said. "I'm Tim Simmons. Sylvie and I are old friends."

Richard appeared bewildered to find a strange man at the table, but his politician's instincts kicked in. He stuck out his hand. "Richard Woodruff. A pleasure to meet you. Are you a Fairview native?"

When he was through charming Tim, he made his way down the table, to where his daughters were waiting. "Lizzie," he said, pulling her into a bear hug. His voice was a warm rumble. "You doing okay?"

"I'm good," she said, blushing—and, Sylvie saw, undeniably pregnant—as she stepped into her father's arms.

"And Diana! Look at you!" Diana smiled faintly. She, too, looked different—no makeup, her hair loose and wavy, in leggings and her tunic, her body rigid as she studiously avoided looking at Gary. Sylvie wondered whether Richard, with his instincts, his sense of people, would pick up on the rift between his daughter and his son-in-law, or Lizzie's pregnancy and her boyfriend, but what he seemed to be noticing most was the food.

"You made all of this?" he asked. "You really did?"

"My Sylvie is a very accomplished woman," said Selma. "She can do lots of things. Dress herself, cook a turkey . . ."

Richard gave his mother-in-law a tolerant smile. "Selma. Good to see that not everything's changed." He gave Diana a hug, gave Gary a handshake, kissed Milo on the cheek, and introduced himself to Jeff, then settled into his chair. "Just tell me somebody saved me a drumstick."

I can't believe this, Sylvie thought, taking her seat as Richard filled his plate and started asking Tim about the Connecticut governor who'd been caught in some kind of kickback scheme. Her mind was racing. Lizzie pregnant! Her husband and her . . . whatever Tim was, in the same room! She lifted a bit of Diana's cranberry chutney to her mouth, then set it down, untasted, knowing she was far too tense to swallow.

"So," said Richard, looking around the table. "What's new?"

Lizzie started laughing first. Selma joined in, cackling loudly. Diana managed another dim smile. Even Gary looked a little amused as Richard looked more and more puzzled.

"What?" he asked, as the laughter grew louder. "What am I missing?" It was Milo, grave and stern-faced, who finally spoke up.

"Aunt Lizzie has a baby in her tummy from . . ." He paused, pointing at Jeff, having momentarily forgotten his name. "That guy."

"Jeff," Jeff supplied. He gave an embarrassed wave, then took Lizzie's hand. *Good for you,* thought Sylvie.

"My mom and dad are having grown-up problems, but Bubbe says nobody dies of divorce."

"True," Richard managed, pausing to give Diana a concerned look. "Anything else?"

"I saved the best for last! We got a Wii! Can you believe it?" A smile brightened his face, and Sylvie felt herself relax—she'd been worried, she realized, that Milo would start talking about his fishing trip with Grandma's special friend. "I thought I'd never ever have one. My mom is opposed to them."

"Not Wiis, specifically. I just don't want you having too much screen time," said Diana. She reached out and smoothed Milo's hair (he'd worn a hat downstairs, but Diana made him take it off before he came to the table).

"But my dad brought me one, and Tim and Daddy hooked it up, and now I have Wii bowling and Wii tennis and Wii golf . . ." A shadow crossed his face as he turned to his father. "We get to keep it, right? And take it back to Philadelphia? It doesn't have to stay up here?"

"If your grandma doesn't want to keep it . . ." Gary said.

"It's all yours," Sylvie said.

Milo jumped up and down, beaming. "Okay! All right! A-plus! Who wants pie?"

When dinner was over and the dishes had been cleared, Sylvie slipped out of the dining room and sat on the glider on the porch, pulling the cardigan she'd grabbed tight around her shoulders, breathing in the frosty night air. Her guests were still gathered around the table, finishing their coffee and dessert.

She thought she'd cry—all through dinner she'd felt herself on the verge of tears—but now, out in the cold, she felt calm, even confident. Whatever storms came, whatever happened next, whether she stayed with Richard or not, she could take care of herself and her daughters. Her time at the beach had taught her that. She thought Richard would come join her—Richard or Tim—but instead it was Diana, who wandered out onto the porch. She had a knitted ski cap on her head, red fleece gloves on her hands, a blanket wrapped around her shoulders, and another one in her arms. She handed the second blanket to Sylvie and sat next to her mom on the glider.

"Hi," she said, in a strangely muffled voice. Sylvie turned and saw a sight she hadn't glimpsed in years: her daughter in profile, crying. When had she last seen Diana cry? She thought back through the years, finally remembering a volleyball game, a shot she'd failed to block, and how she'd sobbed for hours on her bed. Diana had been twelve at the time. Maybe thirteen.

"What's wrong?" she asked. "Is it Gary?"

"What's wrong," Diana said, in a choked voice. "Everything's wrong." She took a gulping breath. "I almost killed a little girl. I wrote the wrong dosage on her prescription, and if one of the nurses hadn't caught it, she would have died, and I did it because I was distracted. I was in love with someone else." Her voice was tiny as she wiped her fist against one eye, then the other. "But he doesn't want me."

"Oh, Diana . . ." She was stunned. If she'd had a lifetime's worth of guesses, Sylvie would never come up with the double whammy of incompetence and infidelity. She would have sooner guessed that Gary was cheating. Not that he seemed to have that kind of energy—sexual or otherwise—but Diana? Moral, judgmental Diana, Diana the absolutist who saw the world in blacks and whites and had no patience for shades of gray?

"I was lonely," said Diana, and wiped impatiently at the tears as they spilled down her cheeks. "I know it's not an excuse, but I was. I was very, very lonely."

Sylvie knew she should say something, make some comforting gesture, except Diana had never been an affectionate child and she'd grown into an adult who didn't like being touched . . . although, Sylvie supposed, if she'd fallen in love then she'd been getting touched by someone. She placed a tentative hand on Diana's arm. Her daughter buried her face in her hands and cried, and Sylvie sat there, at a complete loss for words as she tried to separate her own experience with infidelity from what Diana had done, and what had prompted it. She'd been happily married when her husband had strayed, and Diana . . . had Diana ever really been happy with Gary?

Her daughter's sobs were tapering off. Sylvie had to say

something. "Sometimes," she began. "Sometimes the worst thing that happens to you, the thing you think you can't survive . . . it's the thing that makes you better than you used to be."

Diana's voice was muffled, but not so much that Sylvie couldn't hear every word when she asked, "Is that what you told Dad?"

Sylvie didn't answer, even though she thought that what she'd told Diana might have been as true as anything else she'd blurted, or screamed, or cursed at Richard in the heat of the moment and the shock of discovery. These things happened, God knows they did, and sometimes, couples even survived them. And she was better now; better than she'd used to be.

"I'm a terrible person," Diana cried.

Sylvie said, "Oh, no. No, you're not." She opened her arms and let Diana collapse against her. She held her as she wept, patting her arm and murmuring soothing words: *don't worry* and *you'll be okay* and *I love you, and your father loves you, too.*

Finally, Diana wiped her face and said, "I never wanted to get divorced. Never. It's one of the reasons I picked Gary in the first place. I wasn't, you know . . ." She paused, staring off into the darkness. "I decided to marry him because I saw . . ." Again, she paused. "You were always so in love with Dad, and I thought . . ." Sylvie waited, dreading her daughter's judgment. "You lost so much of yourself," Diana said. "Every decision you made was about him—what he wanted, what he needed, what was going to be best for his image. I didn't want that. I wanted a marriage of equals, not where it would be one person who mattered and one who didn't." She looked at her mother. "I'm sorry if that sounds terrible."

"No," Sylvie said. It hurt to admit it, but it was true. "You're right."

Diana gave another bitter laugh. "And look at me. I thought I was so smart, arranging my own marriage. Didn't see this coming."

"The other man," Sylvie said. "Are you in love with him?"

"He's . . . I don't know. Maybe I could have been. Him, or someone like him, if I'd given myself the chance." She sat up straight, shaking her head as if to clear it. "Milo's the main thing," she said. "I'm going to make some changes. I want a different kind of job. I want to slow down. Be home with him more. I want . . . oh, I don't know what I want. Just for things to be different, I guess."

"Where will you live?" Sylvie asked. "Will you stay in the house?"

"For now, at least," said Diana. "Gary's got a place. I've been thinking about asking Lizzie to come back and stay with me for a while. She'll be able to see Jeff, and help out with Milo."

Sylvie nodded, thinking how that part of it, at least—the two girls together—sounded good.

"And what about you?" Diana asked.

"What about me?" Sylvie said.

"Are you going to go back to New York?" asked Diana.

"I don't know," said Sylvie.

She turned to look through the window, back into the dining room. Her husband had planted himself at the head of the table. There was a plate in front of him, a bottle of beer at his side. He held his fork balanced in his long fingers and appeared to be having an animated conversation with Jeff and Tim and Gary. About politics, Sylvie figured, feeling a mixture of love and disgust rise up inside her. Always politics.

Diana leaned over to kiss her check. "I've got to check on Milo," she said, then hurried back inside, bundled like a mummy in the blanket. Sylvie sat, waiting. In a minute, the glider creaked . . . and there was Selma, wrapped in her mink. Her four-pronged cane gleamed in the moonlight as she sat down with a grunt.

"Exactly what is going on with your family? I feel like I need a scorecard to keep up! Lizzie's pregnant, Diana's left her husband, except he's here, you've got your husband and your boyfriend at the table. Oh, and you got a Wii. Whatever that is."

"That about covers it," Sylvie managed. "Poor Diana," she said, because, even though Lizzie was pregnant, it was Diana who was on her mind.

"Diana will be fine," Selma said briskly. "In fact, Diana might be happier than she's been for a while."

"She feels like she's failed," said Sylvie. She didn't have to tell her mother, who'd known Diana since her arrival in the world, that her older daughter had never failed at anything before—not school, not work, not motherhood, and certainly not marriage.

"In Chinese," said Selma, "the word for *crisis* is the same word as *opportunity*."

Sylvie sighed as, below them, the wind churned the waves. Growing up, she'd heard that proverb from Selma more than once; more than once a day, it felt like sometimes . . . but in this case it might actually apply. Diana would go through hell, untangling her life from Gary's, working out custody, and finances, and who would be living where, not to mention finding a new job and handling a son who already seemed predisposed to melancholy. But maybe, eventually, she'd build a happier life. Sylvie let herself imagine it: her daughter slowing down, from a sprint to a trot, selling her fancy car, leaving her makeup in the vanity drawer, letting her hair return to its natural color, which was, if she remembered, a pretty light brown.

"And what about you? What about you and Richard?"

Sylvie pushed her toes against the boards of the porch, setting the glider in motion.

"I won't judge you," Selma said. This was another one of her mother's favorite lines, meant mostly as a joke, because how could a judge not judge? *I won't judge you,* Selma had said when Sylvie told her that she was leaving her job to stay home with her girls and then, years after that, that she wasn't planning on ever going back to work. Selma had kept her promise not to judge insofar as judging involved words, but, between the raised eyebrows, the rolled eyes, and the way she pressed her lips together while humming "Mm, mm, mm," Sylvie had felt judgment—specifically, negative judgment—exuding from her mother's every pore.

"I love him," she said, with her face turned toward the sea. That was what she'd felt, seeing Richard come through the door with that bakery box. Even after what he'd done, even after he'd hurt her, she loved him, and she would have loved him even if they didn't have thirty-two years of marriage and two daughters and all of their history between them. Maybe it was chemical and probably it was pathetic, but she loved him, and she suspected that she always would, that no matter what happened, her first and truest feeling would be what she'd felt as a young bride, watching him descend into the subway every morning: *My husband. Mine.*

"I know you do," said Selma. "But can you forgive him? Can you trust him?"

"I don't know." Sylvie felt as if she were being torn in half, love and loyalty pulling her one way and shame and betrayal tugging her somewhere else. And then there was Tim Simmons, who had been honorable and sweet. What to do about Tim?

"Let me tell you something," said Selma, which was how she prefaced a great many of her thoughts and pronouncements. "Whatever you do, Sylvie, it's nobody's business but yours. Yours and his, I suppose, but you shouldn't make a decision because you're worried about what people will say."

Sylvie nodded, smoothing the blanket around her legs.

"People will want you to behave a certain way, to make a certain choice because it reinforces the way they see the world. The feminists want you to leave him. They're still pissed that Hillary didn't dump Bill. The Bible-thumpers will want you to stay because that's what Jesus wants wives to do, I guess, and ever since Jenny Sanford filed, they've got no one to put on their pedestal. Ceil's going to have an opinion, and Lizzie, and Diana. But you have to do what's right for you."

"And Richard?" Sylvie ventured.

"Him, too, I suppose. But I'm your mother, so you're my concern. I want you to do what's right for Sylvie."

Sylvie nodded. What was right for Sylvie? What would feel best, what would sustain her over the years she had left? "I want Richard," she said. Selma nodded, unsurprised. "But I want things to be different. I don't want to be the kind of wife I was before. I don't want that kind of marriage again."

Selma rocked. "Would Richard be happy with a different kind of marriage? A different kind of wife?"

"I don't know," Sylvie said. Maybe she was valuing herself, and the pleasure of her company, too highly, but she thought that Richard wanted her back; that he was a little lost without her, and maybe lonely, too. She also suspected that he was also feeling so guilty that he'd agree to any conditions she cared to impose. She could tell him, for example, that she would no longer make public appearances. It was too much pressure, having to stand beside him and submit herself to the world's scrutiny, to the bitches of Boca Raton and elsewhere who'd look at her face and her clothes and the body they covered and find it all wanting. No more rallies, no more picnics, no more parades. No more fund-raising, no more wasted hours with groomed, toned, coiffed ladies who'd see her as nothing more than the afternoon's entertainment, who'd whisper about how much her clothes had cost and who was doing her hair. She'd spend part of her time up here, in Connecticut, by the ocean, maybe with Richard, if he could spare a day or two each week. Ceil would come for a long weekend and they could continue their cooking lessons in person. Come summer, she'd walk by the ocean, maybe she'd buy a kayak. She and Ceil, the girls and their children, could charter a boat and catch fresh fish and cook them out on the grill. She'd throw parties for the whole family, even crazy cousin Jan; she'd redecorate, repaint, turn the house into a place where everyone was welcome, where everyone had a bed to sleep in and a place at the table.

"And the other fellow? The Simmons boy?"

Sylvie sighed. "I don't know." Maybe that was a better answer. Tim was solid, and steady, and she sensed that she could learn to love him, and that the two of them could be happy together. She knew, with a bone-deep certainty, that he would never betray her the way Richard had. She also suspected that she wouldn't ever love him the way she loved Richard . . . but, perhaps, there were other, better kinds of love.

Selma cackled with delight. "More drama. You've made me a happy, happy woman."

"Well, that's something," said Sylvie, and looked through the window again. Tim was clearing the table, and Richard was still sitting, talking to Ceil and Larry, who'd helped themselves to slices of pie. Selma picked up her cane and thumped back inside.

Sylvie sat for a few minutes, listening to the murmur of conversation through the windows. Then she went into the warm house. She found Richard standing in the foyer, putting on his coat. Someone—Tim, she thought—had packed up all the leftovers, and Richard had a Tupperware container of turkey and stuffing and cranberry chutney in one hand. She reined in her desire to smooth his scarf and ask if he'd remembered his hat and his gloves, to tell him to listen to the traffic reports on his way into the city. Instead, she just watched as he buttoned his coat.

"Thank you for coming," she said. "It was nice to see you."

"Can I call you?" Richard asked, and then answered his own question. "Well, I know I can do that, so let me rephrase. Will you take my calls? I love you," he said before she could answer. "I never stopped loving you, and I love the girls, and I want us . . ." His voice was raw. "I want us to be a family, Sylvie."

That was what she wanted, too. But she wanted it on her terms, or, at least, on terms they could agree on instead of terms he'd dictated and she'd gone along with. She wanted a chance to fix what was broken. She wanted to change her life.

"How about this? I'll call you," she said, and walked him through the door. They stood on the porch and, after an awkward moment of fumbling, she kissed him lightly on the lips before squeezing his hand and saying, "Goodbye."

Back inside, her mother was sipping coffee at the kitchen table. Larry was playing a video game. Tim was in the kitchen, loading the dishwasher, and Ceil was leafing through one of Sylvie's *Gourmet* magazines. "Gary left," she reported. Sylvie nodded. She told Ceil and Larry which bedroom they'd be using—she'd laid out fresh towels that morning—kissed her friends, and told them she'd see them in the morning.

She found her younger daughter curled on her side on the bed, covered by a puffy down comforter with nothing but a hank of blond hair peeking out. Sylvie bent down and kissed her cheek. "My baby," she whispered.

"Your baby is having a baby," Lizzie said, with her face toward the wall. "I'm an MTV special waiting to happen."

"No," said Sylvie. "You'll be the same age that my mom was when she had me."

"Except with no Yale Law degree. And no husband," Lizzie pointed out.

"There's no right way to live a life," said Sylvie. "You just do the best you can. And you'll always have me to help you."

"Thanks," Lizzie said from the depths of the comforter. Sylvie kissed her again, then tiptoed down the hall.

Diana was sitting cross-legged on her bed, with Milo in his Batman pajamas leaning against her. From the stains on his cheeks, and the trace of whipped cream in the corner of his mouth, he appeared to have been crying . . . crying, and eating pie.

"I miss my dad," he said. "Why'd he have to leave? I wanted him to stay."

"Oh, honey," Diana said, and looked helplessly at Sylvie.

Sylvie sat with them. "Do you want to call him to say good night again?" She supposed she should have checked with Diana before making that offer, but her daughter, looking relieved, found her telephone and held it out to Milo, who managed a quivery smile.

"You know the number, right?" Diana asked, and Milo nodded, tongue between his teeth as he pushed each button. Diana mouthed the words *thank you* at Sylvie, who nodded and slipped out into the hall.

There was a nook between the bedrooms at the top of the staircase. The nook held an armchair covered in a light-blue toile fabric and a small table with a lamp and a telephone. When Sylvie was a teenager, this had been the home of the single "upstairs phone" (the downstairs phone was in the kitchen), and it was where you'd sit to have a conversation with your people back home, or with your friends in Fairview, to make plans for the coming day or the next night. It was here that Sylvie sat. She sat until Milo's murmur subsided, and she could hear Diana talking to her son for a while in a low, calming voice, until the light went out. She sat while her mother ascended the stairs and Tim came up to say good night before he drove home, and Jeff came upstairs with Alka-Seltzer and a glass of water, giving Sylvie a whispered "good night" and a sheepish grin before slipping into Lizzie's room. She sat as the house quieted around her, until the last log in the fireplace fell down in a shower of embers and ash. She sat, alert but peaceful, the way she had years ago, as a young mother, in a rocking chair next to Diana's crib and then, years later, Lizzie's crib, touching their chests to make sure they were breathing, watching their eyes roll under their lavender-colored eyelids as they dreamed. *Come to bed,* Richard would call, half-asleep himself, and she would tell him that she was fine here, fine right where she was. She would doze in the rocking chair, coming awake as soon as they stirred, to whisper lullabies into their ears, and reach for them as soon as they began to fuss and stretch out their arms for her. She would tell them that she would love them forever, that she would always be there for them, that nothing bad would happen while she was there.

LIZZIE

"Remind me again why we're doing this," said Diana as they pulled off the Beltway, heading toward Georgetown.

"Because we want to see," said Lizzie from the backseat. The week before, she'd had to break down and buy a few pairs of actual maternity jeans to supplement her drawstring skirts and pants. She lifted up her tunic and scratched her belly idly—it seemed as if it itched all the time. Poor Jeff was a nervous wreck about it. He'd read all the books, had downloaded birth plans from the Internet, and insisted on playing classical music to the baby every night after strapping headphones on to Lizzie's belly. When she told him she was itchy he'd gone online and found that itching was the symptom of some extremely rare liver disorder that pregnant women could get. She'd pointed out that it was also a symptom of the extremely common stretch mark, but Jeff still worried every time she scratched.

"This costs a fortune," Diana complained, turning her car into a parking lot and handing the attendant her keys and a twenty. "Are you sure we're in the right place?"

Lizzie climbed out of the car and pulled a map out of her purse. She had maps, she had news reports, she had photos from Google Earth, and she was positive—almost entirely positive—

that they were where they were supposed to be. She led her sister two blocks north and one block east, until they arrived in front of a little yellow clapboard house with green shutters. She looked down at the picture, then at the house, on a pretty, narrow tree-lined street with rows of similar little houses, all painted shades of yellow and cream. "This is it," she said.

For a moment, the two of them stared in silence. Diana was still too thin, lean as a supermodel and looking like a spy with her skinny jeans tucked into high-heeled boots and a belted black leather coat. Dark glasses covered her eyes and a fur hat was pulled down low over her hair, which she'd had cut upon her return to Philadelphia. Now she had bangs, and her hair, long ever since Lizzie could remember, barely brushed her collarbones. "You look like you're twenty-five," Lizzie had said, and her sister had smiled sadly and said, "But I'm not."

"What should we do?" Diana asked.

Lizzie considered. "We could get coffee," she said.

"Decaf," Diana reminded her.

"Maybe some snacks. And then we'll just wait."

Diana thought for a moment, then shrugged and walked to the wooden bench just down the street from the house in Lizzie's pictures. Lizzie sat beside her. "So what's the plan again?"

"Let me do the talking," Diana answered. "I'm going to ask her why. For starters."

Lizzie nodded. "Why" was a good question, maybe even the only question. But would the woman have an answer?

She'd discussed this with Jeff the day before, when they'd carried Milo's old crib up from the basement in pieces and set it up on newspapers in Diana's empty living room (Gary had taken the couch and the television set and moved both items to his bachelor pad). Personally, she didn't want to say anything to the woman, or ask her anything. She wasn't sure she'd even have the courage to speak. All she wanted was a look.

"You don't think you'll change your mind when you see her?" Jeff was stirring the pink paint they'd chosen at the Home Depot that morning.

"I guess it's possible," Lizzie said.

Jeff had nodded agreeably and picked up his brush. Their plan was to paint the crib and assemble it up on the third floor, where Lizzie and the baby would live when the baby came that spring. That was the plan for now . . . and Diana had replaced the single bed with a double so that Jeff and Lizzie would have the option of staying there together. Lizzie wasn't sure, but she thought it was what she wanted, and what Jeff wanted, too—to stay together, either in Diana's house or in his apartment or somewhere new that they'd find together, Lizzie and Jeff and the baby.

Beside her on the bench, she felt Diana shift and sigh. Her sister was thinking about Milo, she figured. His dad had him on Saturdays, and while part of Diana undoubtedly relished the free time, the chance for a long run or a movie or a nap, part of her would always be with her son, worrying about him, wondering if he was all right, maybe even regretting that she and Gary weren't a couple anymore.

"Look!" Diana hissed, and pointed her chin at the house's front door. A woman, a little short, a little plump, with curly brown hair tucked under a red fleece cap, was stepping out onto the street. She had a purse in one hand, a briefcase in the other, and, as they watched, she locked her front door, put her keys in her pocket, and started off down the sidewalk.

"Wow," Lizzie breathed.

"She looks better than she did on TV," said Diana, who'd become, Lizzie thought, a lot less judgmental in the past weeks.

Lizzie stared as the woman turned the corner. The famous Joelle Stabinow, without whom none of this would have happened. Without Joelle, Lizzie would have never taken Jeff to her bed, and never gotten pregnant, Diana might have never left Gary. Or maybe all of it would have happened anyhow. Maybe it was fate or destiny, the great wheel of karma, endlessly spinning, that her old friend Patrice had liked to talk about when she was stoned and *I Didn't Know I Was Pregnant* was a rerun.

"Hey!" Lizzie turned. Diana had gotten to her feet and was walking, fast and purposeful, down the sidewalk, toward Joelle in her jaunty red hat. "Hey, excuse me!" she was calling. Lizzie groaned, got up, and gave chase.

Joelle had turned around, her face round and winter-pale, friendly and expectant. She looked, Lizzie thought, completely regular, the kind of girl she might have sat beside in a psychology class or on the subway. Her hat was the same fleece one that Lizzie had in her closet back in Philadelphia, only Lizzie's was orange. "Yes?" she asked politely.

For a moment, Diana didn't say anything. The silence stretched out. Just as Joelle's expression shifted from polite to puzzled and a little bit afraid, Diana pulled off her sunglasses. "Do you know who we are?" she asked.

The puzzlement lingered for an instant as Joelle studied their faces. Then the other girl's face flushed red. "Yeah." The word came out of her as a sigh. She straightened up, her face still red and blotchy, and adjusted the strap of her purse on her shoulder. "Yes. I know who you are."

"Who?" said Diana, like a stern teacher prompting a timid pupil.

"You're Diana," Joelle said. "And you're Elizabeth."

"Lizzie," Lizzie said automatically. Diana glared at her with a look that said, *We're not here to make friends.* Lizzie shrugged. She couldn't help it. Nobody called her Elizabeth unless she was in trouble.

"Do you want to go sit down somewhere?" Joelle asked. Lizzie admired her bravery—if it had been her, she thought, she'd have said she had no idea who these two strangers were, then gone trotting off as fast as her legs could carry her (not very fast, these days) in search of a subway stop or a police officer.

Lizzie looked at her sister for guidance. Diana nodded once. "There's a coffee shop on the corner," said Joelle.

Did you go there with our dad? Lizzie thought of asking . . . but she kept her mouth shut and her hands off the camera, even though she badly wanted to snap a shot of Joelle's round, flushed face.

A minute later, the three of them were sitting at a round wooden table in the back of a busy coffee shop. "Can I get you anything?" Joelle asked, and Lizzie was reminded, vividly, of her mother, who had that same knack for playing hostess, for putting people at ease.

"Nothing," said Diana.

"Um, chamomile tea?" Lizzie said. Her sister gave her another evil look, as if having a cup of tea with this woman—this woman who in person was feeling more and more like someone Lizzie would like knowing in real life—meant that she endorsed what she'd done.

Joelle got up to get the drinks. Diana leaned forward. "Would you stop acting like you're on a date or something!" she whispered.

Lizzie bit her lip and bent over her cell phone, texting Jeff their new location. Then she looked up at her sister's face. "So you'll ask the questions?"

Diana nodded once coolly and said nothing else until Joelle came back to the table. She had Lizzie's tea, and a mug of something for herself, and she was carrying a cinnamon bun and a croissant. "In case anyone wants something," she said, setting the plates down. She unzipped her jacket and pulled off her cap, causing her curls to spring free and bounce around her cheeks. "So," she said, sounding, Lizzie thought, less like her mother and more like her Dad. "What can I do for you?"

You can apologize, Lizzie thought. As if reading her mind, Joelle said, "I'm sorry, of course, if that's what you wanted to hear. I felt terrible . . ."

"Not terrible enough to keep your legs together." Diana's voice was low and carrying, sharp as the crack of a whip. Joelle flinched, and flushed again, but nodded.

"That's right. You're right. I . . ." She dropped her head, so that she was speaking more to the pastries than to Lizzie and Diana. "I fell in love with him. And I was lonely."

This time Diana was the one who sighed. Lizzie looked at her sister, the faraway stare in her eyes, and thought that Diana must have been lonely, too, when she'd taken up with the name-tag guy.

"It was wrong," Joelle continued. "I'd never done anything like that before. It's not like me. I'm not like that."

Lizzie had a hundred questions—whether her father had been the one to seduce her, or if it had happened the other way around, and if he'd loved Joelle, and how he'd ended it, and how Joelle was doing now, without Richard in her life. But before she could ask one of them, Joelle started talking again.

"You should know how proud your father is of both of you."

Diana gave a sharp, unpleasant laugh. "Is that what you did for pillow talk? Discuss your boyfriend's daughters?"

Joelle's flush deepened, but she didn't stop talking and she didn't look away. "He wasn't proud of what he was doing, but he was proud of both of you."

"He was proud of Diana," Lizzie said, because surely this was true. What parent wouldn't be proud of her fast-moving, high-achieving sister? But Joelle said, "No, you too, Lizzie. He said you have the most unique way of seeing the world of anyone he'd ever known. He said he didn't know where it came from—he wasn't artistic, he said no one in his family was—but he said that the way you looked at things made him feel like he was seeing them for the first time."

Lizzie sat back, surprised and pleased. Her coat fell open. Joelle's eyes widened, but she didn't say anything.

"I think we're done here," said Diana, getting to her feet. Joelle stood up, too.

"I am sorry," she said again. "And if it's any consolation, I knew that what we had was temporary. Your dad loves your mom. I think I was just . . ." And here her mouth curved into a charming smile. "You know. The female version of a sports car or something."

"Or something," Diana repeated, and Lizzie could tell she was trying for that hard, mocking, whipcrack tone, but not quite getting there . . . that she was amused in spite of herself.

"I wish . . ." Joelle's voice trailed off. When it was clear that she wasn't going to finish her thought, Lizzie took her hand and squeezed it.

"I hope you'll be okay," she said, and found that it was true. Whatever ill will, whatever anger she'd harbored toward the other woman, it was gone. She was just a girl who'd made a mistake, and Lizzie herself had made so many of them that she was in no position to judge. Joelle nodded gratefully. She pulled on her hat, picked up her briefcase from where she'd set it beside her chair, gave Lizzie and Diana a brief, shamefaced wave, and then hurried out the door.

Diana watched her go, then pulled on her sunglasses. Lizzie trotted to keep up with her as she stalked down the sidewalk, heading toward the car. "I think," she said a little breathlessly, "that it went okay. Don't you?"

"As well as could be expected," said Diana, handing her ticket to the attendant.

"I think," Lizzie ventured, "that maybe we could have been her friends. Not now," she added hastily, as her sister's face darkened, "but, you know, under different circumstances. In a different lifetime." She stole a glance at her sister, then blurted, "You know, you're kind of scary."

For the first time that morning, Diana smiled. "Serves her right."

"Oh, come on." The attendant brought the car around, and Lizzie slid into the passenger's seat. "She wasn't so bad."

"Maybe not." Diana flicked on her turn signal, looked right, then left, then right again, and pulled out onto the street that would lead them home.

SYLVIE

So here she was, right back where she'd started, in a car hurtling down a turnpike, heading toward a rest stop, where there would be news. Only this time, the rest stop was in Connecticut, and Sylvie was behind the wheel, captain of her own fate, master of her destiny. This time, she wasn't alone—Tim Simmons was at her side, with an overnight bag in his lap. This time it was February instead of August, with a sleety sky and the promise of flurries in the forecast for the afternoon, and six inches of snow overnight. And this time, the news might not be bad.

"You want me to drive?" Tim asked.

"I'm fine," Sylvie said. She was dropping Tim off in New Haven—Ollie's a capella group was doing a concert at Yale. Ollie had a car, and would drive with his dad back up to Fairview for the weekend.

Sylvie zipped along the highway with her thoughts not on the man in the passenger's seat but on the man she was going to see. After a few weeks' worth of awkwardness, she and Tim had decided, in a short and excruciating conversation, to be friends. "You're not done with him yet," Tim had said, and Sylvie had acknowledged, a little ruefully, that it was true. He'd broken her heart, he'd shamed her, but still, she wasn't through with Richard Woodruff.

She steered around a curve, her heart in her throat and her hands tight on the wheel, past the exit to the mall where she and Richard would stop on their way up to Connecticut when the girls were little. There was a miniature train in the middle of the mall that cost a quarter to ride. She had pictures of Lizzie and Diana on that train every single summer from the time they were old enough to sit by themselves in the little wooden cars to the time when they were six or seven, and almost too big to fit. They'd stop at the mall every summer, even after the girls had outgrown the train, to use the bathroom and have lunch. They'd walk past the train on their way to the food court. Richard would buy an Orange Julius, and the girls would look at the train and say, "Remember when we were little?"

When she'd decided she was ready to see Richard, to talk with him face-to-face, the mall was the first place she'd thought of, before realizing that it would be too painful to sit across from her husband somewhere that they'd once been a family, never mind the spot that had occasioned one of her marriage's oldest jokes. "I'm taking you to court," Richard would announce when the girls were little, holding Diana's hand, lifting Lizzie in his arms. "Food court!" Diana would roll her eyes to show the world how lame her parents were, but Lizzie would laugh. "Food court!" she'd chortle, waving her fists in the air.

"We could meet at a rest stop," Sylvie said.

"A rest stop?" Clearly, this was not what Richard was expecting . . . but, after a minute on his laptop, with which he'd grown at least minimally proficient in her absence, he located a spot on the Merritt Parkway halfway between New York and Fairview, and Sylvie said she'd be there at noon.

A picnic basket sat in the backseat. The day before, she'd flipped through her file of recipes and called Ceil to talk about beef stew. Dredge the meat in flour, Ceil instructed. Season with salt and pepper, brown in oil, remove from pan. Brown onions and garlic, scrape up the browned bits with a little beef broth. Add more broth. Bring to a boil. Add carrots and potatoes, crushed tomatoes and tomato paste, a bay leaf, a glug of red wine ("How much is a glug?" she asked, and Ceil said, "For me, it's whatever's in the bottle that I'm not planning on drinking"). Slide the stew into a slow oven (by now, Sylvie knew what that was), and let it cook. "You can't ruin it," Ceil promised, leaving Sylvie to think about all the things that could be ruined, and whether her marriage was among them.

That morning Sylvie had reheated the stew, scooped a generous portion into an insulated Thermos, and added a loaf of crusty bread, cut-up radishes, butter, and salt. There was a plastic cooler in the pantry—the very one, she thought, that Uncle John would use to ferry his beer to the beach every afternoon. She filled it with ice, and a bottle of pumpkin lager, and a bottle of iced tea. She poured another Thermos full of coffee, wrapped up a handful of the magic bars she'd baked, and headed down the highway to meet her . . . husband? Estranged husband? Soon-to-be-ex-husband? *To meet Richard,* she thought. That was enough for now.

"Up here," said Tim, pointing toward the exit. Sylvie slowed the car and followed her GPS through the tangle of unfamiliar streets until they found the corner where Ollie, bundled in a fleece coat, was waiting and waving. Sylvie slipped him a package of magic bars.

"You sure you'll be all right?" he asked, hugging her a little longer than technically friends should have hugged. "Not nervous or anything?"

"Of course I'm nervous," she said, which was true. Her knees felt like water, her skin was clammy. "But I think I'll be fine."

"Call me if you need me," he said, and pulled out his own phone to show her. "I'm right here."

She nodded, hugged him again, then got behind the wheel again and started driving.

By eleven, she was at the rest stop, an hour early. Ever since her days of waiting for Richard's trains or Richard's planes, she always kept a book in her purse. She could pour herself some coffee, nibble the heel of the bread, keep the heater on, and read until Richard arrived. But Richard was there waiting for her, standing outside a car she didn't recognize, with sunglasses over his eyes and a baseball cap shadowing his face.

She sat for a minute, looking at him. He'd dressed for the weather in stiff blue jeans that looked as if they'd just come out of a box, and a plaid shirt, just as new-looking as the pants, and lace-up rubber duck boots with a fluff of fur peeking out of the top. Sylvie smiled, thinking of how his feet must have sweated during his drive up, because she knew, with the certainty only thirty-plus years of marriage could bring, that there were rag wool socks under those boots. Even though he'd grown up in Harrisburg and seen his share of hard winters, New England snowstorms terrified him, and he'd outfitted himself as if he'd be making the trip by covered wagon, as if blizzards were in the forecast instead of a paltry few inches, as if bears might come charging down the embankments and start attacking his BMW. She bet that there was a bag of snacks on the passenger's seat—string cheese and beef jerky, nonperishables that would have survived intact if a bomb dropped, or if he'd been making the Middle Passage in the hold of a slave ship, as opposed to a two-and-a-half-hour drive in a luxury sedan on paved roads, with convenience stores and gas stations never more than a few miles away.

She put her book back in her purse and opened the car door. Her voice was calm and her hands were steady. "Hello, Richard," she called.

He spun around as if she'd goosed him, his new boots tangling briefly on the pavement so that he almost tripped, and Sylvie was reminded so vividly of their first meeting, when he'd fallen through the ice, that tears sprang to her eyes. *Oh, Richard,* she thought, feeling her heart brimming with a complicated mess of emotions: fury, still, and scalding shame, but underneath it, an intractable affection. And love. Still, love. "Jesus, Syl!" her husband cried. "You scared me!"

She smiled, and collected their lunch. It was chilly out, with thin sunshine peeking through a scrim of clouds, but no snow was falling yet, and the fresh air felt good after the drive. She'd worn a sweater, and a down coat and a scarf, and the way Richard was dressed he could have sat outside through an ice storm. "Picnic table?" she asked. There was a thin strip of grass between the parking lot and the woods, and in one of the parking spots, an old man was trying to coax his bulldog back into his car. ("Come on, Brutus!" he wheedled, as Sylvie and Richard walked past. "I've got chopped liver!") Of the six picnic tables, only one was occupied. A mother balanced a snowsuited baby on her lap and ate a half-sandwich one-handed while her husband squirted sanitizer into the outstretched palms of two little boys.

Sylvie set out their lunch, scooping stew into the bowls she'd brought while Richard opened the lager and poured them each half a glass. She wondered if he'd offer a toast. But Richard just spread his napkin on his lap. "You cooked this?" he asked, taking an appreciative sniff as Sylvie passed him the bowl. "I can't get over it. You, cooking."

"I've changed," she said, and passed him his bowl. She didn't think she would be hungry—she'd had an image of herself nibbling at a salted radish while they talked, but the stew did smell good, and she hadn't had much breakfast.

For a few minutes the two of them ate in silence. In the parking lot, the old man gave up his attempts at persuasion and, with a grunt, bent and hoisted his dog into the passenger's seat.

("You're killing me with this, Brutus," he said, before getting into his own seat and driving away.) At the neighboring table, one of the little boys whined that he hated peanut butter, they always had peanut butter, and he wanted ham and cheese and why wasn't there any of that, and his father said, "Because life sucks, then you die," and the mother said, "Really, Jamie? That's really how we talk to the five-year-old?" The father subsided for a moment, then said, in a stage whisper loud enough for Sylvie and Richard to hear, "I like ham and cheese better, too."

Richard tore off a hunk of bread and buttered it. "I'm glad you called. I wanted to tell you something."

She stared at him, waiting, as he chewed and swallowed and finally said, "I've been thinking about it, and I've decided . . ." He paused, tore off another chunk of bread, and said, "I think I'm just going to quit. Hang it up before the next election. Start a foundation, or join someone else's. Do some good." He smiled at her—that old charming grin, the smile that said, *I'm going places, and you can come with me.* "What do you think about that?"

Sylvie knew what she wanted to say to him: that she missed him, that she wanted them to try, that she wanted to be part of a family again—but she couldn't say it yet. Not until she was sure that it was what he wanted, too.

Since Thanksgiving, Richard had called her every night, and they had long conversations, not just about politics but about everything—a piece of music he'd heard, an art exhibit she'd read about, trips they'd taken, trips they'd like to take. The conversation would move to their daughters. "Can you believe Lizzie?" Richard would ask. "She's big as a house." "Richard," Sylvie chided, but she, too, could hardly believe how Lizzie had blossomed. The last time she'd been in Philadelphia, Lizzie, in maternity cargo pants, was sorting through a bag of baby clothes she'd found at a secondhand store. She and Jeff had told Sylvie they were taking classes in something called the Bradley birth method. "No drugs," Lizzie had explained, and Diana, who'd been making lunch in the kitchen, had rolled her eyes and whispered to Sylvie, "Bet you she's begging for an epidural before he parks the car."

Lizzie had gotten a part-time job assisting a wedding photographer and was starting to make a name for herself for her offbeat, black-and-white candid shots that caught the couples at unexpected moments—a bride licking frosting off her fingertip as the groom paid the caterers, a tiny flower girl asleep in her grandfather's arms. Gary had moved a few blocks away and saw Milo almost every night. Diana had gone back to work at the hospital. She'd cut her ER shifts down to two a week, and was helping to run a program for mothers who'd been born with their babies addicted to drugs. "I thought you didn't believe in addiction," Sylvie had said, and Diana had given her a sad smile and said, "I've changed my mind."

She told Richard stories about her visits with the girls, and he told her about what happened when he saw them, and about life in D.C., and back in New York. In all their conversations, he'd never asked about Tim, and Sylvie had never offered any information.

Across the picnic table, Richard wiped off his spoon with his napkin and set it on the table. "I've been thinking about you a lot." He then reached out his hand, brushing his fingers against her cheek. His voice deepened. "You look beautiful," he said.

She waved away the compliment, feeling shy. She looked different, that was all: she'd let her hair grow longer, and stopped dying the gray and straightening the curls. She'd put on a few pounds, but not as many as she'd expected—all the cooking seemed to have been balanced out by all the walking on the beach and to the grocery store. Her cheeks were rosy—normally she covered the flush with foundation, but she hadn't worn makeup since she'd arrived in Fairview, and hadn't wanted to start that morning. She wondered what he was really seeing. She felt different, but that didn't mean she looked that way . . . and had Richard really been seeing her at all over the past years?

Richard took her hands. "Do you want to try again? Is that why you wanted to see me?" he asked. When she didn't answer immediately, he said, "Or are you . . ." He broke off and gave a rueful chuckle. "I don't even know how to have this conversation with my wife. Is it serious? You and that other guy? Is that what it is? You wanted to give me the bad news in person?"

"We're friends," she said. "That's all."

Richard squeezed her hands. "I don't want to lose you."

She scooted herself backward on the picnic bench, taking her hands back and folding them in her lap. "Maybe," she said, "you should have thought about that before you—"

"I know," he said, before she could finish. "My God, Sylvie, don't you think I know that?" The mother and the father and the little boys at the next table had turned to stare. Richard lowered his voice. "Don't you think," he said in a hoarse whisper, "that I would take it back if I could?"

She thought about it. "I don't know," she said. "I don't know why you did it in the first place, so I don't know whether you regret it. I'm sure you regret the consequences, but as to the act itself . . ."

"Stop talking like a lawyer," he said, but he didn't say it angrily. He sounded tired, more than anything else. "And as it happens, I do regret it. The act itself."

"You do?" she asked lightly. "She looked pretty cute in those pictures."

"Without going into details," Richard said, "I can tell you that Benjamin Franklin had it right with regards to the charms of the older woman."

"So why, then?" All the lightness and high good humor was out of her voice. Why, then? Would he even have an answer?

He exhaled, running his hands over his head, a gesture she'd seen him perform thousands of times, when he was irritated, or tired, or stalling for time. "I think I was flattered, more than anything else. Flattered that a young girl like that would be interested." He looked down, sighing. "Tell you the truth, she reminded me of you a little bit. And that made me feel young."

"So was it worth it?" she asked.

Closing his eyes, Richard said, "Of course not. I lost you, I lost the girls' respect, I lost my reputation, I lost everything I'd worked to build since I was twelve years old and decided I wanted to be president."

"You were eleven," she reminded him. She was trembling again, shocked at how simple it was to slip into her old role as the institutional memory of their marriage, the one who kept track of the anecdotes and in-jokes and the vacation photographs, the curator of the family history.

"Well, I was twelve when I figured out that wasn't going to happen. And if I'd known being in office was going to be this much work . . ." He looked down, giving Sylvie the chance to see new threads of gray in his hair, and that his bald spot, the one that he despaired of, had gotten bigger. Politicians worked until they dropped, running for office, even for president, into their eighties and holding those offices until they were dragged off the public stage (occasionally after they'd collapsed on top of them), but in the world of regular people, there were plenty of men who'd retired at Richard's age.

"I screwed up," he said.

"Yes," Sylvie agreed. "Yes, you did." Even as she was saying it, she felt that old spark, that familiar connection, the sense that they were playing on the same team, that she wanted what was best for him and he wanted what was best for her.

"It was stupid."

"Yes. It was."

"I think of what I threw away, and I just feel sick. Sick and sad." She nodded. She knew about sick and sad. "I know you'll probably never be able to trust me again . . ." He rubbed at his hair again. "Will you come home?"

Sylvie waited before giving him the answer she'd arrived at on the drive down. "I don't think I can come back to New York. Not yet. And I have to tell you, Connecticut feels like home to me now."

He nodded, as if this news did not surprise him. "Is there anything I can do to change your mind? We can do counseling, if you think that would help."

Sylvie couldn't imagine the two of them sitting in front of some stranger talking about their feelings.

"Or, if there's something else I can do . . . if there's any way I can convince you how sorry I am . . ."

He gazed at her, chin tilted slightly down, eyes looking into hers. Always the politician, she thought, a little amused, a little disgusted. And always, still, her Richard. He'd gotten a haircut in the past week or so, and there was an eyelash that had fallen off and gotten stuck high on his cheek. She pressed her fingertip against his skin and pulled until the eyelash came free. "Make a wish," he said, and she closed her eyes and blew and thought, *I want my family back.*

"You miss the lashes?" Richard asked while her eyes were still closed, and she smiled. Richard had always been vain about his lashes, which were unfairly long and lush (Lizzie had inherited them; Diana had not). Once, when they were dating, Richard had gone as Elvis to a Halloween party, and Sylvie had convinced him to let her put mascara on his lashes. "You're so pretty," she'd said (she'd had, at that point, a few preparty glasses of wine). Richard had looked at himself in the mirror, turning his head from side to side, batting his lashes like a parody of feminine flirtation. "Well, what do you know?" he'd said, and smoothed the glistening pompadour that Sylvie had helped him shape. "I am."

Sylvie refolded her napkin and slipped it back into the tote bag. She had thought about a speech she might deliver during her drive, so she was prepared. "I'm not sure what I want right now. It feels good to be by myself."

"Can I see you? Up there? I miss you." Richard rubbed at his forehead. "Nobody else laughs at my jokes."

"Not Joe Eido?" she asked, even though she knew what he meant, and that it was more than laughing at jokes. After all their years together, they shared a common dialect, the language of the marriage, shorthand references, the abbreviations and bits of shtick they'd do. Whatever he'd done, whatever he'd become, Richard was the one who knew what she liked on her pizza, and where she liked to be kissed. She wondered if he knew that those were her happiest memories—not their wedding, certainly not Diana's wedding, which had been an expensive, overblown affair with the bride corseted into her three-thousand-dollar gown, cursing in the ladies' room because her groom had gained ten pounds between his last tuxedo fitting and the wedding night and now he was busting out of his cummerbund. Not that first victorious election night, not the inauguration, down in Washington, where she'd held the Bible and the girls had held his hands. Her favorite times were the ones she'd spent just sitting with him in their den at the end of the day, with a cup of tea for her and a bottle of beer for him, half-watching whatever was on the TV, half-reading whatever book or magazine was in her lap, talking about what they'd done that day, what they'd do during the week, and the weekend ahead.

So that's that, she thought. They'd talk. Maybe it could be a start. Feeling exhausted from the adrenaline rush and the driving—and, as always, his closeness—she began packing up the remains of their lunch, sliding the dirty dishes and used silverware into a plastic bag she'd brought, setting out the Thermos of coffee and the dessert she'd packed. Richard poured coffee for her and a cup for himself.

"These are really good," he said, eating a magic bar.

Her husband sat before her, under the slate-gray sky, sweating in his plaid shirt and long underwear and wool socks, looking like a man who'd just strapped a heavy backpack onto his shoulders and wanted only to take it off. A ridiculous figure . . . and yet, still, part of her wanted nothing more than to walk to the other side of the table, put her arms around him, pull his head against her chest, and tell him that he could rest, that all was forgiven. But there was a tiny, icy seed inside of her heart, a place in her mind where that first piece she'd seen on CNN would be playing eternally on a kind of hellish loop. She was different now. Whatever she'd been before, now she was a woman who did not make excuses for Richard, or instantly forgive him, or put what he wanted ahead of everything else.

"So?" he asked her. "So what do you say? You and me again?"

"Big question," she said.

"Take your time," said Richard. "As long as you promise you'll give me a chance." He reached for her hands again, and she laced her fingers through his, squeezing tightly, not wanting to let go. He was her husband, and she loved him, and they could get through the rest of it. She could have her new life, and he would have his, but they would be together—all that she wanted, all that mattered. "I know I don't deserve one, and if . . ." He swallowed, and when he started talking his voice was hoarse. "If things end, then I promise you I'll be fair. But I want a shot at making things right."

She nodded, imagining what the coming years might bring. Maybe once he left the Senate he'd join her in Connecticut. Maybe she would go to cooking school, learn to kayak, learn to fish. She would be the mother she hadn't been when her girls were young, she would do what she could to be there for Milo, and for Lizzie's baby, when it came. She would take care of herself, not just Richard . . . and maybe he could learn to take care of her.

They sat across from each other at the picnic table, husband and wife. Cars full of travelers zipped past them on the parkway. "Look!" said Richard, as something light wafted into Sylvie's coffee cup. Snowflakes flurried down, melting on her cheeks, as Richard, smiling, pointed at the sky.

ACKNOWLEDGMENTS

The book you're holding in your hands actually got its start ten years ago, before anyone had heard of Silda Spitzer, Elizabeth Edwards, Dina Matos McGreevey, and Senator Larry "Wide Stance" Craig.

Ten years ago, in the spring of 2000, I was a lowly newspaper reporter with a manuscript and a dream, querying agents to try to find one who'd take me on as a client. I'll never forget picking up the phone at my desk and hearing a tiny little voice saying, "I loved your book! It spoke to me!" (I remember, very distinctly, thinking "How?")

That book became *Good in Bed*, and the agent who loved it was Joanna Pulcini. She and I worked on the book together for months, cutting and trimming and revising and rewriting, before she started making the rounds of editors. She'd take them out for drinks or lunch and say, in her tiny little voice, "I have three words for you! Good in bed!" Then she'd refuse to say any more, or tell them whether the book was fiction or a how-to guide with pictures.

In May of 2000, Joanna took me to meet the editors who were interested in working with me. All of them were lovely, but one stood out—the one who told us that she missed her subway stop because she was so engrossed, the one who prevailed upon her entire marketing and publicity team to read the thing in a weekend, the one who had the clearest vision of the kind of books I'd go on to write.

That editor was Greer Hendricks, and she published *Good in Bed* in the spring of 2001, and it did well in hardcover and then took off in paperback . . . and a team was born.

I've been lucky enough to work with Greer and Joanna for ten years, over seven novels and a short-story collection, and I can't imagine that there's a writer who's luckier than I am to be with such dedicated, smart, funny, hardworking, visionary, lovely women. I hope we'll be a team for many years—and books—to come.

Other women I'm blessed and lucky to have in my writing life—Judith Curr at Atria and Carolyn Reidy at Simon & Schuster, who believed in me from the beginning, and Meghan Burnett, my unbelievably good-natured and hilarious assistant, who's unfailingly friendly and diligent and doesn't bat an eye when, for example, I ask her to look up the lyrics of all twenty-two chapters of R. Kelly's "Trapped in the Closet," and then sing them. I'm also grateful to the wonderful Terri Gottlieb, who takes care of my girls and makes my writing life possible.

Love and thanks to my thoughtful and generous first readers: Curtis Sittenfeld, Elizabeth LaBan, and Bill Syken.

Marcy Engelman, my genius publicist, is the best workout partner and dining companion in all of New York City. I am by far the least famous and important person she works with, but she never makes me feel that way. I adore her, and Dana Gidney Fetaya, a Marcy in training, and Emily Gambir.

My thanks to Joanna's assistant Alexandra Chang, Greer's assistant, the unflappable Sarah Cantin, Nancy Inglis, copy editor to the stars, who knows that, after all these books, I still misspell *tee shirt* and don't know how to make my computer do ellipses.

I'm grateful to everyone at Atria who works on my books:

Chris Lloreda, Natalie White, Lisa Keim, Jessica Purcell, Lisa Sciambra, Craig Dean, Rachel Bostic, and Jeanne Lee, who has much better taste and a better sense of what book covers work than I do.

My love and thanks to the good people at Simon & Schuster UK: Suzanne Baboneau, Julie Wright, Ian Chapman, Jessica Leeke, and Nigel Stoneman, who gave me the Jackie Collins treatment in London and Dublin.

A special shout-out to Jessica Bartolo and her team at Greater Talent Network, who set up speaking gigs so that I can leave the house in grown-up clothes, spend the night in a nice hotel, and tell stories about my gay mom.

Thanks to my family, as always, for the love, support, and material: my husband, first reader, and traveling companion, Adam; my daughters, Lucy and Phoebe; my mom, Frances Frumin Weiner, and her partner, Clair Kaplan; my sister Molly and my brothers Jake and Joe. Finally, thanks to all of my friends, near and far, on Facebook and on Twitter, for making me laugh, for helping me feel connected, and for reading the stories I tell.